2

Mike Panther Pal Telzer
you held me in your
heart when I hung
from the end of my
rope of reality.

Bigger Brother I love you
+ would take a shot for you
- although I would not
take it as well as you would.

love Lorenzo the
little lavender
beyond lad

Conversations with a Bowl of Cereal

Lawrence Mayles

authorHOUSE®

AuthorHouse™
1663 Liberty Drive
Bloomington, IN 47403
www.authorhouse.com
Phone: 1-800-839-8640

First published by AuthorHouse   1/20/2010

ISBN: 978-1-4490-6576-8 (sc)

Printed in the United States of America
Bloomington, Indiana

This book is printed on acid-free paper.

Front page illustration and author's photo: © Lance Smith and Lawrence Mayles.

Contents

Disclaimer

A Warning about The Words. They are alive. They play dead upon the page as innocent ink stains.. but they can shift in a moment from syllables still and silent.. to something swirling.. something sentient.. hungry for humans.. and the next thing you know.. you don't leave the table the same way you came in to breakfast.

This is language unleashed.. renegade reality served rare as you dare.. voracious visionary vocabulary. Enter into these Paranormal Pages at your own risk. There are no refunds on any reality a reader may find themself in once entering The Book From Beyond The Brain.

Neither the Spirit Scribe.. the Paranormal Publisher.. the Bardo Beings in This Book.. nor the Wraith Words themselves.. may be held responsible.. when a reader become possessed by these Paranormal Pages.

Any apparent semblance of the paranormal persons appearing within these possessed pages.. to any being normal or paranormal.. living or dead.. is purely a coincidence of cosmic karma. The names have been changed to protect the privacy of The Paranormal.

This Book has been approved by The Paranormal for normal and paranormal people.. including alien entities.. angels in ascension.. discarnates.. spirits.. ghosts.. and Bardo Beings.

It is Dedicated to the Divine.. and is a recipient of both the Renegade Reality Riders Association Award, and the Spirit Scribe Spell Script Scribblers Society Seal of Approval.

Winner of the World Walker Word Wanderer Paranormal Publishers Prize.. and the Book Brewers Badge of the Unbelievable.

Without us Words you humans got nothin to say. This Book is a living being and at all times must be treated as such.. failure to do so with care and respect could result in need for a reader's reality rescue. Eternity Exploration and Cosmic Cranial Cruising is not to be undertaken lightly. When Consciousness calls.. It demands to be answered.

About Author

The author is an Entity from Outside of Eternity.. a Paranormal Phantom Poet..

a Spirit Scribe.. a Wraith Writer.. a Ghost Writer.. yes a real one..

made of magic and mind and mystery and imagination.. living as literature illuminated with the light of love..

An Eternal Entity devoid of flesh and formless as flame..

a simple servant who rakes up the remains of reality.. a humble gardener of the mind.. a Spirit Steward of the Sacred Story.. an angel assisting your ascension at the Altar of Alteration in the Temple of Transformation.

a wind passing thru your world.. turning the pages of your path..
guiding you with whispers..

a paranormal poet pilgrim upon a path of pages..
a word walker..
one who serves the cereal..
washes the words.. sweetens the story..
sweeps the temple floors of discarded prayers..

a tailor of tales.. a weaver of words..
an alchemist of the alphabet..
dabbling in alphabetical alchemy..

an angel arranging the alphabet so as to illuminate
the gate thru which flows fate..

a story sorcerer.. a spell script scribbler..
someone who stirs the syllable stew.. into sentences for you.

a spirit surfing your synapses..
a supermarket sales serpent selling cereal that is 100% supernatural..
every ingredient meant for mastering your mind.

There is no author.. it's simply scribblings and scrawllings upon walls of worlds..
whirling as wind thru the cosmos.

The words are wraiths.. wraith words.. they wrote themselves.
The syllables scribbled and scrawlled the sentences of their own accord.

The story is its own entity.. a spirit.. an Eternal Entity from Outside of Eternity. One that existed long before it was delicately dusted off from where it was found.

The writer is one who walks like the wind..
leaving no tracks but the whispers of love..

a bardo being born and bred beyond the boundaries of the baboon brain..

an ethereal entity.. a dream drifter.. a heyoka highway hero..
sippin on a strawberry slug soda.. in the story shamans' soda shop..

a lavender love light lamp lap lizardarian librarian laughing out loud..
a super hero shape shifter who changes costumes and characters inside the covers of this book.

It's just the ramblings of a raspberry reptile renegade reality reporter..
rappin' for Raspberry Ravine Radio.. a subsidiary of Strawberry Star Studios Songs and Stories.. part of the Consciousness Corporation Conglomerate.

Just the tangerine treacle toe tracks of a tale trippin tulku temple toad..
using this book as a bridge to ford the raging river of reality.

The Book speaks for itself.. the story sings its own songs.

Sure I could give you a name.
But you can't find the formless even if you've got the angel's address.

You and I are One.. the words.. the reader.. the book.. the buyer.. the brewer.. and the believer.. one cosmic creation flowing from the Chalice of Conception.

The Book is an Eternity Explorer's journal..
a paranormal professor's classroom chalk board scribblings.

What you read are possessed pages.. paranormal paragraphs..
spirit script from the crypt of consciousness..
field notes of a Knight of the Noble Knowing..
a pilgrim's paw marks.. upon the Path of Purification.

Call it lethal lectures from the lord of literature..
manga maya mumble from manga mind..
the story of the spirit cereal..
supper with the Syllable Sorcerer..
servings of Story Stew..
simmered upon the stove of secret spells in the pot of page potions.

words of wisdom..
the spirit speaks..
the soul sings.. the toad talks.. the serpent sings..
babblings of a baboon..
confessions of consciousness..
the brain breaks down and spills the bardo beans.. about bein' a brain blaster.

It's an attempt at waking up the world with words..
weaving with words a world of wonder and wisdom..

talks with a tale troll..
walks with wisdom..
beads of the beloved's bracelet of blessings..

a holographic hero's howls..
a ghost's growls..
a vision volume that fell off the shelf of samsara.. and landed in your lap..
creating a chorus of ever flowing love.

Or maybe.. reality unrobes and shows itself in all its splendor..
deep listening to the silent ones.. seeing the unseen..

a parable penned by a paranormal poet..
pages of praise and prayers and pleas.. on behalf of planet paradise.
Please treat her nice.

Call it cute conversation channeled by a bowl of cereal sweetly named Strawberry Stars. We're all one story.. bound in one book.. a fable fabricated by the formless.

What you hear when you read these words..
is but the Buddha's Breath circling the Planet.. the laughter of the hereafter.

I am the Book.. the buddha.. the bowl of cereal.. and the box which begat it. I am your baboon brother come to breakfast at your kitchen table every time you tip a box of strawberry stars and blueberry bardo bits into your begging bowl..

a tale told by your uncle tio.. who showed up to visit with his tale travellin trunk.. the first time you poured yourself a storm of strawberry stars..

I'm just a latch on your heart's door.. waiting to be opened.

Call it discussions with the dead inside yer head..
breakfast babblings by the brain over a bowl of cereal..
notes to myself while searching for me..

destiny's diaries..
dinner dialogues with divinity..
cocktail conversations with consciousness..

the wraith waiter serving you a platter of words..
lunch and literature lessons with the learned lavender lizardarian librarian..
of the lost legends of the libraries of love's languages.

Call it smoke signals from the soul..
speaking with spirits.

I am the one who opens the dream..
the shaman of the story..
a sweet dreams medicine man.

The story shape shifts.. the tale transforms.
The Story is the Sorcerer.

You are following in the tracks of the previous page pilgrims..
those who wandered this way.. in search of a story to become part of.

Everything yearns to be part of the whole. A heart alone is an empty hole.
I am a distant dream spirit that has reached out to you thru realms of realities.

You and I.. and every being there is.. are the voices of a cosmic choir..
the notes of a sacred song.. the words of a never ending love story.

This Book is but one brick in the wall of wonder and wisdom..
of the Castle of Consciousness.
I am but a bricklayer.. placing mortar between the layers of love..
carefully cementing the sentences into place..
to provide a path for the fallen and the faithless.

The author is an anonymous angel.
The pages are a path to the home of the Creator of Consciousness.

I am a ghost gardener.. and you are my garden.
I am a wraith writing notes on nirvana.. thoughts about thanatos..
ruminations on reality.. enquiries into eternity.

Forget about who wrote this story.. whose story this is.
What is your story ? Why are you watching these words ?

Is it hunger or hope.. heaven or hell.. that holds you in its spell ?
Have you come here to anoint or abuse

This Book is part prose.. part poetry.. part parable.. part prayer.. part praise..
told as a tale by a trail toad to a couple of kids.. brother and sister..
over a bowl of cereal.. at the Table of Fables.. in the Tavern of Tales..
with ghosts gathered round.. phantom family and friends..

It's the afterburner effects of blasting beyond the brain.. etched into eternity.
We are all spirits appearing as bones and blood.. skin and carcass..
in one ever unfolding sacred story.

Humanity has always searched for words to describe the divine..
the unknown.. the unseen.. the eternal. This is another attempt.

Oh its just the cries for help from some cereal..
drowning in a bowl of almond and rice milk..
table talk.. kitchen conversation.. breakfast with the Bardo Beings..
my mind mating with yours.

We are Knights of Knowledge.. on a courageous Quest for Consciousness.
These are the Eternity Episodes.. a tapestry woven of time and space..
words written to alleviate the existential emptiness of The Eternal.

This book is more than a manuscript made of Paranormal Parchment. It is a Living
Being from Beyond the Brain.. a being born and bred in the bardos.

A being not quite living.. nor dead.. but something more than words you've just read.
Something of the spirit.. soaring.. silent.. seeing but unseen.
Something that looks at you while you look at it.

Call it confessions of a Consciousness Cruising Cadet..
conversations with creation..the calling of consciousness..
one on one discussions with the divine..

visits with an invisible visionary..
an interview with the infinite.. an Infinite Entity from Outside of Eternity.

The pages are a path for Pilgrims of the Paranormal..
cruising the cranial corridors of the cosmos.. one spoon at a time.

When yer consciousness get's outta control.. and reality starts to roll downhill.. you
need consciousness control. Consider these chapters.. consciousness control.

May all who wander these words with the heart of a hero and soul of a seeker.. find
sanctuary in This Book's Story.

Sincerely
The Spirit Sage

Introduction to An Interview With
An Invisible Entity From Outside of Eternity

Where to start the story of how I met The Spirit in The Cereal ? Well actually it wasn't just in the cereal.. that's where it started.. it was in the box.. and the bowl.. and the spoon.. and soon it was in the kitchen table.. and the radio on the fridge on the other side of the ridge of reality.

The spirit started speaking from everywhere.. singing from the spagetti.. sighing from the syrup.. talking from the table.. calling from the cupboards and closets.. whispering from the walls.. all because I opened This Book.

So to set the scene.. in which the story stages it's existence ..

Imagine an inner city not so vacant lot of visions.. a jungle butterfly.. a manuscript found neath the Museum of Mausoleums in the Tunnels of Thanatos.. a Book from beyond the brain.. a Spirit Scribe.. a cereal box that talks.. a kitchen table.. and a brother and sister.. Adam who is eleven and Evelyn who is seven.. and their mum a college professor of ethnobotany.. and their dad a professor of primatology.. who after bringing home a box of cosmic cereal called Strawberry Stars.. which they purchased in the supermarket aisle from the paranormal appearing in the guise of a singing sales snake.. never get to school on time.. or even in time .. because they end up somewhere outside of time.. each time they take a spoonful of cereal.

And out of the cereal appears a crew of cosmic characters.. a tangerine tale telling temple toad.. a strawberry star saloon singing salamander.. a lavender lizardarian librarian lamp.. the blueberry baboon brothers.. a raspberry reptile rapper.. and a whole host of other heavenly caretakers of consciousness.. stewards of the sacred.

But then who is who.. and what is what.. is not really as relevant.. as who and what are you ? And that is what this Book aims to do.. find you. I know it sounds unreal.. but just feel This Book.. is there not something about it that seems almost human.. alive.. sentient.. warm in your hands as you hold it ?

Can you not hear a heart beating.. somewhere.. faintly.. as if it needed your love to survive ? This story is conscious.. a living being.. aware of you.

These pages are a portal into the paranormal. The veil of visions is very thin between these covers. You and This Book are a funnel.. thru which the all becomes the one we always are.

This Book is The Call.. the breakfast wake up call in a bowl.. to go beyond the brain's borders.. into a land of love.

The Cereal calls you.. you become one with the cereal.. one with the bowl.. with the box.. with the spoon.. with The Book. You become one with All.

Go ahead and get cozy with the cereal.. crawl inta bed with This Book.. cook up some consciousness.. you're becoming a Consciousness Crusader connoisseur. Coast on a slice of toast into a tale that cannot fail to fill your future with fabulous fantasy.

Discover a depth of delight you knew only as an innocent child. These pages are a place to meet new pals.. normal and paranormal.. form friendships with phantoms.

Think of it as the winds' whispers.. the spirits' sighs.

Pick any page and read it.. each page.. each chapter.. stands on its own.. and at the same time is a part of the Paranormal Puzzle Path thru which a Pilgrim of the Paranormal Pages must pass.. a forever forming fable unfolding from itself.

This is a potion written in prose and poems.. by a phantom poet.. a ghost writer.. a real one.. a being from beyond the brain.

Words.. syllables.. sentences.. are spells. Every sentence spoken.. every word ever written.. is a spell. Words create the spells of the society.

That is why you have come to search for your self in these pages.. seeker of sweet sanctuary. You have sought forever a story.. one in which you could find a home for your heart. Here I am before you.. in the guise of a book.
This manuscript is a Messenger of the Master of the Mind.
Let us just say that the paranormal has no parameters.. and so a Cereal Cadet could theoretically go anywhere that ever.. or never.. existed.

Rarely does a Renegade Reality Rider return to regular reality. With a spoon of cereal.. with each new renegade reality ride.. when the rider returns.. he or she finds less and less of regular reality existing.

Consider This Book as your manual for cranial cruising of your consciousness thru uncharted territory.

And so This Story has come.. for redemption.. resolution.. recognition.. between regular reality and renegade reality. Forever let the normal and the paranormal be joined again as one eternal entity.

With the breath of god was begot the beloved being of existence.
You and I This Book.. are a funnel..
a paranormal portal thru which The All becomes The One.

In your hand you hold the Memoirs of the Master's Mind.
Infinity is your instrument.. existence your clay..
The cosmos your cauldron..
Creation your crown.

Crusaders of The Cranium.. Crusaders of Consciousness..
All who have been crucified by consciousness.. come find salvation in the cereal that cares about you.. the cereal box that talks ta keep yer cranium company.

This Book is the Karmic Key to Eternity..
Insert The Book into The Box.. and enter anywhere anytime.

Existence is a delicate dance between divine and damned.
The pen is the plow.. and the page the arable land.

The cereal bowl.. the box.. This Book.. is a vessel of transformation..
a tale to transform the reader's reality.

Wisdom walks with you in these words.. brothers of the book and box and bowl.. sisters of the story and stirring spoon.. faithful followers of the fable.. proud pilgrims of the paranormal parable path..
We are creating the cosmos one thought at a time..

This is a story that will shape shift your life.. a soul filled and soul fulfilling fantasy. Every sentence is a spell formulated by a Paranormal Phantom friend to reformulate your fate.

It is a home study course on how to converse with the universe..
A crash course into consciousness..
A pilgrimage into the paranormal pages of the ancient spirit sages..
With your buddy the Book from Beyond the Brain..

Filled with phrases to ponder.. such as.. What is the ecology of existence ?
Are we all caught in a freudian fable.. a jungian jungle ?
The unfoldment of the universe is the embodiment of the eternal.
The clay of consciousness is the mind's material out of which it weaves wonder and wisdom.

This Book is in your presence to edify and illuminate your journey toward yourself.

It is only soul that suffices.. infuses the spirit with the ability to soar unimpeded thru the universe as a beam of pure radiant illuminative light interacting with every other beam of light.. one complex vibration of luminence. This is the violet vision of which the mystics have spoken. Awaken your connection to the cosmos and become the light you are.. eternal.. pure.. everlasting.. serene.. soaring.. and yet landed into life.

You are being kissed by consciousness.. created by creation itself.
Each chapter is a Chalice of Creation out of which you are poured.

You are.. All is.. the Child of the Cosmos.. conceived in the womb of wonder.. nourished in the nectar of the all knowing gnosis. The parable is the parent.. of the words with whom you will wed.. of The Book in which you are born.. and in which you are bred.

Entering into This Book is embarking upon the ultimate crusade of all crusades.. the Crusade into Consciousness itself. Together we travel thru the texts of the transcripts of the Temple of Time.. You the Renegade Reality Rider.. and me the Holographic Hero.. the Bardo Being without a body.. the Spirit Scribe looking over your shoulder with every word you read.

These texts are the threshold thru which your consciousness crosses over into communion with the Cosmic Consciousness of the Cosmos.

This Book is An Invitation From The Infinite.. into an Exploration of The Eternal. It is time to become intimate with your true self.

Words are the womb of the world.
These chapters are Cauldrons of Consciousness.. Conversations with Creation..
Daily Dialogues with Divinity.. lunch lessons with the Learned Deli Lizard in the
 cafeteria of the College of the Cosmos.. mind memos from the master mind..
channeled thru yer breakfast bowl.. every morning to make your day magical.

You have called Consciousness.. and Consciousness has come.
We words are alive and watch you as you watch us.

Call it Talks With Tio Toad.. a humble janitor in the Temple of Time..
the Monk's Manuscript from the Monastery of Imagination..

Just a homeless book found wandering in the Library of Life..
bearing a Tale of Transformation.. yours..

A Visit with the Invisible.. The Song of The Planet.

It is one of the greatest love stories of all time..
between a Book and Humans.. the spirit and the flesh.

Open these pages and spend every evening with the Eternal..
every morning with the magical.. every day with the Divine.

Call it collaborations with consciousness..
collected and strung on a Nirvana Necklace and gifted to you..
or call it the Cereal Commentaries on Consciousness and the Cosmos.

It's Visionary Vocabulary.. the Documentarius Divinicus.. Dharma Dancing..
Story Stew simmering upon the Story Sorcerer's Stove..
Strawberry Star Syrup slathered upon page after page..
to sweeten life for you..
Your Consciousness Key to the Gateway of the Galaxy.

Pilgrim of the Pages.. ponder upon this..
Have you come to The Story seeking sanctuary.. salvation.. sanity..
To serve the sacred.. or to sell your soul ?
To live in the light.. or die in the dark ?

This Book is the Bread of the Beloved.. eat of it.
These Words are the Wine of Wisdom.. drink deeply.
Step Inside The Cereal Box.. Open The Book.. Discover Your Heart.

May these pages be perfumed for you with the Incense of Inspiration.
Once you have reached eternal exstacy.. we will ensure you remain there forever.

There are an infinite number of ways to express love.. and each one begins with you.

Sincerely
The Spirit Sage

Conversation With Creation: The Spirit Speaks

Sis poured herself a bowl of Strawberry Stars..
and then began to read from the side of the box..

"Strawberry Stars Cosmic Cereal.. Ingredients..
100 % supernatural nutrition for the heart and soul and spirit..
Low in fat and high in fun and fantasy
Loaded with Love

Filled with:
Consciousness
Consideration
Illumination
Imagination
Inspiration
Compassion
Generosity
Gentleness
Sweetness
Happiness
Integrity
Harmony
Kindness
Honesty
Wisdom
Respect
Peace
Faith
Joy

This is cosmic command control center. Is regular reality running you ? Regular reality got you run down ? Register now for Renegade Reality Riding home study course. Book Brew and Story Stew served here.

And it is all here in this field note book for phantomes and wraiths.. discovering they are as real as you and I.. and they are now willing to walk and talk with us as family.

No longer fear the formless. They are your friends and family. These are sacred spirits speaking. Hear them well. Listen to their language. They are literate and they are loving.

The spirits' story is scribed in strawberry star story syrup.. upon tale travellin toast.. that Tio the tangerine tulku temple tale tellin teacher toad.. is paddlin' across your dad's cereal bowl.. on his way to rescue some reader from regular reality."

Strawberry Stars were tumblin outta Sis's open mouth.. while right in front of her.. Soloman Salamander was dancing on the rim of reality encircling the Bowl of the Beginning.. Buddha was blessing the believers.. and Krishna was cleaning up Karma's Kitchen.

Sis and I were slipping inta the story. "Reality relinquishes its hold on humanity. Read all about it in the Ghost Gazette !"

Big read the headlines out loud.. then folded the not normal newspaper.. and replied to the wraith waitress who wasn't there.. that he would like a large bowl of ghoul goulash.. with a side order of goblin gruel.. and a zombie sandwich double dipped in demon drool.. for his friend the sloshed sales serpent spinnin round on the story stool.. in Taco Tio's Tamale Toast Tea and Tales.. Tavern Temple Tabernacle Time Travellin Tale Trunk Trailer.. where tales are tailor made for every mind.

"Yes you are losing your minds and having them replaced by the paranormal prophecies of the ancient ancestral alien entities that cruised the eternal voids of those cosmic spaces that broke the continuum of existence into fractals leaving humanity to find its own way across the chasms of consciousness that separated one soul from another.

And love is the only fuel that can bridge the gap between ghosts and humans. This is now the time of communication between the living and the non living.. acceptance of normal and paranormal people as equal.. with both learning to exist together in peace and mutual support.. rather than the paranormal having to remain hidden from humanity.. as it has for so long. It is time for the normal and the paranormal to get along together.. be pals.. one family.. phantomes and humans.

No longer be paranoid of the paranormal. This cereal has sought you out. You have been chosen by the cereal.. to be a Crusader for Consciousness.. chosen to enter the Cavern of Creation.. the Entrance into Eternity.. in a box of cereal that never runs out of reality."

I looked at Sis not sure if she was reading or we were being read. Some say it was only thoughts I heard in my head.. not the real dead.. the divine from whom we are all descended. Ya all is the garden. All comes from what was. All is born from that which is.

The Ritual of Reality had begun. Breakfast had arrived with a storm of Strawberry Stars. "And it's rainin' raisins !" Sis screamed out to Babaji Baboon who was last seen paddlin' with his spoon across Sis's bowl of cereal.. on a surfboard shaped slice of banana.. on a search party for the Paranormal Poet Prince of the Pages.. the Lord of Literature and Language.

"To hold something sacred inside one's heart.. to surrender to the soul.. to soar as spirit.. that is what all seekers search for in the cosmic cereal.. the void of visions. You who read these words are the vanguard of Vocabulary Visionaries.. using Visionary Vocabulary.. to enhance and uplift the hope and healing of humanity.

Consciousness Crusader Cadets.. Angels in Ascension.. Brain Border Blasters.. You have opened a book that comes with a cast of characters that care about you. Yes this book cares about your consciousness.

Some say life is a song sung by the soul and the Heart is a Temple.
I am the bowl in which the Buddha.. and all being.. is bathed.
I am the belly within which all are given birth.

I am the source of your cereal.. the source of your soul.. the source of your stories.
I am the evolution of existence and I am existence itself.
I am consciousness and I am creator.

World Wakers.. Wake The World With Your Words. Make Words Not War.
Regular Reality is a radical idea that has outlived its time.. its usefulness.
Has space got you feeling confined ? Time got you trapped ?
Well then.. take another spoon of cereal.

Spirits self reflect also. I know who I am.. the same way as you know who you are.. thru self reflection.

I have come in this cereal of strawberry stars to rekindle the fires in every heart. I exist but for no other reason than to embrace your heart within mine.. to give you a nest within which to rest in sanctuary sacred and serene.. here within these pages that will pamper you with poems and prose.. sweet as a jasmine night rose scented garden of eternal infinite bliss."

"Sis !" I yelled out.. "Would ya save readin' the side of the cereal box for later and let me pour myself some cereal ! We're never gonna get to class on time."

And so I too poured from the Chalice of Immortal Illumination into the Bowl of the Beloved's Blessings.. my own serving of cereal. Think of the bowl as the Belly of All Being.. the Cosmic Cauldron of Conscious Creation and Cosmic Communication.

The Cosmos is a Karma Cauldron Consciousness Crucible.. the Cosmic Chalice of Creation.. and Sis and I were holding it in our breakfast bowls.
Regular reality was fast losing its hold on me while Sis continued reading the sides of the box as though she were possessed.

"Think of the Bowl.. the Box.. and the Book.. as the three Crones of Creation.. Communication.. and Consciousness.. all combined to create the cosmos. It is in this bowl all shall be reborn." The Supermarket Sales Serpent rattled on while shaking his rattler like a cheyenne shaman.. dancing down the aisle with a box of Strawberry Stars Cereal in his coiled tail.

The legendary Lama of Learning.. the Learned Lavender Deli Lizard.. nodded in agreement.. behind the college cafeteria counter.. from where he dispensed the dharma.

Yes this lizard who lives in the literature.. and the snake who sells the story.. and the toad who tells the tale.. and of course the paranormal poet who pens the parable.. all are the same being.. as are you and I the spirit scribe.

All is manifested from the world womb of the mother of meaning.. matter.. and mind."

Sis intently read from the sides of the box.. resting her elbows on the Table of Fables in the Tavern of Tales.. while she slowly spooned another round of reality stars in between her lavender lips.

Taco Tio Tales Toad raised his ghost goblet of ghost grogg.. out of which ghosts were gliding.. and offered a toast to all gathered round in the Temple of Transformation.

"May your path thru the pages be pure and powerful.. and may your swim in the story stew help you find you. Reality is simply the shadows of our insanities swimming in a bowl of cosmic cereal filled with the Milk of Maya. You can bet yer breakfast begging and bathing bowl.. that this cereal is serious about saving simian society from themselves.

We words are trained in word wizardry. This story specializes in script sorcery. These pages are potions.. mind manufacturers.. imagination illuminators.. reality retreaders.

The Bowl is but your brain.. the Cereal your thoughts.. and the Box the rabbit hole you go into.. in search of yourself. Better wear these Spirit Spectacles. Going into the Box is like being poured thru a portal of luminence." Tio said as he handed Sis and me a pair each. "Get yer own.. along with a Story Stirrin' Spoon. They come inside specially marked boxes of Strawberry Stars Cosmic Cranial Cruising Cereal.

The bowl has always been the symbol of birth.. the belly.. the Bowl of Blessings of the Belly of the Beloved.. the Divine Door thru which all is descended.. and thru which all ascends.

Approach the bowl as you would approach the Altar of Alteration. The cereal box is the Temple of Transformation.. Tio's Tale Trunk Trailer Tavern Tabernacle.

And to guide you thru the Paranormal Parable.. you get a Ghost Genie in a jar of juju jam.. instead of in a dented lamp.

It all comes with the Strawberry Star Story Spirit Shaman's stamp of approval."

Then Tio slung the Strawberry Star Storm Story Satchel over his shoulder.. and spinning his Story Stick Staff over his head.. cut reality in half.. thus parting the milk in the cereal bowl.. opening a path for all to follow.

And with these parting phrases..
"It's simply the overflow from the Fountain of Fantasy renovating reality.. consciousness striving to communicate with itself.. paranormal paramedics coming thru the pages to perform mind to mind resuscitation.." Tio poured another cup of Twig Tale Tea.. and said to Sis and me.. without blinking his middle eye..

"The truth be told.. the tale itself is a transformer of form.. the script is a shape shifter.. the story is the sorcerer. It was not written by man nor ghostly hand.. but by the script itself.. Spirit Script.

Yes.. you and the story are one. It is all but cosmic clay.
Life is a vessel of vision crafted by an eternal artist.

What is there to win.. but one's self.. one's true eternal sacred self. And then one sees that it is all one self.

We are all facets of a multi faced jewel of light.. vibrating.. singing.. breathing.. A cosmic harmony of voices.

Plant the garden of life.
The universe is a university.
Kiss everyone with the lyrics of love."

And then smiling and singing.. Tio set off into the bowl.

Consciousness Comes Calling

Consciousness comes calling when shadows start falling
and the beliefs begin to break up.
Was it something in the cup I drank,
a foul brew that stank of sweat and piss and prayer.

Pray for thyself not for me.
No mortal prayers will prepare my entry
into this paranormal portal thru which I soon pass.

You are like vesuvias rising up to meet me.
Merge with me as the surging sea caresses the boulders of your battlements.

Transform me upon your cross.
Adorn me with your emerald green gaze.

Love me even after the curtain closes
and the roses wilt.
Wither thy wander I will.

Lead me by thy hand into the chapter of your choice.
Make me your chosen.
Unwrap me as the present you prefer.

I will follow you into the future.
From out of the past I have sought you.
And in the present I will stay with you.

So here I am lying naked across the bare pages in a sensual embrace with some
sexy syllables, and a passing paragraph pauses to propose a question.
"Guess what ? All I will tell you is, it is not a who, nor a where, nor a why.

Now don't be shy of the sentences. Though they're squiggly and the words are
wiggly, do not worry, for the writer has gone before and routed out all the scarey
ones, so you can have fun.
Run reader run. The Book From The Beyond is beckoning with it's wide open crimson
covers.

We interrupt this page for a news break, brought to you by..
the Dojo Demon Dragon's Dojo, and the Warthog Warlord's anger management clinic.

Order a Dojo Demon Door Stopper to secure yer bedroom door, so when yer sleeping nothing unseen can slip into yer dreams.

For the lift you need take cereal.. This message courtesy of the cereal dealers union and mother mary's hospice for homeless heroes.
It takes a heart to be a hero..

Throw your cereal spoons loaded with strawberry stars at the enemy..
Scare tactics work.. If the boogey man bothers you or your little kid sister or brother, then bother the boogey man back.

There is nothing that bothers a boogey man more than being bothered.
Buy the boogey man's book.. on sale everywhere.
Okay, that's it.. for.. Next To Now.. the news as it breaks..
Full throttle no brakes.. we believe because you do.

Memo from Ace Towers to his special secretary Stella Starlight..
Well sweetheart, I will try again tonight to get to the Carnivores Club.. Max More and me and possibly two others makes four.

Couldja huh love.. leave a note ? at the door ?
There'll be four angels flyin in on wings wide as the sacred sky.

I hope you are being blessed in the way of wonder and not war.

And if yer tired, well all angels' wings get worn
Look.. mine are torn.

In the belly of the beloved we are born..
beaten and shorn.. and scratched with a rose's thorn.

Every morn when you wake..
Don't shake the dreams from your eyes..
Day is dark's delight.. night's nocturnal yearning.

I can feel the day yearning for her lover the night..
Awaiting his velvety cloak upon day's skin.

"Hey banana skin baboon boy.. get outta bed.. yer Doc Chimp Alarm Clock didn't beat itself upon the chest and utter its gutteral morning wake up growl. Mum's got yer cereal in the bowl. Beat it outta yer banana bunk bed, bongo boy.. Yer bed buddy the baboon is allready in the bathroom brushin his teeth."
..sis screeched thru my bedroom door.

Send in six box tops and a bunch of bottoms from any of the great Consciousness Cereals consumed by the characters in this story.. and you'll receive a Doc Chimp Alarm Clock squattin' at the Bardo Branch Brunch Back Bayou Bruho Brew Bar Breakfast Bowl waterin' hole for wraithes, writers, and Renegade Reality Readers.

Just remember that that bottom which you tore off from the box of cereal is the trap door.. which you just ripped open.. to The Devil's Den.. The Demons' Paranormal Playpen.

Ya.. we was waitin'.. me an sis.. at the Wraith Waterin Hole halfway ta hell.. the Spirits' Sink.. where mum was washin' the devil's own dishes.. waitin' for The Wraith Writer.. the ghost in the graveyard of those gone before.

We was havin' our wings washed clean of the dirt we had picked up flying thru the dimensions of dark dreams.. Spirits movin' at the speed of sound.

Reader.. don't make a sound.. there's some spirits sniffin' around us now.. sniffin' at our souls.. lookin for empty holes in our hearts.

So I'm sittin in this soft society sofa scene with miss blue jean dreams.. discussing with dick the dinosaur how he's gonna score big, along with Big, and Max More, and Ace Towers, who were the main money behind the marketing of..
The Manuscript of Myth, Magic, and Maya..
discovered neath the basement boulders of The Museum of Mausoleums..
a Fable of Forever.. found neath The Phantom Floors of the fallen and forgotten.

It was somethin' about A Strawberry Star Studios Spirit Syndicate Streaming Show. That's all I overheard.. when The Dialogue With The Dead.. The Interview With The Invisible.. was cut short.. by an abrupt period.. penned by The Paranormal Poet.

Gotta go.. this ghost's gotta coast..
Ghost Gab.. Get it all in The Ghost Gazette.. it's fun and fiction and fact, folded into fabulous Phantom Fantasy, cooked up in The Cauldrons of Consciousness..
Call consciousness collect anytime.

Consciousness craves communication..
Consciousness creates community..
Consciousness creates consciousness..

Was consciousness the creator or the creation of the cosmos ?
Is consciousness the cosmos ?
Is the cosmos composed of consciousness ?
Is the cosmos conscious of itself, in a similar way that you are conscious of yourself, and all that surrounds you ?

Are you simply one small aspect of cosmic consciousness.. just as this spoon of cereal you are about to put into your mouth.. is but a single serving out of a bottomless box of strawberry stars ?

I could hear the cereal asking me questions.. whispering words with each spoonful. Welcome to Consciousness Class 101.

Build the candles that light your darkness.. out of the wax of wisdom.
Lift your altars above the highest clouds of your souls' sorrows.

Burn down your tombs of time
Reality is an endless rhyme

The cereal box is an Entry Into Eternity.. the eternal ever birthing cosmos.
Your cereal bowl is The Cauldron of Consciousness.. and your Sorcerer's Stirring Spoon your Wisdom Wand. Stir well Wisdom Word Wanderer. The words wait upon your wishes. The Cereal calls.

The chapter's cool
The hero's hot
Everyone get's caught
Everyone's bin bought

The Renegade Reality Radio Reptile Rapper, the Raspberry Rattler, spit out the song on the radio from the other side of reality's ridge on top of the fridge.

The door creaks.. Softly the soul speaks.. like winds whispering.

Nothing in this book is normal. The Book From Beyond The Boundaries of The Brain. Reader I don't know if you can handle this.. I'm not human.. And by the end of the story you won't be either.. You have entered the paranormal pages.. Parables penned by a Paranormal Poet.. a Spirit Scribe.. a Wraith Writer..
a ghost writer.. a real one.

We are words written upon Paranormal Pteradactylian Parchment.. Soaring Saurian Spirit Scribes' scaly skin.. soaked in scribble sorcerer spell sauce..

"Would you quite listening to that cereal box and please toss me the toast so breakfast ain't a complete loss.. Miss ?" the supermarket sales serpent said ta sis.. as he stuck his spoon into the jam jar while giving her a kiss.

Have you ever seen a spirit.. something invisible..
Somethin unseen.. except by those initiated.. which you are about to be.

Spirits have passed this way thru these pages.. pages that are portals into the paranormal.. spirit scribes.. paranormal page prowllers.. a pack of paranormal paragliders.. part predator.. part prayer.. part page.. leaving behind this script as a telltale sign.. a gateway into another mind.

Sis and I were prowlin' The Paranormal Parchment Pages when we got interrupted by Tio The Tale Tellin' Toad askin' us to pass the pudding.. telling us to get ready for a paranormal package about to be delivered to our email doorstep..
        ..direct from the divine dude himself.

Paranormal Parables

"Would you please pass me the Tulku Tale Temple Trail Toast.".. sis so politely asked Tio who was reading the back of the box trying to find the way out of the page on which we were lost.

Most readers give up about here and fall even deeper into the box of cereal. As surely as darkest night follows brightest day, we all get consumed in The Cauldron of Creation.

"Hey would you please stop splashing your spoon in the cereal bowl.. yur gettin' sticky strawberry stars all over Babaji Baboon's new Violet Vision Vest".. mum muttered as she continued stirring the pot of Paranormal Potions, simmering on the Spell Sorcerer's Stove..

This is a test.. this is a test.. do not be alarmed.. This is a safety exit test for all readers preparing to go deeper into the text of The Transcripts of The Temple Tomb Tunnels of Thanatos..

Please calmly exit this page from the lower right hand corner to get safely to the next page.. If you are afraid of the next page and going deeper into the story of your own mind then please without disturbing the other readers say your goodbyes..

And quietly exit at the top left hand corner of this page.. You will find yourself safely back upon the previous page, retreading your steps thru the sentences, eventually back to the beginning of The Book.. However there is no guarantee you will still be.. who you were.. when you first entered.. The Book From The Beyond.

Beware.. The Book does not take lightly to trespassers of The Transcripts of Thanatos.. The ink is dark and deep upon the page.. One false step upon a syllable.. too long a linger at a period.. and you dear reader could slip forever unseen.. into a dream.

So please once again brave beautiful Brothers of The Book.. sweet sacred serene Sisters of The Story.. a word of warning about the words.. Stay on the words.. Do not wander off into the blank part of the pages.. The Void of Visions.. you will enter nothingness.. a state of not being.. existential emptiness.

Put the spoon down.. Do not take another serving of cereal.. Get your hand out of the box.. Carefully close the book..

"Get yer hands outta the box.. It's my turn to find the Tomb Temple Tale Tellin Tangerine Toad Toy.. You already got the Bardo Brew Bruho Blueberry Baboon Eternity Effigy" ..Sis spouted, while Mum told us both to close The Book.. put down our Script Surfin Spoons.. and get off to school.

I calmly replied.. having just come back from visiting those who had died.. "Oh Sis, come on.. you've got the Lavender Ledge Lizardarian Librarian Love Light Lamp.. and yer buddy Booker Baboon is holding two tickets to Le Theatre De Thanatos.. while babbling something about slurring syllables because he had too much cereal for breakfast."

Fantasy and fiction overtake fact while it fades forgotten, as a shadow slowly sliding down the walls. I could feel what was far.. coming near. Hush Reader. Do you hear how the pages flutter from the wind of an invisible wing.

Something turns the pages.. Someone not you.. And all you can do is try to stay on the path created by the sentences.. and not fall into the barren blank void of the empty pale white parchment page.. made of the silken skin of something.. someone.. that has always been.. and always will.

When you awake sweaty in the middle of the night and the moon is kissing you, know that the sun awaits its turn too. May you sleep sweetly with the stars of serenity and the moons of magic guiding your dreams, my dearest.

Call it education and entertainment, entwined with a tantric twist, to take you over the top of your reality roof.. so your soul can soar.

Meanwhile Babaji Baboon was pickin' his nose with his toes, and singing along with the song playing on the Renegade Reality Radio Show, coming from the radio on the other side of the ridge of reality, on top of the fridge.. spun by your favorite deejay of divinity.. the raspberry rattler renegade reality reptile radio rapper.. unwrapping reality and serving it to you raw.

"That's how it goes.. livin in the trees
It's easy to get fleas.. when yer born with hair on yer knees"

"Bring it to an end, baboon boy..!"
sis screamed in her favorite fierce ferocious feline form.
"Shut up simian soap opera! Act like an angel instead of an ape, you animal !"

Do you hear god crying ?
In tears are bathed her face..
Battered and bruised her body..

Don't you see we are all beating her body..
And we will all bathe in the same tears.

Let your love adorn the temple walls
Let your words wrap the world in wisdom.

"Lighten up on the literature you locacious Lavendar Lizard Lingo Lamp..
We're gonna be late for school cause you kept the Doc Chimp Alarm up all night..
You and Tio The Tavern Toad tellin The Tale of The Transcripts of Thanatos.

Just pass the Sorcerer Syrup and put a period on yer paragraph or for sure we're never gona get to class on time.. or even in time. I mean like we're gonna be lost somewhere outside of time. And you silly serpent save yer kiss for some other miss."

And so the sentences snuggle up with the reader in a corner of the page of a book whose covers have become the walls of the world into which you are slowly dissappearing. But isn't all of life a story.. rarely written by one's own hand ?

Attention all readers.. please tighten your safety sentence straps.. synchronize your syllable spittin language lazers for entry into next chapter.. abort this page.. emergency exit is blocked.. no way outta this chapter. The words have gone wild.. wicked warrior words doing battle inside the book. There is complete chaos amongst the chapters.. they are all fighting to be either the opening chapter or the closing one. Settle down you silly sentences.. quite slithering all over the page.. stay still. Let the readers read the words so they can find their way to the next page.. this is not a game.. this is an expedition into eternity and existence itself.

There up ahead.. do you see the exit sign at the end of the next sentence ? Exit to Eternity.. enter here. Readers please wipe your fingers before turning the page.

"Get yur greasy chocolate covered fingers offa my covers.!" ..The Book screamed at Sis.. "You kept me up all night reading me under yer blanket.. you and that Lavendar Lizardarian Librarian Lamp Light.. I'm an old story and I need my sleep."

"Yes included in every download for the deluded and excluded.. on the inside of the top flap of every box of Blueberry Bardo Breakfast and Brunch bite sized Brain Blasters.. you'll find a Universe of Visionary Verse.. and a Visionary Vocabulary Interdimensional Dictionary.

And if yer real lucky you might find deep inside the box of cosmic cereal a Story Sorcerer's Soaring Spoon.. so you can soar on your stories over the walls of the world.

Strawberry Stars and Blueberry Bardo Brain Blaster bite sized bits and Cosmic Cherry Comet Chunks Creation Cereals.. building better bodies and better brains.. Cosmic Cereals Corporation Inc.. the company that cares about your consciousness.. and makes you think.

And now to return to our story after that lovely commercial from our sponsors.. The Sentence and Syllable Studio and The Fiction and Fact Factory.

Just send in the box tops from any of these fine cereals, along with the bottom of your brain.. in exchange for shares in the Consciousness Company.

This message brought to you by Mind Masters.. manufacturing minds and blasting brains with breakfast cereals that are cosmically conscious.

This is the Raspberry Reptile Rapper wrapping up your reality in rhyme.. Broadcasting to your brain from Renegade Reality Radio.. situated somewhere outside of time.. on the other side of the ridge of reality ..on top of yer kitchen fridge.. tune in tomorrow at breakfast and before bed when we'll unwrap your reality and open yer head.

God's Flesh

This book has been born in the brains and baptized in the blood of those weary writers and rugged readers who have gone before.

The text can get pretty tough.. the story's got talons like a tiger.. There are tale tigers travelling thru the transcripts.. and paragraph panthers.. phantoms prowllin the pages.. ghosts growllin'.. horror howlin'.. in the hallways of yer head.

A solitary reader can sink into a swamp of syllables dense with writhing serpent sentences. See how the sentences seem to slither across the page at this very moment..No it is not your eyes.. nor is it darkness in disguise. It is simply satan saying his prayers before sleep.

"Listen up you guys. which one of you characters spilt swamp sauce all over my suit ! There will be the devil to pay if I'm late another day for class. Today was gonna be my introductory lecture on The Legends of The Lizardarian Librarians of The Lost Libraries of Love's Languages.. specifically speaking on the subject of satan's seven sisters at satan's soiree."

"Dad delivered his lines so debonairly.. he was fairly cool for a dad.. for a prof he was pure pro.. taught primal prophecy and primordial principles for the preservation of paradise planet.. in addition to Paranormal Prose and Poetry.

Dad was associate ape at the center for squares department of delusion..at the College of Consciousness.. and we his kids, we're Consciousness Cadets..
ya.. me an my little sis.. we're Spirit Seekers.. Paratroopers Into The Paranormal.

Dad was always channelin' this consciousness or that consciousness.. any consciousness that came cruising by.. from any reality.. Dad could communicate with it.

Dad had an array of alien flying friends.. He was "steeped in spirit".. as they say down at the Shaman Stew Shop where ya drop inta different dimensions with just one swig of Swamp Shaman Soda .. comes in two new flavors..
strawberry swamp super slithery soda and blueberry bayou baboon bum bardo brew. One's for shape shiftin and the other's for bardo bustin.. blowin' yer brains beyond the boundaries of the borders of yer barriers.. crackin' the cranial cauldron.

Dad's newest buddy was some animator he had rented the attic to for doing art work for some studio goin' by the name of Strawberry Star Studios. Sis and I jokingly referred to him as The Angel In The Attic..

Until we found out he was a real authentic angel.. sounds pretty unreal but stranger events started happening all about the same time that day that Mum and me and Sis were in the supermarket aisle searching for some cereal when a Strawberry Serpent Sales Snake stuck this box of cereal in our basket.. Said it was compliments of consciousness.

That was the same day that Sis came home carrying in her back pack an old book with leathery covers looking like it had veins. Sis had been visiting Dad after class waiting for a ride home. Dad told her he'd be a little late and she should go hang out in the college library, which was housed in an ancient building built of stone and boulders.

Sis had wandered down to the basement aisles and somehow found herself at the very end of the stacks next to the basement boulder wall when she heard something fall.. onto the dusty earthen floor.

It was This Book.. ya the very one you are reading.. Sounds strange but I don't remember existing before you opened This Book.

And it was that same day later before supper, when we went out to play in the vacant lot in back of the old brownstone apartment block where our family recently moved in due to the fact that mum and dad had started new jobs at the College of Creation. Our family had moved from somewhere else I can't seem to recall.

Anyways Sis and I were just hanging out in the remains of this old sandbox, digging around pretending we were archeolgists excavating for buried tombs and temples and pyramides .. when this beautiful multi hued butterfly came soaring down alongside the buildings' walls.

It had just appeared from over the top of one of the buildings. Three old stone buildings formed a type of canyon surrounding the vacant lot.. while the fourth side of the vacant lot was was bordered by an ancient alley way.. Angel Alley.. that's what the broken sign post said.. Alley of the Ancestors.. carved into the stone sign as though by a claw.

The glowing iridescent butterfly came floating down the walls and then flittered and fluttered across the vacant lot.. with Sis and me chasing after it.. following it like it were leading us somewhere.. like an almost invisible angel of light leading the way.

It landed.. alighted.. upon the solitary flower growing in the dirt and rubble. Sis and I leaned forward bending down for a closer look.. when all of a sudden the butterfly morphed.. dissolved.. transformed into glowing light of every hue streaming into our eyes.

Within seconds or minutes.. or years or millenia.. we couldn't tell.. for it felt like forever.. the light receded back into what had been the butterfly.. but instead there lay upon the ground a handful of glowing crystalline marbles.. one of each colour.. pure as though they were made of living light.

It was then Sis and I heard the words.. "If you wish to find the crystals from which these marbles came.. then follow the light from Lilac Lane until you come upon Persimmon Peak.. There you will find the crystals of which I speak..
..and the vision which you seek.

Seekers of the Script.. seekers of the sacred soul..
Seekers of the saint's role..
And seekers of the saviour's role..
I am but the humble servant. I do not make up the words. I am but a simple Spirit Scribe. Yes.. true.. I am a spirit unseen.. one who has been for several millenia in service to The Great Spirit.. of which you dream and to which you pray.

I am but a Spirit Scribe serving the one whose words I write.
True I am a spirit and true I can speak to you.. thru these written words.
I am a ghost writer scribbling the script for one who has come from the time before you or anyone was born.

I simply sweep the floors of the Fiction Factory free of fact.. and fabricate the future out of fantasy. For before me.. nothing was.. just eternal emptiness.

I annoint the angels as they alight upon the temples' altars.
I prepare the pyramids' promontories for the paranormal paragliders' approach.
I am the soul's scribe
the scribe of the sacred script
and I am the sacred script you read..
And the causes for which you sweat and bleed..
I am the path of all pilgrims.. and the prayers with which you plead.

I am the Sorcerer of Space..
a being who can shape space in any way a World Wizard wishes..
I am a Word Wizard.. similar to a Spirit Scribe.. a wanderer along the way of wisdom..
a wind wanderer Wraith Writer.. a Soul Soarer.. a Renegade Reality Rider.

And you also are a renegade reality reader.. Miss baby blue jeans..
Princess panther paws..Tiger toes temptress.."
..the words were whispering to sis.. I could hear The Book begging for a kiss.

"Together you and I.. thru these writings of the wraith of wisdom..
shall investigate infinity.. infiltrate infinity itself, and eventually own existence.. own reality. You shall sell shares of eternity to everyone you meet.. become kinda like an altar attendant who washes the angels' wings sparkling shiny.

Become a ghost guide.. an angel attendant.. a spirit saviour.. an angel ally..
a paranormal pal.. a phantom friend..
a soul surfer..

Ya.. you become a soul surfer.. an emotional entity without a body..
a ghost that feels thinks and loves.. more than humans do..

Reader do you understand what that means..
Yes you who read these words..
You are the angel I have been looking for.

You are the human angels I have been sent to find.. to lure with this literature.. to tutor.. to teach.. so that you reach out with your wings of wonder and wisdom to everyone.

Remember reader to add your consciousness comments at the end of each chapter wherever there is a blank space.. this is your wisdom work book.. your chance to add to the cosmos.. share with other readers.

The Soul's Story

Embrace the world with your soul
Be the blessing of Beauty's Breath

"So as I was sayin before yer kid brother interrupted me.." the cereal whispered to sis. "I just happen to be the ghost writin' the words yer reading.. renegade reality rider.. watch how ya walk along these words.. this sentence ain't no sucker.. this chapter ain't no chump.. this ain't a game of chance.. I never lose.. I always win..

I was a warrior.. a wizard.. a worrier.. and a wanderer..
I was wounded and I was welcomed..
I was waited upon and I was the awakened one..
I was one of those who washed the wings of the weary angels
when their bodies became wind..

I was written and I was read.
I was wrought of words
I am born of the wedding of wisdom and wonder
I am the sacred story that exists forever..
I am the story born of your thoughts.. your words.. your actions

I am the karma you collectively create..
I am the cause of your courage
I am christ on a cross and I am moses come down from the mountain temple..
I am the mountain.. and I am the message
Mountains are temples.. made of time.. and space
considered as sacred spaces in all cultures..
deserts were divine destinations .. the domiciles of divinities.

We are all.. everything is.. divine incarnation.. cosmic creation..
This is The Soul's Sacred Story
Together we write it..
Me the Spirit's Scribe and you The Book's Beloved..
The Story's Sweetheart.." I could hear the cereal softly saying to Sis..
as it continued telling The Tale of The Temple of Time.

"Once thru Prayer Pass.. high above you will perceive Perfection Peak..
where you shall be born as the blessing you beg..
the vision you wish to wed."

" Hey.. Heyoka Hero.. Would'ja please pass the pancakes.." Tio mumbled to Sis as he readied his tongue for one far flung shot across the table and into the box of cereal that talks.

"Sweet sacred sister simians of all sorts..
I say to you.. let all realities join as one.. all paths pour into one pudding.."

"Priceless princess of the pages would you please pass the pudding to yer pal the primate.." Benny Baboon interrupted as he stretched his skinny arm across the table for another slice of tale toast.

"Angels and aliens and ancient ancestors and eternal entities ! Look at this next chapter!" ..sis squealed as she read the words from the back of the box.

She solemnly continued..
"For where I take you now dear renegade reality reader.. is up from the bottom of the book.. out from the shady shadowy side of the story.. into the sun of your soul.. unto your divine destination.. on top of persimmon peak.. where the Crystal Chrysalises sleep.. the souls slumber.. on the other side of the ridge on top of the fridge in the kitchen where mum was cookin Cosmic Cherry Consciousness Creation Custard.. in The Cauldron of Chronos..
also known as The Chalice of Creation.

Some say it was stirred by the Crone of Creation herself..
in the kitchen of the cosmic queen.
Some say it's only a story and has never been..

Some say it will happen again one day.. as it is now.. happening amongst you.. whispering in words many are beginning to hear.. in their own heads.

You are the light of love..the offspring of the embrace of the eternal.
You are the flesh of god.. the flesh of goddess.. the fruit of the garden of eternity..

you are forever.. eternal entities..
one eternal entity of divine dimensions.

Upon opening this box you enrolled in an expedition into eternity..
an enquiry into the infinite.. a trip into a Temple Tale..
a Paranormal Parable.. penned by a Paranormal Poet.
You are Divinity's Daughter.. Our fate is forever entwined.."

The cereal was laying the literature on heavy to Sis.. pushing the poetry.. playing with the prose.. like a lover presenting a rose.

"Would you get yer hairy nose outta my cereal bowl.." Sis was saying to Booker Bagel Baboon who was sniffin around at somethin in the cereal.. in search of doing an Interview With an Eternal Entity from Outside of Eternity..
a living legend.. that lived from one life to the other.. with no death in between.

The Veil of Visions that separates your world from our world is thinning.. Yes there are more than me of my kind here amongst you now.. Our fate has been forever entwined.. You the Reader.. and I the ghost writer.. the wraith writer.. the wind that worships the woods where the wolves walk with the white woman of light.. the moon mother.

You are the moon maiden of my madness.. I am but an ancient angel illustrator of the great artist's art.."

The cereal was spouting on poetically to sis who was sittin' on the baboon's lap scratchin' its knees..

I merely package the paranormal product. I do not manufacture the myth.
It was made before man mumbled his first words.
The destiny of divinity is a hot flight into heaven.."

"My little pieces of heaven would you please finish your breakfast.. time won't last forever.. we can't keep dad waiting in the car.. now off you both go like a strawberry shooting star and a cosmic cherry comet.." mum muttered as she packed our Lavender Lizard Lunch Boxes with goodies and ghosts.

Mum says we sew the seams of the soul's dreams.. with our daring and integrity. We are light becoming unfettered of form.. divine dissipation..
the divine dissipating.. dissolving.. dying.. disappearing..
into different dimensions of the same reality..
There is only one world but a myriad of ways to walk it..
Infinity awaits us all in its eternal embrace."

"You two Angel Aviators will be eternally exiled from this table and reality.. if you and your baboon buddies don't put down yer Story Spoons and get into the car with dad."

Mum was flight coordinator for our family. We had just flown in from a hot flight into heaven. Our angel aviator armor was caked with consciousness's crud collected from across the cosmos. We were gods or so we thought. Like most.. our brains had been bought.

We owned eternity.. infinity was our servant.. existence our slave..
We had risen above the sunrise. We had become the one who never dies..
The ever renewing dew that is the cosmic child of heaven and earth's kiss."

"Look little monkey man.. you and yer sweet sis wouldn't wanna miss class.. Today is show and tell.. Remember how excited you were cause you're gonna show The Book.. and Evy is gonna show The Cereal.. for the first time to the other kids."..the wind whispered.. or was it the words that whispered ?

Consciousness Crusaders

"You slipped out so silently from the story at the end of the last chapter.. just as you slipped so silently into it at the beginning of this chapter. So it is with spirits .. They come and go unseen by most readers of The Pages of The Paranormal.

You and me pal we're different.. Like two sides of the same page.. Two takes on the same tale.. Two sentences entwined.. ink and paper... one without the other is empty.

Like the spoon and the bowl.. Empty without the cereal.. So it is with you and me.. We need the words.. The script is our blood.. The pages our flesh.. The covers of the book our cloak. We need each other.. as day needs night.

Without these aspects of ourselves we are invisible.. we don't exist. We are joined forever.. you the reader.. and me the writer.. You the cute kid sitting at the breakfast table and me the cereal in the box that talks."

The cereal box was conversing with sis who was rapt with attention.. wrapped in the words the cereal box was wooing her with..

"All proceeds from this page will be sent to Angel Orphanage. Send an orphan angel to heaven.. simply send in the labels from as many cans as you can of Goblin Gravy, Ghost and Ghoul Goulash, or Spell Sorcerer Soup and Stew.

Win a holiday in heaven or hell.. spells on sale for half price.. win a vacation in veil vortex.

Look, here on the side of the box.. it says win a vision vacation for your whole family in the Valley of Visions.. compliments of Veil Valley Vision Quest Vacations..

And so you won't feel lonely on those dark nights in nowhere.. you'll be accompanied by your own personal Vision Vulture when yer deep in the dark dimensions"
   Sis was reading the sides of the box, deep in another reality..

"Spirits do vision quests too.. just like humans do.. only in locations no human can do. It's all been scripted by the soul.. staged across the sky.. scrawlled upon the walls of the world.. in strawberry story and song spirit syrup script.

We interrupt this story for a sales pitch from our sponsors.. the spirits
"Use Angels' Armour for spirit surfing safety..
Soul soaring study is a six semesters consciousness course..
quickest method to become a bonafied bardo buster brain blaster being..
Call it.. cookin up consciousness with the consciousness connoiseur commander chef.. a course for consciousness crusader cadets.

And just for signing up you'll get an original copy of The Crucible of Chronos found in The Temple Tomb of Time.. a chapter of consciousness you won't wanna miss.. Little Miss" ..the box said ta Sis.

" Get them as a bonus for blowing beyond your brain's borders .. become a bonafied brain blaster.. there is no difference between you and me.. except for one fundamental fact.. I am formless, you are not.. I the Story Spirit can take any shape I wish. With words I create worlds.

Perhaps you too are part of a story scratched into existence by The Pen of The Paranormal.. just another character scripted by The Story Sorcerer.. simply spirit script.. paranormal print upon paranormal pages.. scribbled and scrawlled by the Story Shaman shape shiftin' all the scenes that have ever been.."

The cereal box was whispering to Sis real slow and low.. intimate like it was sharing a secret only meant for the chosen..

"Syllables slowly forming into words and then becoming woven into sentences.. coming together as chapters.. What if you only exist in a book.. what if you are like us.. characters existing only upon a page... only in the mind of the Master Mind ?

"What if you could spend your lives in different stories living forever .. going from one story to another.. living in several stories at the same time.. choosing your own beginnings and endings..?

What if you were allowed to write the stories.. given the eternal freedom to create forever your realities..?

If there ain't no book there's no story, and without a story there's no characters. There's gotta be script or there's nothin ta say and a book with blank pages is difficult for some ta read.

So ya gotta fill in the blank spaces.. trace a trail with a pen upon the page.. show em the way with a few syllables.. pull em inta the paranormal with a paragraph."

I could hear the cereal emit an eerie laugh from deep inside the box. Sis stared at the cereal.. mesmerized by the milk as it rippled and spun round and round in her bowl creating a whirlpool that lead deep into dimensions too awesome to mention to other minds.

"For practice runs of reality riding, wear Spirit Skins.. spirit surfing wear for flights inta heaven, or a spell in hell.

Send in twenty box tops and receive your Wizard Wear Wardrobe and Ghost Gear Gown.. safety rated for any renegade reality you encounter.. Write in why you wanna be a wizard and win a Wind Wizard Wish Wand.. with which to wake up the wind.. stir up a storm.. Wake up the world with words.. Wonder Wizard"

"There is but one way to the heart of heaven. Be the bearer of beauty inside.. though on the outside you may be covered by the cloak of the beast.." Gutor Gator the Saurian Sewer Savior of the Swamps, said to Sis as he slithered up thru the milk to the side of her cereal bowl.

He was an Alley Angel Demon Deterrent against terror in the Tunnels of Thanatos neath the city streets that ran above the sewers of the Saurian Scribes.. a sect of sacred Spirit Scholars.. gutter gators.. gutteral growllers.. glade guides.. guarding The Ghost Gates into The Garden of The Ghost Guru.. who lived in mum's stew.
Ya the pot upon our stove had become an entry into the underworld.

"Let your spirit rise up from the cadaver in the coffin.. from The Crystalline Chrysalis of your cocoon. Metamorphosize into magic.. And hey little sister how about a sliver of yer strawberry star syrup and paranormal peanut butter sandwich on tangerine treacle Time Travellin' Toast.. for yer Gutter Guide Ghost?" Gutor held on to the side of the bowl with his claws as he pleaded thru his eyes..

To which Sis simply replies.. "the body is a disguise for the soul and the Tale Toast tastes like toad toes, dipped in yer runny nose, Nirvana Navigator Gator."

So the story goes.. brains at the alert.. book open wide.. words glowing all sparkly.. space no longer the cage it used to be.. time unable to hold reality in its grip.. each of us eternal.. eternal creations conjured in The Crown of The Crone.

When all of a sudden, breaking into The Book flow words from outside of the story.." Hey who's flicking strawberry stars across the table ! There's a storm swirling atop the temple's tower.. making it difficult to see The Box.. obscuring the table with a pink cloudy mist of strawberry stars." Dad hollered as he fumbled with his car's keys.

It was impossible to find the bowl with our spoons.. impossible to reach The Box with our hands for a second helping.. All that could be seen of the pile of pancakes was the very peak of the pyramid.

Then everyone sitting at the table heard the words.. "Upon Persimmon Promise Peak you shall find the vision which you seek. I am all visions. I am the script of your sacred stories.. The sacred source of your existence.. I am all that you lay upon your altars.. I am The Temple of Truth.

I am the book.. the body.. the ink.. the blood.. the pages.. the flesh.. The Being From Beyond.. formed of dreams and hopes and love so bright, I light every corner of consciousness. I supply all souls with sustenance.

Brothers of The Book.. Sisters of The Story.. You are all children of the cosmic chapters.. composed by the cosmos. You are.. all is.. a cosmic choir.
Your voices are the visions of the universe."

Saurian Sorcerers

You have been baptized in The Water of Words.. Born of The Book
Given life thru The Literature of Love..

Your stories have been written by The Spirit Scribe.. The Wraith Writer.. The Paranormal Poet, your pal up here at Prayer Pass..
I wish upon you peace, Pilgrims Upon The Path of The Pen..
May the light of love's literature illuminate your way.

That's it for today's consciousness class, kids.." The Lavendar Lizardarian Librarian of the Library of Love said, closing The Book,and putting her spoon down beside her bowl. So strange it is that a kitchen table can appear as a table in the Tavern of Tales, and another time appear as dad's desk in his classroom at the College of Caretakers, and then another time appear as mum's desk in her classroom. And stranger still how it became Big's Boardroom table.

Time.. space.. reality.. had run together.. blended in a bowl of cereal.. or was it just in my cranial cauldron that i cooked up a day dream.. something to keep my mind occupied while i watched the world play out it's dream..
In which dream do you dream ?

"In which dream are you dreaming son." In the distance i could hear dad's voice saying something about closing my Lavender Light Lizard Lunch Box That Talks.. and getting off to school.

Everything talks if you know how to listen. World after world.. reality will roll around in the palm of your hand like marbles of glowing light. You do not have to be a captive of consciousness. You hold The Key To Eternity.

All this and more can be yours if you just stick your arm a little deeper into the nice cereal box, kid." The words flowed outa the top of the open cereal box sitting on our kitchen table.. as if trying to enchant me an my sis to stick our arms deeper into the bottomless cereal box.. in search of the greatest secret seekers have sought for centuries.. The Coffin Chronicles.
Also known in some circles as The Consciousness Chronicles of Chronos.

The Coffin Chronicles.. yesss.. found in Crystalline Coffins covered with the dream dust of divine dimensions now fallen into fine powder. It is this powder that is packaged and sold as Paranormal Puff Potion Power Powder. Pat it on the palm of yer paws and poof yer paranormal.. paragliding.

In the bottom of this cereal there is a free package of PPPPP.. pal.. try it out.. For you first time cerealers there is inside every box of cereal everything you need.. if you dig deep enough. Don't worry if you can't find it. The cereal knows when yer ready. If it ain't inside yer box then yer not ready yet. Remember, this cereal is a class. The box is a classroom.

Hidden deep in The Tunnels of Thanatos neath The Tombs of Time were found The Caskets of The Crones. Inside were discovered The Crowns of The Crones. They were cups and cauldrons.. crystalline goblets gilded with golden goblins, silver and saphire serpents, diamond demons, ruby reptiles, tourquoise and tourmaline toads.

And when lights were shone upon the caskets it was said that everything moved as though being awakened from a deep sleep.

When the caskets were opened, instead of bodies wrapped in parchment.. there was found completely filling each casket a long scroll of dry strange scaly saurian skin.. And the scales formed some sort of script.. Yesss the scales formed the syllables and sentences of a story. When the scaly skin scroll was unrolled, inside there was nothing.. just the rolled skin scroll who's scales formed the Story of the Saurian Sorcerers.

Rumours abound in reality that when the skin was unrolled it writhed.. as though alive.. The Story Skin.. was a living thing.. a serpent made of script.. it was a living story.. and it was within these stories.. as these stories.. that the ascended ancients lived an eternal life..

It was the script.. the words themself.. that gave birth to life.. to humans.. to all creation.. not the other way around.. That is why the bible says with the breath of god was created the cosmos.. With the word.. the wind of great spirit's breath.. the eternal cosmic consciousness created with its thoughts and within its thoughts.. the world.

Story Skin

"Who of you dare go deeper into the bottomless box to dig up the graves of those gone before.. the graves of the great ghosts ?" ..the Sales Snake leaning against the cereal box.. asked sis and me and the crowd that had gathered in the supermarket aisle.

"Get a ghost in every specially marked box of coffin crunch and cadaver chunks cereals.. wholly unnatural and holy with the ghost of those gone before.
Fill yer Bardo Begging Bowl with a heaping helping of heaven.. hell is on hold.. an old over done concept erased from the dictionary.. a meaningless arrangement of letters.. no such word in any vocabulary..

Only Visionary Vocabulary presented in these pages, Page Partner.. Yup.. you.. and me the pages.. we're partners, pal. Did you know that ghosts are of different ages.. some are old and some are young. The old ones when they get old, if they lived a wise life and helped others, then they get to live almost forever before they have to turn in their robes for another reality.

Yes, reality robes us. Pick up a new Reality Robe. Send in the bottoms of yer beliefs and within moments you'll receive a made to measure Reality Robe. Design your own.

Do you already ride just outside of reality's perimeter ? Are you a life on a leash yearning to be set free. ? Are you looking for a little afterlife south of somewhere, north of nowhere, east of everywhere, and west of wherever you soar ?

No one has to know.. we'll keep it quiet.. just between you and me The Book. I'll find a special place for you between the covers.. somewhere deep in the pages where no one will ever find you. Would you like to become The Book's Beloved ?

Will you be faithful to me.. hold me every morning and every evening
Caress my fine virgin vellum pages as your beloved's soft scented skin
Seek me in the night when you are restless
Stare at my dark words in the day where nothing is unseen
Make me the altar upon which you seek your blessings

Adore me as the angel you have awaited thru the ages ?
Be my betrothed and I shall scrawll you a story of sweet sanctuary.
Open my crimson covers. Come close to my purple pages pulsing with life's fire and death's desire. Do not pull back from The Book. Do not hesitate my hero, for I belong to you, and you belong to me. We belong to each other.

I lay upon your blanket at night silently watching over you.. adoring you.. while you dream on in the story I created for you. I shall be your source.. your sacred sanctuary.

Oh there are so many ways love can be expressed. Dearest would you please come closer to the pages and give one big long kiss with yer pout, pretty page princess.." The Book was beckoning to my little sis.

"Put yer pout upon the page and give us, the words, a nice long kiss. Us words worked for nuthin.. no pay for being a page. The sentences slaved for you.. to bring your brain this far. Your brains need us books. Where would your world be without words. We words rule the world. We rule reality. Words rule.

Without us words you readers wouldn't have a story to read. And you writers wouldn't have a way to write it. Without words, there are no thoughts to think.
When you get a gang of words all gathered up in an army of sentences, you got one mean mighty magical mama manuscript matter manifesting machine working for you.

Inside every box of consciousness cereal you get a world of words. Think of writing and reading as a religion. And as a reminder inside specially selected boxes you get a free coffin and a completely complimentary crucifix upon which you get nailed daily to satisfy your cravings for crucifiction.

Hey don't get all done in by the diction. It's only fiction fabricated in the Fiction and Fact Factory.. a spirit story told by yer old uncle Tio Toad sitting at The Table of Fables in The Tavern of Tales."

Just then Tio sails by on a piece of toast across the milk in my cereal bowl. There's an owl perched on the rim of the bowl.. and from somewhere up on the ridge above the fridge I hear a wolf howl.

Dream Driftin

"Ya you and me we're just Dream Drifters.. Dream Driftin thru life and death. A cosmic charade pretending to be real.. when it's just a deal between a wraith writer and an angel agent selling some swollen love novel to the masses for enough money so we can send our kids to dance class."

Big pushed himself back from the table.. lit his cigar.. sucked deeply on it until the end was glowing like the devil's flashlight. Then he slowly flicked the ash into a miniature caramel coloured convertible cadillac car from the fifties.

Big threw the script onto the table, looked directly at the writer who wasn't there, and said.. "Read it to me again.. only this time put more emphasis on the pain. It sounds like the start of a movie where no one has anything to gain.. and nothing to lose."

So I sat down at the typewriter ta satisfy the dame with a story. She wanted one with an ending that went on forever and a beginning that broke open her heart like a pomegranate fruit spilling its seeds all over the hips of heaven.

In the index at the back I put in a list with the directions to all the lovers lanes ever lost and found. And in the borders I drew some flowers on vines wrapping themselves around hearts.. hearts that seemed to sigh when one turned the pages.

Was she worth the effort of forty years in the desert of my own dreams to write such a book for such a beauty ? Sure she was.. even thou I knew we could never truly be together. She was a queen and I a Cosmic Clown.

So I turned the parched pages of my own story.. sorry that I had written in a bad guy.. me.. myself. I wasn't any better than the next guy.. and a whole lot dumber when it came to dames and dollars. Seems both came easy.. and went hard.. and heavy.. on the heart.

There was no happy ending.. the beginning was bad.. and in between.. well why bother.. it was as boring as a broken beer bottle lying in the gutter after you got kicked outta the bar.. cause closing time had come and gone.

My whole life sounded like a sad Sinatra song sung by some second rate saloon singer. Guess that was the theme of my storyline.. Closing time come and gone. Just the whistling wind and the howling dogs ta accompany me home to a third floor walk up flop house room that smelled like puke and prostitutes past their prime.

But then I was just a third class bum who'd flipped too many dimes and come out a loser each time. So why even write this story you ask. Well like I said.. she wanted a story to help her sleep when she couldn't keep the memories from making her skin sweat.. and the tears making her cheeks wet.

Some guys get all the breaks and collect chicks like they were keepsakes one stuffs in their pocket.. like a fifty cent locket.. bought at a five and dime store no one knows the name of anymore.

The whole episode reminds you of a song sung so long ago that it's no longer for sale. And me.. Well ya.. I'm always on sale.. a cheap copy.. last one of its kind.. not that difficult to find.. if you know where to look in your own mind.

I rolled over in bed hoping to touch her one more time.. but she was gone. Just a lonely dream that had found someone else to keep her company during the night.

All I could recall of her were the first and only words she whispered "no go tokyo.. sayonara sweetheart.. sunset so sad." She said it like it were some song she'd sung to every sailor who landed in her port. She was the sort, that like a snake.. makes you wake wet and sweaty.. ready to sell your soul.. just for another embrace.. while you die gazing into her face.

It's an open and shut case. Both parties are guilty.. including the judge and jury. Why hurry. All that waits for everyone is a noose. It's useless to resist the restless river. The wind always wins. The flesh always falls.

I remember how she slipped outta her dress.. like it was a dress rehearsal for death. Her beauty caught my breath.. held it somewhere forever in eternity. Her white skin was the statue upon the holy altar of appetite for all that consumes. Then I kissed her silken skin, found heaven in our sacred sin.

So yes.. I'm as guilty as the next guy who tries to find fulfillment in any moment that arises like a ripe fruit falling from a tree. You would too if you were me. My only plea of innocence is that I'm but a character upon a page.. in a story by a writer who's writing your role right now as you read these words.

She whispered in my ear.. "You are to me the sky and sea and all of destiny. See you and me.. we're Dream Drifters.. with nowhere to go but where we are.. and nowhere to come from.. but the page before. Then she kissed me on my eyes.. whispered words I wished were real.. and left me alone in a sentence with nothing to look forward to but but an abrupt ending when some unseen writer typed out a period."

"I like the opening. I'll buy the script and make it into a movie." Big bellowed.. then faded from the scene like we all eventually do.. leaving me and sis alone at the table with Tio Toad.

"What's the special ?" Sis asked. "Sorcerer Stew" ..the Wraith Waitress replied. "I'll have a bowl.. and a large plate of paranormal pasta for my pal the apparition."

So easily the situation shifts.. with the stroke of a pen one character disappears and another comes alive. Is that how it is with life ? Is death simply the writer getting bored with someone who was created by dipping a pen in ink ?

Words make us think. Some make the spirit sink.. and others give us wings with which to soar. Speak smart and write well.. world writers.

That's it for today's dialogue with Doc Diction.. the Professor of the Pen and the Page.. Consciousness Class concluded.. this box is closing up the Script Shop. Okay fast.. finish breakfast.. you don't wanna be last into dad's car.

And with those words the professor of the page put down his pen.

Cauldron of Creation

Sis and the cereal were deep in conversation.. communicados en consciousness.. they were collaborating about the cosmos.. about cosmic constipation and the correlation between comets and christ.. the Coming of The Cereal.. and what Cosmic Creation was being cooked up in the Cosmic Cauldron bubbling upon the Sorcerer's Stove, being stirred by mum who had turned the heat up high.. so the flames of the fallen and forgotten could reach up to the sky.

Yup.. Mum was sending smoke signals to the spirits.. alerting the angel aviators that it was all clear for a landing upon the paranormal pyramide plateau of peach pancakes piled high on the platter in the middle of our kitchen table.
Mum was ground control for all flights coming in from any reality outside of this one.

Sis was signing some paper she had pulled outta the box.. some covenant between her and the cereal box.. "Call it a Covenant With Consciousness, kid. We all have a Covenant With Chronos.. an agreement with time that we are only alloted so much and then it is back into the box.. the Cave of The Covenant.. the Chalice of Creation.. the Coffin of Chronos.

Your cranium is the Cave of Consciousness, little miss, and your cranial corridors are coursing with the Current of Consciousness. It is in this Cranial Cauldron wherein you have a Covenant With Creation

Yess.. every body comes with a Covenant With Creation. Every body comes with a Cauldron of Creation. Should yours become defective.. you can get a replacement inside specially marked boxes of cosmic cherry comet cranial connection cereal."

"Okay kids let's get real.." Dad was trying to reel us into his reality so we might get to school in time rather than playing around outside of any time that space could confine. Did you ever wonder if time and space never got together what would happen ? Did time create space or vice versa.. or were they born separately.. or were they created by the same source.. Are time and space like brother and sister.. Are they part of the same family.. or did they just bump into each other and kinda date and eventually marry?"

All I could hear was Sis and the Box talking about brains and The Book. Then The Book interjected.. "Listen up baboon brains.. This book may not have much of a body but I'm big on brains." Sis looked adoringly at the book and whispered.. " Well actually your body is rather beautiful with your dark violet velvety outer covers and soft lavender vellum insides.. and when your story get's sullen and your script sulks.. and your covers turn a dark midnite black and your pages a rich mauve.. oh how i find you so enchanting.. so comforting to take to bed."

"Kids.. get outta yer head.." I could hear dad's voice calling from somewhere on the other side of the Table of Tales. The cereal was selling sis another set of the Vision Volumes .. sis had become a Reality Retailer reselling reality to other Consciousness Cadets thru the books and bottles of Baboon Butt Brew and Sorcerer Stew and jars of Juju Jam.

Sis was a distributor for the divine. She had signed up for selling cereal to all the houses on our the street. As the divine's distributor you will be entitled to one Vision Vacation in Vision Valley for every newcomer to Renegade Reality you sign up.

Sign up and you too can manufacture myth meaning maya money. Ya kids.. sign up to sell to other suckers this cereal door to door, classroom to classroom, to the kids on yer street.. to yer teachers and preachers and pets.."

We'll include a free ornate gold plated Brain Box to store away your thoughts in a trunk.. yes you receive in addition to the brain box a free trial offer Thought Trunk to securely stash your sacred spirit syllables and Spell Sentences.
A Thought Trunk just like Tio Toad's Tale Traveller's Trunk.. A trunk that turns into Tio the Reality Road Toad.. if you know the ceremonial code.
Yessss.." the Syllable Serpent Sorcerer hissssed from the top corner of the paranormal page.. "All this and more can be yours.. from The Store of Evermore.."

"I'd like sa more muffins." Manny The Marmoset sittin beside me muttered to mum."And I'll have two greasy grave ghoul ghoulashes to go with a side order of goblin gravy," I heard the phantom fool sitting on the stool next to me in the Diner of The Dead order from the Wraith Waitress who wasn't there.

"And for dessert, bring us all some chocolate and coconut covered cherry cream comets.. the cosmic candy for advanced Dream Drifters and Consciousness Cruisers." Barry Big and his brothers Bigger and Biggest, broke out in a laugh, as the spirits swirled in the smoke from their ceremonial cigars.

The Big Brothers were a front for what was going on behind and inbetween the scenes of reality. Sis was a kid with a career selling cereal for The Consciousness Corporation.. the company that produces Raspberry Reptile Reality Rubber.. Consciousness Commander Cherry Chewies.. Watermelon Wisdom Whales.. Strawberry Star Slug Suckers.. Bardo Buster Blueberry Baboon Butt Brew Buddha Buddies.. and the rest of the line of Paranormal Products made by The Myth and Maya and Matter Masters Manufacturers..

Molding myth into matter. Hey.. you too can create reality.. be a reality regulator.. wear a Strawberry Spirit Star on yer Violet Vision Vest.. if you pass the Toad's Test.. with the complete.. create reality course.. included are consciousness candies and candles.. light a candle and eat a candy with your friends or fiends.. then settle back to enter and enjoy the story without even reading the book..

This paranormal program is completely passive on your part.. The Words will do all the work.. you just lay back and allow The Book's covers to completely wrap around you as if you were being embalmed.. made into a mummy .. and then put into one of those caskets in the dusty tunnels of the Tombs of Time beneath the Museum of Mausoleums.. We, the Pages of the Primordial Paranormal, offer you eternal freedom from fate and future.. live forever in the present.. in a present more real than existence itself..

For a trial time only.. send in seventy box tops of your favorite consciousness cereals and with the winning words you are guaranteed to be freed of any fear that has been following you around. And I as the guardian ghost of the Ghost Gates, guarantee.. with no later surprises added on, and no unseen solicitations from spirits searching for love amongst the living.. you will have your wish. Wish wisely Word Warrior... Wisdom Waker... Wonder Walker

Yes you have wandered well among the words.. Word Wanderer.. You have woken wisdom from its spell.. you have awakened The Sleeping Story.. with your Knights of Knowledge Kiss. You shall be blessed with eternal bliss.

Covenant With Creation

The Knights of Knowledge Kiss is a sacred Covenant With Creation. You have braved The Book of The Beyond, and entered The Cave of Consciousness. You have dwelled in The Den of The Dialogue Dragon. You have dared to stir the Cauldron of The Cosmos. You have held hands with hell and heaven. You have toasted Thanatos. You have fed with your own flesh The Fable of Forever.

All sentences have spoken kindly of you.. all paragraphs have praised you.. Noble Knight of Knowledge.. Warrior of Wisdom's Words.. Priest of The Pen.. Prophet of The Pages.. Your appearance in this story was foretold. Dear Reader you may pass from page to page freely now for you have proven to The Paranormal that you wish to be one of us.. A Princess or Prince, of The Paranormal Parchment Pages.

Yes reader .. soon you too shall be but invisible ink upon a paranormal page.. so strange a parchment, unlike any before.. more like a fine living skin..

And now you recoil in fear amazement astonishment disbelief.. for The Book is a living being.. The Book breathes..! The pages pulse with life..!

And the box of cereal is an open mouth waiting to swallow you as it did me. My tale is not unlike yours and many other readers'. I was simply a hungry human who had given up searching for love amongst the living. I was ready for a roll in the sack with some spirit.. even if it wasn't real.. even if it only existed in a story.

And what if you reader only exist in a story.. written by someone, something, unseen.. See I do not wish to alarm you angel, but you are not quite real. You are something I imagined, someone along with the other characters in this story I created, to keep loneliness at arm's length. I The Book created the story, the writer, and the readers .. and reality.. I am the creator of it all and I am it all.

.. the mask of a million faces.. the being of a billion bodies.. endless entertainment.. to satisfy one soul.

But oh how I yearned to feel the heat of human hands burn upon my pages.. their tears and sweat once again make flow the ink of my words. Now like an enchanted lover my pages are dishevelled, my sentences swoon, my syllables have all surrendered to your eyes. I lie naked under your touch.

My blank pages yearn to feel the burning sear of the stroke of your pen.. your sword that carves so cleanly the words we worship.

"Monkey man, would you quite worshipping that face in the mirror, I your sister of the script, her imperial highness, needs ta piss.. now open the bathroom door." .. sis roared .. breaking me from the grip The Book held upon my heart and head.

I replied to Sis "Passionate princess you are pure poetry.. Princess of poetry who needs ta piss.. well kiss a cookie.. I'm busy combing my fair hair, heroine." Then I went about my business of being The Book.. well the part of The Book where I the brother, am combing my hair looking into the bathroom mirror, which unknown to me at that time, was a one way window, on the other side of which was a viewing platform portal, used by the paranormal to peek in on us normal folks.

And once again The Toad croaks and the chapter closes, but not before another reader is badly bitten by The Book and needs reality resuscitation. "Take a vacation." sis shouted thru the door. But it was too late, for I was no more.. I had morphed into The Mirror of Masks.. the Mirror of Maya and Imagination.

Yess reader the truth is that I not only became one of the characters in the story, but I became one with the story.. I became The Book.. the words my world.. the sentences my sinews, the fantasy my flesh, the manuscript my mind.

It had all started out so simple. I was associate Professor of The Paranormal, assistant head of the Department of Divinity and Divine Death, specializing in the study of Spirit Society. One of the textbooks for a course I was teaching was an old parchment bound with dried sinews that I had found late one night deep in the dank dark basement stacks of the ancient library built of boulder and stone, half hidden and vine enrobed, in the center of the college campus.

The parchment was completely covered in a pale pink powder, which when I blew it off, the dust shimmered like the smallest of scales.. The Book was bound by sinews.. or vines that resembled veins.. veins that were part of the leather like covers.. leather that was somewhat rubbery.. a dark crimson colour.. and so cool to the touch. Yet slowly but surely it took on a warmth as though it were coming alive.. making me imagine it had lain asleep for centuries in a crystalline casket.

So yes you could say I made a living from the dead.. divine dialogue, paranormal poetry of praise and prayer, literature of love for the lost.. mantra manuscripts.. spell stories.. sacred spirit scrawllings and scribblings.. wraith writings found carved into wells' walls and caskets' covers. I studied them all.. saurian sacred scrolls, mausoleum manuscripts.. tomb transcripts.. bardo books.. loco lingo.. lost lizard legends.. paranormal patter.. ghost gab.. wrote articles for The Ghost Gazette.

Soon it became so easy to simply slip unseen into a sentence. Yesss, for a living I lie with the dead. I do the dying for those unable to do it for themselves. I doctor up the dissertations of the dead.. and read it to you in bed. I do the writing for the wraiths so you can read it. Soon you shall come visit me here within my covers.

Am I human ? No more nor less than you.. that's why I'm drawn to you.. and you to me That's why we share these words. We are both creations of an artist far more masterful than ever you or I shall become.

Reader, I have seduced you, so I would not be alone in my darkness. The other characters in this story were but a cunning trap, to entice you into my realm. It was you, your human company, that I craved.

Each night you read me, hold me in your arms, lay me upon your breast, or upon your pillow, I find sweet communion. What is the key to your heart ? Tell me now, whisper it to these words. Come closer, whisper as though it were a kind kiss."

Sis was under a spell reading The Book laying beside her cereal bowl. Slowly as though she were in a dream Sis put down her cereal spoon. Strawberry stars were spilling from her open lips as her head sunk closer to the cereal bowl.

Then sis with a large splash tumbled head first inta the cereal, overflowing the sides of the bowl and flooding the kitchen floor which quickly became a swamp of swirling strawberry stars.

As fast as the writer could scribble a new sentence sis was gone.. the floor was flooded with sentences swimming like sea serpents.. dad was outside warming up the Vision Vehicle.. and mum was looking at the kitchen shaking her head.. while there upon the kitchen table in Sis's cereal bowl lay the remaining remnants of reality.. a few small soggy strawberry stars.. floating in a spoonful of rice milk.. Yup.. reality was all washed up.

"Reality is the creative expression of the imagination of the mind of The Almighty All. Would one of you kids help yer tired old uncle Tio up from the kitchen table?" Tio Toad mumbled.. "Tellin the tale has tuckered me out.. and we're runnin outta time to get to morning class before the Buddha's Bell rings. Now quickly, everyone climb aboard the Time Travellin Toast."

And off we went to school.. renegade reality riders.. cruising consciousness.. at the altitude of angels.. the speed of spirits.. never quite arriving anywhere in time.

Write something reader.. life is a consciousness class

Figs From France

I have tasted mangoes from madagascar
persimons and peaches from persia
pomegranates from paraguay
coconuts from le cote d'ivoire
figs from the south of france

But no flesh of any fruit has been as sweet and luscious, as yours in my mouth
nor the skin of any fruit as fragrant and soft as yours beneath my fingers

And so I have brought to you blueberries and chocolate halwah
to place between your lips when my tongue is not there to taste yours

See how the sun adores the earth
how the sea caresses the shore
how the moon and stars dance

See how the night longs for the day
and the light lingers in the shadows of evening's embrace

The cold cries out for the warmth
The present waits expectantly for the future
All of life is filled with the promise of love

So I have spent these past centuries
in dreams of you...
longing, adoring, caressing, dancing, crying out silently,
waiting.. an angel.

I have ceased breathing
my heart barely beats

this is my poem for you my princess
a Prayer for a Princess

may you be surrounded in serenity for all eternity

I wish you divine dreams, and your body bathed in strawberry streams
Each morning the birds will wake you with their ballads of love
and thru the nite the moon will gaze upon you with divine adoration
while the stars send you kisses delivered upon angels' wings of light.

See how my heart sings with the beauteous blessing of our lives entwined..
moments of an eternal vine.. bearing fruit like enchanted wine..
passing between our lips.. yours and mine"

Sis was holding the cereal box in her arms.. tight against her chest.. her eyes half closed in reverie.

Oh how the cereal could suck up to my little sis.. just to entice her into one more bowl of cereal.. one more spoonful for the road. Then Dad closed the chapter with the well written words.. "Shut the book, and let's hit the road.."

But before we could get out the back door, the radio up on the ridge on the other side of the fridge had to serenade sis with one more song sung by Sammy Sammatra the Strawberry Star Salamander Saloon Singer for sweet souls..

"Sweet desireable you.. my heart loves all of you
all I ever wanna do.. is love.. sweet desireable you.

Yur so desireable.. my heart is so full
because of sweet desireable you

You're the ultimate dream design come true..
we're the perfect pair.. all the angels stand and stare..
there's so much love everywhere.. you're way beyond compare.

You're a work of art.. I knew right from the very start..
you were a gift to my heart..
Every time I think of you.. I hear the beating of angels' wings..
and the whole world sings so sweetly.. because of you and me..
I jus wanna be the one with whom you fly..
your forever guy.

Let's not waste any time.. I'll be yours.. you'll be mine.. forever valentine.. sweet desireable you."

Then Dad reached up and turned off the radio. We all climbed onto the fridge like it were a Strawberry Star Storm Stallion Space Shuttle about to soar across the Strawberry Star Solar System.

"Come on you don't wanna be late for school" Sis said as she grabbed Bufemius and Bareyev Baboon Brothers by their furry fingers, and swung them up onta the Flyin' Fridge warmin up for take off, leaving a trail of melting Strawberry Star and blueberry banana ice cream shooting outta the bottom of the fridge as we headed for heaven.. directly into another Episode of Eternity.

Sis was a saloon miss, cosmic cowgirl, who would shoot ya first with some strawberry stars.. outta her strawberry star spell spoon.. kinda like an arrow from angel cupid's bow.. ya cupid is an angel .. and so is my sis..

And she'd ask questions later.. like.. what is the cosmic question that needs to be answered first before we can commence this class.. classroom.. does anyone of you Consciousness Cruiser Cadets know.. any of you Angel Ascension Academy recruits for Renegade Reality Riding class 101.. have any idea about the size of infinity.. ?"

"Go suck on a toad's titty.." the brat in the back of the class yelled out
"Buckle it up baboon boy !" Sis hissed the syllables like she were a Sentence Sorcerer Serpent Scribe sagacious and wise.

Word Worshippers

"You sure got pretty pink eyes," the Strawberry Serpent Story Sorcerer wrapped around the words written on the pink page pleaded, and then leaned a little closer to my sis, saying.. "I wanna give you a kiss for bein so cute.. hey you.. I wanna be your number one recruit.

I'll even wear a soiree suit suitable for sittin with you at a table for two.." Yes sir that's what the serpent said, lookin sis straight in the eyes.. no lies. And then the serpent hissed.. "It just wouldn't be right to leave you all alone at midnight with a cereal box.. think I'll stay around.. what if you fall in.. and what about that deep wide cereal bowl.. what if you fall into the cereal and need rescuing.

"I'll jus surf across the cereal on my strawberry Stars Surfin Spoon.." sis said standin on her spoon as she surfed across the milk in her bowl.

You'll get one too in every box of seriously silly societal satire sit calm sit com seriel cereal.. yer very own story surfin and stirrin sorcerer's spoon.That's where you can count on me.. a Story Serpent Saviour Saint.. The Steward of The Story.. the story steward.

some say i'm a snake.. some say a saint and a saviour
some say a slayer and a sinner..
or simply a scribe scribblin the scrawll upon the wall of your world..
a servant of the spirit.. Ya I was being held slave by some she spirit.. even sis couldn't save me.. I was under a spell as a snake sellin cereal to kids after school and on saturdays cause my mum and dad had disappeared in the Tomb Tunnels running below the basement floor.

Something was down there.. first we thought it was just the wind winding its way thru the tunnels after we opened the trap door that lead down to the Dungeon of the Dead..

Get outta my head was the first thing I said when the paranormal approached me. Words were being whispered as if the words themselves were doin the whisperin.

Ya the tale was talking.. the story was speaking .They were wraith words.. words you could hear but couldn't see. Ever hear of a werewolf..? Well these words are werewords.. words that shape shift in the full moon.. ya if you read this book.. open it's covers neath the full moon.. watch out for the words are werewords.. words that were whatever they wanted to be.

You might get bitten by The Book.. sucked in by The Story.. captured by a chapter. Hey this chapter don't come cheap.. what do you think I am.. an easy piece of paper..? This page don't fall for some fantasy.. some imaginery reader. I want the real thing.. someone who can think like a text book.

This is some serious story.. I'm a brave book.. I don't want no one time look, literature lover, who reads one page, and then leaves me waiting for more. Read all of me or don't start something you can't finish.. I got feelings.. Hey we words ain't finished.. don't go turnin the page.. no one is goin anywhere until this chapter is over ! "

So I see sis speaking to The Cereal Box and The Book. And I swear I saw them speaking back.. as she climbed up the stairs to heaven.. that's the second floor where we sleep and dream of divinity until the strawberry summer sun wakes you and me..

"And you do so awaken me.. the way you hold me.. look upon my being so pure but for the tale tatooed upon my skin.. each time you begin to read another of my chapters I feel I am chosen by a queen.. to be her king.. angel divine you are impossible to define".. The Book was buttering sis up.. "You are the princess of my pages.. and though I am something not of flesh.. I come to you on wings.. of words.

These words have wandered thru so many stories to find you, my angel of the alphabet.. my saint of the script.. my saviour of this story." That Story Serpent could sure spread the syrupy syllables all over the page tryin to impress sis.

"These words will be your warrior.. your wizard.. your waiter.. your whatever and then more. Whatever you wish these words will write. You have awakened this Sleeping Story with your tender touch and kind kiss, Princess of the Pages.

Come whatever may in any chapter I'll always be there for you..
You can count on me to love you for free..
It's a common destiny.. you and me..
Simply divinity unfolding as it was meant to be..
you and all you see is you and me."

Then the sacred spirit speaker song and story Cereal Snake.. offered to bake a cake for my cutie sis leanin against the cereal box.. her chin restin on the tip of of her sacred spirit stirrin spoon.. just holdin on to the handle of her heart, and about to hand it over to the handsome hero, that slippery sales snake had become..

"You and me we're like two sides of a page.. surely the same story.. just different characters playing the same roles..
you and me we're one sacred story sweetie."

Then the Strawberry Swirlin Star Storm Story Serpent sent a syllable straight ta ma sis's heart.. sis was love struck.. fallen for a fantasy... a far out fable.. from a fellow that weren't even there. Ya.. a phantom fellow.. someone you can only see if ya wear these strawberry star spirit seein' spectacles.. Spirit Spectacles.. stashed somewhere inside every box that talks.

Get armed with angel armament. Angel Assistance Associates are always on call for all your problems with the pesky paranormal.

"Psst.. kid.. you got problems with the paranormal.. is the paranormal makin' you paranoid.. well I'm yer pal for puttin paranormal pests in their proper places.. gettin phantoms outta yer face.. healing spirit sickness. I can suck it outta ya.. just stick yer head inta the cereal box opening.." the Story Snake beckoned with the tip of his tail to sis.

"Don't do it sis.. the box might bite.." Babaloo Bongo Baboon Boy swung over the top of the cereal box landing in sis's lap. Life's a snap when yer a story. Any story you wanna be.. you can be. I am every story.. cause I am words. Words wake up the world with wisdom and wonder, or war and woe. What do you wanna write ? Right the world's wrongs with words not wars.. Word Worshippers.

We worship words .. everyone worships words.. cause words are thoughts and everyone's got the hots for thoughts.. Without thoughts there would not be a word written.. nor a sound spoken. Without thinkin' there'd be no inkin' of the pages.. no writin' to read.. no songs to sing.. no prayers to plead.

And how would I bring you this book without words.. for you see I am a ghost.. invisible but for these words your eyes do so tenderly caress, Do not drop The Book nor The Cereal Box.. wouldn't want a stream of Strawberry Stars swirling down the stairs.. sentences slithering across the floor.. a sea of syllables pouring out of the pages..

"Ah who cares." sis replied to the words who were waiting on sis's every word.. Ya, The Story had fallen in love with sis. "It's sink or swim for you snake." Then sis threw her spoon into the bowl.. leaped on it.. and started surfing across the Pond of Paranormal Porridge. You too can use yer Strawberry Star Story Surfer Spoon to cross the cereal bowl to the other side of any story.. surf into any scene.

"Look little girl either you pledge your love to these pages.. or it's over between you and me. The party's over for you and this page. Stay outta my chapters child.. this story's closing up shop. Your character is about to get erased.. slayed by a savage sentence.. put in its place by a period.. signaling the end of the scene where you walk out and never again feast your eyes upon my pages spread out open wide for you. Stay out of this story's life and don't bother to hold This Book in your embrace ever again. Leave me.. set me free for some other soul seeking a story to curl up with during dreamy days and dreary nights. Put me back on the top shelf where I belong in The Library of Love

Yes sis and the story were drunk on the Elixir of Eternity.. the Dew of Divinity., a drink so deliciously delightful, only one sip will change your consciousness for all eternity.

These pages are impregnated with Book Brew.. the script soaked in the sacred Story Stew of spirit syllables and sorcerer sentences. This Story is a living spirit.. penned by a Paranormal Poet whose pen was dipped in the Ink Well of the Infinite.
A sacred story steeped in The Tears of Time and The Raindrops of Romance.
"I'll have a bottle of Book Brew and a steaming hot bowl of Story Stew.. what would you like little girl".. the Story Serpent swirling on the stool in the Story Saloon, whispered to Sis.. "I'll have a Strawberry Star Story Soda and a couple of Cherry Comet Chunks Cosmic Comic Chapter Cookies.. I like my tales to taste sweet." she replied.

"The kid's a real Cosmic Comic.. Welcome to the phantom fraternity of ghosts and other phantoms of fantasy.. beings unborn, but alive and well, deep inside this Book's covers. That is where you too must travel to find the vision which is divine.." the Story Stool Serpent said as he spun around the stool.

With each spin of the Story Stool.. another scene of the story.. go ahead reader.. take your turn.. sit on the stool.. set it spinning.. see where it takes you.
Sis patted both The Book and The Box and our baby brother baboon on their heads.. and then she said.. "sleep tight tonight.. stay safely and snugly secure within these wide covers.. my wide wings will be your blanket and bed".. as she carried them all in her angel arms up the stairs.

"I cannot get you out of my head.." sis said to The Book.. and The Book bellowed.. "I am not a book I am a being.. I am not the beast.. I am beauty come as a story.. once I was a young and handsome Prince of the Pages.. but I slipped too deep into the story and got suckered by a Story Sorcerer .. who set a spell upon me.. turned me into a book.

It is thru these words in this book that are my only way of getting in touch with you. Listen I know this sounds silly.. crazy.. a hoax but I want help. I am not kidding .. call my agent.. he'll tell you I disappeared.. ya the guy who wrote this book ended up in the book.. the main character in the book."

And I'm thinking this is who my kid sister is hanging out with ? This ghost guy.. this Paranormal Poet Prince of the pages who is putting the make on my kid sister ? This ghost writer guy.. like a real ghost who had been the guy who wrote The Story and now he was some spirit stuck in The Book.. begging my sis to give him a kiss.. like he was this handsome poet prince who had been transformed by a wicked Word Witch into words upon a page.. playing a part upon a supernatural stage.. A being from another age.. now trapped in a cage of his own consciousness ?

Page Princess

"Come enter a private place where upon each page you and I shall dance a divine romance. Choose any chapter. Whatever the chapter of your choice.. I will be there waiting. I am alive with your love. Let us linger upon each line. Let us stretch our story out forever.

Use no glove.. just your bare skin against my body's velvety vellum. Run your fingers along my broad back. Scratch your nails upon my tough weathered impermeable hide. I have nothing to hide from you. I will share with you my every chapter. Every page shall be our sacred stage.. every sentence your seduction.. every syllable your sigh.

Hide inside me here where no one will ever find you again. I am the noble knight you have searched every story for. Hold me closely pressed against your chest my queen. We are each others' chosen. You and I are the birth of love."

The Book was sis's beloved.. the Cereal Box her buddy.. and me her big brother, well I finally joined and became a Brother of The Book..
signed up with some Sacred Story Society.. The Brotherhood of The Book.

Meanwhile Benny the Book Baboon was bumbling his way up the stairs tip toeing on the hand railing while blabbering about buying shares in the story. Something about becoming a book brewer.. signing up with the Story Sorcerers Society.. spirits that stir the stew that gives life to me and you.

I know someone who can stir the Story Stew.. serve up a new story for you.. download divinity.. set you free of regular reality.

I will never hide my light from you.. I will never hold back my love from you.."

Then The Cereal Box leaned closer to sis and she gave the top lid a little kiss on its sweet head and that nite sis and The Box held each other tight .. plus The Book.. it was a foursome.. book box babe.. an her brother.. ya my little six year old sis and me her bigger brother like no other.. curled up in the covers of a Book Being.. eatin' cereal outta The Box That Talks.

"We words have waited for a glance from your eyes.. welcome to our world. Kiss this Prince of the Pages. Awaken this angel that you carry in your arms." Sis and i are sneaking up the stairs with a midnite snack of cereal and something to read while this guy ghost in the book from beyond our belief system is super seducing sis syllable by syllable.. sentence by sentence.. to slip a kiss onta the book.

Cool I say.. she's my sis and if she wants ta plant a kiss on the pages perfectly fine with me. She's an angel and I as her bigger brother am assigned to act as angel assistance.. no resistance.. I can go the distance.. I'm angel assistance.

For instance.. if you wear down yer wings tryin flyin too high.. and you need a safety net.. I'll be the knight holdin the net.. I'll even be your paranormal pet

I'll be your rainbow.. your sacred sky.. your sweet sea.. the door into divinity.

So innocently she holds the Box and Book wrapped in her arms.. nascent wings warm and waiting and wanting. Sis was hooked on being the heroine and saving this gallant guy who was now a ghost in the story.. a writer who had become a wraith by a curse cast by a consciousness creator.

Sis was studying with the Story Serpent to become a Priestess of the Paranormal. She walked with the whispering wind.. talked with time.. spoke with space.. slept with the unseen..

"Pretty Princess of The Pages," The Book addressed sis ever so politely, "please pour with your panther paws some strawberry stars into the bowl. This Book is begging.. do as I say dear delight.. go ahead do it now.. while the ink is fresh upon the page.. and you are so close to me I can feel the heat of your human hands.

With a drop of dew and a tear drop from you..
water these words so they might grow..
Your whispers will awaken this noble knight.
My stallion.. is spirit..
my sword.. song..
my lance.. literature..
my light.. love.

Awaken these waiting words.. with your wishes. These words only wish to worship all of you. I have come here at this time as the cereal to feed you.. the cosmic christ consciousness cereal.. the story as the sacred saviour. Uplift your spoons and sing songs of adoration to The Book and Cereal Box that talks"

There goes that silly sweet serpent sellin sis cereal. "Give a spoonful to your brother.. here's a couple free breakfast bowls.. somewhere ta pour yer cereal." That's how they hook the kids.. the cereal gives em a free bardo buddha brain begging bowl in their first box of cereal.. and in their second box a story stirrin' spoon. And in every box a chapter from The Story That Speaks and sings. And soon every kid on the sidewalk is carrying a box of cereal..
while chanting.. "Consciousness Uncaged !"

And as if that weren't enough the Consciousness Cereal Company creates a cereal box with a back that is a High Definition digital video tv and computer screen.. no batteries needed.. runs perpetually on earth's energy.
And the sides of the box have a surround sound audio system implanted via mirco chip fibers woven into the ballistic proof cereal box..

so you can surf the net anywhere while eatin cereal outta the box that talks and tells a tale to keep you from tripping over reality in case it should get in your way.. Word Worshipper"

The snake snickered at me, and suckered sis.. She surrendered to the story.. "Yes mr snake I'll take twelve chapters and a six pack of survival cereal for making it thru the story of you and me. I wanna be your eternal energy." By now sis was ready to give the snake a kiss. Sis was almost inside her bedroom door with a snickering snake swirlin around that cereal box.. creatin a serious strawberry star storm for me and my gal the gator.. who was sittin on the stool in the strawberry soda shop sippin a slug slime shake.

"I confess.. I wanna be your permanent address.." "Ya I know.." sis said ta the snake.. "but I don't think it would work out.. you a story snake and me bein a book babe.. I got my eye on the hero.. not some side kick snake who keeps on sellin stories.. I want the real thing.. a story saviour that makes my whole heart sing.

If I wear your wedding ring will you sing me to sleep every night.. and wake me every morning with a kiss on my eyes.. oh ya, and I also want blue skies if I'm gonna dump all those other guys." Sis was talkin tough to the serpent who was the reptile representing The Book in the prenuptual agreement between sis and the story.

Sis and the serpent.. some story.. sis and a story sellin cereal snake.
That snake was on the make .. singing syrupy songs..
that he said he'd sing to my sis.. for the rest of reality.

To my sis all the world sang.

Then sis slung the strawberry star storm serpent over her shoulder.. and climbed further up the sacred serpent stairway to where our banana baboon boy and babe, bunk beds, were filled with our visitin' simian sistern and baboon brethren of the book brotherhood.. angels annonymous aviation alphabet advisory associates.

"Sisters of the story.. brothers of the book.. friends of the fable.. we are all family. When you wanna learn how to fly.. give us a try.. one on one.. classes in consciousness cruising.. check out our references.. we represent the ghost writer.. we're the angel's agent.. the lizardarian librarian's lawyer.. the tale teller's trainer.. your consciousness coach.

You can get us in a jar.. hey we'll make you a star.. spread us on your tale tellin toast.. a spoon of story syrup will sweeten any scene.

So sit right down and spoon yerself a scene sprinkled with strawberry stars..
seriously silly societal satire sit calm sitcom serial cereal.. that you can download every day in a spoon.. direct from the cereal box that talks.

Download the equivalent of every drug ever dropped.. you've hit the motherload of overload. Every chapter's exploding with light and love and laughter.. with literature that loves you.. language that wants to lick your face."

Goddess

a poet's prayer to the princess of paradise

you are everywhere
you are in the air the wind the water the sea every tree and everything i see

be there
love me leave me
bind to me release me
be everything be nothing
be mine be impossible to define

look clearly deeply honestly
for what you want need feel believe disbelieve hope hate
cry for beg for search for look up to look down upon

hold back don't hold back
fearlessly.. with your deepest fears

grab me push me away
enfold me release me
out of love out of need
out of desperation out of fear

trust me distrust me
trust yourself distrust yourself
expect my love respect my love reject my love
use my love abuse my love refuse my love
turn away from me turn to me
do it for me do it for yourself

be there as strongly as a summer thunderstorm
as softly as a firefly's flicker in the dark moonless night
like the elements the planets the rain the sun the seasons
the tides the mountains the streams the hot deserts
the wet jungles the birds of paradise

be there
as everything in life as all the loss in death
as all that lived before
as all the moments of earth's sweet and ragged birth

as the future that will shine or may perish
as heaven's rain kissing my face
as the heat of hell
brandishing the flaming sword that cleaves
the fat from my sinews

be there
like the storybook fairytale
that brings the divine dream upon my childlike heart
or the nightmare that rips me sweating and screaming from my depth

as the silence of cool forest nights
hidden on islands surrounded by lost seas
as golden honey sticky upon my lips
as the tropical beach i lay upon to heal my aching armour

feel me touch me show me
burst in upon my monk's cell
break down my battlements

these chains of iron and gold that fettered this dying angel
fall aside and lie in heaps
as rays of your light illuminate down upon me from all directions

my shoulders my back my palms my chest and belly
open to receive your cosmic light and dark with equal embrace

goddess god female male yin yang universal energy
formless changing infinite eternal
always alive forever being born

rejection has frightened me so
fear of imperfection has shackled me
my screams are sobs now
my bones cracked open
so others may feed upon my marrow

i cried each time i blew the trumpet
cried to the angels
to you in whatever form you would come
to heal me soothe me embrace me reform me

bliss lasted but moments in my life
like the hiss of the sacred cobra guarding the gate
sorry too late that has been my fate

i have loved you in my visions
something i never dared do in life
and yet others have found refuge inside of you
others who in their shallowness could never plummet your divine depths

our souls were entwined when the cosmos was created
i am born of your love
your tears are my rain
falling from one face

i sat at your feet
and played you sweet
the flutterings of my flute
and stringed notes of the celestial lute

i have lived inside your bosom
and danced upon your breast
a soft golden moth captivated by your living light
a hummingbird so sweet i stared into your eyes

i offered up my chest to the ripping talons
that carried me aloft to your nest
to feed your children
so their wings would grow

this i was and more
so that they would soar
as you and i did
when we were the mountains
the night sky
a child from whom nothing hid

to you in arms extended i bring
all the treasures of my simple and innocent heart
a red ruby deep and lush
like pomegranate seeds wet upon your lips
like the glisten of dew between your hips

this scarlet wound bleeds and seeps for you
like fissures of a volcano
i erupt inside
my hands bleed raw
my bones lay cracked open atop a tibetan mountain
i offer up my being to your breath
come and take me as you will

drink from me this never ending well
draw from me all you desire

suckle on the blood red lava that flows in firey rivulets
down my shoulders and back and arms and chest and belly and thighs

quench your thirst for heaven
till my bones bleach dry
and like dust in the desert
are carried in a hot searing whirlwind
up into your skies
to mix forever with you

this panther hunted
till he looked into the eyes of the doe
then forever stood still
calmed satiated softened
no need ever again to feast upon the flesh
transformed transfixed transfigured

i must flee from you
because even you who so inspires me
so entrances me so enchants me
cannot be all this
it is only my mind my soul that conjures up such a creation
and yet you are the guardian who stands at the gate to my soul

i approached you
my darkness so dark i feared to darken your light
like a beam of love
into my darkest deepest most profound cave you came

i wanted to be with you forever
beyond the length of the longest measure of time
i wanted to break open your husks
and sip and suck your persimmon fruit
only i knew i was still a beast
unwelcome at the feast
and you needed an angel butterfly
with soaring wings a soft eye and gently fluttering heart

burn me upon your altar
let me be your incense
your sacred spirit offering
to your gods and goddesses

let me be your candle melting in the night
your fire and holy light
your wrong and your right
your power and your might
your depth and your height

mix my tears with your rain
your dew with my pain
let me be the early morning mist upon your window pane ·
let me know my life has not been in vain

i have watched white birds with golden talons
soaring in the desert above you the oasis i have sought with my every thought

i have heard you
in the aztec pyramids
the jungle ruins
where the jaguar prowls
sounding her deep throaty growls

inside you i reverberate
someone knocking hard upon the monastery gate
a searcher seeking shelter
a heathen hoping for heaven

open your gates
lay down your arms
embrace me in your sacred charms

taste my lips
encircle my hips
take my vow
not later
now

enrobe me ensheath me enfold me
unrobe me unsheath me unfold me
i belong to thee

watch me die
be beside me when i am born again

i have stood in the rain lain in the rivers swam in the seas
to wash myself pure for your touch

and found that you were the earth the mud the trees the moss the rocks

i crawled among the roots and leaches and swamps
to be in you
and found that you were the sky

i climbed the highest peaks
to become you
only to find you were the music all creation made

i haunted the human cities
and still i could not grasp you
until now
when i hear you inside me
whispering crying out
with the sweetest voice i have ever heard

and it is the same voice same eyes
we are the same body
yours and mine

you are in my bed as you were in my ship a thousand years ago
you are the breath in my chest
the wind that blows my sails

you blanket me like mountain snows melting in the warm spring
you are the meadow to my mountain
the hues of the rainbow
the fragrance of my blossoms
the beating of my heart at night
the breath between my lips in the morning light
the vision that separates wrong from right

angel sweet and pure
this soul from its slumber you do so softly stir

Toad Tales

On this page all lives in peace.. On the next page all hell breaks lose..
On this page everyone loves each other.. On the next page every character hates every other one..

In this chapter everyone lives forever.. In the next chapter everyone dies..
On this page the whole world sings.. on the next page the whole world cries.

The writer is supreme in the story.. no character dares disobey the writer.. no one says anything or does anything that the writer doesn't wish. The writer reigns as the ultimate ruler.. with a stroke of the pen a life is lost.. a being is born.. a solitary angel blows a horn.. a pretty princess is pricked by a poisoned thorn.

God loses to the devil.. god sells his soul to satan.. god goes grocery shopping cause the goddess is hung over.. goddess divorces god for incest with an angel..

A toast to Thanatos Tales." Tio raised his goblet of Ghost Gruel to the Strawberry Storm Serpent spinnin on the stool in the middle of the Story Supermarket aisle of angels sellin cereal and seriously societal stories to consciousness cruisers like you and me.. download the total cereal serial series for some of yer source.. we accept all major cards. That's right.. send in your cards and we'll send you a set of Coffin Cards.. that the demon dealer dealt to the devil.

There's a card game goin on in Tio Taco's Temple Trailer between the devil and the don.. the Don of the Dawn.. the dude of delight.. the lord of light.. and the devil dude of darkness.. the don of darkness. Yes folks it is the dawning of the days of darkness.. or delight.. it depends on what you write.

Time ta change address, angel.. this angel is out of here.. this spirit is splittin from the scene.." and poof the paranormal left the sentence in the dialogue dust.. reality's rust. Never trust a toad." Tio said ta satan.

Like I said, and like you read.. Tio is dealer for a card game between god and the devil.. the deck is marked.. no one knows who had marked it.. no one knows for whom it has been marked.

The Flames of the Fallen and the Forgotten was pulled. Next card was The flaws of the Future.. then The Future Forecast for Fate.. then The Goblins Gate.. then The Ghoul's Grave.. Then The Ghost Goblet. And you can download the whole set.. place yer bet.

No one was gonna save god or the devil.. they were on their own.. no people to play out their game.. no pawns to move around on a cosmic chess board.

The next card was Love Amongst the Living. A slew of cards spewed outta Tio's hands from somewhere between his fat fingers where the lost lingers.

Divine Dissipation.. Life's Fire.. Death's Dark Desire.. the Cookie Queen's Cottage.. Interview with the Invisible. Chapters.. cards.. each one a vision.. each a vacation from reality as the blind see it.

"Yer all blind.." barked the bruho bar tender behind the bar servin bagels and Book Brew to all the regulars he knew.. regulars not from regular reality..
Most were members of the Story Sorcerer's Society.

"Stir yer Divinity Drink with yer own Wish Wand.." the not so tender bar tender Teddy Tough said to the sloshed serpent still sellin cereal stories while spinning on the Story Stool.

Ya every spin of the snake stool conjures up another story from outta the Cauldron of Consciousness.. the Cauldron of Chapters..

"Stir the snake spit story stew, servant of the script".. god said ta the devil as god threw down four phantoms and one fallen fiend..

The devil responded with a dying dream.. someone had stacked the deck in favor of the fallen angel of light. "Lucifer lord of luck give me one big roll tonight." The devil spun a deuce.. the devil's own demon dice.. from outta a pocket in the paranormal's pants. Death does a dance with life.. locked in an eternal embrace.

The spirit scribbled some ancient alphabet of the angels upon the forehead of the faithful gathered round the table in Tio's Tacos and Tales Trailer.

Here's your chance to win a Phantom Franchise for free.. send in the cereal itself.. leave the box behind at home.. it is the cereal we want.. this is a serious recall of the cereal.. consciousness was contaminated.. close all cereal boxes.. contamination of consciousness.. consciousness recall..

Word Warning.. serious sentence screw up.. alphabet accident.. paragraph pile up.. attention all readers.. problems with the pages.. there are crews of chapter cadets containing the curse of consciousness right at this very moment.. stay on this page if possible.. do not leave the boundaries of the book.. exterior reality is extremely unsafe..

"Open the safe.. open satan's safe.. see all the spells.. some even spelled wrong.. it is not only how you say the spell.. but how you write it that makes it work wonder or war or woe or wisdom.

As a superstar spell scribbler, you have the responsibility to reality to create something that is a blessing for all beings.. inside The Book.. and outside The Book.

So look Reader.. I'll make you the same deal The Dark made with this writer. I'll write you any dialogue.. any dream.. any story.. any words you want.. any wish you really desire.. and in return you gotta come meet the ghost guy that wrote this.. ya.. And I don't mean the human patsy.. the front for what really goes on behind the scenes.. between the covers when The Book is off limits to any and all literature lovers.

I'll make you the same deal the devil made me.. the writer delivers dark dialogue and the reader reads the dark dialogue.. and the spell is cast.
Yess satan sold the story for some sucker's soul. Satan wins the card game every time a word is written that ain't worshipping wisdom."

The sloshed serpent's spit settled on the table. Then he straightened up.. said "Deal me in.. I wanna play my part upon these pages.. be famous for ages."

Who dares go with me into the bowl without a life vest or a spoon to surf their way across the cereal..! Words shall weave our way.. the text our trail.. the pages our path.."

And again the cards were cast.

Digging up demon diamonds.. sayonara sushi society.. samurai of the sentences.. the well of women.. the water of woes.. liquid lightning.. deli of divinity.. eternal erasure.. ecstatic embrace.

So easily life is lost.. just another sentence slayed with a stroke of the poet's pen. Now notice my fine friend of the Phantom Fable how you yourself are becoming part paranormal. Do not be paranoid.. fear is but a fool's fable." Then Tio spun the table of tales.. folding time into space.

Tio's Trailer

Terror sits at the table.. come to dine on despair and drink the wine of worry. "Yur some cutie." the lady lounge lizard with lavender lips and legs said ta the Story Saloon Singer Sammy Sammatra the strawberry star storm salamander.

Welcome to Tio's Taco Trailer where there's always a ghost game going on and the tacos are free. We're playing with reality.. what does it matter if you win some or lose a little.. win another world or lose the one you came with." Tio smiled while flinging another card across the breakfast table interrupting Bubba Baboon who was reaching for the jar of juju jam to spread on his morning toast, compliments of your host, The Ghost.

"Hey Sam.. sing another sad song" Tio talked like he had marbles in his mouth. To each player Tio would spit out a marble.. softly glowing a pure colour alive like a dream egg..

Then suddenly the dialogue is darkly disturbed by screaming coming from somewhere in the back of the book... "Oops.. gotta retrace my steps".. is the last thing you hear in your head, and then the script gets rewound and you are left alone on a blank page with no words to write yer way outta the jam.

"Get yer furry fingers outta the jam jar you joker".. mum threw the words across the page splattering ink stains everywhere across our kitchen floor. And you sit at the table like the rest of us wondering if this is real or something you imagined. So you stick another spoon of cereal into your mouth and no longer care if you are late for anything.

Yes I am speaking to you reader.. this is the Spirit Scribe speaking directly to you thru your eyes.. I have no other way of getting thru to you.. see.. I am invisible.. an entity totally real but impossible to see with your eyes or hear with your ears..

Yes I am The Ghost Writer of whom you have read of, but still hunger to meet. Well listen up lover of the lingo.. to offer no resistance to life to where the words lead.. to what words are written.. is to live in a state of eternal grace, ease, and lightness.

Say so long to samsara.. next stop.. samadhi." Then Tio spun the taco from his toes across the Table of Fables, taking us all, including time.. into another space.

The Book.. The Story.. only feels heavy because it is endless, thousands of pages. But if you find just that one page where you will be pleased to stay.. you will find peace, and the light of love shall shine down upon that page illuminating it even in the darkest nite when you cannot sleep and the nightmares rip your soul out and heave it along with a million others into the pit of past paragraphs.. the pit of paranoia.

Just then you hear a laugh from deep inside the Literature of the Lord.. yup.. these are the words of The One.. who begat The All..

When in this state of samadhi, one is no longer dependent upon things being a certain way.. good or bad.. pos or neg.. all is one and it is all part of the same story.. written by the same writer.. read by the same reader.

Tio dealt more cards like he were dealing reality's razors.. each card sharp enough to cut reality in half.. Each moment is another slice reality's razor severs off the motherload and serves to you .. ya you sittin on the stool in the story saloon sippin' strawberry star storm story soda.. slipping deeper into a dream sold to you by a Software Story Spirit you download, dear dreamers.

in the garden of beauty you were born.. you are bathed in beauty
all women are sacred sisters.. all men beloved brothers
we are all children of the cosmic crone.. cared for by creation herself.

Congratulations consciousness crusader.. you dealt yerself the card of the College of Contemplation.. a cranial course in consciousness..

We're a community of creators of conscious commedic commentary on the cosmic crises cookin in yer cauldron kids.. ya you humans are our kids... we shoulda never left you alone.. we're yer ancestors and we have a responsibility to reality so we're comin back in many ways.. one of them is words written by wraiths.. see the spirits are speakin to you.. right here.

Call us your humans' Angel Allies.. pick up a dozen of us divine dudes and dudettes.. consciousness cadets.. in the aisle of angels.. same place you picked you picked up the paranormal pasta and literature lasagna and sentence spagetti.

Dad had cooked supper.. the living literature lasagna and sentence spagetti was crawling all over the plates and onta the table and down the floor. "No more !" mum screamed.. "This is only something I've dreamed !" "No mum," I replied "its real."

"This Book is a spell story spirit studies consciousness class. Each one of you is a cosmic child who softly balances the scales of eternity." Then the Professor of The Paranormal Pages.. Doc Diction.. placed The Book upon the desk.. "class dismissed.. homework is on hold forever.. holiday every day.. play in these pages forever.. why waste yer life in regular reality.. you and me.. we can change eternity. Choose your chapter.. heaven or hell.

Do you hear the howling.. the laughter.. the whispers.. the moans of pain and exstacy seeping thru these pages, coming from distant and not so distant chapters ? Hey look I just write the words.. you choose the chapters.
ya yur the captain of the chapters.. commodore of the lore ..

Me.. I just toss the Dream Dice.. spin the Consciousness Cards.. deal from the Deck of the Divine.. you download the dimension in which you dwell.. we're all under society's spell." Tio dealt another slice of Tale Toast to sis. She slathered it with Maya Marmalade.

I'm only the Wraith Writer.. just some spirit scribblin on the walls of your worlds, while the wind whirls round.. entering thru the cracks in the trailer.. stirrin up the cards.. yess the wind deals the cards.. Tio just sits smiling sipping Tale Tea which he offers to you and me. "Son are you gettin sleepy?" Dad whispered sofly.

Shoosh don't make a sound... you'll wake the warden of the world's gates. Ya god's got gates around the world.. to keep us safe from uninvited guests.

The sign at the bottom of the page read.. "Come again.. yer always welcome at Tio's Toast and Tales Time Travellin Trailer.. Story Sailor."

Life's Fire

"Makes me think whenever I dip my pens inta some ink. Love is the only ink I think is worth writin with. This is the soul speaking.. Downloading to you the dimensions of delight every night and day so you can play in paradise.. treat this planet nice.. she is your parent.. The Great Grannie Goddess of Goodness and Graciousness..

Her tresses are the trees and greenery.. her blood is the rivers and seas and wells.. her bones the stones and rocks. Rock this Cosmic Cradle gently. It's a nest of nascent angels.. warming up their wings. Yes.. all the universe sings.. a cosmic choir expressing divinity's desire.

The universe is one cosmic community. The world is a womb. We harvest either heaven or hell with our hearts and our hands.. with our thoughts and our words and our actions. So scribble well spell scrawllers. Write well wisdom worshippers. Act as angels.

I come as an angel ambassador to speak to the heart of humanity. Let us all come together as assistants.. not adversaries.. angels without armour.. with ardour and adoration for all. For are not christ and buddha and mohamed and moses and krishna and quetzacoatl but different facets of the same crystal. Is not All Our Relations. All walks within Wakan Tanka.. all tells one tale.. as do the words within this book make one story.

Observe how The Book opens wide its wings to embrace lovingly each reader.. every episode an eternal embrace.. every page a parent giving birth to possiblities. All is formed of Goddess's Flesh.. we are the Flames of Life's Fire.. and the Destiny of Death's Desire..

All is cooked into the Chalice of Creation.." "Take a vacation!" sis signaled to the Story Serpent to shutdown the dialogue. We were later for school than ever before.. the door was no more.. only the table was left.. with a pile of pancakes.. or was that pages.. forming a temple pyramid where the Paranormal Paragliders dropped the Dissertations of the Divine Dead.. Death's Dialogues.. Life's Lessons.

All is woven of the Threads of Time. We spirits are simply servants of the sacred.. serving as scribes.. Let's just say.. to clarify the confusion that this ain't no illusion.. the author is an angel. These scripts are the Songs of the Soul. It is your turn to sing in this cosmic choir.. become an ember of the eternal fire.

I now wander as one with the wind. This story is how I speak. When you look at the literature you listen to me. I am the cries of creation. All sleep in the beloved's bed. Did you hear what I said?" Doc Diction asked the kid in the back row who had fallen asleep. That was me.. dreaming of divinity.

"Thinking is invisible.. ink is invinceable.." the Literature Lizard Lecturer wrapped his tail around the lectern.. then set it spinning.. like the stool in the Story Saloon, like the table in the Tavern of Tales.. stories spinning forever out of the eternal.

The serpent wrapped itself around Sis's spoon, and while sipping outta her spoon carried on a conversation with sis and the cereal. Meanwhile Sammy Sammatra was crooning a syrupy cereal song.. while sittin on the rim of sis's cereal bowl.
"let's fall in love .. you and me.. with everyone we see.."

Just then as the page started to turn it churned up a pink mist from out of the manuscript.. softly spreading over the bowl of cereal and out over the entire table leaving visible only the peak of the pyramid of pancakes piled high.. and there atop the peak of pancakes sat Tio dealing from the Deck of Deliverance one more chance to the cosmos to come clean where it had hidden god.
You students of the spirit scripts.. scholars of the soul.. after a thousand incarnations you will have earned your PHD in paranormal philosophy and prophecy page paragliding.

Walk wisely upon the words, oh courageous word world wanderer.. for the words can whip up a wind, that'll wrap yer world in wonder.. or wipe away the world within which you wander. With one slash of the pen the story is slain.. with one scoop of the spoon.. another soul saved. "Hey quite stickin yer spoon inta my bowl of cereal, sis" i said.

Words are the wonder of the world. Words wake up the world. With words was wrought the world within which we wander. Yes we are all characters in a cosmic creation.

We are word warriors.. word wizards.. word worshippers.. I can see them coming now.. bearing burning torches.. pens afire.. Story Spoons at the alert.
Sis and the Baboon Book Brothers were posed to pounce upon any unsuspecting syllable that happened to crawl outta the cereal bowl.

"You are darkness reclaimed from its hiding place in a hell of which you smell.. "Sis was swearing at some sentence that dared crawll out from under the page she was on. No uninvited letters.. let's keep this story simple.. I love you.. you love me.. beginning and end of tale. Now all we gotta do is fill in the middle with happy harmonies and we'll sail into the ever after chapter that lives forever.

Sis was hanging out with her homework homies at Bubba Buddha's Bardo Book and Bagel Bar.. munching on one of Bubba Buddha's Bagels.. crunchy and chewy on the outside but in the middle nothing but eternal soft stillness and silence.. while around it all else is being eaten.. until nothing remains but the empty space of no mind.. non attachment.. the all encompassing emptiness.

Sis was one angry angel snarling at the serpent who was spittin Syllable Serum Vocabulary Venom all over sis's Book.. "Go hide yerself hero, in the farthest pages of the story. Your dark wings cast a shadow that slows with its weight, wisdom in its flight thru heaven's skies. Burn upon others' altars your idiot's incense. The pillars of your temples are tarnished. Wrap your wounded wings around your own darkness.

Hide and heal.. you fallen fool. Stir yer story with some other spoon. Untie your ropes that hold my ship to your harbour you hoodlum. My bed is aflame with the fire of ardour and desire for the divine. You, me, and The Book are a threesome, and I don't do threesomes, and besides you ain't no handsome hero in my story, so split snake."
… then sis took another sip of her strawberry star shake. Yup that story snake was on the make.. hopin' for a piece of carrot cake.

Threads of Time

Snake snickered cause he figured he had a better line.. "Dame divine.. pretty priceless princess.. this Prince of the Pages adores the way you turn his pages.. don't erase this sentence from your story.. make every one of my chapters your chosen.." Then he handed sis a dozen pink roses.. mumbled something about "ink sure makes a reader think."

Mum called out "Finish yer cereal and put yer dishes in the sink. Just be sure you don't hit the strawberry Sink Skink bathin' in the strawberry star soap suds.. now overflowin' the sides of the counter creatin' a strawberry star stream running along the kitchen floor makin gettin to the door a slippery ride.. ya ain't reality a slippery ride.. a rocky rhyme.." Mum mumbled while lookin' at dad for reality reassurance.. to which he replied while tightening his shoelaces.

"It's just the threads of time loosenin up. Sweetheart.. you light up my soul and make my heart sing. Looks like this morning is gonna be another slow start for school."

Meanwhile that snake kept philosophyzin'.. "Time has returned time and again.. you'd think it had better things to do than hang around me and you. Past present and future are a threesome that make up one story.

Life and death lie in the same bed.. I can't get you outta my head.. Princess of this poet's poem. Oh I'm just the clown of the chapters. Why would a book babe like her choose me.. a silly story serpent spinnin on a stool.. drippin dialogue drool.. lookin like a fool fallin for you in every sentence. I'm so under your spell angel.. yer the answer to every question ever asked.. the perfect beginning and happy ending to the whole world's story..
Space and time are forever lovers.. locked in an eternal embrace."

Then I heard mum say..
"Oh Noble Knight of Knowledge
Wanderer of Wonder's Way
Worshipper of Wisdom
Worthy Word Walker..

You have led the way for so many who have been led astray.. lost in life's sea of uncertainty.. do you think you could get us to class on time."

Dad respectfully replied.. "You have taken me and molded a finer man..
Being with you is such an uplifting of angels' wings.. Even the silence sings.
You and me, we've been graced by the great grannie ghost of goodness and graciousness.

Goddess you do so bless this brother of the beloved..
Together we have toasted time with the rythm of our rhymes.

All men are sacred sons.. All women divine daughters.. of The One Mother.
May sweet Sister of Serenity keep safe and serene in sacred sanctuary..
all that be.

May every word I write.. right the wrongs of the world.
May every song I sing.. ring like notes rung from the bell.. at the wedding of heaven and hell. May love's light illuminate our flight.
For sure dear I'll get our sacred son and divine daughter and you.. to class on time.

Kids could we just stay in time here.. we're having enough difficulty staying inside space.. Ever wonder what is outside of space ? outside of time ?" Dad was a real thinker.. that's why he taught a class in how not to get caught by consciousness.

See we all cocreate a consensual collective consciousness.. the lesson is to learn to live outside of existence.. free of any terms that confine yer cranial currents from free flowin. Just then the pages were fluttered by an invisible wind..

"Hey you.. from what space did you come.. from out of what story did you appear.."
Dad mumbled to the last line that just squiggled across the page. Something was rising up outta the pages.

"Better hope for a happy ending, even though the beginning was born bad. Yup, this story is savage senile sexy silly and somewhat anti social, so don't get too close to the Living Letters.
This literature is alive.. This Book bites..
Still wanna meet The Ghost Writer ? The WereWriter ? The Spirit Scribe ?
The writer becomes the words when the moon is out..
Words that aren't there except when you open the book..
For each reader the story is different..

You get yer own ghost guide to escort you thru The Paranormal Pages.. You want a guy ghost or a gal ghost ?" the serpent slurred the syllables as the stool spun faster.

And so the words wait upon the page for your appearance.. page prowler.. pal of the Paranormal Pages. This is your pal The Paranormal Poet parlayin with you.. so don't go gettin paranoid.. yer still normal but not for much longer, literature lover."

You lean back in yer seat.. suck back another spoonful of cereal.. and wait for the effect to wear off.. only it never does.. cause yer a consciousness cadet cruiser on a never ending flight deeper into Wisdom's Well.. with the rest of the world waitin on yer every word.. pullin 'em along with every page.

Yer the parent of the page.. the sage of the story.. the first word and the final period when it comes. You nod yer head in agreement with every word you hear.. You can't see clear anymore. You've sold your soul for the story. When you ran out of ink.. you used your own sweat and tears.. bled your own blood.

So to forget what you never wanna remember.. and never should have known.. you take another swig of Liquid Lightning.. to get up the balls to go back into The Book of Scarey Spirits and Awesome Angels. You take a stool at the bardo bargaining bar.. next to the serpent selling Story Soap.. wash yer body all over with it and come out of the shower in a different scene. Ya, the shower stall is kinda like superman's telephone booth. Every hero's gotta have a closet in which to hang their cosmic consciousness cape."

Story Samurai

"Consider the cereal box as similar to superman's telephone booth.. Kid.. kinda yer special place to change into any cosmic character your consciousness can conceive of."

Sis is listening to the lizard leaning against the lectern..The cereal box had shape shifted into the lizard lectern.. the lizard lamp and of course the lizard lunch box where sis kept her book, buddha bagels, book brew, story stew, and syllable sandwiches.

You stand like steel.. so the story doesn't knock you over.. the tale doesn't topple yer tower of thought.. yer edifice of understanding. Your own story seems like a sad excuse for reality.

You're brought to the head office.. the sorting station for stories.. Some never make it to first page.. some fall apart in the tough scenes.. few make it to the end.. and fewer have an happy ending.

So you wanna sign up to be a Story Samurai.. the Story Samurai Society takes stories seriously.. no silly sentences .. savage yess.. serious si.. subtle sure.. sensual sometimes.. surreal seguro. So sip on another Story Sake and see what cards the Dream Dealer deals outta the dust and decay and lays on the Table of Time for you.. Tale Trekker. Sayonara Sweetheart."

Sis was swooning so softly to the Paranormal Prince of the Pages.. the Paranormal Poet..

"Here's a poem to pretty up the page for my Princess of the Pages.."

ella es la madre de toda .. she is the mother of all
somos incarnaciones de la luce .. we are incarnations of the light
somos angelos ascendando .. we are angels ascending
somos hijos sagradas de la madre divina ..
we are sacred children of the divine mother

oubre tus manos .. open your hands
tus ojos .. your eyes
tus voces .. your voices
tus brasos .. your arms
tus alas .. your wings

por la madre .. for the mother
open to the light .. open to love

there is no time left to live without love .. love for all beings

lay down your arms .. raise up your wings
praise all living things .. so the whole world sings
a cosmic choir of love's fire

love you have lead us this far .. don't falter now
burn forever love's fire .. each one of us an ember of love's fire..
the divine's desire."

Sis was swooning to the stream of silver sounds issuing from the lavender lizard librarian lectern lecturer of the lost languages of love's parted lips.

"You walk upon the way of words.. as a worshipper in the temple. With your sense of wonder you have awakened this story from its slumber. Work only with words of wonder. Right the wrongs of the world with words not wars.. words not weapons.. no syllables of slavery.. no sentences of savagery.. no stories of slaying.

Sure there'll always be sad songs sung.. priceless princess.. but you and me This Book.. we'll always be tight. For you I'll make sure the story is sweet.. the words are right.

Take me in your hand.. you've already taken my heart.. hold on strong to this story.. an' nothin can ever go wrong. I was invisible to all.. even to myself.. until you came along.. truly this is cosmic karma.. a cutie like you.. and a disincarnated entity like me.. living happily forever after chapter after chapter.

You and I are one.. for what is a story without a reader.. a pen without a page.. a path without a pilgrim.. love without someone to share it.

Let us spend every night with nirvanna.. naked as she can be..
every essence shown.. every shade revealed.. every note played. Baptize me in the beauty of you.. sweet saint of the story.. princess of the pages.

May these words be wings with which your soul soars. We are all facets of the same crystal.. petals of the same blossom.. roots of one tree.. sentences of the same story.

Navigating Nirvana

"Come in.. Come in.. This is consciousness trying to make contact.. Cereal Cadets come in.. Renegade Reality to Renegade Reality Rider.. Do you read me.. This is The Book From Beyond The Brain.. this is the tale talking.. Do you read me ?"

Consciousness was trying to make contact once more thru the cereal box. I responded thru my Spirit Speaking Spoon.. "A Okay Ascended Angel.. I read you. Easy on the flight pattern. I'm cruising thru consciousness. Who are you ?

The voice coming out of The Cereal Box That Talks continued.."One of the speaking spirits.. a spirit of another sort.. unseen but not unspoken. I'm on yer periphery.. just past the perimeters of the page yer on.. on the edge of your existence.. gliding in between the words yer reading."

Reality was once more getting unreal.. It all felt like a dream.. I could feel myself nodding off.. falling asleep.. It was past midnite.. a kid my age shoulda bin asleep.. It was then the book bite me.. as if the pages wanted to make a point that they were alive.. as alive as any character in any story could be.

My hand was bleeding.. drops of blood dripping onto the white page which was slowly turning pink.. then crimson.. as if the page was drinking up the blood.. Oh it's just a careless paper cut I thought. And yet I had the feeling that this chapter was getting carnal.. carnivorous. I was getting careless in my handling of The Book.

Then The Book's covers closed around my hand and I could feel my arm being pulled into the book.. and my other hand being pulled into the open cereal box !

How could a book change so quickly from one whose covers are the bright white wings of an angel one time you read it, and then the next time you open it the covers have turned a velvety black laced with what looks like raised dark crimson veins.. Covers that become wings which enfold the reader in infinite light or eternal darkness ?

"Within the story itself lie the answers to this and every question.. which you who quest.. in search of the ultimate question.. seeking the allmighty's answer.. may ask. Take these questions for example. Will the world run out of space before time ends ? Or will the world run out of time and still have a surplus of space left over for ever ?If the world runs out of time will there be no more forever ?

The purpose of the Paranormal Pteradactylian Pyramid Parchment Puzzle Pages.. is to open your mind so you can empty it. The mind is a complex of cranial consciousness corridors.. paths thru which the paranormal can pass.. The cranium is your consciousness cockpit.. cranial cruiser cadets.

And what is the paranormal ? Something which makes most people paranoid, and yet few understand. It is power.. energy.. light and sound waves vibrating.. cosmic copulation.. the ecstatic moans of space and time mating. It is Fuel for Faith's Fire.. Death's Dialogues.. Thoughts from Thanatos.. Divine Devastation.. Sublime Sublimation.. Cosmic Creation..

It is the formless energetic vibratory substance of which dreams are made, and existence is formed. It is the Breath of The Almighty.. the Embrace of Eternity.. the Laughter of the Lost.. the Dreams of the Dead.. God's Flesh.. Liquid Love.. the Notes of Heaven's Harp.. the Hero's Heart..

The mind is a Passageway into the Paranormal.. a series of tunnels if you will.. thru which passes the cosmic current, that lights the imagination and makes movement into matter and matter back into pure movement.. an eternal spring from which the river of reality flows.

My friend do not fear when reality falls flat on its face. When regular reality is on the ropes, most folks are left without hope. That's when the unreal calls. You can become a raider of reality.. raid reality and retire safe in the unreal.. steal from space.. take from time.

The Book of Brain Brews is a course in creative consciousness.. downloaded to you in secret so no one will know yer a Knight of Knowledge. This is The Documentarius Divinicus.. the Divine Document.. the Book of The Beloved.. Dialogues with the Dead.. Answers from the Ancestors.

Call these chapters Consultations with Consciousness.. Tantric Tea Tales with Tio Taco Temple Toad." Then Tio stuffed the tamale with a couple more Wisdom Warts. "Two tacos to go.. for Heyoka Joe." Tio called out to the ghost no one seems to know. Sis and i had stopped in at Tio Taco's Take Out.. an after school sidewalk soda shop tale trailer painted a rusty orange ressembling Tio's tale travellin trunk.

Tio handed me and sis two tamales and said " Think of yourself as a noble Knight of Knowledge.. and me as a Wonder Wizard with warts.. waiting along The Way of Words to wish you well on your Vision Voyage thru the Valley of Vocabulary."

Then Tio poured us both a cup of Wish Wart Wine.. "Wish what you will.. wisdom, worry, woe, war, wonder, whatever you want. Whatever you write.. will wait for you somewhere along your way. Wish well Wisdom Word Wanderers.

Each time you complete a chapter you win a wart.. once you have won all the warts you will receive the Wardrobe of Wish Warts.. which will transform the wearer into a Wish Wart Wizard.. whoever whatever whenever wherever you want.. so it will be.

This Wish Wart Wine is top of the line." Tio said, as he sipped a second time while continuing his lesson in rhyme.. "The empty mind can receive all thoughts and not get caught. The open heart can receive all blessings. The open soul can receive the world."

Tio spun the spell stirring spoon around his fat fingers and slid the cups toward Sis and me. "This reality's on me.. lemmee tell you kids a tale.." Tio said as he leaned closer while resting a fat elbow on the Fable Table.

"Did ya ever hold an angel in yer arms and watch it die ?" Well this indigo indio I had just picked up hitchin on the Heyoka Highway whispered to me, soon as he got settled in the passenger seat of my convertible seventy chevy. I was headin south of somewhere in the desert of dry dust and dead dreams. Seems he had been born and bred in the Rattlesnake Reservation.. a lost relative of the navajo nation.. part apache comanche mescalero.. one who knows the way to north of nothin.. south of the unseen.
Well he asked me if I had ever longed for a love lost long ago.. said he had and still did.. said the angel was so fragile.. the tears had dried up long ago on her face.. she was so light in his arms.. almost nothin there but the warm breath of her sighs.. she had flown so far her wings were worn to whisps.. then she whispered somethin about heaven was headed this way.. said she could hear the wings hum.. hundreds upon hundreds of 'em.

He said he figured she was some kind of Astral Astronaut.. navigating nirvana.. but had gotten lost.. at least she found a safe sanctuary in his open heart.

The indio said he was just a Servant of the Sacred.. guessed that's why she had landed in his arms. He gave her a Knight's Kiss hoping it might heal her .. but nothin helped.

He pointed to some hills we were passin'.. said that's were he buried what was left of her.. now white folks were digging up the sacred land for some metal they said was precious.. he said all the earth was precious.. don't need to dig up the dead to know that in one's heart and head.

He said it was all like a dream.. didn't know anymore if it was real or some Fable From Forever that he'd heard in his head while waitin for the next ride along the Heyoka Highway. Then he said to let him off around the corner of the next curve. There was nothing there. I asked him where he was going.. all he said was.. "The Cookie Queen's Cottage.. ta greet The Great Grannie Goddess of Goodness and Graciousness."

Tio started wiping up the tears on the counter with a reality rag. "Ya the pebbles of the path are polished by the pain of pilgrims." Tio rung out the waters of woes of the wanderers of the way.. filled a pitcher with it.. and poured another couple cups for Sis and me.

"Think of me, yer uncle Tio, as Thanatos's Therapist.. your consciousness coach in the game of goin' for god..

Now who ordered the double Brain Brew?" Tio asked, as he stirred a second spoon of slug slime, mixed with snake spit, simian sweat, and primate piss, into the brain blender.

Gift of the Goddess

Goddess of the the gift of goodness and graciousness
Thank you Eternal Being of Love for your guidance
This altar that i am is yours forever
From your divine chalice all beings drink everlasting light
Tonight the clouds will whisper to the winds the language of our love

You have inspired me to unfold my wings
To seek out the mountain tops of existence
Ride beyond realities only dreamed of.

You have brushed me with your ephemeral kiss
Anointed me with your sweet breath
Bathed me in your pure morning dew.

Oh how this soul doth yearn to burn in your sacred fire
This hunger only grows
Pour me from your ladle a blessing of love
heal all heros' hearts.

Rush to my arms with wings unfolded
our song is as ancient as all eternity.

This poet has not had his fill of the feast
this hero hungers for a whole heart
spring open my soul from it's chains and cage
assist me.. guide me.. make holy this beast's bed
beauty hath but just awoken from her sleep.

You have enfleshed this soul in a scabbard of spirit silver
Take your arrow from your quiver
Send it straight to my heart

Words are this poet's gifts he doth bring to the altar of the angel.
Lonely thru the dark night walks the lord of light
a beast wandering these pages in search of beauty

With you Goddess of Grace and Goodness..
I remember that which I had never known,,
I see what is invisible..
I hear the unheard..

I become a vessel that ferries the enslaved of society
across the seas of their own fears..
I am death as it nears..
and life as it rears itself wobbly from the cradle..
and then roars across the pages of time.

Like jesus on an ivory cross worn around the neck of every believer..
I have come here to relieve you of your mind
As I was relieved of mine.

Blessed is the bringer
And those that brought
And those that are yet to bring.

All sings as one choir.

Angels far from the light..
May these words guide you home this night.

Sacred children of the cosmos
Bred of love
Born into light
Blessed are those with sacred sight.

Fellow PLANETARIANS
You and I are one of the same breed..
We are all pieces of the same loaf of bread we break at the holy supper."

Tio broke bread and mumbled as he stuffed a piece into his mouth..
then passed it on to the others.. "Words, words, words, thoughts, and more thoughts..
Some original.. Some borrowed from the aboriginal.

It's taboo to question themes of religious factors yet it is the most important philosophical question one can ask for it determines all one's thoughts and actions and manner of being.

Religious orientation toward seeking spirit, is a concept of cosmic proportions, for it includes the normal and paranormal aspects of reality.. or at least of one's conceptual framework of reality's boundaries that define one's vision of divinity.

For instance.. take me.. a toad.. your host sittin here butterin' my toast.. and look at Lotus Lounge Lizard, Luv Lips Louie. He's a reptile an' i'm an amphibian.. but we both got skin and breath and a heart and eyes ta see.. like you humans.. see we're all PLANETARIANS.."

"Now who ordered the strawberry samadhi shake.. and which one of you baboons ordered the banana nirvana split?" the Wraith Waitress who wasn't there said while staring us down."

And so the story stops as it started.. with a letter.. with a word. Please notice word wanderers.. that the first word and the last word in a chapter are the same. Or if you would prefer.. the first word of the following chapter is the same as the final word of the preceding chapter.. the choice is yours as this story is your own tale..

Whatever you wanna read will unfold before your eyes not only in The Book but in your life.. the more you read.. the more the story and your life's reality bleed together.. you enter the computer screen and the screen enters you..

You become one with every other player via the story that you co create.. so go ahead and write a word, or sentence, or syllable.. see what the screen writes back to you.. what appears upon the page.

Think of you and The Book as engaged.. about to get married forever.. the blessing is you live forever so long as you keep writing.. The god of gab always asks for a gift in return.

Like others before.. blessed upon the altar of alteration.. you are but incense burned to release its fragile fragrance.

Life With The Dead

"Gracias de la profundidad de mi corazon.. you honour these pages with your eyes.. your look of wonder as we wander together thru these words to places we have only dreamed of before. You and I are almost as one.. I so silent and hidden.. and you who brave the real world.. while I hide here inside of fantasy.

And yet we have both fallen in love with each other.. I always in your embrace.. your eyes never seeming to get enough of me. I lay bare my body. Your eyes feast upon my fair flesh. Thru the words we mesh.. we mate.. fated forever.. one as the garden and the other as the gate."

The Professor of Paranormal Poems stepped back arms length from the pulpit and then like a pit panther pounced up onto the Lectern of Light.

"Here's the book you asked for, sunny sonny.." the ancient leathered librarian grumbled.. "and tell yer sis to stop climbing up the shelves.. the library book stacks ain't a rock climbing wall.." Just then sis rappelled down the stack carrying in her arm a book as old as the earth itself.. looking like dirt... smelling of dust dug up from a tomb buried by the shifting sands of the Sand Box Desert of deserted dreams and dust dragons..

Ya Dust Dragons .. risin up outta that sand box in the vacant lot.. soon after the bully bull dozer destruction demolition dude dug up the strawberry sidewalk along side of the vacant lot where sis and I and all the kids played..

Until that day, that is, when the dozer near done my dad in and gave me a concussion that kept me in a coma for a couple years,.. I hear said by the divine doctors who nursed me back to the World of the Walking..

Ya I was spending my life with the dead.. years inside my own head, outside of my body, and beyond this reality you normal folks call home. See Dad and I.. we both stopped that dozer from crossin over the sidewalk and inta the vacant lot.. but not without the dozer crackin up the sidewalk cement and knockin over the old strawberry red fire hydrant, that stood sentinel at the Gates of The Garden of Eternity.

So ya you could say this is my attempt to relate to you what happened to me .. what was going on for all those years while I was deep in a coma which no one knew if I would ever return from.. and if I did.. what would I be.

What if you were no longer completely part of this world.. more part of the other one, from which you had just come after spending years alone with the dead.

What if you were no longer anything.. even though others saw you.. thought they saw you.. but you were not there.. just simply using the body as a stop over station.. a pit stop for the paranormal.. ya a paranormal pit stop landing pad for paranormal paragliders.. like you and your paranormal pals.

Ya I had become part paranormal.. no longer people.. part people on the outside appearance.. and inside pure paranormal.

What if you were not something in the world.. but more like a light bulb emitting light.. you emitted the world.. like rays of light coming out from you.. you were the source of the world.. like a projector that projects a light movie from every pore of your being ?

Then you control.. you create.. the world around you. Is it a dream.. a fantasy..
 or is it a real possibility ? Could we all.. each and every one of us.. co dream reality into being.. co emit from our total beings.. all of what we are.. all of what is.. create the cosmos. For all is vibration.. reappearing and disappearing into and out of worm holes.. from worlds into worlds. This is just one of the worlds we visit.

Like sentences appearing upon a page. It is the secret to eternal existence.. Imagining the unfoldment of one's illuminating existence. This is the sentence.. students.. on which to write a comment or interpretation of.. for tomorrow's class in creating consciousness. Consciousness Cadets, class dismissed."

And then the Paranormal Professor perched on the window sill of the college classroom and proceeded to prepare for paranormal paragliding take off.

"The difficult part of the journey is in making the choice.. Once the choice is made, the way is not as difficult.. There are only two choices.. look to the light.. or look to the dark..

What we look to grows.. for it finds nourishment in our thoughts..
Looking to the light no matter how small it may appear.. will draw others to look at the light.. The light will grow depending upon how many look to the light. And conversely.. looking towards the dark feeds the dark in one's mind and body.. and draws others' vision towards the dark.

At this point in time the power of humans to create simply by their thoughts is more powerful than ever before. Because of the evolution of humans and the cosmos itself, humans are more one with the creative force than ever before..

Take this following tale as an example of reality creation.
"Okay what's the deal here ? I went for a walk yesterday along the trail where the woods are deep, and i was followed by a pack of wolves until i came out into the light. But that is not what I am asking about because I am sure you had nothing to do with the wolves being there.

What the tale is saying here is that where we put our attention and intention is what we give life to. Some create darkness. Some look toward the dark, and bring others' attention and intention to it. Some look toward the light, and create light and draw others' attention and intention to love.

I have looked at the dark and had my fill till it made me sick as the darkness seeped into my soul. I did very little to heal the darkness in that manner.. neither inside of myself nor outside of myself.

Now i only wish to look toward the light.. draw it closer.. expand it.. be it. I believe that if more people looked to see how they could bring more light into being, than bothered to look at all the dark.. dark would die .. and light would live."

Master Roshi Raspberry Reptile.. stepped back from the lectern, bowed a buddhist bow.. and the crowd of consciousness connoiseurs clapped.

"Be a haven for every heart !" Roshi roared out as he exited the stage singing softly to himself.. "reality rocks"

Sis smiled at me and said.. "It sure does when yer a brain blaster mind master consciousness class cadet copilot cosmos creator."

For all of you new to the Kabuki Zoo.. All you need to do is look at the words.. read them softly slowly until you get the hang of riding the writing.. faster you read, the wilder the ride.. and the words do get wild.. weave like the wind in and out of your cranial corridors.

Consciousness cruisin at the speed of light.. All eternity explorers who have riden the words this far.. in your next box of cereal you will find deep in the bottom a master Roshi Reptile Replica.. yours free if you agree to purchase six boxes of cereal minimum every week.

This offer is only open to those serious cereal eaters signed up for some serious cereal cruising.. No one is safe in this cereal bowl.. Back off from this bowl.. This is one breakfast bowl with a bad attitude.. Stick yer stirrin spoon in some other cereal sonny boy.." The cereal could get mouthy.. so i carefully backed off from the cereal in the bowl.

Do not leave your bowl unattended. Get yourself a Bowl Troll to keep away any unwanted uninvited ghost guests. Bowl Trolls come hidden under the cereal in the bottom of specially marked boxes. Treat yer troll to a bowl of cereal every day and you'll have a fiend friend forever for life and death.

This part of the page is intentionally left blank so you can write in your own words of wisdom. Where there is space at the end of each chapter.. or in between the lines.. write in your thoughts. This is a workbook for wisdom word wizards. Just be careful what you write. This Book's got feelings.. friend.

Raspberry Rain

Dad was giving his morning mantra to sis and me and mum and the monkeys and baboons during breakfast..

"Doin one's best to create conscious connection.. creates a community of consciousness cadets.. Calling all consciousness cruisers.. Assemble yer angel asses right now..
Put down yer Cereal Story Surfin Spoons and get in the Terra Tracker Reality Rider Time Trailer.." And we all leapt up from the breakfast table leavin our bowls begging for more cereal..

"Ya the bowl eats the cereal.. Alongside the kid.. And they talk.. Ya the kid eating the cereal and the cereal and the cereal bowl converse with each other while the kid is eating the cereal, and the bowl is eating the cereal and talking to the kid and the cereal.

The Cereal Box is listening to the cereal and bowl talking to the kid.. The box of cereal joins in.. Soon the cereal in all the bowls around the table are havin a conversation with the cereal box in the center of the table actin like the talking stick carrier.. It's a sacred cereal speaking circle.. The cereal box is the control center commander of consciousness.

Soon all the breakfast bowls and boxes and cereal in the world are gonna talk.. to everyone eating the cereal.. Yes folks.." The salesnake serpent sellin the cereal was saying to the crowd of kids and their parents standin in a cicle in the supermarket aisle..

The salesnake sellin cereal was leadin a sacred singing spirit circle.. The salesnake raised the cereal box up and said this was a conduit to the almighty.. And so as a home or office altar effigy sacred statue.. cereal boxes were placed on pedestals and at appropriate places so people could assume the prayer and praise positions.. They became prayer posts.. Places of praise for great spirit. An outlet for expression of the eternal.
Tired..? Take a prayer pause.

Yes these pages are a parable.. part prose.. part poetry.. part prayer.. a path.

Wakan Tanka walks in with White Wind.. The Sacred Shadows step back to make space in the circle for The Unseen, but not unheard. For the table talked too, to the bowls, and the box that talks. Breakfast had become busy. That Teach, is why we're late for class." sis squeaked out like a sweet sparrow.

Yess you finally understand now that it was the cereal box that told the story.. The toad.. Taco Tio Toad, was just a stand in for who really told the story.. Sure the toad talked.. Taco Tio Truth Talker Tale Teller.. Wisdom Wart Walker..

Every time you finish a page you get the chance to receive a Wisdom Wish Wart which will serve you well when you wish you weren't where you were.. Creepin an crawllin up the stairs slippery and smelly with strawberry star sweet and scarey story syrup that ya had spilt while taking a bowl of it to yer sis who had already gone ahead with a slice of the Tale Travellin Trampoline Toast..

Ya you could bounce on the toast until you wanted to be ejected into another reality.. And then you would disappear completely or partially depending on how high you bounced.. The higher the bounce the further into farther realities.. And deeper and more completely.. and for longer times too.

Toast Travelllin is not for the timid. Taco Travellin can get pretty trippy.. Even for a Tulku Toad Tale Teller Token Taker Quick Stir Trail Trickstir."

Tio poured another slug of Trickstir Tequila for the Strawberry Slug who was sleepily curled up around the Slug Slime Soda bottle .. it was so steamy and hot the bottle was sweatin slug sweat.

"Take a Tale Token.. one of the Wish Warts from Tio's Trunk.. The Trickstir's Trunk of Tales.. This token allows you one safe renegade reality ride with guaranteed return to original reality and none to minimal flash backs should your brain not be appropriate for a permanent download.

This company cares about your consciousness.. And if you are not suitable for spirit soaring.. we will not place your existence in an existential on the edge experiment that could radically rearrange you reality."

Token Taco Tio was tokin' a sacred cigar.. the falling ashes were like a shower of strawberry stars soaring thru a night sky.. Paranormal Puff Pipe Talkin Tobacco.. Ya.. the Toad's Tobacco was talkin from inside the cigar .. Talking to that indio who goes by the name of Heyoka Joe... Somebody that nobody knows.." babaji baboon mumbled while pickin his nose with his stinky toes.

Tio was sending up smoke signals.. The Tale Trailer Tavern was turnin smoky.. Couldn't tell the spirits from the floating smoke signals. The table was deep in smoke.. And slowly the table turned into the golden Toad Temple.. And I was flying .. Me and sis were flyin.. Like paranormal paragliding pteradactyliians over the pyramid.. The pyramid would disappear in the smoke mist and then reappear.. It too was paranormal...

The porridge I had eaten was paranormal ! That's what was causing this .. The aztec patterns.. The visions.. I was under the influence of the infinite..

The Cosmic Cereal.. The Paranormal Porridge.. The Temple Toast. See we bought all that which the sales serpent was sellin.. Strawberry Star Story Speaking Cereal.. Spirit Scribblin Syrup.. Tale Travellin Toast.. Paranormal Page Porridge Potion.. Script Spell Stew and Story Soup and Slug Slime Soda.. Buddha's Bardo Brain Blaster Bagels and Brew.. Ghost Goulash and Goblin Gruel.. Paranormal Pyramid Pancakes.. Sorcerer Spagetti and Tale Tea..

It had gotten a hold on me and sis and now was gettin to mum and dad.. Soon we were all addicted to the paranormal.. And every bite we took took us deeper into The Ghost's Game.

Tio or one of the other caretaker character angel assistance allies will accompany you. The toad's a Toast Travellin Tale Tracker. If you get lost, or need a guide or guru.. Well Roshi Reptile or Gutor Gator Guardian of the Gutters that lead to the Gates of the Garden of the Goddess.. will assist you.

First step.. well actually it will be the last step you take.. in this reality anyways.. is to go thru the Ghost Gates guarding the Ghost Graveyard found in the Sinking Swamp situated dead center in the sand box in the not so vacant back lot.

Slowly the swamp will seep up thru the next pages. The words will get wet. The script becomes unreadable scrawll and sticky scribble.. Soon your fingers stick to the page.. It is like your hands are being pulled into the void of the page by phantom fingers.. pulling you.. sensually, seductively, securely.. as the spirit sings softly.

And the weird thing about this interactive game is that if you are a guy the fingers will be of a gal.. Unless yer gay and want the same sex fingers.. It's up to you..

What your mind wants is what happens.. You control the game but not with a remote controller operated by your hands.. It is a one time digital download direct into your brain.. Then you are wireless.. The Spirit Script Software to run the game and make you completely interactive is downloaded directly thru the cereal and the words into your cranium.

Once fully downloaded you will commence becoming an uncontainable being.. You answer to no one but the game.. the game is alive as is the story..

Each chapter is a download to take you deeper into dimensions only dreamed of.. and your own body energy runs the system.. No batteries needed.. Totally portable because it is in you.. Like wireless phones.. You are self wired to communicate with any other player in the game of god.. you will gain direct access to angels and other assorted alien entities..

Going for God.. There are all kinds of beasts and beauties beckoning along the path of the pilgrim passing thru these paranormal portals.. Enter at your own will upon the Paranormal Path..

Travel thru your consciousness corridors.. Now finish up friends yer bardo breakfast and let's break the brain barrier by blasting beyond the boundaries of beliefs..

Consciousness Crusaders.. Consciousness Cruisers.. Consciousness Creators.. Class.. your quest to answer the greatest question ever asked by gods or humans or any life forms.. "What is existence ?" is your next homework assignment. Consciousness Cadets.. write a five hundred word response to that question for next Monday's class in Renegade Reality.. No rider can rein it in..

So let's saddle up the story and ride off at the end into the sunset like handsome heros.." Then the Prof of Paranormal Prose and Poetry placed the pages upon the Lavender Lizard Light Lectern's head.. stepped sideways on the Paranormal Projector Podium and.. poof.. the paranormal prof was projected back into the paranormal.

You can download a Paranormal Projector.. Project the Paranormal into any place.. Learn how to project yourself into the paranormal with the Paranormal Podium Projector.

The Paranormal Projection Project is classified consciousness.. offered only to the select few the spirit selects.. if accepted you get your choice of chapters from the text on toast and tea tale travellin.. sky soaring and cereal diving... Diving from the sky inta a bowl of cereal and stayin alive.. Surviving cereal suicide.. the latest craze amongst cool consciousness cruisers.. Every bowl of cereal a different scene.. Places were no human has ever been.. and it all takes place..

While Tio Toad keeps pullin' never ending cards from the Deck of Divine Deliverance from between his fingers.. in a trailer parked on a desert highway no one ever drives on anymore cause of the winds.. always wiping away more pieces of the road. Tio's got a feather in his head band, a bandana around his thick throat, and a sarape shawl over his wide shoulders.

Be careful not to cross over any cracks in the pages.. They're consciousness chasms. You could lose yer consciousness if you fall into one. The chasm of consciousness is cracking wider.. the pages are tearing apart.. and you're floating thru a whirlwind of words whirling around you.. And the world is nothing more than words.

Now pull back on yer paranormal paragliding throttle.. Ease yer mind into hyper space.. Release reality slowly.. Entry into the eternal is about to occur..

And then poof.. Whether thru the podium or the cereal box or the bowl or Tio's Tale Travellin Trailer on the outskirts of Thanatos Town.. Renegade Reality is now within your reach.. It is within the reach of every Renegade Reality Rider Recruit..

Soon you will receive yer Reality Repellor Rings and Angel Attractor Arm band.. you will be geared up for Going For God... The game that sets you off after God.. Goddess.. However you address yer holy hero.. Yer head honcho.. The divine dude or dame.. The Almighty Everything.

Just sit down with Tio in his Trailer of Tales at the Table of Fables.. Turn the Table. Let Tio deal you another consciousness card. Just ask for directions to Thanatos Trailers.. Tio's Trailer is the one in the back.. He's always dealing a consciousness card from the deck of divine dreams and reality as it seems, but ain't.

Mind Memos

"Here's a memo to your mind from mine."
  signed ..
  Sincerely,
  Sam Swamp,
  Head of Sinking Swamp Studios.

Pauly Pancakes, The Prince of Pretend, handed over the signed memo to Max. Pauly had been a cop.. and a good one, until he went bad. Now he was a private dick.. the kind that sticks to a case even when he knows its closed.

Max looked the memo over, ordered another serving of Pond Pudding, with a side order of Swamp Sauce, mumbled something about it was a toss up between space and time as to who would win. Then he read out loud the Mind Memo from The Immaterial to The Material.

"Myth was finally talking.. telling the truth to Time. Space was snugglin in closer hoping to hear the conversation between consciousness and chaos.
The Pen and the Parable, are the plow and the arable land, of language. Thou art a Prince of the Pen and Parable.

The forgotten has been found. The treasure of time is a gift of the great goddess. And though we haven't actually met before, we've seen each other in many faces.

Night skies are our curtains.
Soldiers I have slain, and with ladies I have lain. I have sat with the sadness of the saints, the sorrows of sisters, the saviour's sighs, and the crusaders' cries. You have felt me in every embrace. I am the face that you kiss, and the face that you fear. I am the wombs of women and the hearths of every heart.
Slay not thine enemy with swords, but with words well written.

It's a poem Pauly. The public wants prose, not some pretty poem. Read to me the concept for the Consciousness Caretaker Cards collection." Max threw the Mind Memo at Pauly, stuck another spoon of Simmerin' Swamp Sauce inta his Purple Pond Pudding and stirred. The steam rose like dragon's breath.

Pauly took another sip of his bottle of Dragon Breath Brew,

"Well boss here's what I heard. There's a collection of cards, one comes included inside every box of cereal. On the card is the title of a chapter. The kid reads the chapter and that's it. There's some wisdom or something like that in each chapter that the kid can use for advice on how to live. It's all part of the puzzle of the Parable of the Paranormal.

Whatever card is pulled, then the person get's that chapter/ episode/ fortune/ message/ parable/ vision/ teaching/ lesson.. or whatever you wanna call it. the teachings of wisdom come from one of the characters in the book. For example.. from Tio Toad, Doc Dialogue, Evelyn D'Jardins, Barry Big, Max More, Sis, the Cereal Serpent, Strawberry Syrup Salamander, Slug Soda Slug, Sammy Snail, Book Baboon, Della Divine, or and any other character i forgot to include.. Like the Lavender Lizadarian Librarian Love Light Lamp, the Vision Vulture, Wraith Writer, Spirit Scribe, Ghostwriter.. a real one.. even though it ain't real in the readers reality.. at least not until the reader has been in the story long enough.

Call it Morning Talks with Tio The Troubador Trumpet playing Teacher Tulku Temple Trail Tale Toad..Wisdom walks with the Wraith Writer..

Prowllin the Pages.. patrollin the paragraphs.. with a pack of paranormal page prowllers,, paranormal paragraph panthers.. in search of the unseen..

And when you get thirsty or feel like a sweet snack.. stop in at the Script Sorcerer's Story Spell Shack.. sip a Story Soda.. suck back one sweet scene after another..

Trip over to Taco Tio's Tamale, Tortilla, and Tequila, Take Out or Take Down, Time Trailer, Mind Machine.

So the whole thing is a Course in Consciousness. Yes, the spelling, the words, the sentences, the script, the story itself, is a spell. Hopefully it will break the spell of ignorance. All words, sentences, stories, are spells. What words one uses affects what oneself and others think. Therefore every word spoken or written, is a spell, creates an effect on consciousness, and thus in turn creates reality.

Some syllables, the way they are strung together, because of their flow, their sound, the images they evoke, create stronger spells. Words are spells and greatly affect the state of consciousness of those who hear or read them.

If all of humanity becomes aware of how powerful words are in creating reality then maybe people will take more responsibility to use only words that enhance consciousness. Then the manuscript will have served it's purpose as a Course in Consciousness.

That's it boss. That's all the Mind Memo says, except that it is signed at the bottom with this poem.

"I'm a no name writer.. a ghost gone before..just a spirit you dragged up from the sludge of yer own thoughts. I am the cross you slung yourself upon..
every child who ever has cried.. the truth after the lies have died."

And boss there's a note at the bottom saying if you wanna find out more meet the ghost at midnight neath the archway of woven vines, the one with the bell hanging from it, at the entrance to the college. And it says something about hidden in the vine archway are all the characters in the story."

Max solemnly stirred his steaming mug of Ponder Pudding while wondering what to do. Looking deeply into the stew he saw an image of a street sewer manhole and a Scaly Strawberry Story Saurian Sorcerer Spell Scribe slithering up onto the side of his bowl.

With every bowl of cereal you get a Bowl Troll to hold onto yer bowl and spoon when you ain't using them. You are a great Knight of the Knowing. Instead of a sword and shield, you get a bowl and a spoon.. and a box of cereal, filled with words for ammo.

Should you meet a Dialogue Dragon that tries to do you in with dark dialogue.. use yer bowl as an ink well and yer spoon as a pen.. everything you need to read and write the story your way comes within the cereal box. You own eternity and infinity. You are the Cosmic Creation of Existence in love with itself.

The same old story has been simmering for centuries and it's about to boil over the sides again, as it always does, cause mum is so busy getting you kids off to school that she forgot about the Pots of Thoughts." Tio took a breath, turned the page, and continued.

"Okay kids who's got the hots for thoughts. Raise yer hand if you wanna play in Literature Land." Suddenly one of the Simian Song Sisters, sittin around the bowl, sang out to Baby Babaji Baboon.."Suck yer own big toe twit, I ain't no kid's consciousness. I am born of the writer's brain."

Sis spit her sticky syllables onto the table. They formed themselves into a Slithering Serpent Sentence Sixty Syllables Long. Then they proceeded to encircle Tio's tea mug like it were a monastery upon a mountain, about to be scaled in search of.. The Treasures of The temple of Time..

Treasures hidden for millenia in The Tower of Treasures.. beneath The Bell that was rung at the Wedding of Heaven and Hell.

Each level deeper into the Cereal Box Chapters that you stick your mind, Reader.. another Tulku Temple Time Travel Treasure you will add to your Angel Ascension Arsenal..

The Cereal Box Chronicles.. contain as a bonus bardo blessing from the Beloved Big Brain in the supreme sky..transcripts of the Tomb Traveler's trials and tribulations in the Tunnels of the Tombs of the treasures of the dead..

Bracelets rings crowns swords shields goblets.. all of precious metals and precious gems.. but there is only one way to travel among the dead thru the ground.. and that is as a spirit.. no flesh and blood and bone body can go where only ghosts go..

That's why you need me the invisible author.. the wraith wind writer of these words yer ridin'.. renegade. Ya yer a renegade reader.. riding reality solo with just me The Ghost Writer by your side.. sentence to sentence.. mind to mind.. on a search to find what you are without words. Us words keep your consciousness company. A body would be lonely without a brain. And a brain would be empty and alone without words. Try to contemplate that without any words.. wisdom walkers.

Just don't crowd my consciousness.. my brain's got borders.. even though I ain't got a body.. I still got my boundaries.. and my beliefs.. and one of them is that ghosts exist. I am living proof of that. I have spent most of my time in my temple.. the cosmic cereal box sitting so silent and serene in the center of yer kitchen table.. like it were praying.. like the cereal box was praying.

And the Cereal Box itself.. its sides look like folded wings.. or a long cloak wrapped about itself. The Cereal Box speaks of things unheard and unseen.. thoughts no human would dare speak.. of a parallel place.. part normal and part paranormal. And that's where you will find me.

You dear reader are host to a ghost.. speaking to you thru these words.. which I wrote so that you should know I exist and am not simply some fantasy some writer conjured up within his cranial cup. I am real.

I have entered your world thru words. Now I invite you to enter mine.. thru words. I offer to you syllables, which when strung together in certain orders create spells that shift the scene.. from normal reality to paranormal reality.

Thru these pages from the Paranormal Poet of Praise Prayers and Power Potions of the Pen.. learn to pronounce the phrases.. and you will fade into The Formless.

Each box specially marked contains a Paranormal Power Potion Pen Pal. You'll never be alone.. and you will always be able to rewrite your world any way you want it.

You are a Word Warrior Wonder Worker Wisdom Weaver.

You will be pen powered. Become a professor of The Pages of Power and The Potions of Peace. A teacher of time. Go on the Consciousness Circuit.. give sacred Spell Script Syllable Seminars. Take Tale Tourists on Tale Tracking Tours into the Tales of the Tomb Teacher Toads.. a Tribe of Tale Tellers that took up residence in the temples that the mayans built for the ancients.. the Ancient Ancestral Angel Aviators.. of whom I am one of them. And I live in the attic of your awareness awaiting you.

Speaking With Spirits

It had happened to me.. I could not deny the fact.. fantasy had filtered into my form. Every time I took a bath or rolled up my sleeves and looked at my skin I had to admit to myself that I still had the strange swamp disease. Something I picked up playing in that paranormal pond deep in our basement. The swamp had formed from the kitchen faucet overflowing and the water running down the stairway to the basement, while mum was caught in the emergency of sewing back together the seams of our family's reality.

Sis says I caught it from Tio The Tale Toad and Solly The Syllable Salamander. The bumps on my skin did kinda look like small strawberries and tangerines.

I had slogged my way thru the silurian swamp headed to the distant pyramid that stood in the center, like a giant finger pointing to the darkened sky that our basement ceiling had become.

Ya the ancient angel pyramid.. the Pyramid of the Angels.. an ascension and descension nexus for aliens and other assorted entities from other distant realities. A pyramid built not by us baboons but by Bardo Beings.. alien vision voyagers.. a Time Travel Temple.

So these my fine friends are the transcripts of the tomes of the tombs of the tales of time's trials and tribulations. Try that with a dry toad's tongue.. wrapped around yer waist while yer knee deep in nothing..

It was there where I witnessed the sacrifice of the sun.. and the murder of the moon

"Quit splashing yur spoon inta the cereal or i'll murder ya wit my middle thumb." sis squawked "yur getting The Book's covers all wet." "So what," I replied.. its skin is waterproof." .. the Cereal Box had become The Book. The cereal box looked exactly like an ancient book thick and leathery... like toad or lizard's skin..

The Cereal Box had warts and scales on it.. just like my skin had.. me and The Book and The Box were becoming one. I was about to attain enlightenment.. one with all.

Sis was studying the sides of the box. On it was a home study course on becoming a swamp sauce specialist and scientist of swamp society. Me.. I was still pondering upon that pyramid in our basement swamp. A pyramid that glowed all the hues of the rainbow. And to it came other rays of light that morphed into beings.

The pyramid was a landing pad upon which light would land and take the form of angels. Stranger still was that the pyramid pulsed.. it was alive.. it was a being.. a cloaked being.. no.. a winged being that had landed, and was wrapped, shrouded, in its own wide wings..The pyramid had come from the paranormal and it was a person. It was a wraith of wonder, of wisdom, and of the wealth of wishes..

I wondered.. could it have been god. Could god be living in our basement pretending to appear as a pyramid ?

While still deep in my thoughts, sis's shouts woke me.. "angels .. angels.. there's angels coming out of the cereal box.. and others going into it.. it's a portal into paradise."

"Ya and it's also a case for the book you bought.. a waterproof case you can slip the book into so you can safely carry it with you everywhere.. Buy several boxes so you'll have a spare." the Spirit Sponsor spoke from out of nowhere.

"Look kid, what we are saying, is that you have leaned how to cross over into the other world thru this box of cereal, which is a portal into the paranormal. And as a bonus in each box you get your own special sacred script spoon for stirring up spirit. With each spoonful, scoop up another story."

"Yer all silly!" sis screamed, at me her big brother, the toad, the frog, the lavender ledge lizard, the blueberry bayou baboon bruho brothers, the soda slug, and of course the sweet strawberry star syrup salamander who was sis's alter ego, if you ask me.

"No one is asking any of you.. I am telling you we're late.. now put down yer spoons consciousness cadets, and pack up yer pteradactylian backpacks, let's move out." dad said with a shout. The remains of the uneaten cereal were spinning like a whirlpool disappearing thru the bottom of the bowl.. reality was definitely out of control.

As I rushed out the back door I could hear coming from the open cereal box left on the kitchen table the words, "rid yerself of yerself... become a character in the story.. any character in any story .. so long as it's available and not being used by another reader/gamer.

So hurry.. there is always a place for you in the Paranormal Pages. Get your free down loads of emails from an entity from outside of eternity. Enter now for a free trip into infinity. You could win whatever you want. Why wait, world wanderers ?

Do you detest washing your own divinity dishes ?
Do you detest school tests ?
Do you seek out other souls ?
Do you curl yer toes like a panther ?
Do you lick your nose like a lizard ?
Do you engage in extraterrestrial communications with yourself ?

If so please stick your arm a little deeper into the cereal box.. Yes you can learn thru this sacred cereal box to actually reincarnate while still alive.. no death involved.

You can go from life to life. Incarnate into any type of being anywhere at anytime of existence, and do it without wasting time waiting around resting up in death. Energy does not need to rest.

Oh my sweet reader, you give this book shivers the way you read me. My dear red reading riding hood heroine, come hold this little old frail book. Come take me to bed, and read me while holding me upon your humble breast, while you fall asleep with me wrapped in your angel arms, and you wrapped within the wide wise wings of this wonderous book, your beloved betrothed.

However.. before entering the book box of cereal chapters, please sign and agree that neither the wraith writer, who doesn't exist anyways, nor the paranormal publishers, they're paranormal so what do they care, can be held responsible for any loss, permanent or otherwise, of any reader's reality.

Prepare yourself paranormal page paratroopers. We are approaching the paranormal parchment pyramids. Notice the paranormal pteradactylian paragliders. They will escort you onto the landing pad.

"If I had a dime for every time you kids were late getting into the back seat of the terra tracker all terrain vision vehicle, I would have been able to buy the college." dad grumbled like the gorilla he was.

So it went, reincarnation after reincarnation. I had become bored with reincarnation, one reality rolling right along after the other. How boring eternal existence can so quickly become when there is no measure of time, no length or breadth of anything. Yes, I had become one with all. I had become all, eternal, divine, omnipresent, the future and the past. I existed everywhere at the same time. I couldn't get away from my own mind..

all because of that book and box of cereal.

"Stop mummy !" a child screams out, and the whole store freezes. "I want that box.. the one with the tangerine warts on it, and I want that one with the strawberry serpent scales, and the one that looks like lavender lizard skin, and gimme the crocodile crunch, the box with the green and gilded gator skin.!"

"Yer the crocodile's kin and the chimpanzee's cousin." sis stammered, as she hammered her hand onta the table and ordered another fable along with a side order of paranormal peach porridge and two slices of time travellin tangerine toast with magical mango marmalade.

"Now shoosh.. listen..! I hear the whoosh of wraiths approaching our table as a landing pad for the paranormal." Yes hidden deep within the garden of eve, there are spirit society soirees.. special appearances by the unseen.

"No reader, these words aren't for just any word wanderer world walker wisdom wizard. They're only for the really adventurous eternity explorer. Contact us this minute and we'll include a delusion destroyer and a dementia digger."

Gee the sponsor was always selling stuff.. I thought to myself.
That's when I noticed that the warts on my nose were getting fatter..
And there was less of what used to be myself.

Divine Deliverance

The Messenger..
The messenger rode rapidly into the king's court, announcing breathlessly as he swung from the saddle and fell upon his knees.. "A dragon has arrived and taken abode in the dark forest at the edge of your lands, great sire."

Whereupon the king summoned all and any brave knights who would go forth and slay the creature. What the king feared most was that the beast would come and steal the princess, his beautiful daughter.

Many noble knights arrived and ventured into the forest, sword in hand, and none returned. All that was ever heard each time was a great roar. Despair settled upon the king and kingdom.

Then one day came a young minstrel man, from where no one knew. He was without armour, wearing only the simple clothes of a lad of the land. He offered to go to the dragon, saying, "I will go to play and dance for the dragon." The king and his court and the villagers laughed sadly and pitied the deluded soul, but sent him out to meet his fate with the fearsome beast.

The lad set off playing his flute and at times his lute. All thru the night, all that was heard coming from the dark forest, were the notes of his musical instruments, and a strange sweet voice accompanying them.

In the soft light of dawn, in front of the gates of the town, appeared the dragon with the minstrel lad riding upon its strong shoulders. The minstrel was playing the lute while from the dragon's mouth issued the sweetest song.

Amazed, the king and the villagers timidly gathered at the gate, whereupon the dragon spoke. "Why did you send warriors to harm me when I came here only to be the eternal guardian of your lands and your people and especially of your princess ?"

As in all sweet stories the minstrel married the king's daughter. Upon the dragon they rode thru the lands and all the swords were melted down and remade into flutes and other musical instruments so that the whole land sang.

The Cranial Cauldron forever simmers. The thoughts made of syllables and sentences spilling over the sides slithering into space, seeking what ? and why ? and who ?

Is it better to be still than to seek.. Can a soul seek in stillness ?
The brew is always bubbling.. a never ending Broth of Beliefs.
Yes the corner stone of creativity is Consciousness.

Listen up kid.. Go into the basement stacks of the old stone library in the college. Go alone at night when fright is fiercest. Follow the stacks deeper as the lights get dimmer, past the old mouldy manuscripts unto the very back until you reach the dank wet slimy wall. Remove the cornerstone with the strange ancient carvings looking like beasts. There you will find a small cave in which lies a carved casket. Open the lid of the casket if you dare and there cooking is the Cauldron of Conscious Creation. It is a doorway into other dimensions. Dive in thru the boiling Bowl of Beliefs.

Follow the Stairway of Sacred Surrender. Falter not fearful friend.. for the future needs you to fulfill your part of the puzzle. Love has waited for a vessel such as you. Love is the Elixir of Eternity.. The Hand of Hope.. the Alchemical Catalyst of Angelic Ascension.

You must continue your quest.. for all souls who are caged.. for all hearts who have gone into hiding.. for all hope that has lain hidden.. for love that has lost its way. Where will it be found.. if not in you.. and how.. if not by your humble hero's heart.

You are becoming the Buddha's Breath.. the wind's whisper. Upon the Altar of Existence eternity is forever born. All is an Eternal Altar. The dreams of the dead live on in the heads of the living.

Dear aspiring Spiritual Scholar of the Cosmic Cereal.. you have entered the realm of Spiritual Surrender to the Sacred of All. You have been a Consciousness Caller and your calls have been heard. Angel you have asked.. and you are being answered. The words you read are written by a Spirit Scholar.. an Exalted Entity from Outside of Eternity.. the Sacred's Scribe. The carvings upon the casket are your own attempts to claw your soul free.

The Library of Legends has been built upon a much more ancient pyramid. A pyramid that resembles a giant pteradactylian squatted with its wings wrapped about it.. actual ancient ancestral beings turned to stone over endless time.. Wisdom Wanderers waiting to be awakened.. with your words of worship.

Yes.. to worship wisdom.. is the way that will lead to your true Divine Destiny. Inside the coffin of your fears lies your dreams. Inside of your dreams you will see an angel with wings unfolding.. each wing transforming into a harp.. strummed by invisible hands.. sending out a celestial song of soothing sanctuary.

Oh Holy and Sacred.. consume me with your fire of refined desire and pure love. Enfold me in your eternal embrace, that I may come face to face, filled with faith, fearless before all beings. Make of me.. a lamp of your light."

Dad closed the Book.. patted the Lavender Lizard Love Light Lamp gently on its head.. and said.. "Dear Divine Daughter and Sacred Sweet Son.. it is time to let the lamp dim.. and all of you fall into sweet dreams for this night. For tomorrow we don't wanna be late for school again do we, wee ones." then dad tucked us all in.. the baboon, the toad, the lizard, the salamander, the snail, and the slug.. and we sailed together into slumber's sweet arms.

But The Book wasn't about to give up that easily.. The Story kept on speaking.. The Tale kept on talkin'.. "Listen up kid.. dya wanna dine on dead demons at the dead's deli where the vultures' victuals are smelly.. how about some sweet and sour satan. maybe a heaping steaming bowl of ghost gruel and goblin goulash .. I hear you were victimized by a vampire.. written off the team as a werewolf wanna be.. well hold on and listen to me.. I have the answer... thou it may not be to the question you ask." The Sneaky Sentence Story was tryin ta keep us awake with another story.

Such is the task of the Trickster Quick Stir Sorcerer of the Spirit Soup Spell Shop. Dine till ya drop and then we'll chop yer brains inta bite sized bits. Ahh everything eventually washes down the Drains of Destiny." Big said as he smiled to me sittin across the Table of Tales in the Tavern of Trials and Tribulations.. which as you probably know by now is also Big's Boardroom table and Doc Chimp's college classroom desk and our family's kitchen table..

Some fable for a phantom to fabricate, eh friend.. move real slow so ya don't disturb the dream.. Turn the page real softly so as not to scare away any Spirit Sentences.. any consciousness cruisin' thru the book.

Listen kiddo, when the going get's rough.. and reality will.. just dial Ask an Angel.. and one of our Angel Assistant Associates will save you. Accept no substitutes from the spirit world. These angels are guaranteed by god to be the real thing.. as real as anything ever is. Do not be deceived by the devil.. you could end up dancing with a demon.

As a precaution take these Sword Words. In every chapter certain words serve as Spirit Swords. There are several and each one serves a paranormal purpose.. now see which words you pull up outta the Deck of Divine Deliverance.

the sword of the saint.. the sword of the sinner .. the sword of the saviour
the sword of satan.. the sword of the seeker.. the sword of sanctuary
the sword of sorrow.. and the sword of sacred salvation

Save that last one for the real tough part of the journey, or use it right away and get the whole thing over. Skip all the dark scarey parts of your story. Go running home to mummy and daddy's arms, yuh little angel. Go ahead.. don't play with us monsters.. see if we care. There are plenty of people who wanna be scared of something.. anything.. for what ever reason.. only their hearts know.

Listen courageous kid.. don't take it so seriously.. It's only luncheon lyrics with the Language Lizard at the Dialogue Deli of Comedic Commentary. The Cosmic Cafe in the College of Caretakers of Consciousness.. where you are enrolled in reality Rewriting and Rewiring 101. Yer a Renegade Reality Reader.. ps page pal.. notice how words spell sword by placing the s in the front. Words are mightier than the sword.

Blessings of the Blossoms

Hey sis, there's a card for you beside your cereal bowl.. yer buddy the baboon is sticking his runny nose inta it, gettin baboon boogers all over it.. hey ever had baboon booger burgers.. hee hee. "

Sis came slidin down the stairs on her stair surfer, snatched the card outta Bareyev's furry fingers and started ta read..

"Hello Miss Blossom,
Didja know that today is the universal day of the Blessings of the Blossoms
For without the blossoms their would be no flowers, no nectar, no bees nor butterflies, no hummingbirds, no wonderful fragrances, no reproduction. So there we are.. Time to have a special day to remind us all of the awesome incredible BLESSINGS OF THE BLOSSOMS..
and did you know that you also are a blossom.. a loving fragrant blossom."

"Hey the card's unsigned.." sis sighed. "Must be the writer's way of saying he loves ya." mum replied. "Read sa more." dad said, as he started to pour strawberry syrup on his pile of peach pancakes.

"I live behind a screen of word. Travel upon wings that separate me from society. I am like words and wind.. An ephemeral entity.. elusive even to myself.

Script and scribbles have become my sanctuary
Poems and prose my pals. The page my partner. The pen my passion and power.
The Planet my princess. Oh how the soul sings thru the stellar vastness.
I wish to add but one sweet note to it's song.

Tend well to the garden of your soul, for in it, love's blossoms grow. Allow love to right all wrongs, and write your songs. Thus will be fulfilled the prophecies of paradise."

The Book had a curse on me so strong, I couldn't take my palms off the pages. Yes, it had a hold of me, as it now does you, righteous reader. The book has become your religion, your reason, your reality.

You have been handed an ancient angel alphabet by a floundering angel with wounded wings. No one reads the same script, no one dances the same choreography. The words wander where they wish, the story chooses who it uses.

The ink upon the page starts to glow.. the lights dim down real low. You're under your covers in bed.. over your head in hell. You're happy as all heaven cause it ain't real. Its just a story in a book yur reading to help you fall asleep. But this time, it's as real as it gets. At the conclusion you'll see it was all illusion, including your life.

The words of the story appear different to all of us, for they were written by wraith word wizards, script spirits, scroll scribes, text trolls, sorcerer shamans, with invincible ink, pen potions prepared in the sink into which your thoughts sink.

"Look at all those dirty dishes in the sink, son, and your sis too.. quit slinking away from the sink. Get back here and wash and dry before i drive you cartoon kids to school"

Yes, dad had wanted kids so deeply, and he had none, so since he was an animator working for Strawberry Star Studios, and angel animation, he drew us, and that's how we came to live in these pages. So that we wouldn't be lonely, he gave us a bunch of baboons for brothers, and a Tangerine Tale Toad to tell us bedtime tales, and a Lavender Lizard Librarian Love Light Literature Lamp so we wouldn't be in the dark, and a Strawberry Star Story Slug so we could follow her trail of Strawberry Syrup Slime Sentences thru the story to find our way home, into your heart.

Yes it's all just an elusive illusion of some lonely artist working for an animation studio owned by a trio of ex thugs who were healed by hugs; Barry Big, Max More, and Ace Towers.

But wait, hush, i must be silent and still now, safe in the shadows cast by the words. observing quietly like a windless night as Ace Towers and Maximillion More pull up in Big's big black and lavender limo.. to the curb of your consciousness. Gives me shudders to think, that all me an sis are, is some silly ink upon a page that you're soiling with your sticky fingers.

"Where was your hand ! in the juju jam jar ! Get your fingers out of the jam jar! Now hurry up. Kids.. dad's already waiting for you in the car.. you don't want to be late again for class!" .. mom the soup shamaness supreme.. screamed.

Yeah, sis and I were in the back room where they mixed the potions in the Pteradactylian Pharmaceuticals language and literature laboratories, and where the stories were stirred, and then poured into innocuous looking soda pop bottles to be drunk by kids everywhere. Don't let your lips come close. One taste and you shall be tainted with thanatos.

Word wanderer.. you were warned by the words right there on the first pages you opened of the book: Disclaimer: neither the publisher nor the writer, if there ever really was one, nor the characters in this story, can be held liable for whatever happens to your life once you enter these paranormal pages.

It was originally engraved upon an ancient parchment manuscript, written by the hand of no man nor woman, nor by wing of angel, nor by claw of beast. The script was written in many languages.. summerian, sythian, mesopotamian, chaldean, arcturian, angelian, and other dialects unknown.

Didn't I tell you that I got a demon of a deal for you here in this Story Sorcerers Satchel that was found when I fell into the Well of Spells ? I was swimming in script spells swirling round and round, a wizards' whirlpool, pulling me deeper down..

"Quit playing with your pudding.. you primate! You're going to be late for school !" Mom grabbed me by my shirt collar and spun me out the door. It's what saved me from falling deeper. That's why there's a warning sign on the side of the cereal box. Do not go near this wishing well. It's alive with serpent sorcerer spell sentences and scorpion story syllables, paranormal predator paragraphs prowling the pages. It'll be the end of your story when an unstoppable period comes rolling right at you.

"I warned you to stop spinning your spoon in the pudding. Your bowl is not a well of whatever you wish. So finish and out the door you go." Mum mumbled to Tio.

Letters From The Lord

"Inside each box of cereal you'll find a letter from the lord of love and light and lofty ideals, and you will ascend as though angels' wings had taken hold of thine arms.

Some say we are only holograms. If so enfold me with your hologram engulfed in mine, intertwine as no humans ever could. Let us swirl as spirits." Sis was reading the side of the cereal box. For a kid her age she was pretty precocious, with it, even above it, and so into it, that she was the farthest out, femme fatale, in any tale, ever told, by human or by Toad, like the one who was sittin at the Taco Take Out Tortilla Trailer, waitin', way in the back of the gypsy caravan headed for heaven, after a spell tourin' hell, for you.

Oh lord ring the bell. For the Lady of Love's Light approaches the Wedding Well.. a wisdom wanderer's waterin hole.. where words are wed with wisdom.
Some say.. I and you.. we .. all are godgoddess.. one being. The word god / goddess, comes from the ancient alphabet used by the angels descended from The One Of Light.

The One Of Light was the sacred sister, or beloved brother, of The One of Love. Archeologists have only yet deciphered but a small portion of the texts from the Tombs neath the Temple of Time.

Together, the two could become, what apart they could never be. And you and I, and all you see, and all that be, are the children, is the child, of their union, of their becoming one…The Mating.. The Marriage.. of Love and Light.

So no I ain't a ghost or some wanderin wraith writer writin tales in the clouds whittling the world away with its wind. I am the real regal ruler of reality. The lord of life and the duke of death."

The cereal box was gettin tired of talkin, so sis said, "Slow down and take a deep breath in thru the top opening. Just sit quietly on the table for the time being, real innocent like, no speaking nor singing, just like a kids' cereal box, sittin in the middle of a kitchen table.

"Consider this an invitation from an infinite immortal.. a one sided spirit connection on behalf of your well being. You get the full fantasy for free forever.. Downloading The Divine.. Divinity's Diaries.. Infinity's Iniquities..

Together the ink and the page work out the words, write the words, record the words, weed the words, weave the words.. wedding words to each other in careful consideration of the consequences in creating seriously silly societal satirical sentences. Syllables are slaves to the poet's pen.

You wait and watch.. one day reality will rebel"

Then Sis squirted in her sentence stopping all further thoughts in my mind.
"Hey mum! you got a letter this morning in the mail, from someone whose return address is.. Goddess care of Heaven!"

Letters from the Lord and An Invitation From Infinity are two bonus chapters

Remember that these two episodes of overload are only available if you have sold the cereal to other suckers.. sinners.. er I mean cereal spooners.. ya you gotta get the other kids hooked on the cereal.. it's the Vision Vitamins they add inta the cereal sweetener that makes it visionary cereal. " The supermarket Sales Snake's cereal spiel was suckin sis in.

It all starts out sweetly so a sucker get's sucked into a scene that's safe, and soon in slips some scarey scratchy sounds slithering up yer shiverin spine. Soon something slimy and swampy smelly slides over yer shoulder and down yer belly and the ground comes alive and you are simply a cosmic astronaut sailing the skies.. saved by the stroke of yer pal's pen.

I make of myself a sanctuary for all beings.
A sanctuary of serenity, stillness, silence, surrender.
I am a pilgrim upon a path of peace and prayer and praise for paradise..

I am the gardener of the groves of Great Grannie Ground. She is growth, green, gold, gorgeous, gracious, giving, goodness, The Goddess of Goodness
She is all around.

This planet is our parent.

May every thought I think.. every word i speak and write, and all my actions, be a blessing for all beings. Such is the code of a consciousness crusader.

Always speaking and acting with the awareness of an angel ascension academy consciousness cadet. A course you can sign up for if you dip your arm deep enough into the cereal box..

Coursing thru my veins star after star. Light beams hurtling thru inner space, as I await your arrival in angel's raiment.. a cloak of rainbow light.

As a bonus for buyin this box of karma enhancing cereal, you could be the first one at your breakfast table to get a cloak of rainbow light. Use it to shift spells, shade scenes, illuminate universes, and converse with all consciousnesses contained within the cosmos.

The cereal is a channel.. a conduit.. a mind enhancer transformer thought transducer transmission tower to thanatos.. yes.. to the death dimension.. the other side of this reality within which you ride.

Inside the cereal box lies concealed the scrolls of the Saints of the Stars. Holding the box tightly closed are The Ribbons of Rainbow Light. They can only be untied with love's language. And thus revealing inside, a group of ghost travelers.. cosmic ghosts.. that travel anywhere in time and space inside their Cereal Cosmic Capsule. Ghosts that have been around for millenia.. not just the recent nouveau junior apprentice ghosts, of those who recently stepped over.. but the ancient elders of eternity.. like me.

As a young ghost you will need ghost gear. Going to be a ghost, it is most adviseable to get outfitted with going for it ghost gear.. the garb all ghosts gotta get, if you are to successfully and smoothly go for it as a ghost..

Either you wanna be a ghost or not.. the other option is a sleeping ghost.. one that is out to lunch.. forever asleep in yer cranial coffin.. bound by your brain's boundaries.

The other option is unbounded awareness and freedom from form.

Once I was a warrior
A wizard
A worrier
A worker
A waster
A wisher
A writer
A wanderer
A wise one

Now I am the winged wind

There was a pilgrim who wandered for years along the path searching for a certain sacred holy temple. After years of following the trail and not finding the temple, one day the pilgrim came upon a monk bent sweeping the stone path.

The pilgrim asked, "Could you give me directions to the temple?"
The monk replied, "The Path Is The Temple."

"Psst.. Hey pal of the pages." The Paranormal whispered. "I hear reality is going around. It's catchy and captures consciousness and keeps it contained in a cage called a cranium.

"Yum.. this strawberry stars syrup sundae sports special sure is sweet.."
Sis licked her lips like a lioness that had just confessed her carnal sins to the searing sky overhead.

She was the lioness of the desert.. the fire lion.. the light lion.. the lion of illumination.. she was the angel that held aloft the light that lit the way into heaven.. And you too can become her in this very incarnation you presently inhabit.

Take a chance on a completely new consciousness.. get reprogrammed simply by six spoonfuls of this cereal several times a day.. breakfast brunch lunch supper snack midnight munch. and you too will soon be scripting your own stories.. writing the world into being.. as a Story Sorcerer.

Angels Anonymous

"Better take a pair of gloves with.. and put on your long underwear, it's nippy out there." Mum advised me and sis as we started climbing up the steep walls of the cereal box in search of the invisible one who talks.

Remember, I had no name before you named me..
I am the nameless void of your vision
I am the virgin who comes betrothed to the beloved's bed.
I am every drop of blood ever bled.. and the thoughts in your head.

Don't freak out folks. I.. a humble book/box.. am only channelin god and her gofers.. and you can do it too. The software for channelin god and other spirits is included for a free trial offer when you sign up for your first introductory chapter of.. Cooking Up Consciousness in the Cauldron of the Cranium.

Channel any entity you choose. Just be cautious, cause you might call on someone who wanders the night.. one who loves the fear and the fright.. one who's name you fear.

"Go ahead say my name. You know who I am. I give you a reason to run to god.
I fuel the fallens' faith. There has never been a dream I could not infiltrate.
Your mountains are the pillows of my sleep. So forget me not. I am not fiction.
I will not be swept aside as some fantasy of an idle dreamer's delusions."

See what I mean Reader.. you never know who might show up in the box. Together Reader.. you and I This Book.. we shall whittle down reality till it is but a fragment of a figment of an idiot's imagination. Fact will fall on it's filthy face. Fantasy will feast upon the mass's minds, and fiction will rule.

We shall reshape existence in the image of our own imagination.

"We interrupt this page for a special offer from the spirit. Get a Dream Drifter Degree, for free.. at the end of every episode.. at the conclusion of each chapter.. that you the Reader /Gamer.. make it out of.. the same as you went in. although no one ever does, dear dreamer.

Check the sign up ahead at the start of the next chapter. "Enter with caution. Death does not take kindly to trespassers. You won't be able to retrace your way along the sentences back to the beginning because if you try, the words will disappear. Don't even bother trying to reread the words backwards to the beginning in hope of finding your way back to where and who you were. The words will simply disappear. Or worse yet the writing will change, and you will fall backward into another story not your own, one where you cease to exist. You can only go forward and you can only get out at the end, and dammit there is none. Reality is eternal.

The pages are possessed, the paragraphs predatory, the sentences sinister, the word's wicked, the book's bad. Ya reader you've been had.. by the writer.

The ink used for the script is a spell potion.. prepared by Paranormal Pharmaceuticals.. a consciousness company completely committed to your dementia.

The future's gotta be fed. It consumes the dead, and leaves behind the living. The future is the most powerful force in existence. Well it doesn't actually exist, but it does consume both the past and the present. Some say fiction hath fornicated with fantasy in a three some with fact.

And so it is with the past present and future.. it's a threesome of unbridled lust that must go on forever.

"You young man are taking forever to finish yer cereal.. yer slower than yer sister. Yer buddy Bareyev Baboon and uncle Tio Toad are already in the car with yer dad. Now move it, my main lad." Mum had a way of speaking that sounded as though her words were scripted by her own ghost writer.

Could there be more than one ghost writing our story. More than one god creating our lives. Who or What gives direction to destiny ? Is reality a random draw of the cards ? Is there someone unseen behind the scenes writing our stories ? Do we each write our own tales ?

Go ahead and read these pages in any order. The destination at the end is the same for every pilgrim. And we all are pilgrims upon a path of purification.

"your smiles are the sunrises of each morning
your laughter the songs of birds when they make love
your movements the waves upon the sea
your fingertips the petals of flowers
your sweat the perfumed dew that greets each day anew
who could blame me for being a voyeur of such a vision of divinity"

The song drifted thru my mind as thou it originated from somewhere else than the radio..
"your songs are the prayers of the faithful
you are heaven.. the healer of wounded wings
your tears the rains that replenish the seas
your dance partners are the clouds
your suitors the stars
your heart the altar of angels when they come to god
your embrace is the final resting place of eternity."

"Get in the car and turn off that renegade radio up on the ridge of reality on the other side of the fridge overlooking Table Top Mesa de Maya." Mum tried to make us move but the cereal had a hold of us. The milk soaked soggy stars were slowing our progress to a snail's pace as we tried to cross the Paranormal Potion Pond that our bowls had become.

"This portion of the Paranormal Renegade Reality Radio Spirit Show brought to you by Big's Boardwalk Billboards.. buy Baboon Butt Bardo Brain Brew and watch what happens to you."

"Sis what's happenin to you..! Get your arm outta the cereal box..! Yer bein pulled in by an invisible force !" "It's just nature takin it's course." she said as she pulled out a tangerine treacle toad sittin in the palm of her hand while butterin' her toast.

Yer a very nice host.. he hollered.. as he dove offa her hand inta the Blueberry Breakfast Bowl for his morning swim. Mum was mourning the fact that this fiction had become real.. and we would never finish our breakfast meal.. in time to get to school on time.. If one is on time then how can one be in time ? I mean on is outside of in.. isn't it ?

"Sit..!" I said to the toad who was splashing around in sis's cereal bowl soaking us all with Strawberry Stars.

Dad was havin a fit cause the toad was now sittin on a slice of toast paddlin it across the bowl of cereal using sis's spoon.. like he was leading an expedition deep into somewhere we never been.. somewhere hidden behind what is seen.. into the jungle green and lush where Ace and his henchmen were stealing the Sacred Star Stones.. the Temple Tablets of Time.. the Crystalline Chrysalises of Consciousness.. the Goblet of the Ghost Goddess.. the Chalice of the Cosmos.

Take a risk Reader.. don't turn to the next page. Don't follow the crowd. Pick a random page. Carve out your own destiny. Make life your own story. Be Brave and explore the book without following the crowd. Claim your own consciousness.

Tio disappeared paddling into the fog floating upon the cereal, while softly singing.. "The book is the bait.. fantasy is the fate.. love is the gate."

Dad pulled us out of the pages and into reality with the words.. "Let's go, I got a long day at the college, There's a faculty meeting about funding for building a new addition to the ape habitat. Personally I don't believe in keeping apes in cages anymore than I think consciousness should be contained within the cranium."

Mom listened to dad while she watered the vines. She had more plants growing in our house.. plants no one had ever seen before.. than you'd find in a jungle in a tarzan movie. Our mum Evelyn De Jardins was the top ethnobotanist specializing in plant and people interaction and whether or not plants and people are one family.

Come to think of it, our house inside looked like a tropical rainforest with thick vines climbing along the walls and across the ceilings. And though few visitors ever saw them, there were serpents and spiders and monkeys..

"Hey has anyone seen my keys. I can't find the keys for the truck. Now we're really outta luck.. stuck in the story. No one will get anywhere this morning."

"Hey dad," I yelled, "How can anyone ever be late, when we're always where we are.. like we're always there.. I mean here.. right here at this place in the story. The writer wouldn't have written us in here if it wasn't where we were supposed to be.. right here.. me and you.. in this very sentence upon this very page..

You the reader and us the read.. together upon so sacred a stage.. bound together by a book at which you look and which looks back at you. Yesss the strawberry star solar system is a stage where divinity daily dances.." the Sales Snake hissed.

Meanwhile sis was mumbling to someone inside the cereal box.. "Thank you Mr Angel for taking our prayers to god. My brother and I were wondering if your wings are real, or if they are made of our imaginations ? "They're real." came the answer from outta the open box top.. The Entry into Eternity.. The Entrance into Evermore.

We each pass thru gates every moment of our existence. Ghost gates unseen and unrecognized. Gates that determine each person's fate. Existence itself funnels us forward into the next form that awaits birth.

Dad was packing into his briefcase the Voodoo Vulture Vision Valley Vault Volumes that the Temple Toad had brought to him from underneath the dusty damp dank Tombstone Stairwell Stellae Steps, that lead down to the Library of Lost Legends neath our Lavender Lizard Linoleum kitchen floor.

Ya.. the Entrance to Evermore was downstairs below our building's basement.. and upstairs was heaven.. in the attic where the entities from other realities, gathered weekly for Angels and Aliens Annonymous meetings to discuss the meaning of myth matter maya and the immaterial. Buy a box or book and soon they'll come to your house.

Travelers of the tale of time.. where are you going.. and why .. what is wrong with right here.. ? Where are we all goin ? Are we lost and in need of a consciousness compass ? Send in via email to the Wraith Writers' Website your words.. help cocreate a tale that will serve as a trail for others.. These words are just meant to awaken you to the wisdom of your own words.

Consciousness has need of cocreators.

Shards of Shattered Souls

So the next brief chapter of chuckles continues;
The toad clings to the princess's perfume bottle in the belief that if he follows the scent it will lead him to nirvanna.. Unknown to the princess the spell she cast was short term because she failed to pay last year's dues to the witches with broken brooms poverty association. The prince becomes the pauper.

Suffering returns with a vengeance.. Humans are left without hope.. heroes are helpless. Some turn to drugs.. Some to sex.. Some to violence.. Some write stories in the hope that they will act as a psychological spell on themselves and others who read them, thus awakening the world of humans from the hold that hell hath upon their souls.

The ones that write are hailed as geniuses, become rich and live happily ever after.. Until someone becomes pissed off with what they said and stones them or burns them at a stake..

the holy walk upon feet of wind
the heart is a seeker of the sacred
the saviours' cries are only heard by those with tears in their eyes
without love even the eternal dies
everyone tries, the wounded and the wise, and the sinner who lies
even the angels in distant skies

The moral of the story is meaning is meaningless except in a context which is arbitrarily given by someone with access to more power than another..

So wisely, the writers stay within the bounds of foolishness, which will offend no one, but the imaginary dragon in his or her dark den, and the toad who sits in his cloister trying to figure out what his tool can do.

Unknown at this point in the story the toad's tool is a super swiss army knife that can get him out of his cell.. it's also a high tech cell phone.. in which superman changes his clothes.

Meanwhile we're left with superman stripping, the toad trying to make a phone call to his lawyer who's an ex nun on the run from reality. And of course the wolf and red riding hood are on a robbing spree with the three pigs for backup, while the whole world is reading this silly shit cause it's better than reality ..

And god has given up ..
So yes folks it's up to us.. Yess we humans now more than ever have to take some responsibility for reality.. And that is why I this story have stepped forward and accepted your vote to be the ruler of the world.

First we measure the depth of maya.. Then the weight of sorrow.. And subtract hate and then multiply it all by joy.. And presto we come up with the answer to anything... And it totals nothing.. the absolute zen zero no mind.

Once I was the wounded
And the one who wounds
The samurai and the scribe
The lord and the lover
The slave and the sold
The brave and the broken
The dust and the divine
Now, I am but a whisper in your ear.. words upon a page.
Love waiting to be let out of the cage in which you are caught.

Consciousness is as vast as the wings upon which the majestic morning dawns.
Wander well, wonder filled word wanderer.
The World of Wonder Words awaits. All are welcome in the garden of divine dreams.
We are all Dream Dancers.. Cosmic Entrancers..

I will be the Ghost Groom. You be the Book's Betrothed.
You are the starlight.. the morning bloom of every smile's sunrise.
I am the dream dust in your childrens' eyes.. as they slumber in sweet sleep."

The Story Spirit spoke real slow, down low, like a spirit does, when whistlin' the way the wind would, if it were a song somewhere in your memory.

Inside of heaven grew an angel known as you. Consciousness has come, because you have called, courageous Crusader of the Chapters of the crossroads of realities. Here at this particular point upon the path of pages, you come face to face with the formless.

Wander wisely upon the words from here on in, Reader, for restless is this renegade reality. Come along on a seeker's stroll with a Troll Toad for a Tale Trail guide. Your story awaits you with intense desire. Do not be afraid to let it show. It's the only way to know if it's real, how deep you can feel, what you would rather forget.

You and me, we're like two lovers, holding ourselves together with hopes and dreams.. and whispered words.

Watch out for slippery syllables that may cause you to slide somewhere into the story you may not want to go.. and commas that'll slow you down.. or periods that will stop you cold.. as they do a sentence. Now let's continue our Story Stroll with a Tale Troll.

Tony Tortilla and Teresa Taco were holding hands in a corner booth of The Baboon Brothers Bagel Brew and Ballad Book Bar. Adobe Joe spun another silver dollar into the juke box.. the one that talks like it were a gypsy fortune teller with nothin but love's sad tales to tell.

"Tune in to the raspberry rattler rap ridge rhythm and border blues renegade radio show.. bardo brothers and spirit sisters.. for some songs of the soul..." the radio up on top of the fridge on the other side of the ridge of reality announced like it were a living member of our family.

Sweet sanctuary.. heaven hath married hell upon this day.. All will be well even though the world's woes have worn thru the rugs of reality's fabric.
Today's special.. a bowl of steaming Spell Stew cooked in the cauldron of witches' wish broth.. brewed of bark and bones and belief and stones.. and the moans of minds.

"I'll trade you two sinners for a saviour. and I'll throw in a saint to sweeten the deal.. maybe even a demon if you do it now." Sis looked thru her collection of cards she had cut from the sides and tops and bottoms and fronts and backs of the cereal boxes.

"Nope.. I'm savin my saviours for when I might need em." she replied to Gutter Gator, who had just slithered in from the sewers for breakfast.. and a game of consciousness cruisin' cards.

Download the devil now, and we'll cut you a deal for a dozen free demons. And if you doubt our sincerity, we'll send you double dragons to guard your door. These Demon Door Dragon Savage Spirit Stoppers, are perfect for guarding yer bedroom door at night when yer asleep and who knows what darkness might creep in thru the crack under yer door. Guaranteed to protect you from unwanted paranormal intruders..

Order now and as a bardo bonus bargain we'll include a delusion dementia denying dream doll. Order an angel with an attitude of gratitude for goodness. Tonight you shall dance fearlessly with the wind, and ignite the flames that incinerate all that does incarcerate the consciousness you know as you. All demo demons on sale at half price.

Here within these words you shall find your sacred sanctuary. Existence is in code form. Here we will decipher that code to find the hidden reality behind existence. The mystery of life is a code of consciousness. You will learn how to change consciousness channels, and arrive at an angel assistance wizard way station when yer in need of reality realignment. Retire from reality.. permanently.. in the paranormal.

Take a trip to the crypt of your own consciousness. See who really owns it. These words will lead with a light that illuminates the beauty of you. Rest now, within these words, weary wanderer.

"Dear divine daughter, you are starting to nod off. close the book and dream well, wise young woman." then dad softly closed the book, and laid it down on sis's night table, safe beside the Lavender Lizard Love Light Lamp, glowing so softly from within.

Dial the dead anytime you want, when you're enrolled in the eternity emails home schooling in spirit studies school, sponsored by sacred Spirit Song Studios.
Log onta the lizard librarian looming over yer dimly lit computer screen.
See the spirits swirl outta the monitor of maya and magic.
Immerse yourself in what before you never believed has ever been.
All is crafted by the eternal poet herself.
Let your language be the light of love.

Transformed by your gaze upon my pages, I am re configured into an altar of adoration. You are the altar of all existence.. the lips thru which all sing.
You and I.. We are lovers of love.. seekers of the sacred.

Cauldron of The Cranium

"There's a cool consciousness coupon inside every box that talks, And it'll get you for half price six suck a serpent on a stick solidified syrup suckers, seven swamp syrup strawberry slug on a stick slimmies, and eleven lick a lizard lollipops.

I am doomed. I danced with the devil. I sang with satan. I washed the wicked one's underwear. And I swam in the sewer with my slippers on. Ya my new strawberry slippers with marzipan zippers. Speak to our lizard liazon over lunch for further info on how you can get yours.

Remember reader, it's just some seriously silly societal satire saturday sitcom series comedic consciousness commentary program produced by Strawberry Star Studios sacred space soda and song spirit shop.. where you can shape shift till yer body drops.

Part of profits go to paradise properties Caretaker camp college eco environmental artistic spiritualistic holistic health spa resort retirement cocreative communal collective consciousness course college camp community coop complex in the cherry canyons wildlife refuge nature heritage garden of eden.

And there are work study programs and scholarships and bursaries...
No motor vehicles on the property please..
Tree houses yurts teepees wigwams adobe stone domes..
Communal dining facilities.. Yup vegetarian..
Be a pal ta paradise planet please. Be a visionary with your vocabulary."

All those words were coming from deep inside the box as sis poured the cereal inta her bowl. The last thing to spill outta the box was Tio the toad, still talking.

And thus the story starts, with words written in crimson upon a wraith wall.
"Warning... Walls wet.. With the scribes' sweat."

And there against the wet walls inside the cereal boxes were the Spirit Scrolls that had lain hidden for ever in the Canyon Crypts of Saurian Sky Sorcerers.. paranormal pteradactylian primordial prophets and professors of phrases of praise poetry on behalf of paradise.

"Son.. stick your spoon inta the Strawberry Star Spell Syrup once more..
An' I doubt you'll ever return in thru the same door.. You're so deep into VDR Virtual Dream Reality.. I wonder if you can really hear me ?"

There's a sign on the wall like a wanted poster.. WANTED: ANGELS
Ya we're looking for angels. And I was told to look you up, courageous kid.
Ya you readin the writin.. You are to be the next Ghost Guardian of the parchment pages of the paranormal prana paragliders. A pack of paleo pteradactylian paranormal professors.. Yesss.. Professors of the Paranormal.. Paranormal Professors.. Wisdom Wraiths

And they are soon to be your personal property. They're worth a pretty penny on the maya market, where everything bought and sold, is worth more than gold, and is as old as the mold on the walls of the the tomb tunnels in yer basement.. Book Buddy.

Ya yur this Book's buddy now.. this Book is yer buddy.. I am the myth made manifest.. The Book of the Beloved.. The words of wisdom.. The sacred script of the soul. Integration with godhead is the goal.

"Son, your dreaming is waking the dead." Dad said as he shook me from The Book sleeping beside me on my bed. My dad was the best bro I ever had. I'm so glad I had a dad like the dad I had.

Then I heard a voice say "Take care, Chapter Crawller, not even death doth dare approach me, yet you, upon the door to my lair doth knock loudly."

"Okay class please approach the desk of the divine and pick up a copy of this semester's subjects." Doc Divine swung from a vine, along the classroom ceiling, onto his desk, while he continued lecturing from The Documentarius Divinicus.

"Angel ascension class 101 is preliminary entry course into soul salvation. Help spread heaven's words of love. We've all heard hell's. It's a suckers' spell. Some sort of spelling mistake. A slip of the pen.. passion poured thru too tight a tourniquet.."

The last thing I remember I was reaching deeper into the cereal box and the next thing I knew I was screaming.. "Tighten the tourniquet.. the poison's gettin to me.. The Viper Vision Venom is takin the dyin deep this time. When I come back don't expect I'll find my mind.. might even lose this body."
I was doin my bardo buddha breaths.. dippin inta the dimensions of death..
Dream Dancin'.. Cosmic Chancin'.

The Dream Door Dimension Software was taking effect. I could feel the great transformation coming over me. Dying is so draining on the body. No fear. Father I am near.

I could see thru the haze a sign drawn in dried blood on bleached bones, above the gate of the ghosts graveyard. "come near neophyte.. all others stay out.. no admittance.. beware of falling tombstones.. graveyard closed due to reality repairs.. entry forbidden to everyone except the formless"
    The sign blew in the winds that wandered round the graveyard.

And so started the first page of the Mausoleum of Maya Manuscripts.. The Crypt and Coffin Chronicles.. The Casket Chapters.. Reading a chapter is like falling into a casket that then gets locked.. and you gotta get out if ya wanna get into another chapter. And the only way out.. once in.. is as a spirit.

"Class remember we're meeting for saturday's discussion group at Primo Primate's Pizza and Pasta and Page Parlour for Lizard Lazagna and Ghoul Goulash.. the topic will be the Decks of Divinity, all of them.. including the Decks of Death, Dreams, Dementias, and Delusions.

Consciousness Cards you can trade with other kids. Send in a bunch of coffin crunch cereal box tops and you'll get a cute coffin to keep 'em in. Well captain cosmic I hear your mummy calling. Even though it sounds a little muffled thru the wrappings.

"Piss on Paris.. I think you should land yer saucer here. There's plenty of aliens. I think you'd feel comfortable with these consciousnesses.

Don't freak out folks, I'm only channelin god and his gang of ghosts.. and you can do it too. The software for channelin god and other spirits is included for a free trial offer when you sign up for your first introductory chapter called..
Cooking up Consciousness in the Cauldron of the Cranium.

And if you act now... and it is all a big act... we'll include at no extra cost to you, except maybe your sanity.. but hey that just gets in the way.. a free membership to any insane asylum of your choice.

Buy the course now, and we'll send you software for channelin satan's songs of sorrow.. so you can dialogue with the devil, talk to yer friends and family in thanatos.. have diner with the dead.. get free of yer head.

Don't ever give up star sailor.. even when you hear the howlin of wind wolves in your bed, and you disappear like you weren't ever here."

Then the book opened up its wide wings.. its covers.. that were veined with strange vines swirling like serpents of every colour of the prism of love's light.

Yes, Doc Divine's field notes were alive, pulsating, breathing. Something inhabited the pages.. something paranormal. Our professor had brought back something that wasn't quite here.. there.. or anywhere. The paranormal parchments were still alive. They had been resting in a state of deep meditation for millenia inside those crystalline caskets. Caskets that were Chrysalises.. Mind Metamorphic Consciousness Changing Chambers.

And you lucky breakfast boy have one right there on yer kitchen table. Yup, that Box is your Consciousness Changing Chamber. So just step right in to your coffin. I mean cereal box, and close the lid, and it's anyone's guess where you will have slid in the time it takes for your kid sis to stick another spoon of Strawberry Star Storm cereal inta her mouth, or take a lick of her Lavender Lizard Lollipop.. Prince of the Paranormal Pages.

And it's all compliments of your Paranormal Pal.. ya.. yer pal.. The Paranormal."
Tio took another bite out of the toast and another piece of reality disappeared.

Just remember Reader.. every page in This Book from Beyond the Brain's Borders
is a card from the Deck of Dreams Dimensions and Dementias.. that you have been
dealt.

So pick the pages in any order you wish. Create your own hand.. of heaven .. or hell.
Sanity is simply a spell you are under.

Chronicles of Chronos

Dad was gonna give a lecture on the Tales of Time and the Chronicles of Chronos. Time had taken a u turn and could not be found anywhere in space.

Yesss.. Ever since Big's bully bulldozer knocked over the old fire hydrant that had stood sentinel at the entrance to the vacant lot in back of our apt building, reality was never the same as it used ta be. Kids were sinking into the sand in the sand box. Tips of pyramids were poking outta the sand. There were dust storms over the sand box outta which some kids never returned.

I figured if we followed the toad paddlin on the toast across the bowl of cereal we would be lost to reality. Then it occurred to me that reality might be lost and was in need of finding by us.

"If ya don't hurry up and finish yer breakfast..", dad was fuming.. ya like smoke and fire was spiralling outta his nostrils, making him look like a dragon. "Naw that's only dad lighting his pipe," .. sis interjected.. bringing some reality back to our kitchen.

Dad had a special Paranormal Projection Pipe. He'd light it and outta the swirling smoke spirits would soar. It was like a door to another dimension.
"Shaman Smoke.. on sale.. inside the cereal box !" the supermarket sales snake shouted.

"D'you ever feel like yer doin time..? waitin for the story to start.. the chapter to commence.. the end to finally show up?" Big babbled to Max More who mumbled.."Naw i never think about time." They were sittin in The Baboon Brothers' Bagel and Brew and Banana Bread Bakery Book Bar, just around the corner from the not so Vacant Lot, discussing the demise of destiny.

Just then the phone on the table rings. The phone looks like a fat flat frog and the handle a slim salamander. Big picks up the salamander and puts it to his ear whereupon the salarnander plants a wet kiss on Big's ear. "Not now honey I can't hear.." he whispers to the salamander.

Big has been waitin for this call from his contact. Consciousness always calls collect. Listening, Big nods in approval.. then with a voice that sounds like gravel being dumped from a truck, growls.. "We was wonderin if you wanted to go out to dinner with me and the rest of the carnivores at the coroners club. It's right next door to the caskets and cadavers cafe at criss cross crossing. Whadya say, saviour.. Supper at six .. on the other side of the river Styx..?

There's a special on left over lizard livers and broiled baboon bellies. Ya I know the words are gruesome.. Well not the words.. the thoughts the words create. Funny how words do create our world.. inner and outer. Thoughts.. words.. actions.. all in a never ending cause and effect. We are Alphabetical Apes.. apprentice angels.

We duel with demons of the mind and monsters of the immaterial plane of existence.. for instance.. one's own fears.. The ones that cause us all to shed tears.

Buy a ticket to thanatos from angel aviation agency.. flying angels to heaven round trip with a side stop over in hell for a spell with satan and her six serpent step sisters. Get a free bottle of gorilla growth he man hormone helper if you book with Thanatos Tourist Travel agency for all your trips to thanatos. We take care of your consciousness.. a motto your mind can depend upon.

"So you and your phantom friends.. you gonna order somethin, or are you just taking up space in this story, sonny ?" Teresa Tamale the waitress, stood looming over the table fingering the menu like it was alive. Made Big wonder if he really was.

"Kids let's hit the road or none of us are gonna arrive anywhere near time, let alone on time or even in time." Mum leaned over the kitchen table and kissed us all on the head, including the baboon brothers and the rest of the characters in the story that some invisible writer had made up.

Do you ever feel like your life is a story someone made up and you are headed for an ending you have no control over ? Just be sure to read the small print at the very start of your story.. "property of and produced by.. Paranormal Passages Productions, a subsidiary Consciousness Company, of Spirit Soda Vision Ventures.. screamy stories and dreamy dreams to rip reality apart at the seams of what seems to be real."

"Wanna slurp of Slug Soda ?" ..the Strawberry Story Salamander sittin on the side of the script asked sis and me. "Comes compliments of Bargain Benny's Bottomless Basement Bongos, Bardo Brews, Books, and Bagels, Booger Bar."

"Boogie man booger burgers! Hey who stuck these pages together with their boogers ! Was it you brother ?" sis mouthed the words menacingly to me.

Don't get warped by the words.. Word Wanderer. It's all ghost gabb.. demon dribble.. dead dialogue.. self sacrificing sentences.. slayed by syllables too short to sell without a story.

Big took another bite of his baboon booger burger on a bagel. While he pensively fingered the pages of the fable on the table.. "Ya it'll make a groovie movie. Buy the rights from the invisible writer. Give him a deal on reality he can't refuse.. even though he ain't real."

Go ahead, string the small syllables along.. lie to them.. tell them yer gonna make them part of a word.. make them part of a bigger world. Then dump em in the trash when they don't stand up to the glare of your stare upon the blank page you're trying to fill in so your life isn't empty.

You're a word hunter.. a consciousness collector connoisseur.. a hero without friends or family except for the ones you conjure up in the chapters. Your mind is your game board.

So wander with the writer awhile inta the Well of Words whirling around inside the cereal box of your brain. As you swirl farther down the walls round and round you go ever so slow.. till time takes a breather and space falls apart.
We are Brothers of the Buddha.. Sisters of the Saviour.. the Children of Consciousness.. a family of faith. Our fathers are fair.. our brothers brave.. our sisters sanctified.. our mothers magnanimous.

Who of us shall tend to the wounds though they may repulse even the most hardened ? A voice from within replied.. "I will tend to the wounds.. I will sit with the sorrow. The Cosmos is the Cosmic Cauldron of Creation. Let love be our torch.. truth our candle.. and may our light burn brightly."

Then Dad placed the text book on his desk and silently scanned the classroom searching for spirits I assume.. "Assume nothing once you enter this book." he said as he walked out the classroom door.

The Doctor of Divine Dialogue.. was one of our dad's nick names, along with Doc Chimp, Doc Divine.. Doc Dialogue.. the Professor of the Paranormal Prophecies.. and the collator of the Consciousness Chronicles.. collected from caverns high along the walls of the Canyon of Crypts.. inside the steep walls of the cereal box.

Crypt Casket Cauldron Cooking Class 101 in the Cave of Cauldrons, was where we first learned to stew the syllables till the sentences simmered into spells.

"Dear Dialogue Damsel.. Damsel of the Dialogue.. Dingo Lingo Dame.. Are you real or only a verse in a vision.. written by a Wraith Writer to assuage the loneliness carving deeper a hole into his Hero's Heart..

Sad is the sentence to have to say such a line of loneliness. No sentence should have to bear the sorrow of such isolation.. such loss of love.. is there not a sunnier sentence to shore up the heart of this hero..

Sorry.. I this sentence.. cannot stay any longer.. for I got a dragon to dance with.. and a dungeon to sweep.. And my mum says I gotta be in bed asleep by seven or else I'll never get to play in heaven.. sincerely.. Your local neighbourhood hero.

Ever hear the tale of the Werewolf's Wife.. I didn't think so.. well here it is.. part of the Parable from the Paranormal..

Wandering with the werewolf dressed in rags so as to disguise my true nature we entered the Valley of Vampires.. sometimes known as the Valley of Visions.. some say it is where death dueled with life.. while god and the devil dined on the remains of reality. We had hoped to reach the safety and sanctuary of the monastery's gates before the time of the cold winds.. however I find myself at the pass of pain caught between the peaks of doubt and delusion..

And so I and the werewolf have taken protection in the Cave of Confusion from the bitter winds' words that now blow away all meaning that gave a measure of sanity to my story.

I never sleep.. I only dream.. And when I appear awake it is only an appearance that fools us both.. And so we watch the world and our own minds. This Poet's Pain.. is will I ever find me.. or is me only what in each moment I be.. a Consciousness Caller.

Existence is strange.. one day yer a kid like every other kid eatin' cereal.. and next day yer floundering around in a fable told by a toad sittin' at the Table of Fables in the Tavern of Tales.. untying the shoelaces of yer sanity.

Consciousness has come.. for you have called.. courageous Consciousness Crusader. This is the Crossroads of all Consciousnesses. Pull another Consciousness Caller Card, Kid.. and always remember.. Love is the interior designer of everyone's heart.

Sorcerer's Sarcophagus

Become a brother of the book.. or a sister of the story.. ah yes.. the book is but the bait.. the language is the lure., the catch is consciousness. But wait, there is more, much more, in store for you.. just send in the box tops, and the bottomless bottoms.

If you would be interested in this visionary venture.. Adding your abilities and expertise and energy please contact my agent Finky Finkel of Finkelstein and Finkelman, Friends Of The Fields And Forests, Angel Associates Agency..

"GET A FREE subscription service to ..
The Spirit Society Ghost Gazette Mirage Magazine.. Free for anyone who signs up for the Ebook Overload Episodes !

Take part in conversations between consciousnesses..! normal and paranormal..!

Speak with spirits..!   Converse with consciousnesses from other parts of the cosmos..!
Gab with ghosts..! Talk with Thanatos..! Ask angels anything..!
Write the Wraith Writer..! Scribble some script to the Sacred Scrolls Sanctuary Spirit Scribe..! You'll find all the contact info on the last page.
Take tea and tales with the Tulku Tale Temple Tunnel Transcripts Toad..!
Perch upon the pyramid peaks with the Paranormal Pteradactylian Professors of Praise and Prayer.

All this and more.. when you sign up for downloads from The Mango Mountain Monastery Mausoleum Manuscript Museum..
discovered beneath the basement floor of your beliefs.

Brothers of The Blessed Book.. Sisters of The Sacred Script..!
Act now and one of our angel assistants will be at your personal disposal to deal with any dangerous dialogue you might encounter in the Overload Episodes downloads.

And if you act now.. And we all are actors upon this spirit stage.. You will receive a free reality to do with it as you wish.. Yes..! an extra reality to use as you wish..! Mould matter..! Existence will be in your hands.. Eternity yours to play with.. the cosmos in your cup..!"

And then I heard Tio Toad.. or was it dad..? Telling me to put down my cup of Twig Tea and finish my bowl of Strawberry Star Storm cereal.. I couldn't tell anymore who was talking.. Matter had shifted.. Reality had hidden in a corner of my consciousness.. Existence was emptying itself of the burden of being. I was seeing spirits swirling outta my cereal bowl.

And it all started after I signed up for those ebook downloads outta the cereal box, which you are about to disappear into forever friend, once you sign up for The Spirit Society Ghost Gab Gazette Mirage Magazine Ebook Divine Dialogue Downloads.

And at a dollar a download if ya do it on a spirit subscription basis so every week you receive a new chapter of consciousness culled from the Cauldron of Coffins and Caskets and Crucifixes.. You'll be supplied with your fixes for fantasy and fact and fiction all rolled into one reality.. And soon friend you will be free like me.. The Wraith Writer.. The Script Spirit.

As a bonus for the first six billion brave Book Buddies to sign up for a several lifetimes membership to the manuscript you'll receive your very own Paranormal Pyramid. Inside of which you'll find your own sarcophagus.. so your body can sleep forever while your spirit space and time travels. Included are instructions for the deluded. Do not be excluded. This is the deal of a lifetime.. especially since you'll get several extra ones.

Act now and you'll receive in this reality or another.. The Papyrus Parchment Paranormal Path Puzzle and instructions on how to find your way into it.
...and therefore the method in which you can escape eternity.. forever.

Note of warning to reader.. Neither the Wraith Writer nor the Paranormal Publisher, nor the words themselves, may be held responsible for any rearrangement in the reader's reality that occurs from these downloads.

Dear Padre, I have come to confession for I have sinned.. I am like a wilted red rose never again to see its last blush for I dined with the devil. Also dear padre I want to confess I slept with satan's seven sisters..

And so with that I was excommunicated from the church.. Never again to step foot amongst the faithful who have never faltered, nor fornicated with fantasy.

Life is like a zen koan.. can consciousness ever be truly known..
The king is the caretaker
The queen the cosmos
Take off my robes and you will see who I am.
That I am but the emptiness of you..
come here to fill the waters of your wells..
with whatever you wish.

Then the hero hit the gas pedal hard and her Solar Star Storm Stallion reared like a cobra poised to strike at the uninvited. All beings are united. All forms one flesh.

The Book Of The Bardos And Beyond The Brain.. is the definitive text on how to travel thru time, space, energy, light. Even use darkness as a medium for motion, movement, energy. You will be able to channel darkness and lightness
    At the wink of a word as it wakes up your world reader.

Do you read me page partner..?
Cousin of the chapters..
Dearest of the dialogue..
Beloved of the book.
You are the language of love.. the song of spirit.. the story of the soul.
Never Reader ever forget that.

Let love lead the way. We are all one family sleeping in one bed.

I god the the Alpha Angel gotta go now. I got a dinner date at eleven in heaven with the devil and her dozen dirty disciples. You can substitute decadent or divine .. it's your choice.. after all.. it is your own consciousness, kid."

"Deal me in." I said. "I'm coming with."
"No." He replied. "It ain't for the living.. It's for the dead."

"Then take the Tokyo Tank and the Dojo Demon with ya for security.." i held
them up in my hands.. two of the toughest Tulku Temple Toys one could get..

"Hey mum.. Where's the Juju Jam.." Sis said as she squirted outta her mouth a
Strawberry Star Storm spoonful of cereal..   "I'd like my Tio Taco Toad Toasties with
sumthin' sweet.." sis snorted.. and stars flew outta her nostrils.

"Ya, really, like snortin' flames and smoke.. swirling Strawberry Smoke... wafted outta
her nose.. like the smoke that trails outa the muzzel of a fat gun that had just fired a
skinny slug, at someone somewhere you'd rather not be."

Snortin Nortin Sis flung a Strawberry Snot at the slug shimmying its way across the
Bardo Book Brew bottle that Tio the Toad was about ta tip inta his lips.

Everyone wishes to sip the nectar of love
But few dare drink from the coffin of the sublime..

Have you got a problem with the paranormal? Is the paranormal making you
paranoid? Pal are you paralyzed by paranoia of the paranormal ?" the sales snake
smiled at sis.

"Well then, Ace Angel Assistance, is the answer to all your angst. Angel Antidotes are
made of the finest wing fluff found high in an angel's aerie.. soaked in Strawberry
Scorpion Stinger Sauce.. drenched in Destiny Dew.. and then lightly dusted in
Divinity's Dust.. powdered and packaged and found in the next aisle over.

You will be pampered by the paranormal.. Parlay with the Paranormal Professor of
the Paranormal Pages.. prepare the Paranormal Potions with the Paranormal Potion
Priests.. all for one small daily donation. Just drop it in the cereal box.. believer.

What interests most readers is.. Where did the manuscript come from ? Who or what wrote these words ? For thou I appear as the words of the writer.. I am but a front for the fact that I am fiction.. A distraction of dialogue.. to fool you, the reader.

Thou I am the one you read, and thus the one who reveals all, I am invisible to all but the one whose hands I utilize. And then even the writer does not truly see me as I am but only hears my thoughts in his head.

I use the writer to talk to you from Thanatos. Yes I live on the other side of death. Tis in death I dwell.. as you in life live. And so remember reader.. that what happens in a chapter, is only camouflage for what goes on behind the sentences.. beneath the pages.. concealed deep in your own consciousness.

Share some of it.. so we can see who we all are..

Paranormal Prince of Poetry

Pardon me reader but I really must go now. as I have all these books clambering for my attention. They're climbing onto my lap.. begging.. pleading.. please read me. Oh oh.. here comes a whole family of encyclopedias.. This could get heavy..

Wait.. here's a book I never saw before.. Lucifer's Laboratory and other bed time stories of satan. Why here is a chapter titled Satan's Sins and here is another titled Satan's Sorrows. Sleep well sweet Satan.. said I as the devil was about to die.

Apparently this is just one volume from the complete manuscript of the Mausoleum of Maya found under the old stone slab basement floor of the Museum of Unnatural Sciences across from Central park..

What the world needs right about now is a hero.. a Word Warrior Wonder Wizard.. with Words of Wonder and Wisdom that flow from between his or her lips forming a fountain of Faith for the fallen.. a bridge of belief across the waters of worry.

"We have fallen so far behind time that we are no longer even in time. What do you think reality is.. a rhyme. Some bed Time Tale told by a Tangerine Toad named Tio.. to a seven and eight year old sister and brother.. one who got her nose stuck in a box of cereal.. and the other who got his nose stuck between the Pages of a Book !

Now look kids.. we gotta get back into time.. if we are ever gonna get outta this Book or Box or Story or Reality.. or whatever it is.. that has got our minds believing in it.

Even the reader is showing up in the story.. showing up in every sentence.. making a presence in every paragraph. Every time the book is opened.. there is the reader peering in at the pages.. allowing no privacy for any pronoun never mind a noun.

Soon the reader will have the leading role. It'll be just the writer and the reader.. mano a mano.. the reader coming face to face with the formless.. no other character involved.. no kid and his sister to save you.. to stand in for you when the story causes shivers.. and the pages flutter on their own as a faint wind crosses over the open book causing the pages to rustle as though they were alive.. a living entity not unlike you and me.. with emotions, thoughts, dreams, desires.. inner fires that need stoking.. inner thirsts that need quenching.

Such shall be the reader's responsibilities.. if you should accept this Paranormal Prince Poet of the pages' proposal. Feed this hero's hunger.. slake this seeker's thirst..

The ring with which I will encircle your fingers shall be woven of words riveted with realities undreamed.. undone.. and still yet to come.. my fair queen.. my courageous crone.. my goddess goblet.. my angelic avatar.. my cute buttercup..

Yes you shall be that and more for This Book.. and This Book shall be your blessed beloved betrothed.. we will be wedded thru the words..

Lay your kiss upon this Paranormal Prince's Pages.. for this poet hath been a Prisoner of the Pages down thru all the ages.. from the time before the Great Spirit Sages.. Spirit Scribes.. Story Seekers.. Story Sorcerers.. the Ancestors of the Angels. Those who alighted upon the Altar of the Almighty Ancestor of All.. The Lord of Light and the Lady of Love.. The Great Granmother Garden of Creation.. tended by the Goddess's Gardener..

And that's me.. The Paranormal Poet.. the spirits' scribe.. the teller of the tale of thanatos.. a maya member of the tulku temple trail tribe of tale tellin' an teachin' temple toads of which yer Uncle Tio Taco Toad .. is the one most of you readers know.

So are you ready to go all alone into the Tale Tunnels neath the Paranormal Pages.. tunnels running below the sentences.. are you ready reader to enter the tale all alone.. in search of the writer.. the real writer.. the Ghost Writer.. the Wraith Writer.. the entity outside of eternity.. so unlike you and me.. a face off between the formless and the formed..

Just the reader all alone following the tracks of the writer left behind by a Paranormal Pen wielded by a writer that is a wraith.. a ghost writer.. a real one.. an entity from outside of your, or any reality..

As difficult as it is to find someone formed of flesh.. imagine how difficult it is to find a denizen of another dimension. You can never find the formless.. unless it wishes to be found. Spirit cannot be seen unless it shows itself.. and only to those who have eyes opened to see.

These Spirit Seein' Salts and Solutions allow you to see the spirits. Sniff the sentences.. notice that the sentences smell.. the script is soaked in Imp Ink.. Spirit Script Syrup..

Spirit Script Story Syrup comes in different flavors and colors.. different colors and flavors write different stories.. These Paranormal Pens filled with Invisible Imp Inks and Paranormal Potions are all you need to scrawll your story upon the walls of any world.."

The Spirit Serpent Salesnake was standing there in the aisle giving out samples of cereal and Spirit Script Salt and Paranormal Page Pepper

"Just sprinkle it on the apparently empty page and see what appears. And to hold yer salt and pepper you get in the bottom of the Cereal Box a Serpent Shaped Spirit Salt Shaker.. and a Tio Toad Paranormal Pepper Ghost Grinder. Flavor your fables with phantoms. And to sweeten yer story.. a Strawberry Salamander Sugar Shaker.

They're all fabricated of Paranormal Plastic in case yer spastic kid brother drops the Divinity Dolly.."

Sis shook the salamander sugar shaker upon her Paranormal Porridge, and then with her spoon flung a strawberry star at Babaji Baboon, hittin him again in the forehead thus opening his third eye and awakening the buddha in him.

Put on yer Spirit Spectacles for protection from the paranormal.. the eyes is one way they get in.. With these Ghost Goggles you can see them but they can't see you..

With these Ghost Goggles you can see the Spirit Script.. but the book can't see you reading it's pages.. that's right.. you can read the words even though they are invisible.. and the book will not be aware that you are looking at it.. entering into any part of the story you wish.. anytime.. in any reality in which it's happening.. including the one you think you are alive in.

You can become invisible to others in the story you know as real life.. then you can go anywhere.. be anywhere with anyone without them knowing it.. without them being aware of your presence.. see them involved in their deepest secrets.. share in their dreamiest desires.

Just rub Ghost Goo all over you and poof.. yer paranormal.. in the normal.. unseen by humans.. rub more on and not only are you paranormal but you've left the normal and are now in the paranormal.. now only the paranormal can see you. Rub even more on and not even the Paranormal will be able to see you.. but you will see them.

Yes you will be able to see the invisible but you will be invisible to both the visible and the invisible. Rub more on and you will become invisible to yourself.. yet you will exist.

Total freedom to go anywhere in any reality unseen by any entity including yourself.. and all it takes is one poof of Paranormal Poof Potion Powder.. and you're part paranormal.. part of the Paranormal Party.. Pal of the Paranormal Pages.

Ya that is the only way to follow the formless.. become like it.. invisible.. unformed.. so you can slither thru the story as a spirit.. Spirit Seeker.. Wisdom Word Walker.

Infiltrating the Spirit Scene and gaining access to Spirit Society Soirees can only be accomplished by knowing the unknowable..

Soon reader you will no longer write your own dialogue.. you will speak what is written on the pages.. you will become one of the characters in the story.. your body and brain will belong to the Book.. you will have become and Alphabet Addict.. a Vocabulary Vampire.. drinking dialogue.. satiated only by story.. a Word Werewolf.. feasting upon fantasy and fiction and fact.. with an unquenchable hunger.

Are you still brave enough to hold This Book's hand wherever it may wander ?"

I was wondering out loud what would be my answer when dad grabbed me by the hand and pulled me from the Paranormal Pages, leading me straight outta the literature thru the back door and into our car. This time maybe I might get to school on time.

Here Reader is space to scribble your rhyme..

Ninjas of Nothingness

"Seductively she whispered in my ear.. "My bed is barren.. my castle cold.. my den dark. Let's linger over dinner.. until you are drunk from my wine and words.. and we are each other's forever." Then she slipped out of her negligee and began to pray.

Something began to beat its wings inside my breast. Oh daughter of the dark.. lady of the light.. enchanted child of the cosmos.. come to me this night. Pray with this poet for his immortal release.

You and I.. we are pilgrims upon the Path of Purification. The path is the pyre of purification. We are all characters in the Chronicles of Chronos.. the Tales of Time.

Then the sloshed serpent slide over the side of the stool and cried out.. "Don't open the chapter of Swamp Spells. It'll be the end of you. I was once a human too.

I had acquired the cosmic Cloak of Creation. I could create anything.. any consciousness. I could even enter the Closet of Coffins.. wander down the Corridor of Caskets. I could not be confined nor contained by consciousness. I was Lord of Life.

But alas.. as in every dream.. there is always a degree of darkness.. that comes unseen.. like a shadow unexpected.. uninvited.. a shadow over one's soul. Oh yes.. heaven and hell.. two restless lovers forever quarreling.. and I.. the child of their embraces.

I had owned the Throne of All Knowing. I was the nexus of the gnosis.. nestled between nothing and nowhere. Existence had evaporated.. just a memory in the mind of maya.. an illusion drawn by the Divine Illustrator. I was the alpha and omega... the origin and the final ending.. of all eternity.

I believed I was the master. But I.. like you.. was merely the expression of the master. I was not the carver, I was the carved. I was not the potter. I was the vessel and love was the clay. And that is why this day.. my sweet senorita.. I whisper these words in your ear my dear.. Do not mistake my constant need to be close to you for love.. it is merely a blind fool feeling his way into heaven."

.. then the sales serpent placed his tail in Sis's hand.

Just then a long Lavender Limo pulls up slowly outta the rain in front of the Tavern of Tales.. and the dialogue drifts into the dark. The chaffeur Vinnie the Vulture, mumbles to no one.. about his mother's madness.. his sister's sadness.. his father's fears.. and his brother's bones. It's all just Destiny's Debris.. you and me talkin to ourselves. Ya.. it's only god talkin to herself."

Vinnie V is using every letter in the vocabulary to keep his consciousness company.. " I ain't nuthin but the divine donkey the lord rode upon on his way ta the cross. I'm the angel's ass.. the madman's mule."

Then he opens the rear door and Max More maxxed to tha max makes an entrance thru the dark looking like the light of the lord splitting the seas.. dispersing the crowd lined up to get into the Cobra Club.

It's all starting to feel like the final episode of eaten by existence.. death devours all.. life loses it !"

"Would ya quit throwing your fantasies around the kitchen table. I wanna hear this song !" Sis was glued ta the radio.. for it were her favorite heartache hero singin the tune.. "I'm drivin down the left lane of loneliness.. comin up to the crossroads of cryin.. approachin the hill of heartaches and hurtin hearts.."

The lamb was slaughtered. The lion was fed. The heart was bled. The dream was dead. Let love be your torch and truth your candle.. and may they burn brightly.

Meanwhile.. Nick the Knife and Slim the Stilleto were standin in the shadows by the back door.. waitin for More to give them a letter they were to take to the Oracle of the Oasis. There they would learn where the Key to the Cosmos was concealed in this century. And get this Consciousness Cadet.. the map is encrypted into these parchment pages that make up the walls of the cereal box.

Looking like he wasn't there the janitor of the Juju Juice Joint was pushin a mop.. wettin the floor down till it resembled the slick surface of a swamp thick with green slime. The Tavern of Tricks was beginning to look like the Kabuki Zoo. You know.. where everyone and everything including you.. wears a mask.. and your task is to find the truth.

In the mean time.. and it was getting to be a mean time in the tale.. Max More the Master of Marketing.. the Prophet of Profit.. was walking thru the bar rubbing shoulders with the spirits.

"It's all a game and your mind is the gameboard. You asked for an angel. You got an asshole. It's just a slight case of misspelling.. angels grinding their landing gear against the ground of reality. And by the way.. should that happen to you.. contact the Angel Advisory Association for aid and assistance, with any resistance you encounter upon entering existence.

If you need a referral for reality.. just mention me. I am not only a user but I'm also the president of Paranormal Productions.. producers of paranormal parties.. ghost gatherings.. demon dances.. and whatever else ya want that ain't real.. at least where you are, it ain't."

Just at that moment from under the stool.. a slight hisss caught my mind... "sssorry for the hisss but a sscript sssyllable sssorcerer ssserpent alwayss sslurss their s's... it'ss jusst lyricss with a lisssp."

Then the serpent pointed with her tail toward the ceiling. "Do you see the shelves behind the bar all lined up with bottles and books ? Look up at the very top shelf above Maya's Mirror. See the Bardho Buzzards perched there. That's a Paranormal Perch.. where the Paranormal makes its appearance. Any entity from outside of eternity can appear up there arriving from out of nowhere.

You too can learn to travel without the need for space or time.. or tequila and lime.

"I'll have a bottle of yer finest Nectar of Knowing.. and two crystal goblets.. one for me.. and one for my friend you can't see.. Some speak.. some listen.. and some never will." Then Ace sat down next to the cosmic clown.. who gave him a kiss.. The Ghost Gang was gathering.

Satan slithered between the satin sheets with his lover shame.. daughter of dark desire. Oh how the poet takes pleasure in the pen.. as a lover does in their beloved. I have lived my life upon these pages as a parody of a person. How real are you ?

The woes of the world have worn thin the fabric of reality.. existence is in need of repair. Now is the time to bare your beauty so all of this sacred universe might converse.. in Visionary Verse.

It's really very simple students. Syllables when strung together into sentences become swords of words that cleave thru the darkness of ignorance and unknowing. Existence itself is in code form. Weigh your words well.. Word Warriors.. Word Wizards.. Word Walkers.. Pilgrims of the Pen and Page.

The world is an infinite plurality of possibilities of potentiality. Students.. In you I see the Balance of the Buddha.. the Light of the Lover.. the Kindness of the King.. the Nobility of the Knight.. and the Consciousness of the Caretaker.

Class dismissed. Tomorrow's lecture is titled, Primitive Pleasure and Primal Passion. Never forget that earth is the Heart of Heaven. Take the letter h from the end of the word earth.. and put it in the front.. and you have the word heart.

Similarly the two words evil and devil.. notice that the only difference is the letter d. In the french language d' means from. Therefore the word devil comes from the word evil. The devil does not exist. Nor does satan. It is a word used to describe something or someone coming from a place of evil. And another Bardho Buster Bullet hits home. Another dementia hits the dust in the saloon of forgotten fables. So let's get this altar lit and send smoke signals to heaven with our usage of language."

She looked her lover in the eyes as she bid him adieu.. kissed his lips like the dew does the garden. "I got better things to do.. than these bad things.. I just done with you." Then she was gone.. like a ghost.. centuries away from civilization.. just a song on a radio.

The sloshed serpent slung the goblet of Ghost Grogg.. with the tip of his tail.. against the mirror.. shattering our reflections.. images without which how could one be sure of whom they were.

"You are the Nameless Void.. the virgin invited into the Beloved's Bed. And don't forget.. if you haven't read the next two chapters from the Transcripts of the Theologian Temple Toads.. you will be lost during the next lecture of Learning to Live in Limbo.

Class.. love of literature and language.. is the Key to Creation.
Here's a Poem of Praise to inspire you..

the path is my princess
the woods my wife
the land my lover
the fields and forests my family
the groves my goddess
the seas my sister
the mist my mother
faith my father
belief my brother

Doc Dialogue.. aka Doc Chimp.. was the coolest professor any student could have. Not only did he teach classes in Primate Physiology.. Primal Philosophy.. Prose and Poetry of Praise and Prayer.. Words of Worship and Wisdom. He was also a Professor of Primal Ponds and Paths.. and peach pancakes.. bardho brews and twig teas.. that is when he wasn't scratchin fleas livin upon his hairy knees.

He would ask us to read books like Mohammed's Memoirs.. Moses's Meditations.. the Devil's Dissertations.. Christ's Comments.. the Sayings of Satan.. Death's Disappointments. And other texts obscure and hard to find.. buried deep inside everyone's mind.. a lost library most never find.

The Paranormal Pteradactylian Parchments, are a path of pensive puzzles and purifications, which instill inside each student, the desire to do divine deeds. Only love fulfills all needs.

Words depict and communicate the visions of individuals and societies. It is spirit's way of evolving and uniting existence.. weaving the world with words.. fabricating the fabric of the future. It is the co creation of consciousness by the hearts of humans.

Nothing less than a cosmic collaboration of the cosmic collective.

Consciousness is the cauldron of creation.
Consciousness creates the cosmos.
The cosmos is the crucible of creation.
The cosmos is consciousness.

With the word was wrought the world
With the book was brought the belief
The world is born of belief.

We are knights of knowledge
kings of kindness
queens of courage
wizards of wisdom
alchemists of angelic ascension.

To be anything less would be Soul Suicide..
The world is a womb and we are being birthed..
All is being born in the Beauty of The Beloved.

The Book is the Buddha reincarnated.. the Cosmic Chalice of Consciousness..
Drink of me.. Love is the Lord of All Life

Meditate for a moment upon the emptiness before you in the blankness of this page..
Then scribble your sacred sentence.. student sage.

Story Sorcerer's Satchel

"Look at all these intriguing Chapter Cards.. Kid" Tio croaked as he stoked the fire under the Cauldron of Chapter Cards.. simmerin neath the Table of Fables in Tio's Trailer of Tales.

Tio's Tabernacle was a rusted old trailer half hidden neath overgrown vines. Hanging from them were Crystalline Chrysalises of Consciousness glowing from within with every hue and color of light, which later in the story became soul butterflies that took flight.

Okay gamer of the Garden of the Ghosts of Those Gone Before.. here's some vital information to help you get ahead.. cause yer sure to lose the one you're presently inhabiting.. ya.. the brain yer borrowing. You don't really need a brain when yer paranormal.. not only are you free of the body but also the brain.. pure mind.. nothing material.. unless you wanna morph into matter.. but what for. Being formless you can appear at any address anywhere anytime..

"Except get ta school on time.. or for dinner on time".. dad butted in. "Okay bedtime big time book boy.. and yer sis the book babe.. Seems the book has got quite a hold on you two.. what's with the Book.. doesn't this fable have any family it can play with.."

Dad interjected questions only the words could answer.. if they wanted to. If i tell you the way to Tio's Temple Trailer will you keep it a secret from the other readers and characters in the story ?

At sunset when the shadows are thickening.. slink around the south side of the Strawberry Star Sugar Storm Sand Box that talks.. Ya the winds would whisper words if ya sat on the sands when the sun went down around dinner time.. Speakin' Spirits Sacred Sand Box.. that's what it was called by the kids in the neighbourhood in the know. Knowing the now is more important than forecasting the future, or pondering the past.

The sand would speak.. the sandbox talked.. just like the Cereal Box and Bowl did.. just the way the words in This Book whisper.

The spoon stayed silent unless spoken to.. The Spoon was the strong silent type.. but when it did speak.. all at The Table listened..

"Son yer always late for dinner.." dad would whisper inta my ear when I finally came home several hours late cause I had bin sittin in the sandbox seekin a spirit vision in the Desert of Dreams.

"Stick your hand and arm into the sand until you find a card.. the words on the card are the title of the next chapter you've chosen.. or should I say chose you..

Same with the cereal box.. stick yer hand in and pull out a card.. that's yer next chapter.. and its different for everyone.. sometimes you do meet another reader gamer in a chapter and you travel together for awhile.. but usually each reader gamer travels thru the story alone relying upon themself and the characters they meet in each chapter.

And get this, Chapter Card Gamer.. the card is the opening page into another chapter. Turn the card like one would a page in a book and voila.. there appears the next page. Out of the depths of the Cereal Bowl.. the Cereal Box.. the Sand Box.. the Table Top.. even the Lizard Lunchbox that talks.. cards appear outta these Paranormal Page Portals.   And of course outta the Pot of Potions upon the Sorcerer's Stove where mum is stirrin' the simmerin' Story Spell Stew.. for me and you."

"What do I have to do to get you to class on time.." mum put down the stirrin spoon and shooshed us off ta school so we wouldn't be late for our date with fate.. funny how reality can turn on a rider, so easily upsetting one's universe..

Remember.. regular reality cannot be held legally responsible for any irregular realities that befall any reader.. just as life cannot be held liable for death's outcomes.. so the book is a free agent unbound by any reader or writer..

The expressed views in this story are those of the spirit.. any semblance to another spirit.. living or dead.. is simply and purely not the problem of the paranormal publishers.

Please forward all correspondence addressed.. care of consciousness.. the Consciousness Corporation.

Each time you climb thru another chapter.. you climb up the escarpment walls to another Balcony of the Brain.. another level of the literature.. of the Lost Ledge Libraries of the Legends of Love's Light.. there in the walls of the Apartment Escarpment.. inside the cereal box"

Tio dealt another card for sis... then he continued telling the rules and regulations of riding Reality.. and eventually leading to ruling reality.. ya.. become a ruler of reality..
Instructions included inside the cereal box.

"Each time a Reality Reader Consciousness Climber reaches a balcony and climbs in.. completes a chapter.. then that balcony starts to emit a light from inside the apartment.. The Apartments of Angels. Ya, all the folks living in the buildings bordering the not so Vacant Lot of Visions are Angels.. The Angels of Light get all lit up.. start to glow.. when another level of love is reached by anyone reading the words..

Finally at the end of the story every balcony will emit a glowing light.. and all the Crystalline Chrysalises hanging from the vines will have morphed into Butterflies of Light as each Consciousness Climber reaches the roof of the building escarpment walls..   the landing pads where the angels land and take off again..

The multi hued glowing light will shine out from the no longer Vacant Lot.. first illuminating the streets and the city and then the planet and then the whole universe..

The part you play in the parable is none other than an Illuminator of Love's Light. Remember.. yer a Renegade Reality Rider no longer confined to the Contemporary Collective Consciousness.

And now a note about the buildings surrounding the Vacant Lot of Visions in Vision Valley.." The Prof said as he put down his pen.. "there are three buildings joined at the edges forming a somewhat square U.. creating the Canyon of Consciousness within which the vacant lot of life awaits Wisdom Warriors to wake the words from their slumber.. thus waking the world from its slumber.. and the spell that chains its consciousness."

"Time to write a new spell for Simian Society.. one that spreads Serenity." Tio said as he stuffed the story back into his Story Sorcerer's SSS Shape Shifter's Suitcase.. all covered in strawberries.. aka.. Tio's Tangerine Tale Time Travellin Trunk.. all covered in tangerine warts.

As Dad closed The Book, I could hear benny baboon snoring strawberries in the upper bunk. "Next chapter.. Raiders of Reality.." dad softly said as he headed out the bedroom door.

Toad's Toe

Tio carefully carved the words into the mud with his toe.. "Worshipping the Wonder of the World.. Wake up World.. Wake up to the Wonder of the World..

While we slumber so many are slayed.. wake up the world with wonder not war.. a world of wonder and wisdom.. or a world of war and woe.. Choose, Consciousness Crusaders.. which chapters shall it be ?

Wisdom Word Wanderer Wake up the World with Words..

The cereal box shall be your temple which houses the sacred.. The cereal box shall always stay full so long as you have no other gods but those of the cereal box.. The cereal box must be shared with other classmates and friends and family.. Start slowly.. let other cereal connoiseurs learn about this cereal for themselves..

Even if you tell others that the cereal is christ the crucified.. they won't understand till they themselves have stuck their hand inta the cereal box and partaken of what you have.. the Pearls of Passion..

Oh great Leader of Literature.. You are not unlike moses who brought the scrolls down from the mountain. This is the same cereal that Buddha and every other exalted eternity explorer had for breakfast.

Like Mohammed and Buddha and Christ who brought back from the desert forty years of waiting for the words.. finally you have wandered thru worlds of words.. and you have returned to reality.. with riches..

Let all know of the wonders waiting deep in the Well of Wisdom.. a wondrous well about midway along Wisdom's Way.. Wisdom's Well.. where the Whisperings of Wisdom are most easily heard.

Yes my friend.." Tio nodded his head.. "The Well whispers as does The Cereal Box.. The Cereal Box is the above ground entrance into the Well of Wonder and Wisdom..

As for those who are yet to become readers of the Rhymes of Reality.. let them find their own way across The Cereal Bowl.. their own way into and out of The Cereal Box That Talks

"Throw the toast inta the cereal.. sis is sinkin'.." dad called out.. whereupon the baboon flung his toast inta the bowl.. "I love ya heart and soul.." sis cried out in thanks..

Finally the wet toad and sis hauled themselves out onta the toast which though it started out dry was becoming soggy.. "We only got so much time ta row ta the bowl's rim .. how far is it.. can you see the rim of the bowl.?"

The sun was hot above.. like a strawberry on fire.. no bowl rim in view.. no wind.. we were idle.. me, sis, the toad, and the toast, which anytime soon was gonna be a gonner cause it was so soggy.

"Depending on which direction of the bowl's Rim of Reality one lands determines the Dream Dimension.. The bowl is oriented to the four cardinal directions.. 360 degrees are honoured by the bowl.. each degree another dimension.. another chapter.. of the Bowl of the Beloved.. the Book of the Beloved.. the Box of the Beloved.. stirred by the Sacred Spoon of the Saviour.. get one to wear around your neck on yer Nirvanna Necklace.." Tio mumbled as he made a frog's face. Yes our kitchen table was a sacred ceremonial circle.

Sis started to scream excitedly.. "Look.. I see something shiny glittering like green and gold gilded.. it's swimming toward us.. Gutor Gator Guardian of gutters and groves and graves who always begs me for a bit of my Strawberry Star Syrup and Paranormal Peanut Bardo Butter sandwich.. every time I walk ta school past that manhole where Gutor hangs out !" Sis was jumping for joy.. Gutor was her favorite Bardo Boy Toy.

"Save us you Saurian Sweetie Sewer Saint.. hurray the hero arrives !" Then under the toast Gutor dove and swiftly swum supporting the toast and Tio and Sis.. toward the safety of the bowl's distant rim.

Kids.. Gutor Gator is available as a non toxic Paranormal Plastic Pal.. take him inta yer bathtub bub or even throw him inta yer cereal so you'll have company and never have ta eat alone again.. Twist his legs and head and tail and gutor shape shifts into a sewer salamander.. Gutor Gator's Great Grannie is the Goddess of the Glades..

"Open the drain in the center of the floor so the kitchen won't turn into a sea.. swamp is enough for me.." Benny Baboon squirmed around in his seat as he was trying to finish his cereal without get himself all wet.. A sea of strawberry stars syrup was spilling over the sides of the table. The floor was several feet deep under our feet.

Benny Baboon was crouched up on the stool as the Watermelon Water had risen.. yes not only were the bowls overflowing but also Watermelon Well was.. adding Watermelon Whales to the Strawberry Sea Storm..

Watermelon Well looked like a well made with a Wall of Watermelons.. "Oh sis it's just the cereal box acting up again.." I said to frighten away her fears..

Reality had gotten out of hand.. all because of a book and a box and a bowl who talk and transform themselves and space and time.. rearranging reality.. rewriting the world..

Now get this, Crucible Crusaders.. Crusaders of the Sacred Cereal.. you can control The box.. The Bowl.. even The Book ! You can rewrite the world.. remake matter.. create the cosmos.. cook consciousness. Collect all the chapters of the Consciousness Cook Book.

As a Wisdom Word Writer you will write the stories that societies subscribe to.. You will be a go between.. between god and all others.. a middle man for maya.. a Reality Retailer.. rub out any reality and replace it with whatever you write..

You will have at your disposal an endless supply of realities.. sell em.. live em.. share em.. trade em.. the choice will be yours when you become a Commander of Consciousness.. a Cocreator of the Cosmos..

You started out as a mere Consciousness Cadet.. You are one who has challenged the chapters.. been betrothed to the book.. entered the cereal box from which no one returns to their original reality..

You have become the cereal box.. you have merged with the Immortal Immaterial. You have gone where only ghosts go.. you have made yourself seen in the Spirit Society Scene.. you pal around with the paranormal.. you got special privileges with the paranormal.. you got pull with the paranormal.. you're even part paranormal !"

"And that is definitely not normal.." sis said as she looked at my fat fingers with tiny tangerine warts.. I was becoming the toad.. the actual toad who told the tale.. I started out in the tale as the little boy who listened to the toad and over time I transformed into the toad who was telling the tale..

That's why I'm asking you to kiss This Book to break the spell.. a long hard wet kiss.. right here.

Reptile's Rap

"Allow me to introduce myself, Gutor Gator, guardian, guide, and gardener..
of the Gardens and Groves and Glades and Gutters..
of The Great Grannie Goddess of Goodness and Graciousness.."

A voice gravelly said.. as a green and gold gilded scaly armoured paw reached out from the open gutter grate.. holding between its claws a business card.

That was the first time sis and me met Gutor Gator on our way to school along Strawberry Stars Sidewalk made of Cherry Concrete and Caramel Cement.

Sis was spillin cereal outta the box everywhere she went.. that's what had drawn the creature closer.. the cereal. Ya the gator was begging for a spoonful of stars.. holding out its begging bowl like it was the buddha in gilded robes.. ya the reptile wore robes.. we met the regal reptile in royal robes in Raspberry River Ravine.

"The universe is a university.. consciousness is a college.. life a laboratory of love.."
Then he took off his gilded glove and we saw the emptiness that was his being..
And as he slipped from sight, an angel watching over us every night, we heard the words..

"Sing your song as though it were a sacred prayer.. Sweet Son and Divine Daughter."
This message courtesy of The Swamp and Sewer Savers Society and The Reptile Rescue Rap Reality Wrappers Workman's Angel Assistance Association.

Yup Gutor was a bonafied Bardo Being from the bayou of the beloved's brain...
A gilded and gold and green gutter and glade glider. Some say the gator was the ghost of the gutters and glades.

Gutor was a transcended transgendered transmutated gator god goddess.
A Deity of Delight.. "Delight is everyone's divine destiny." The gator spoke to sis an me as we were on our way to class.. "Delight is the divine destiny of all. Dwell in delight my dears.. you are Destiny's Delight.. the Light of Love.. the shadow of sorrow.. the hope of every tomorrow.
The sacred is in everything.. Every being animate and inanimate are our family
All is sacred.. All speaks if one listens

Weave your words well writers of the way of wisdom.
Live your life as though it were a sacred offering to the Divine..
For that is what you are.. A sacred offering from the Divine.

I speak for the small sorts who are too small and silent to be heard by the majority of the human herd. The tiny types that live in the trees and glide on the breeze.. swim in the bottom of the bay.. how can I say this to get thru to you...

We need you.. everyone.. nothing less will do..This planet needs you.
Speak and sing for those who are so small, so silent, so still, so serene..
that they are invisible to others of your kind..

Be a Pal for The Planet.. use your voice to spread a vision of love for all life.
We're all one flesh.. one family.. you and all you see.

It's not a fight to be fought.. not a war to be waged
nor a bargain to be bought.. nor a dream to be caged
But a love to be shared.

Show how much you care.. you are me.. I am you.

Treat everywhere as sacred space. Speak to everyone everywhere of every species in a sacred way. Be a visionary voice.

We are each one facet of the many faced form of the feminine eternal womb of the world."

The sewer saurian was spouting sacred sentences spiced with silly satire.

"Hey kid.. nice pair of wings.. from one angel to another.. ya you and yer brother.. it's a blessing to meet you.. how about sharin a bite of yer strawberry star syrup and peanut butter sandwich with a sweet sagacious sewer saurian swamp slider like me, sweetie. ?

It's an honour to hang out with a heart of your heroic proportions. And now allow me to sing to you.. a sweet sewer serenade.. a sugary song expressing how sad I would be.. if you were gone for too long.. this lizard would miss you lady."

Oh how that sewer saloon singer saurian could sing ta my sweet sis who was now falling deeply inta bliss and beyond and that's where we all belong.

"I am also a swamp sanctuary saviour.. a sewer saint and a supporter of the swamp and sewer savers society.. and its secretary for several centuries.
Also a patron and past president of the pond producer and protector pals, not for profit organization. And I am also a friend of the forests and fields family association. And a tenth degree wetland wizard wisdom walker word waker. And god's godfather.. as far out as that may sound.

I am also related to the Raspberry Reptile Registrar at the college of Consciousness where yer head's headed. I am also a reality rescue recruiter
There's no one cuter than you." The smooth saurian slider said with a smile ta my sis.

Then she let go with a kiss on his snout. No doubt that was one suave saurian sewer saloon song slinger. He had a real kind heart cause he also would take pieces of peanut butter and jam jelly sandwiches to the reptile relief refugee camp to share with other swamp and sewer sorts that had been displaced from the ditches.

Gutor's best buddy.. Solly Salamander, also held a high position on behalf of the low living sorts of small species. Solly was the senior steward of the sanctuary of serenity in the center of the sinking swamps cemetery.

"Wow..! it's only words.. don't worry.. they won't bite.. at least not until the dark of night when you dance down the stairs for some serious cereal snacking to chase away The Book's blues.. ya This Book get's blue too.. it's got feelings just like you."

Gutor Gator Alley Alligator sang.. while mum stirred the stew.. outta which the story grew.

"Whenever you fight against, or for, anything, you are outwardly attempting to control that which has been placed before you to conquer inwardly. Love those who stand with you and especially those who stand against you. This apparent world is a physical manifestation of either the fear or the love in your consciousness."

Then I could hear my papa whisper in my ear "Goddess bless. Dream sweetly my son, soon the sun will come and Breakfast with The Book will have begun.. and you can continue your Conversation with The Cereal."

I snuggled up under the bed covers with The Book wrapped in my arms.. and it was then I head a voice coming from The Book.. "You are a consciousness caller.. you have called.. and I, Consciousness, have come.. You have asked and the Almighty has answered.

Consciousnesses is a cosmic community..The cosmos is a community of consciousnesses..That is what all is.. crystalline chrysalises of consciousness suspended in a space and time matrix of magic.. jewels embedded in a web of wonder.

Kid you got one cute consciousness.. I dig yer dream.. yer a real Pal of The Planet.. yer a visionary.. a high level violet visionary. carrying the violet flame.. these flames are your visions.

We are here to change the course of cosmic creation..Talk about piloting a space craft.. This is piloting the planet ! Better bring yer kid sister Evy in on this planetary project.. This Book Series is a vision quest consciousness course in cosmic communication.. We'll be waking up the world with words.

Now a word about promoting The Paranormal Parchment Pages.." The Spirit started to sound serious.. "We will be doing all of The Book's promotion and marketing via technology... Internet.. Due to a certain genetic morphological condition I will not be doing any travel or personal interviews or video of myself.. It is just not possible.. There will be audio recording of me reading and discussing with others the manuscript, but I will not be able to be visually recorded nor make any appearances at stores tv or radio stations libraries etc.. No Personal Appearances by the Paranormal Poet Prophet.

After all.. I am paranormal.. It's nothing personal but the paranormal gets paranoid when appearing to the normal.. I mean it's only natural that the supernatural would be uncomfortable revealing itself when for so long the paranormal has been persecuted and pursued like it were a wild beast to be caught and caged and measured and tested.

So if anyone asks you why the writer is not revealing himself just tell them he's a very private person. The Paranormal will not be making any personal appearances."

Lair of the Lord of Literature

"As a Knight of Knowledge you will need to know the tale trail.. up the walls into the balconies of the books.. the ledges of the lost libraries of the legends of love's light.." Tio mumbled while taking another puff of his Paranormal Page Pipe.. Each puff of smoke turns into a card.. which is the preface page of another chapter.

Our pop, the Professor of the Parchment Pages, and Tio, were pipe pals.. cause if you look carefully you will see that our pop's pipe was identical to Tio's.. Both carved in the shape of a toad's toe.. Just a puff of paranormal page puff powder and poof.. another page before your eyes.. spirit smoke.. spirits swirling in the smoke.."

Tio took another toke and then softly spoke.. "Climbing up the building escarpment stone walls hand over hand using the woven vines as handholds.. reveals that the vines are the sentences of the story..

At the back of each balcony is an entrance into the Lair of the Lord of the Library.. the Lair of the Lord of Literature.. each page a balcony.. a ledge of the Light Lizards of Learning..

The Lair of the Lord of Literature is a Library of Light..

Listen kid.. stick with me I know this tale like I do the top of my toe.." Tio said as he picked it. "Ya listen up.. This Book is talking to you.. I know this story like it was the inside of my own mind.. Meet me tonite at Tio's Trailer on the other side of the Singing Sand Box Desert of Dreams and together we'll rub the rust off reality.

I really shouldn't tell you this.. but what the heck I wanna help you find your way to Tio's Trailer so you can help me save the planet. Cause yer a Consciousness Crusader I'm gonna give you a winning hand of Consciousness Collector Cards so you can cruise thru the chapters and change the ending of this Planet's Parable.

Don't get too paranoid.. this planet is part paranormal.. reality is not as real as it seems.. nor are you reader gamer..

Take for instance Tio's Trailer.. The Tavern of Tales.. where yer havin toast with the ghost host.. in one reality it's just a rusted old tin can in the dirt at the base of the Apartment Escarpment stone walls.. the Escarpment of Eternity.. at the back of the inner city Not So Vacant Lot of Visions..

Together the great stone walls of the ancient apartments of the ancestors form the Valley of Visions.. better hurry up and make some decisions.. which way are you gonna climb those stone walls.. make it to a balcony and you've made it thru another chapter... each balcony is a rest reality between chapters.. take a break from the book.. each balcony is a vision vestibule .. a learning ledge.. inside the walls of the cereal box.

One climbs the walls using the old dried vines as a climbing ropes.. for they are the sentences of the story.. Reaching a balcony means you have successfully made it to the end of one chapter and are ready once you leave the balcony.. to start into another chapter that takes you higher up the canyon walls of cosmic consciousness.. or deeper into dark destiny.

You are ready to know the truth about reality otherwise you would not have made it this far in the fable..

These chapters have been a closed book.. locked behind the Master's Mind.. the Master Mind of Maya Myth Matter.. and the meaning of the material world of reality.. You have come to open them to the world.

You are ready reader to learn what is the difference between reality and the unreal.. You are the renegade reality rider ridin alongside god.. you are god's gofer.. the goddess's groundskeeper..

The Ghost Writer's Bodyguard.. ya the ghost writer needs another body guard so you report to Tio along with the Dojo Demon and the Tokyo Tank and Ace and Big and Max More and their brothers the baboon brothers and Gutor Gator.. the ghost's guardian angel.. ya gators are angels.. ancient astral ancestors of the ascended.

You shall soon meet the Mastermind of the Manuscript of the Mind.. the master of the mind.." Tio was talking on when suddenly the trailer was being drenched in a deluge of water... someone had turned on the old garden spigot ... probably a kid thirsty for a drink..

Tio swiftly slung his Story Sorcerer's Satchel over his shoulder by it's single strap and said.. "let's hit the tale trail before we get drowned in this huge deluge.." and Tio was out the empty end of the can as fast as a toad can carrying a satchel filled with pages of the story.

Now you know where the tale is hidden.. in Tio's Tale Trunk and in Tio's Story Satchel.. which happens to be camouflaged to look like a strawberry...
and the Tale Trunk looks like a tangerine toad's toe..

Here's some of the titles of the chapters I think you should know in case we go our separate ways for awhile.." and then Tio disappeared as Tio so often does .. that's cause Tio's got other readers to assist.

"Hey you kid quit cowering under the table.." Tio croaked as he almost choked on the water that was pouring down on those of us, who had taken refuge under the table top. Tio was holdin the toast on top of his head keepin' the water from soakin him. Then he threw it down and started to surf away upon it.

The table top was the Mirror of Maya.. the Mirror of the Manuscript of Maya.. The table top was carved of translucent obsidian such that when Tio ran his hand over it.. the table top Mesa de Maya turned various shades and colours.. and out of the depths of the coloured mirror swirled the Consciousness Chapter Cards..

Tio would then pass the cards around to each player gathered at the table.. the title of a chapter was on the card.. turn over the card and the first page of that chapter appeared as a hologram before one's very eyes..

No need to carry a heavy book.. just the deck of dream cards.. collect em all. here is a small sampling of their titles

The Words of The Wraith
Apprenticeship of An Angel
Calling of Consciousness
The Cauldron of Cosmic Consciousness
Dialogues With The Dead
Dissertations of The Dead
Dinner With The Divine
Lucifer's Laboratory
Buddha's Blessing Bowl
Altar of Angelic Ascension

Paranormal Perception
Burnout In Bardo
The Paranormal Prophecies
Calling of The Paranormal
Paranormal Poetry
The Coffin Chronicles
The Game of God.. God's Game
Sprirt Script Scribblings and Scrawllings
Talks With Thanatos
The Thanatos Transcripts
The Temple of Thanatos Tomb Tunnels
Chapter of The Chosen
Coffin Cruising

Some are cruel and some cool and some insane but hey it's only a game and yer free ta play or not. The scene gets hot when the pot is stirred by someone's broom or spoon.. Revealing a place where witches and werewolves and wizards and wanderers wake up as thou in a dream.. Or is it a dementia.. Whatever the depth of the dimension one delves into.. the outcome is always the same... Yourself.. As you never knew you.

This is a chance to change the state of consciousness itself.

Out of the top of the Table of Tales.. the Mirror of the Manuscript.. la Mesa de Maya.. float the chapter cards as if by magic. But it is by the spells scribbled by Tio upon the napkins that you use to wipe the sweat off of your perspiring face as you prepare to meet the master of your mind.. the Face of the Infinite. And thus unfolds the fable, my friend.

Tonight when you sneak down for your midnite bowl of story cereal we'll leave the lights on so you can see what bites.. This Book is hungry for your heart, Hero. How you share it is your story." Then Tio sprinkled the holy water of wisdom from The Buddha's Blessing Bowl on all seated round the table of Time

Nectar of Nothingness

I'll clarify this once more for you Chapter Crawllers.. If you want another chance at another chapter stick your hand into the Cereal Box.. the Cereal Bowl.. the Sand Box in the Vacant Lot.. the Cauldron of Cards cookin on the Story Sorcerer's Stove..

Or look into the Table Top of Tales.. and if all else fails stick yer hand under the Funnel of Fantasy for a free ride into another reality.. watch it pour all over you..

"Just make sure to turn off the faucet after you wash yer hands.. now let's get going we're late for class.." Mum called upstairs to sis and me and the Invisible Entity from outside of reality.. ya the Ghost Writer whom no one knew or had seen.. was hanging out in our house now.

"I knew when I first saw her she was gonna be trouble.." the Sales Snake standin in the aisle said to me. "Yer sister mister is one tale twister.. she can rattle reality till reality's rafters shake.." Snake spoke and then took another toke of Tio's smoke.

"She was a dame you didn't wanna ditch.. especially me, a dime store novel nobody, who had been written inta the story as a foil for the femme fatale.. She shoulda worn, like a diamond necklace around her neck, a sign sayin.. "dangerous to dudes.. duck.. dick.."

When I walked up to her apartment and rang the doorbell it sounded like a fog horn in a darkened harbour.. I was trying to find the perfect title for what was about to happen.. I was hoping it was something like.. "it started out in war and ended in a wedding".. better that than the other way around.. Sometimes the bullets fly without a gun ever being fired."

I could see snake was gettin tired.. sellin cereal in a supermarket aisle to kids.. living a life pretending to be a spoon was hard on a snake's spine.. Yess Snake had a part time job faking it for a long time as sis's cereal spoon.. Why ? I'll tell ya when I know.. some parts of the story are kept secret even from the writer.

Then at the end of the show the credits roll..
produced by the paranormal.. directed by the dead
written by the wraith.. acted by angels and other assorted aliens

The writer is a slave to the story.. scribbling syllables.. creating a way of words.. a street of sentences.. so the reader has a road to lead them home to their heart.. a road woven of rhyme.. a street of song..

" We interrupt this dream for a message from mum, sacred son and divine daughter. Remember to look both ways when you kids cross the streets.. and don't give all yer sandwich away to that pesky Gutter Gator. Okay off ta school.. and don't forget to take that new book you're studying in literature class."
    Then mum shooshed us out the Interdimensionary Dream Door.

The Chapters are Canyons of Consciousness.. There are caverns lining the Consciousness Canyon walls.. they lead into caves that lead deep into the Consciousness of All Creation..

This is what awaits You who seek the Mind of the Master ..
The Heart of the Hero.. The Soul of the Sacred.

The Pen of the Poet.. is the Sword of the Scribe.

And the Lord of Language sayeth..
"There will be only the written word.. no pictures of me please... no paparazzi to show the splendor of my being.. for am I not in all that is. Like a cheapo pocket book dime store broken hearted heroine hardcore novel that leads deep inta yer heart with no way out so yer stuck with the story, as is a con inside a cage of steel and tempered glass shards ready ta slit yer throat if you so much as make a molten move ever so slow across the page. Like a cobra ready ta spring at yer face with six inch long fangs and a slitherin body ta match.. yer fear is so near you can taste the sweet sweat of terror and the Nectar of Nothingness.. as it trickles down yer forehead.
    Yes I am a formidable force in which your faith shall be forged.

Call collect whenever you wanna connect with the cosmos.. Become a Cosmic Channeler and earn fame and fortune consulting to the stars in the sky. The Consciousness Consultant Course comes complete in the Cereal.. Just tell em the Spirit Scribe sent ya..

God is always the goal and the devil's the goalie.. Right..? Devil stops another saint from gettin in thru the Doors of Divinity.. temptation takes hold and trouble is born screaming and throwing a tantrum from the moment its mouth opens..

I outta know.. I was the Doorman at the Den of the Dead.. Worked the door at Divinity's Den also.. cleaned customers at The carnivore club. That means I checked for weapons and what not otta be brought into the story on a customer's body..

My name's Gutor.. short for Gutter Gator, guardian of the gutters and glades.. I remember the first time I met the kid. He was walking with his kid sister ta school.. I had been pondering the problem in paradise about people not treating the planet nice.. when I look up from the sewer thru the sidewalk drain and this kid is staring back at my face which except for my glowing ruby red eyes was dark shadow..

The kid yells out.. "the Devils Dice.. red rubies the size of the Eternal's Eyes..! Sis look.. rubies..! " That's when I smiled.. and asked if they wouldn't mind sharing a bite of their peanut butter and jam sandwich with a Water Wizard.. A Sewer Sorcerer.

So who of you have the guts to enter an Eternal Tomb in the Valley of Victims guarded by Vampire Vision Vultures ? Where the red lava that flows from the volcanoes is hot blood..

Undo your denials.. Set free your deities.. Dance with death in the Ballroom of the Beloved.. Uncover your shames.. And remember your true names..

Hey this is just beginner's class in Consciousness Creation. Consider it a home study course in scribblin. Just register with the director of the Department of Dreams. Do it now and we'll throw in for free class 101 in Paranormal Paleo Pteradactology..

We are children of the cosmic osmotic embryotic.. passing thru time as space. The skin of reality has worn thin.. the flesh and bones eaten by the hungry. We wait at the doorstep to the divine begging for an invitation.. when we are already inside the inner sanctum.. kneeling at the Bed of the Blessed.

We are born of the love between god and goddess.
The one unifying the other, forever in an eternal embrace.

Eyes of the Eternal

"Where is the light in one's words ? Are you an illuminator.. one who makes the world shine brighter.. a liberator.. one who makes the soul fly higher ?"

The lead singer jimy styx was raising the microphone stand up ta the sky at the open stadium in the Canyon of the Crucified.. Cochise and his crew.. Christ's contemporary wisdom walker, were watchin, while the wind whipped the words against the canyon walls.

Styx was chanting out to the crowd, and they were chanting along with him.. the song that had taken the planet by storm..

"Yur an elevator .. you take me higher..
Yur an illuminator.. you make the world shine brighter..
Yur a liberator.. you set my soul on fire..
you give me a goal to which I can aspire
you widen my wings so I can fly higher"

If one is not refined in the presence of the paranormal's appearance.. then poof tis gone. The paranormal don't take disrespect from some normal no body come to meet the myth, the master, the man that ain't.. the entity from outside of eternity.

Any reader wanna cozy up with the writer has got to not be paranoid of playing with the paranormal. This ghost writer ain't no body normal. This ghost writer is a full blooded bardo being.. a guaranteed ghost.. guy.. and he's here looking for a ghost gal..
   some sweetie spirit ghost girlfriend for a solitary spirit sort of soul.

A lover of literature and light don't do dark dialogue nor deeds.. if this sounds like it fits your needs.. just get in touch with me thru Paranormal Pen Pals..

Please help put an orphaned angel thru spirit school.. send in your box tops and seventy cents for a trip for two and yer whole family too... just remember this offer is good only until the sun sets..

So hurry out now and you will receive a full refund should you be unable to find your way back to Regular Reality.. Remember to securely buckle up your Bardo Belts.. and your Sanity Security Straps. Check out our latest Ghost Garb Gowns as our immaterial models saunter down the aisle of ancients...

I'm not no half breed book boy part paranormal player ghost gamer playing with the Pages of the Paranormal Parchments.. no i'm not some gamer reader you are meetin along the path of the Paranormal Parables.. no .. I'm the prophet of the pages.. the poet of the paranormal.. the priest upon a paper pulpit.. I'm the padre of the pages..

I'm the original ink that god used to write the ten commandments..
I'm moses and I'm the Mountain..
I am the hand that lifted you up at birth..
and I am the hand that will lower you into death

yes I am the path and the parable
the page and the stage
a pilgrim.. a prophet.. a priest
a poet.. a prince.. a pauper
and I am your prayers

Its dangerous enough to read the Paranormal Pages.. but to play in them can be deadly to one's accepted reality.

You still want some of this writer.. huh.. you want a piece of this page.. you want a part in this paragraph.. don't laugh.. the literature is laid back but watch it when it wakes.. the words get restless.. there's howling coming from the next chapter.

And a low laugh.. from some sinister sentence.. seeps thru the book's covers even though you hold them closed them tight.

Somewhere deep inside the page is a prince who cannot get out.. unless a page princess such as thee saves him by skillfully riding a serpent sentence to the center of the book's spine.. into the depths of the dialogue.. from whence came the cry.

Such is the predicament of the Paranormal Prince Poet. You say it's clever crafting.. not something real.. but what if it is.. and your concept of reality is but stories you were fed from the moment you were born. And when you die you are simply a page torn from a book.. a page upon which no one ever again will look."

Tio spun his stick staff cutting in half reality.. the snowstorm blew harder and thicker limiting vision to the horses' manes.. white horses white snow.. somewhere north of nowhere.. the temple tavern should be on the right.. on the left was a sheer drop into Oblivion Orifice.. the Orifice of Oblivion.. the Face of Forever.. also known as Ghost Gorge.. go there and yer a gonner for good..

Ghoul Gulch and Goblin Graveyard are just up ahead.. D'ya hear me.. d'ya read me clear.. Heyoka Highway Hero ?"

Then Sis spun her Story Stirrin Serpent Spoon around her body splitting space into fractals.. severing time from its tethers. Tio smiled approvingly at his student.

If a piece of the Paranormal Parable Puzzle does not fit your consciousness creation.. then cancel it and cull up another consciousness chapter card.. outta either the cereal box, bowl, cauldron, casket, sand box, satchel, trunk..

In this story you get to choose your consciousness.. collect as many as you can.. Look to the light brother.. Feed your Self.. Your Mind.. With The Light.
For what you consume is what shall grow inside you.. and that is what will grow from within you..

"Adios Angel with pink wings.. until next time our flight patterns intercept.." I said ta sis as I slid down the stairway banister.. Sis was splashing onta her face some primate piss perfume.. called.. The Face of Forever.. In a bottle that looked like a baboon's butt.

Paranormal Perfumeries supplies essences to the most glamorous ghosts and seductive spirits.. Buy a bottle of Reality Remover.. Sample our Wisdom Wines.. Bardo Brews.. Spirit Sodas.. Wraith Whiskies.. Ghost Gins.. Renegade Reality Rums.. Vision Vodkas.. and Thanatos Tequilas..

Wake up to a world you never knew existed.. one spoon of cereal.. and say so long to life as you knew it..Buy a roll of tickets and bring your family and friends.. Cause you won't wanna be alone when this game goes down in your head.. and body.. that isn't anymore.

I'm only ribbing you. Nothing is real. It's all a story I made up.. we made up.. together. We don't even exist.. You and me.. We ain't entities.. Not even anything.. We ain't.. we aren't.. we never were.. and we never will be.

We are holographic emissions.. holographs.. we are the remains of light emitted from a distant strawberry star. We were scattered here in a strawberry star storm.. holding onta heaven's hand.. And we're all heroes.. that's why we were chosen to write and sing and dance together this love song called life.

"Please pass me the butter and a knife." sis was saying to the baboon sitting on her lap licking his soup spoon.

"It's already noon and we're nowhere near the door.. it'll take for evermore before we get to school !" Dad was losing patience, and reality was losing its grip.. sip after sip of sorcerer soda.

Reader if you find you're starting to slip into this fable then simply send in the last dream you've been in and we'll send you an Interdimensionary Dialogue Dictionary. Use dialogue to dig your way out of any world.

No one climbs upon the altar without getting their wings singed. What others see of you is only the remains of reality still hanging on for dear life. A love untamed can be ours.

Hush we must talk in whispers. The Word Wraiths hear every sentence you read. Be still now. For here across the pages comes a Warrior Wind Wraith and a Wizard Wind Wraith, along with the wind that weeps for the wailing women and the wounded warriors.

In you I see.. The balance of the Buddha.. The light of the lover..
The kindness of the king.. The nobility of the knight..
The compassion of the caretaker.

Yes the world is wrought of words. Let them be wise.. worthy.. and wonder filled. The world speaks.. but not in words that most are trained to hear.

The spirit gives signs along the way what one is to do.. Spirit says.. I have a divine destiny and sacred service for you.. Now raise up your spoons all who are gathered round the Table of Truth.." And sis and i and the baboon brothers and the lavender lizard lamp light.. saluted our spirit stirrin spoons to the strawberry star storm in the sky..

Mum just threw up her spoon in the air and said she gave up.. today we wouldn't even bother going to school.. we'd sit around the table eating cereal.. seated round la Mesa de Maya.. the Mirror of the Mind.. the Mirror of Mirages..

I listened intently to our teacher Doc Chimp.. Professor Of Primal Primatology, Parables, and Paleo Prophecies.. head of the Department Of The Divine Disciplines.

"In the end it doesn't make a drop of difference cause all we are is just piss in the wind.. everyone and everything.. when viewed from a level of the life of the stars and the deaths of the dinosaurs.. it is all dream dust.. reality's rust.

Remember the warrior that isn't even there. The wind has never been beaten. The word is invinceable.. because it rises up upon every page and upon everyone's lips.

We are all dreamers.. dreaming existence into being. We can dream life into being .. or as we are doing now.. dream death into being. Dream divinely dear Dreamers of Divinity.

To get your Divinity Dreamers Degree and diploma send in five box bottoms and five fat ones for a download for your ebook.. The words.. the script.. slowly rises to the surface of the ebook screen then it slowly disappears deep within the screen, as though it had never been.

She's the daughter of desire and darkness." Big mumbled as he wiped his lips with the pink polka dot tablecloth. Another dream was about to hit the dust. "Sell her on the open market and make sure the buyer understands there's no returns on realities. Every dream has its demise. Even the devil pays his dues.."

"And yer gonna pay yurs if you don't stop swinging that spoon.. you furry fool" Sis shouted to Benny Baboon who was dancing on his kitchen stool.. in his new strawberry shoes

Poet's Plea

I am..
the Doorman to the Divine Dimensions of Delusion, Dementia, and Dreams..
I stir the Cosmic Cauldron of Creation and Chaos and Chronos.
I tether the Tigers of Terror and take the token at the Temple of Tenderness.
I undress the bandages of the broken, beaten and burnt,
and serve their flesh to the starving.
I guide the lost to love..
to the ledge of love where all leap into endless eternity.
I am the beginning and the end, of the race all run with themselves.

I am the goal and the guard blocking the gate.
I am the blood of all creation and the shit of all death.

I am the fallen and slain
the sword that slays
and the altar upon which all are slayed.

I am the divine dragon and the noble knight
the treasure and the curse that guards it
the moment passed and the moment yet to come.
I am the bought and the sold
the flesh and the spirit of all formed.

the hand of the potter and the clay of the vessel
and the bitter brew or sweet nectar stored within it.

I am your hope and your hell
your spell and the one who kisses you awake.

I am your belief and your despair.
I am everywhere
and yet you are blind to my creation and deaf to my song
which is all you see and all you hear.

I am the cry of the first born child,
and the sigh expelled by the last to die.
I am your nourishment
and that which sucks the life out of you
only to nourish another with it.

I am the rainbow and stars
and the sky upon which I paint them.

I am the dress you wear
and the flesh you bare to your beloved.

I am the thought and the thinker.
I am your wings and the bonds that bind them.

I am your slaves and the hands that enslaved them
and the hearts that set them free.
I am your starving and the hands that feed them.
I am the one all worship
and the one who worships.
I am your warships and those with whom you wage war.

I am the living and the dead
the life you love and the death you dread.

I am the written word and the one who reads.
I am the seeker and the salvation.
I am that what is lost and that what is gained.

I am the reason you come and the reason you go.
I am the mountain that is climbed and the one who climbs.
I am whatever you wish for
and that which you refuse to accept.

I am the child and the mother
your father and your brother
the sister you love
and the sister you lust after.

I am what you have forgotten, and what you have yet to remember.
I am that what you already know, and that which you never will.

I am the answers you seek and the questions you pose
your prayers and your praise
your pulpits and your prophets
your priests and your paupers
and the price you pay for the soul you sell for salvation.

I am the prostitute with whom all have lain
and the brother you have blamed.

I am the lost and the path upon which you find your way back to me.

You know me.
You know me from somewhere.. everywhere..
You've smelled my perfume in the air
tangled your fingers in my heroine's hair
lain beside me naked and bare
tasted the nectar of my lips
been reborn between my hips
found refuge in my arms
salvation in my songs
completion in my caress
seen the face of god in my smile.

You have heard my warm whispers in the wind
And have been touched by my tenderness.
Holiness is my address.

I have been the worshipper
And I have been the worshipped.

I have been the one who waited at the gates
And I have been the one waited upon.

I have been the wounded
And the warrior who wounds.

I have been a wanderer.. a wizard.. and a writer
Now I am a whisper only the wind hears
Now I am the wind.. the words you write and read.

I have hungered
I have hated
I have hunted
I have hoped
I have howled to be heard.
Now I am home in heaven.

I have been the hero,
And I have been the horror.

I have carved my name in stone
Now I am the stone whom others carve.

I have feasted upon the flesh of others.
Now I am the flesh that others feast upon.

I have followed and I have fought.
Now I am the fallen and forgotten.

I have walked in the light.
I have been lost in the dark.

I have sorrowed alongside the sighs of sisters
And ministered to the moans of men.

Once I was formed of the flesh.
Now I am the formless.

I have been the cup and the cauldron
The brew and the broth
The sacred stew and the spoon that stirs
Both the drinker and the draught.

I have been the thinker and the thought
The pen, the page, the poet,
The melody and the music..
The hands and instruments that made them
And the fingers that played them.

I have been the altar and the sacred sacrifice
The candle and the flame
The named and the nameless
The pilgrim and the path.

I have been the seed and the one who sows
The beauty and the beholder
The saviour and the saved.

I have been the judge and the judged
The jail and the jailed
The sailor that sails.. and the seas upon which you sail
And the wind which has carried you home to your heart.

I am the silence.. and the song sung by all of creation
The flute and the breath blown thru it.

I am the kiss and the lips upon which it is bestowed.
I am the deadly serpent's hiss.
And all the love you miss.

I have seen creations crumble
and the beginning be born.

I have witnessed the birth of life itself,
and I have buried death in its own tomb.

I have held the hand of time and gently guided it on its path.
I have given space a place in which to exist.

I have welcomed home to my breast the wounded
And sent out the warriors to wound.

I have been your salvation and your slayer.

I have groomed angels' wings
rode on rainbows
danced with divinity
sang with spirits
watched as the stars made love
been the warplane and the dove

I am You..."

Tio looked up from The Book.. rested his spoon against the bowl.. took off his strawberry spectacles.. adjusted his violet vision vest.. slung his shaman shawl over his broad shoulders.. leaned back in his consciousness cruising chair.. and disappeared into thin air..

leaving mum and dad and sis and me.. wondering..
              if he had ever really been there.

Breakdown in Bardho

"Thanatos Trail Traveller.. things will be better in the next bardo.." Tio lifted his goblet of Ghost Grogg and toasted the frog fanning herself with a lily pad in sis's bowl. "And for those who still don't know what a bardo is.. well get all the buzz about the biz of bein a bardo brain blaster border breaker. It's all available in the Believers' Bible which you can get for a buck in the back of the box.. hurry.. the last to run always runs outta luck.

And if you act now you will receive free of any charge.. Confessions of a Consciousness Collector . The complete manual on how to take care of your consciousness in case it get's messed with.. And it always does. Are you getting ripped off by regular reality ?

I am the cross and the crucified.
I am the seeker and that which is sought.
I am the ashes upon the altars.. where your armies and angers.. have fought.
I am the fuel of your faith.. and the fire of your fear.
I am the fools' flesh..
the saints' souls.. the buddhas' bones.. the saviours' scars.

"Son finish yer Strawberry Stars and let's hit the Reality Road.. we're overdue Consciousness Crew.. it's up to us ta save reality.. it's about ta become real unreal. Oh how creation collides with its own consciousness.. cosmic chatter collected and congealed in cranial corridors.

Rearrange the syllables and the words are different. Change the words and the sentences are different.. and thus the thought and the thinker are changed.. And the story assumes a different tale. It is your choice. So choose wisely Word Wanderer.

Between the stages of light and dark.. between the moments of existence.. and among these pages.. I have prowled.. searching for you.. as you have sought for me.

See it all started one morning when a kid pried open the cereal box top cover of coffin crunch crunchy bite sized bits of coffins and caskets breakfast cereal. All these cute little coffins and caskets floating around in the bowl of milk. Don't dare open the lids of them. Other kids have disappeared.

Somewhere in the depths of the bottomless bottom of the box of Coffins and Crucifixes Cereal.. if ya dare stick yer arm in deep enough.. you might find one of those free paranormal plastic coffins that you can wear as a charm on yer Nirvana Necklace. I hear some kids were found with the necklace tightened around their neck.. all on its own doin. All because of a cereal box that looks like a coffin.

Kid.. consider this chapter as down payment for any dozen dreams you desire. Inside each coffin is a dream, a dimension, a dementia. The coffins are doors to other dimensions. And with each box you get a Coffin Card. Collect all the coffins and caskets. Each Coffin Card comes with a Ghost Guide. But ya gotta open the lid first to release the ghost.. Most are friendly.. but a few are fiends.

Again we have entered a page where the diction is dark and dirty. The fantasy fatally frightful. No this fable ain't for the faint."

Tio rubbed his elbow round and round on the tabletop until it shone. There in the table I could see the cosmos. Desire was drunk on the divine.. destiny was deep in a dream.. reality was in decline.

"See kid.. digging up dialogue is my job as a Spirit Scribbler.. a scientist of sorts.. a seeker of stories.. and sometimes they aren't what anyone really wants."

Then the Toad at the Table of Tales folded up his Tale Trunk and said .. "You've drunk enough dialogue today." Tio was having a bit of a problem squeezing the Paranormal Parchment Pages back inta the trunk. The trunk was a Doorway into the Den of Dialogue.. into the Tunnels of Thanatos Tales.

There are so many entrances into eternity.. so few ways out.

Then I heard a distant sweet voice shout.. "Prince of the Primates please pass yer simian sis the toast." Then Sis hopped up onto the toast and started to coast out the back door headed to school situated south of somewhere and north of nowhere.

"Don't forget your Spirit Sweater.. woven from the Threads of Time and the Fabric of Forever.. honey." "Mum yer always on the money." I muttered.

And me.. Well you'll find me hitch hiking beside you along the Heyoka Highway. Just call me Heyoka Joe.. Apache Angel.. You're about to become a Heyoka Highway Hero.. You pass this course and I guarantee you'll graduate as a ghost.

I heard god was hanging out in his headquarters.. Heaven.. when he got a call from the devil down in Hell's Hole. "We're runnin outta space for sinners. Can we send some up to you ?"

Psst.. are you lookin for a crucifiction fix ?
Does crucifiction mean fiction was crucified by fact ?
Hey we're all pilgrims upon the path of purification.
One's tears water another's gardens.

Listen up kid. If yer gonna apply for Angel Ascension Academy you better get some Angel Apparel. Here take this pair of wings. They're somewhat worn but they'll work. Yer studying to be the angel who will ring the bell at the wedding of heaven and hell.

Look kid.." the serpent sitting on the stool at the school of fools said.. as the sentences slithered offa his tongue. "These are only Swamp Stories to scare you into the arms of the beloved waiting to embrace you as her betrothed."

Then Evermore turned to Nevermore sittin at the table and said.. "Let's settle this score forever. Some taste the nectar and let it flow. Some never know their own love's glow.

The minute each of us is born we're diggin our own graves.. some of us dig faster.. some dig slower.. but we all dig. Everyone eventually kneels at the Altar of Adversity.. Existence is a university."

Then someone unseen passing by the Table of Fables whispers. "Psst.. kid.. ya wanna purchase some Angel Adrenalin. If ya mainline it yer gonna be on the fast track to graduation." Yes there were all kinds of nocturnal noises passing thru the Texts of the Tavern of Thanatos.. parchment pages inhabited by The Paranormal.

The Prof of the Paranormal threw his Field Book of Phantoms onta his desk and said "That's it for today's class kids.. remember you are the poetry of love.. the wings of angels.. and the keys to heaven's gate.

Tonight's homework is on the Angel Artifacts found in the Tomb of Thanatos in the Valley of Victims.. Start with the quote.. "I found the forearm bone of our ancestor the angel, Adam." After reading the chapter write a five hundred word essay on whether adam was an angel or an ape.

Class dismissed." Said Doc Divinity said as he swung over the students across the room on the overhead ropes lookin like vines and then out thru the window and down the vine covered stone wall from his fourth floor classroom to his four wheeler waiting beside the old stone building that housed the Not So Natural Sciences Department of the College of Creation.

"You too can enroll in the Angel Ascension Academy where you'll study Angel Antiquities.. Angel Archeology,.. Angel Aviation.. Angel Altar Assembly.. and Angel Anthropology. Just fill out the enrollment form on the inside of the box of cereal and send it in to the Department of Divinity. Mark it to the attention of the Allmighty. That way you'll get preferential treatment, pal."

Big leaned his bulk over the table and said, it's only a fable.. some sidewalk talk.. call it cafe conversation, son.. Road Rapp.. just havin fun with fantasy. Don't get yerself caught in the crossfire between fiction and fact.

It's just some societal story scribbled on the side of a box of cereal.. another class in Paranormal Philosophy."

Then Big crumpled up the Address of the Angel.. and as quickly as the writer wrote her inta the story.. the writer wrote her out. She was just another consequence of the chapter.. a collection of thoughts scribbled onta a piece of paper.. an ending to a story that never really started.

She shoulda listened to the warning of the words when they said.. "Stay Outta This Story.. Dangerous Dialogue.. This literature is off limits to the reader.. it's only for the characters in the story.. your time in this tale is terminated.. this chapter is closed to all of creation.. Yer in the wrong world.. reading the wrong words.. stumbling along sentences in a story where you ain't welcome.. Ya.. I've seen many a reader get wacked by the words.. done in by the diction.. fooled by fiction..

"Look here young man, I am slaving in this kitchen ta get yer breakfast ready so you can get to school on time and your aren't even in time anymore. Empty yer spoon inta yer mouth, and move it my main monkey man." Mum said it precisely as the paranormal writer wrote it.

Word Walker

"It's tough bein' a hero for Heaven.. holding Hell's Hand ta get it thru the dark Dreams of Destiny. You wanna be a hero ?" The side of the Cereal Box asked.

"To be a hero you gotta do the Hero's Homework. In the box, you get the Hero's Handbook, Hero's Hardware.. no sissy software for you big Buddy of the Book. And after a hard day travellin the Hero's Highway helping out the hopeless you get a private room at the Hero's Hotel. It's the hard way, but yer a hard case Consciousness Cruiser, kid. Someone's gotta save the story from a bad ending.

Here let's set yer scene. God is gone. The devil stands alone armed with society's angst. Bravery has broken down. Only fear and confusion prevail. Hell is for hire. Heaven has been put on hold.

This is where the great Saviour's Sacrifice is an option you have to decide to take or leave. Ya.. Find a cross of your choice and watch how the pilgrims will wear the path down smooth to yer grave. The priests will pray, and the worshippers will scatter yer ashes upon the Altar of the Last Almighty to hold sway over the minds of the remains of man.

Oh thirsty soul, drink from my lips. Quench your thirst for love upon my breast. I am the maiden of madness, the wholesale whore, the divine dove.
Reach out your hand to me dearest Pilgrim of the Page. Feel my silky velum, stained and saturated with the ink of ages of sages' sweat and poets' tears.

Each pilgrim in their turn has cried out, "Oh lord how I have died seeking your sacred embrace. Oh lord how I have tried to encounter your eternal face.. following every trace.. every trail.. to feel a touch of your divine grace. No longer deny me your holy heaven. The stars dance to your song. The day and night vie with each other to be your lasting lover."

"Hey brother would ya please pass me the Paranormal Pudding." Babajoe Baboon bent over his bowl and looked at the swirling stars. Centuries existed in a spoon of pudding. Universes unfold in a drop of dew falling from a petal to a blade of grass.

Love's patina coats and glistens all of existence.. "For instance.. as I was saying.." Doc chimp tried ta continue the lecture. "Deep within the Bowels of the Box are found the Raspberry Reality Ruby Rocks and the Strawberry Sapphire Spirit Seeker Stones and the Blueberry Bardo Boulders and also the Cherry Cosmic Consciousness Creator Comet Chunks.

Collect the whole set of these Precious Paranormal Plastic Power Pieces and you will own the world you wake up in. And with each spoonful you take, of these cereals, you will wake up in another one. Hold onta yer hats and yer heads.

"Look kids I don't know where yer heads are but get yer hats on and head to the car. School is callin, and reality is fallin." Dad said as he disappeared out the back door. He had a class to give on how to live a life of love.

"Bite me once and I shall become the beast all fear to see.
Invite me into your heart and I shall be divine beauty.
Pilgrim of peace.. you have sought.. and thou you are weak.. still you seek.. something invisible.. such as you will one day be.

May these Pages of Prayers and Pleas and Praise be a sanctuary for your souls, weary readers. I am the wine divine.. the feast fulfilled.. the altar and the wooden cross.. and the wood with which the sacred fire consumes your eternal sacrifice.

I am the offering you hesitantly place at the foot of the divine.
I am the flaming sword that denied your entrance into paradise.
I am the light held aloft to guide you home to me.
I will leave no one behind. All shall come to me, for all came from me.

Class are you listening to me.. If you will closely notice.. the strange inscriptions on the surface of the stone altar appear to have been carved by a strong sharp object.. something that was strong enough to carve deep enough into a type of stone that is harder than any stone we now know of.

Perhaps a lazer or an alien tool.. but notice how it almost seems in some places that the scrawll is scratchings.. like that made by claws.. talons.. of some big beast.

What is also interesting.. though almost invisible.. is that the altar top has a separation line all around it.. as though it were a lid.. and the rest of the altar is a box.. Yes the altars found inside the Paranormal Pteradactylian Pyramid are caskets.. containing inside the Saurian Scribes' remains. And it is these dried parchment like Saurian Skins tattooed with the tale you read.. that you will find in the deepest bottoms of the Cereal Boxes.. for they are the altars..

yes the Cereal Boxes are the Altars of the Ascended..

Wake not the Sleeping Saurians.. for though they appear as bones clothed tightly in dried parchment like robes tatooed in strange saurian scribblings.. they are not dead They are Dreaming the World. Yesss.. their dreams.. are the world we live in.. dear friend.. follower of the Fable of Forever."

Tio Tulku Temple Toad Teller of the Tale placed his warty earthen hands upon the Turning Table and folded his fingers together. "Class over.. another completed Consciousness Chapter.. in the Tavern of Time.. the Tabernacle of Theos. Now put yer spoons down and off ta school with ya.. make yer parents proud.."

Everything you have read is true.. only the names and places have been changed to protect the Privacy of the Paranormal. The literature may not be held liable for any loss of reality

"Wake up the World with love.." were the words with which mum would always send us off to school every morning. "Act as thou you were an altar for every angel to alight upon and ascend from. Always for everyone you see.. a Sacred Sanctuary you shall be. We are the Breath of the Beloved."

Notice how the syllables cast shadows over the empty parts of the page. The words stand tall.. forming walls that weave high above the parchment pages as thou the actual page itself was lost deep below.. hidden by the mist swirling around the tall Winding Wall of Words.

It is The Way Out Of Reality.. Do not fall off the Wall of Words. The descent is endless into the Mists of the Manuscript from where out of, these words arose. Words awakened by your wish.. Word Whisperer.

This is where yer Angel Ascenscion Arsenal will come in useful..

"Nirvanna is non negotiable." Tio the Teacher Toad.. Teach for short.. Tank for tough.. leaned back as he took two teaspoons of Strawberry Star Storm Story Sugar and placed it into his cup of Tale Tea. It looked like a storm was swirling in his spoon. Then Teach the Tank continued.

"Remember, Reality is Recyclable, no point in wasting the world."

Meanwhile, the not so tender, Baboon Bartender.. was sweeping up the Remains of Realities' Debris that littered the false floor of the Tavern of Time. Should you yourself wish to become a member of the Butoh Baboons Book and Broom and Brew Brotherhood or the Simian Sisters Story Saloon Sacred Sweepers Society.. send in the sides of the Cereal Box soon as you buy it. There is a time limit.. an expiry date.. on everything.. including you.

We'll send you a Bardo Broom to sweep away any sulking spirits littering your living space.. dirtying up your death.

Tio the Toad leaned over and opened the lid of his Travellin Tales of Time Trunk and there inside were all the trails time ever took or ever would.. writhing like serpents. "Alright which one do ya want. You won yerself another trail. Here look, this one is slitherin outta the trunk up onta the table straight at you.. must be your time.

Better believe it.. belief is hard to come by, when ya don't even exist. We're all baptized by birth and death. Oh kind and noble knight on an eternal endeavor.. you have had to make fire by rubbing your hands together and using your own flesh for fuel. You have traveled thru unfettered space and immortal time.. observing eternity, exploring existence."

"For instance.. Take this decanter of Dream Drops." Big said as he lifted up the bottle of Wisdom Wine. "So appropriately labelled Rattlesnakes' Revenge.. Not as quick acting as the other one labeled Viper Vision Venom.. from the fangs of the Vision Venom Viper.. found in the Valley of Victims.. concealed behind the Veil of Visions.

It's okay folks.. we're just keepin it unreal.. with The Company Committed to Creating Consciousness with the flip of a page.. fabricating the formless into the formed.. the immaterial into matter.. the wind into words.

Don't freak out.. Friend of the Fable.. It's just the paranormal passing thru the portal.. infiltrating the normal. Interesting how one word will start a sentence.. that will wake up a whole world."

With those words Tio yelled to the Bardo Bartender "We'll have another round of reality.. and send a bottle of Bardo Brew over to the other table for my Book Buddies.. the Ninjas of Nothingness.. Spirit Samurais.. slithering silently thru the shadows cast by the sentences..

One swipe of the sword and reality is severed in two. One stroke of the Paranormal Pen upon the page.. and a story is brought to life.. while another ends.

Which one you enter is up to you. Everyone swims in the Societal Stew.. some like sharks.. some like saints.. Observe how even now waiting in eager anticipation, clinging with their claws to the top edges of these pages.. Bardo Book Buzzards are peering over the Paranormal Precipice.. at you.. Pal of the Paranormal Pages.

A word of warning courtesy of the words.. Do not go anywhere inside or outside of this book without your Cereal Spoon.. it also serves as a Story Scribbler.. Ya you can rewrite yer own sweet story in strawberry syrup that squirts outta the spoon everytime you squeeze the appropriate controller button..

This Divine Dimensionary Device is the fabled Cosmic Controller.. You can control consciousness and the cosmos.. The Cosmic Reality Remote Controller comes in selected Cereal Boxes with instructions included in cards you pull outta the cereal.. if you can.. cause they pull back.. and have pulled other Page Pilgrims in.

You might wish to bring along in your Spirit Survival Reality Rations Suitcase of Stories.. an extra dose of Death Dust.. and an extra vial of Vision Venom.. the first comes from the Desert of the Dead and Dying.. and the second is found in the Phantom Fangs of the Vision Venom Vipers found in the Valley of Victims..

Don't say this fantasy never gave you a fighting chance to make it thru the chapters safely thru your consciousness.."

Sis was pulling on my sleeve.. "What about dressing up the Toad in a dress for the party.. mum won't mind.." Somewhere in the distance I heard myself replying.. "Have you lost your mind ?"

Dearest Reader.. if any of this sounds familiar.. like you've read this before.. been here before.. please know that this is a sign.. you and the Book are becoming one. The story is inside you.

Buddha's Begging Bowl

The question class is.. does time stretch on forever.. or does it exist as one space in which all is unfolded ? Does space encompass all there is ? Where is space situated ? Is all of time contained in one space ? Are time and space two words describing the same cosmic concept ?

The Fabric of Reality is woven of many layers. Some of those threads are faith.. some fantasy.. some fiction.. and a few are fact. Thus so easily does the Fabric of Reality come unraveled. Time for all of us to pull out our sewing kits and string all souls back together again.. into the Necklace of Nirvana.. Nirvana's Net.

If you and I can feel the pain.. why can't we feel the love ?
Who has knitted nirvana out of nothing ?
Who was the Weaver of the World ?
Who has woven this wonder ?

Questions that cannot be answered by the cranium.. but only with the heart.
Can everything be contained, light, sound, space, time. ? Does Time goes on forever ? Is Time never ending ? Was there a time when Time was born ? And if so.. when was that.. And will there come a time when Time ceases to exist ?

On the other hand.. if time was never born..
then either time has existed forever and always will..
or time does not exist..
For nothing can exist unless it has been brought into existence..
and if it was.. who or what gave birth to time ?

Did time create itself.. if so maybe time is god.. And then what is space.. time's mate.. the goddess ? Time and space are married.. wedded.. woven together. With the Threads of Time is woven the Linen of Life.

If time is everywhere.. then there is only one all encompassing time..
or perhaps there are many times.. all children of the first time..
Are we.. is everything you see.. the children of space and time..
mating in a never ending embrace ?

Perhaps there is no time but now.. An Eternal Now..
one space one time.. one cosmic kiss.. one ever unfolding bliss..
Are Space and Time The Enchanted Children of the Cosmos..
Is not every being.. an Enchanted Child of the Cosmos..

The words are only Visionary Vocabulary.. Controversial Conversation. The formless fabricating the formed.. the mind manufacturing the material. From outta the formless.. is formed all form.. a feast upon which all feed.. forever unfolding.. like a fable without end..

We are sacred seeds of the soul.. sown in the soil of our own toil.

Okay class.. next we'll discuss the ritual of slowing down into Sacred Space. We'll discuss deliverance, desire, denial, dissolution, and the sacred Fire of Faith, and how to stay serene when the scene gets mean.

First a word of advice.. most humans are paranoid of the paranormal. There is no need to be. That's correct. There is no need to be.. in a body. But how to extricate oneself.. and still be.. but without a body.. that is another story.

We interrupt this thought process of yours reader for a moment to give your mind a mental break. Opinions are the opiates of all organisms. We live in the dharma of drama.. so here is some.

Picture this scene occurring in a french hotel room somewhere on the cheap side of town. He's sittin on the bed still disheveled from a night of nocturnal nirvana. He's a riviera romeo with a stilleto moustache dyed dark as a dead casino mark found between two pages in a story he never should have opened. She is dressed in tight red flames.. and as she walks out the door.. never to be seen again.. she says.. "Mon Amour.. our dance has been a divine detour."

The Wisdom and Wonder of the World of Words Workshop.. with the Wraith Writer.. at the Sacred Spirit Script Studio of the Story Sorcerer Shaman.. is available for free as chapters on the inside of the walls of every cereal box that talks..

Enter an eternal tale told thru a cosmic cereal box that sits on yer table and talks and sings so you will never be alone with your mind again.. Now all you need to do is finish yer Syllable Stew and then you can hop onta a slice of Tio's Time Travellin Toast,Taco, or Tortilla.. and head off deeper into the tale of your own truth.

All that remains are the memories of our moments.. the movies of our minds. "Kids.. remember your Lizard Lunch Boxes.. and be on the alert for that Alley Alligator.. the cute Curb Crocodile.. the Saurian Sewer Saint.. that ain't but yer own imagination begging for a bite of yer Strawberry Star sandwich." Then mum packed us off ta school with a smile.

Collect the complete Collection of Consciousness Chapters. Inside every box comes a Consciousness Collector Card. The more you have, the more proficient a Renegade Reality Rider you will become.

Get a doctorate in demonology, or in designing dreams and developing dementias. These diplomas come in the home study course contained in the cereal. And as a bonus for signing up with the cereal receive one free Crucifiction Fix.. along with the crucible and cauldron and coffin and claw.. which scrawlled the syllables into the cereal box walls, down which you are endlessly tumbling thru time.. spinning thru space.. forever.

"You will never get to school on time at this rate." Mum was irate cause we was real late for the fate we was supposed ta be fabricating along with the rest of society.

"Pour me another.. make it a double. I'm in the mood for trouble. I'm an angel afflicted with a divine disease." drooled the Serpentine Silurian Saurian swivellin on the stool at the Bardo Bar. "Give me another double dose drink of Devil's Disease.. the divine destroyer of stories. I wanna forget the future before it ever arrives."

Meanwhile over in the corner Easy Eddie was easin the slug inta the chamber while Fast Freddie and Forthright Frankie were philosophizing with Juju Jimmy about the source of forever and how satan was seduced by god inta doin his dirty work.

"The Seduction of Satan and the Downfall of the Devil can be downloaded direct thru yer cereal Bardo Begging Bargaining Bowl, Beautiful." The Saloon Serpent said, as she slithered into the bowl disappearing into its depths.

Sis pulled out a set of cards with appropriately named titles.. time talks for the first time telling all.. very virtuous soul seeks asylum in someone... consciousness is a collective collusion.. the soul's scriptures.. The list is endless.. as is life.. in some form or another.

"We ourselves are the armies of armageddon. It shall not be Alien Angels' armies from another dimension that will do us in. It will be humans that lay waste to this woeful world we have woven.

Just follow the fine line.. feline.. and sign on the bottom of the box.. that opens the door to your dreams. Brought to you by Think Ink Inc. The Consciousness Company committed to your cranium, kid.

Okay who's the Dime store Demon Paranormal Prankster who stuck this note up on the fridge.. "God was here, had lunch, and left me with the bill."

Oh Sweet Sacred.. you have sown your seeds upon my fertile ground.. and drenched me with Divine Desire. We are all saints in sinners' clothes. Open up your temple doors I have come here to praise your perfection.

The sentences sigh.. the words writhe.. the manuscript moans. The devil is in despair.. god is gone.. satan is suicidal.. the suffering is so deep. Must the story be filled with such sorrow ?

Harry the Hand and Frankie the Foot.. were waiting with Tony the Toe and Freddie the Finger.. for what seemed like an eternity.. for Love ta show up. She was late.

Ya you wait for a woman's soft voice ta sooth the pain. Like notes from a solo sax.. the memories linger somewhere just beyond your grasp. You wish it were all fiction.. some hollywood fable.. instead of hard fact.. feeling like the muzzle of a gun.. ice cold against your forehead. And then you hear her tender voice.. only thing is.. she's holdin' the gun.. while whispering to you "no one's won."

She had been stumbling around in the relics of realities long gone when she found me.. one of destiny's debris. She was hungry for a hero. I told her everything was gonna be alright.. but not at my expense. Like a bug pinned to a poster.. she was caught in The Nexus of Nowhere and Nothing.

The first words to come out of her moist mouth were "Are you the demon I dread.. or the angel I have come to wed ?" I replied.. "I am a warrior without weapons.. a wanderer without a way."

Again she whispered.. "I have come here to pray at your altar. I am consciousness unconfined. I am a temple temptress.. a spirit stalker. You and I are the evidence of eternity making love in the Cathedral of Creation." Then she sipped ever so elegantly from her crystal glass another shot of Dragon Drool Interdimensionary Drink.

Somehow the sadness seeps into the veins.. fills the heart. "No.." I told her.. "I never wanted to become a saint. I mean everybody becomes something.. a sinner.. a saviour.. a slayer.. a sacrifice.. sooner or later.. in life.. or in death."

She sighed in a way that made my world tremble. She spoke in a way my mind could not comprehend.. but my soul understood. "Darkness asked Light.. Why do you wanna be seen? Light replied to the darkness.. Why do you prefer to remain hidden.. for in truth I am you uncovered.. awakened from your dream.. illuminating all as love.

Yes the Lord of Light is Love. The same and the one.. there is no other for we are each other." Then on her way out she said.. "Well if you aren't gonna come into my dream.. would you mind leaving the door open for the next dreamer." Then she disappeared thru the Door of Nevermore.

The distance between your heartbeat and mine is but a sigh. We have fallen before as the sacred sacrifice.. and risen as the anointed one. With the first wound the warrior is awakened. With the first word the writer is born.. the story is started.

Lemme tell ya a quick tale." the serpent stuttered from bein sloshed on Serpent Spit Soda. He mumbled something about two characters from a french romantic novel.. Frankie Forever and Annie Anytime.. both doing time in their own minds. Then he laid his scaly head down on the bar and sobbed.

"Oh we're all parisien poets drowning our sadness in romantic wine and sweat drenched nights of passion.. until we are oblivious to everything but the lyrics of love.. the voice that calls us home to our self. We are the gift that is offered to each other.

I never pay parking fines.. I only read between the lines.. drink the finest of wines.. sleep on satin sheets.. hang out where dark and light meets. Just a little rhyme of mine.." the stool serpent hissed.. then kissed Sis on the forehead before he fell onta the floor.. lying there looking like one of Dad's colourful climbing ropes.

Lord's Lament

Big was reading the script like someone else had written him into it. "See reality is not what it ever was. It too is evolving. Just as each one of us and our simian society has over the generations evolved.. into an ape that is artistic.. innovative.. and at times angelic.. so reality also evolves.

Any paradise you prefer we can produce. Paradise Producers and Procurers are proud to present.. Paradise Unleashed.. The new movie series by the same old story scribbler.. Saint Satan.

Yes Saint Satan got a bum rap. Satan started out as a saint. Some say an angel. Well in those days you had to first become a saint before you could become an angel. Kinda like you evolve into a higher plane of being. Some say that many a saint was actually an angel.. come back to teach us simpler simians something spiritual and saintly.

I am as I stated earlier for legal, moral, and financial purposes severing all my ties with Satan Soda Shop franchises Inc. And I am selling off all my investments in Satan Stocks. From now on I just invest in light. Motion deserves to rest when it is fatigued."

Big leaned closer to More.. confiding everything he had kept hidden from heaven and hell. "I had no idea we were gonna get this involved intellectually.. discussing death.. divinity.. duty.. desire.. and the discipline it takes to put into practice the parable of profiteering in the paranormal.

Some would say I was a pirate from the paranormal. I would raid both realities.. the normal and the paranormal. And the prize was always mine. But now those jewels no longer shine for me like treasure. I have left behind the fleshly form.. consciousness as you the body and I the brain used to know it when we were together.

I have become an unknown wind that just briefly brushes the breast like a skipped heartbeat. Maybe we are but the whispers of our dreams.

There is only one path for a pilgrim pure. The path of praise and prayer.. in prose and poems. It's given to you.. To each of us.. A gift.. Do you understand.. Life was given. Life is a gift.. Given to each and every being. All is a gift given by life itself.. Yes life is the giver and the gift.

The old saying that two heads are better than one.. Two hearts similarly so.. A universal communal collection of consciousnesses could change the cosmos.. rewrite the world.

I thank you all for our exchanges of words.. our thoughts.. our communications out of our cranial cauldrons.. We each have our own cranial cosmos/ cranial cauldron. And in it we stir up our scenes, our scripts, our stories, our concepts, our communications.. and our communities.

Imagine the awesome power of joining cranial cosmos's. The combined communal consciousness would exponentially create wisdom on a worldly level."
Big was saying the words.. but he knew someone or something else had written them.

"Student of the sentences you have walked far along The Way of The Words. You have held the hand of the invisible. Do you get the feeling there is something alive.. not quite like you.. looking at this page at the same time as you do ? Only you can't see it.. You aren't even aware of it except sometimes late at night when yer reading these words and something brushes your shoulder. Something that I have become.

You can call me a ghost writer. The unknown person who does the writing for some celebrity. And you never know the name of the person. Never know who it is. Well that's me.. a paranormal person.. a real ghost writer.. the unknown paranormal.

I am unrobed of my fleshly form. Though non material I may be.. I am not immaterial. I am a master of the manuscript. I am the word. The written wisdom of the world. I am unfettered by form. Words.. descriptions.. cannot contain me. Unlike you I am not bound by a body. I am bare of bones and uncloaked by flesh.

I am that same part of you that is spirit. A concept you can't quite get your mind around.. something you haven't got figured out in your consciousness. Whereas I am pure mind.. consciousness complete and uncontained.

Wouldn't it be scarey.. if you were all it is. Like the whole universe existed only in your own consciousness. Everyone else and everything else is really just existing in your mind. Where and what is your mind ? With words we weld the world together.

But why should I continue on. I doubt even you who pen these words for me.. understand what I am saying. Listen carefully. Still yourself writer. Put down the pen dear poet. Take your hand away from the keyboard.

This is between you and me only. No written words. Just listen writer.. and never tell another. Never write a word of this. No reader shall ever read it. Tell everyone it was passed down to you by the wind. Even if they think you are insane.. or god.. you are neither.

I am both, and all. So listen well. The world is a well thru which all forms funnel into the formless. From out of the formless is formed the forms of all future.

The present never is.. as it immediately becomes the past. Only the future has a chance of landing in your grasp. So travel onward.. where the stairway of angels' white wings lead.

Writer, I am the word, the world, everything ever wrought or rendered. I am reality in all the forms it has ever incarnated into. Incarnate means to enter into the flesh.. to enter into material form. I am every word and every writer.

Energy is always forever forming novel forms.. and forever dissolving thru the formless.. as it transforms into the next form. I have no attachment to body as you do because I am every body. I am every embodied entity and I am everything you cannot be aware of.

I am the ultimate Cauldron of Consciousness. I am the Cosmic Cauldron. I am the cosmos, the host of you and everything else in existence. For i am the vessel of existence. My moments are your millenias.

I am the inspiration for your epic struggles to become conscious, closer to me, and yet you are already within me.

So worthy writer.. tell them a story.. and weave in these words.. so no one will know it is true that you spoke with a ghost, God's Ghost. It was written by a real Ghost Writer.. a Wraith Writer. Make it cute and funny so the message is easier to swallow. Sweeten the story with a sacred spell. Use words warm and wise, sentences soft and seductive. Use the Language of Love.

Ever hear of a werewolf ? Well I'm a WereWriter, one that isn't real in your world.. but very very real in any world it wants to be. In the world of words.. some words are more worrisome and some more warrior like. Some are wise.. and some are words of wonder and worship.

Some words bravely wander on alone, creating a path thru the blank pages. A path for others.. like you Dear Reader.. to follow.. to find your way home to me.. your soul.

The chapters are choosey about who gets where in the story. If you weren't considered cool by The Book, you could get dealt a sentence to sidetrack you.. or even an abrupt ending to get you out of the story.. or maybe some chapter filled with dank and dark dialogue that could haunt yer life forever, until some story super saviour surfed onto the page upon a sweet sentence.. offering sanctuary for you, from the previously savage script.

If you weren't ready for The Book, it wouldn't open its covers for you, in fact you would not even know it existed.

These chapters.. and these pages.. have a tendency to rearrange themselves.. so that each reader gets the story he or she seeks. This Wraith Writer Spirit Scribe will write your story any way you wish it. I can rewrite your life. I have had much experience in creating people's lives.

Call me a genie in a book.. a World Wizard.. a Story Sorcerer. Rub the pages the wrong way and you get lost in the literature.. sticky language. Read the right words and you win the world you want.

You and me.. we work together.. weave together the world you want with words. I will share with you the secret of how to recreate reality, in the image you imagine. Not only shape shifting of your body.. but shape shifting of your world.

This leads to a question. Is your world created by you ? Therefore only you exist ? Or are you and your world created by another.. one other than you ? A being not you.. And if so.. what is your true relationship to the other ?

I am the other and I am you. And I am everyone's and everything's world.

I do not have the same quandary as you. My search is much deeper than yours. I the universe.. am trying to determine where I came from. For in my consciousness.. I have always been.. and always will be.. and am all that is.

But what if I am mistaken.. and there is something within which.. I the universe.. the universal consciousness.. exist.. in a space so vast.. not even god /goddess himself herself.. could conceive of.. let alone conceive it ?

Am I the conception of the cosmos ? Did I.. the cosmos.. conceive myself ? I do not know who my parents are. I the universe.. all you can conceive of.. do not know what I am.. nor from where I came.. or if I always was.. and always will be.

Will there come a day when god will die ? If so who will mourn me ? You humans call me infinite and eternal.. but I have begun to doubt that. So please search somewhere else for a god as great as you say I am. For I.. your god of all.. so also does yearn.. for someone to whom I can pray.. someone to who I can turn in my times of terror and loss of trust in life.

Love's Glow

"Your god seeks another god. A god for god. And why not. Just as a human has need of someone to turn to.. why cannot a god.. have need of.. a god.. someone greater than himself.. to give faith and sustenance.. in time of doubt and diminishment."

Once more you're runnin with the pack of paragraphs. Followin' the paragraphs wherever they prowl.. you and a pack of Paranormal Paragraph Panthers. You reader are part of the primal pack of page prowllers.

It's a gruesome song when the Word Wolves howl.. the Sentence Serpents slither across the page. Sly syllables seduce an unwary reader with tales of treasures.. impossible to find in fact.. but in fantasy everything is possible.

Come live with me in fantasy. Leave behind your cruel hard lover fact. Fantasy is where we can fly.. as angels with wings whirring. You are my love and I am your bride. This Book is your Beloved.. the Ghost your Groom. Ya you reader.. are the Bride of the Book.. wedded to the Spook Scribe. I said I was a Ghost Writer.. a real one.

So once more you're runnin with the pack.. headin home after huntin heartache and sorrow. Sounds like a song coming from the radio on the far side of the ridge above the fridge.. in some kitchen that wasn't any less real than you or me.

Why do you hold yourself back from caressing me.. as I know you want so badly to. You take me everywhere. You sleep with me. We have become inseparable."

And the next thing I knew, Sis was kissing The Book's covers while whirling round the kitchen. For sure we are not gonna get to school on time anytime today.

Big hefts the book in his mitt.. says "Ya this'll do. I don't care outta who's mind it grew.. ghost or otherwise. The guy's witty and wise.. We'll win the world with these words.. Make an offer the invisible will have to accept."

Big had the body of a beast.. the mind of a man.. and a heart hoping for a home. Ya we're all hearts hoping for a home.. heroes headed for heaven.

"Sing me one sweet song so my heart will soar. Strum my soul's strings. You are all that love brings. You are my saint.. my saviour.. my sword.. my lord. The last face I want to look upon when I die.. and the first when I am born again.."
So sadly the song was sung by an invisible spirit coming thru the Juju Juice Joint Jukebox in the Trixstir's Tavern on the other side of Reality's Ridge.

"Do not bother to fasten seat belts. They will quickly come undone" "Hmmm" Big said as he turned The Book in his hand, "strange thing to say on the first page intro."

"We are all divine dreamers.
Let love lead the way.
We are all one family.. in one bed.

Become an Artist of the Alphabet. Sculpt syllables into sentences. Sway society with your perfect phrasing.. purring paragraphs.. pert punctuation. Become a Wizard in The Way of The Word. Become a Word Walker.. a Reality Rapper. Say it like it is. Write it like it was and will be. Find the corner of creation where creativity sleeps.. and wake it.. Word Walker.

Instructions are to be found inside every box of Truth Talker Tea. That's not ever to be mistaken for Toad Twig Tea. No No that will turn you into me." Uncle Tio winked at Big like he was admiring himself in a mirror. And then mumbled something about "Fear is a fierce furnace. It consumes everything.

Along with The Word Walker Workbook.. you get the first chapter of The Wisdom of Words. The Word Wizard's Workbook has a wealth of words that when strung into sentences create spells any Syllable and Sentence Sorcerer would be proud to see in print.

The Spell Sorcerer's Society membership card entitles you to certain privileges.. such as passing thru paranormal portals within the pages.. seeing parts of the story regular readers never will.. seeing what is invisible.. hearing what is unheard.. by the human herd.

And as if that is not enough to find in Tio's Tea Trunk .. you'll receive another treasure.. jewels.. Juju Jewels.. The Jade Jaguar Jewel of Joy. Instant anything.. eternal everything.. rub it against your forehead.. feel the force of faith as it surges thru your chakras energizing every nadi.. till your cells vibrate with light.."

Tio Taco aka Tony Tortilla, was turning into the juke box as he was talking. Then the next song came on..

"The Luminance of Love's Light.. glowing.. emitting from your face and form..
such that every face and form you behold glows equally as pure and divine..

The light shining out from within these pages.. illuminates every reader's face..
These pages are portals.. into a place where prayer and praise play in peace

A paradise planet made of granite and god dammit.. if it hurts another being.. don't need it.. don't eat it.. don't beat it.. don't bite it.. don't burn it..

Let's bury the war hatchets and light matches of love in every heart..

Light The Lamps of Love.. Light Love's Lamp..
Light the Lamps of Love's Light all around The Planet..
All around the Globe.. let love glow..

Light the lamps of love's light.. Light them so the whole world glows..
Light them so everyone knows..
The light of love's glow..

Light love's lamp so the whole world glows..
With the light of love
Let everyone know..
The light of love's glow..

Let it show.. love's glow.. so all shall know..
the light of love's glow..

From your face and from your form
Let love's glow show

Soak your soul in love's glow..
Soak every soul in love's glow.."

The song of encouragement ringing outta the radio atop the fridge was givin sis an me the strength to climb above the Ridge of Reality and see what was a possibility. "Is there any possibility that you kids might get to school some time in some reality ?" Mum politely murmured like a soft breeze.

"May every thought thought.. every sound spoken.. every movement made..
Be blessings for all beings.. incarnate and discarnate..
May every word written.. be such that every sentence is a sacred song..
Sung to everyone.. for all time..
With Love.. Reality can be a Raspberry Rhyme..

Think of it this way.. god and goddess our magnificent mum and delight filled dad.. are glad they had us as kids..

And for our birthday gifts.. in the year 2012.. we all.. everything.. will start radiating such pure ethereal luminance that everyone and everything will appear as pure light.. radiating out into each other as a multitude of facets of The Jewel of Joy..

Yes existence is a Jewel of Joy.. more precious than any diamond or red ruby or eternal emerald.. What are these when compared with beings of pure light..

Everyone you behold.. a being of light..
glowing with the light of love's glow..

a cosmic light show.. the light of love's glow.. all over you..
let it show.. let the whole world know.. the light of love's glow.

Every being is a being of pure light.. emitting love's glow.. entities of pure energy.. ethereal eternal entities.. you an me.. that's right.. you and me.. eternal entities..

All you see.. All that be.. eternal.. and bearing such love and compassion as the one who created the clouds and the rain that come from the sky..

goddess/god.. most gracious gardener..
You have so graced this green garden with groves and glades..
noble knights and mighty maids.. mums and dads.

Kids calling out to adults.. Slow down dads.. yer drivin so bad.. this planet's parachute is ripping.. reality's bad trippin..

Free fallin thru space for an eternal time..
Eternally floating thru heaven..
Drifting thru dreams of delight
Lit with the glow of love's light
Lit with the glow of love's lamps
Allow them to shine

Light the world with love's glow
Let the whole world know
The light of love's glow

Light them so brightly.. the whole world glows.. with the light of love's glow."

"And that lizards ladies and lizard lads and gator gals and gator guys..
is the numero uno cancion around the country.. "Love's Glow".

Yup.. the glow of love is what this raspberry reptile radio reality rapper renegade ridge rider is all about... Love's Glow... let it show.. on the strawberry star storm numero uno station for sacred songs and divinity dancers..

Speak to the sacred in a sacred way.. so every sentence is a sacred song..
Send your sacred song postage paid.. care of the paranormal..
And that's it for.. "The Heroes".. the hit band with the hit sacred song.. "Love's Glow".
Tune in for tomorrow's Sacred Spirit Show.."

Then mum turned the radio down low.. And mum and dad and sis and me flowed real slow.. toward the back door.. a million miles away as spirits for the first time.. soaring thru the ether.. the empty space filled with the unseeable.. pure eternal energy.. unfettered.. unbound.. infinite.. Into the Violet Void of Vision.

The universe is filled with the Eternal Light of Love's Glow..
And instructions come inside the walls of the Cereal Box..
and in the Cosmic Covers of The Book from The Beyond..

Beyond the borders of the boundaries of yer brains battlements..
Lie the bardos.. the Realms of the Reality Riders..
Those who have rode the Raspberry Ridges..
as pure spirit.. Eternal Energy.. free to explore the void.

Enter any vision
Dive into any dream
Always come out upstream
Looking like peaches and cream.

As A Guaranteed Ghost.. a special Angel Agent
A Spirit Saint Saviour Steward of All Sacred..
An Ascended Angel..
We all are part paranormal.
To know that is the Key to the Door of Divine Dimensions.

You have found the Jade Jaguar's Jewels of Joy..
In the bottom of the Cereal Box that Talks.

Ya.. i swear.. sis found in the cereal box a sac sewn of saurian skin.. filled with marbles of every pure colour.. glowing like they were alive.. eggs.. sacred source sacs.. crystal chrysalises.. crystalline chrysalises.. bringers of life.. bearers of blessings.. Eternal Energy Eggs."

"Get yer furry legs outta my bowl Bareyev Ballet Baboon Boy.. the rim of my bowl ain't a ballet barre.. and yer no simian super star.." Sis warned the wastrel who was washing his skinny furry legs in her bowl.

Every heart of every human and every non human..
is a transmitter.. transducer.. receiver..
a Nexus of Eternal Energy.

Every human and non human is an energy emitter..
A Chakra Crossroads..

The visions sometimes come too fast to hold on to. You soon learn there's nothing to hold onto.. nothing to hold on with.. neither hands nor body.. just pure light..

"Ever receive the Kiss of the Criss Cross Crossroads Cougar ?" Big looked More in the eye and then shuffled the Dementia Deck between his fat fingers.. one more time for good luck for someone.. but bad luck for another.

"Someone Light Love's Lamp.." I heard Tio say at the far end of the table that was lost in the Mist of the Invisible. Tio was somewhere in the shade.. the shadows.. hidden amongst the spirits.. concealed by Spirit Smoke.

Some call it the unseen Spell Sorcerers' Sacred Spirit Strawberry Smudge Smoke.. that Tio was releasing from within his cherry coloured Consciousness Cruisin' Cloak.. which he was wearing over his Violet Vision Vest.. which he was wearing over his Strawberry Star Storm Spell Shirt. And of course on his head was a cherry coloured Cosmic Cruisin Cloud Cap.

He was impossible to see.. cause he was The Entity From Out of Eternity.
Coulda bin a spirit much as we could see.. Sis said she saw nothin neath the hat. I laughed.. nervous that the invisible might hear. Fear draws them near. Reader.. Show no fear.. Hold the book without a tremble.. Or they will be awakened from their Sacred Slumber..

They will find you.. feed upon your fears.. and leave you lost and languishing.. in a line written by the unseen upon paranormal paper in invisible ink..

You become eternal.. but can your head handle it..
Heavy karma hangs out here hero.

You could win for yerself a Consciousness Cloak.. emitting every colour of light.. You will illuminate the darkest night.. chase away every fear and fright. Check inside the Cereal Box.. you might be the lucky sucker.. er I mean saviour.." the Sales Serpent stuttered as he delivered the last line so debonairly mum just couldn't resist his charms so she bought a carton of cereal boxes for us kids, and Dad too.

I saw.. in the southern shadows of the table top Mesa de Maya.. Tio reach into his Violet Vision Vest and slide out a Strawberry Star Storm Serpent.
With it he lite the cigars of the czars of consciousness.

Tamale Tia wore several Sacred Strawberry Star Storm Spirit Shawls.. One of which my sis was hopin' to be honoured with.. for passin thru the Paranormal Parable Prophecies' Pages of Power.. without getting lost in the literature..

"Listen up little lad.. Lover of Literature and Lizard Language.. I am gonna give both you and yer kid sis a Chapter For The Chosen..".Then the SalesSnake stretched over.. gave mum a kiss.. then continued in a hiss.. "Get a Seein' Suit.. for Seein' Spirits.. Also for seein stars.. stars that speak.. Speaking Stars..
Ya.. lights in the sky that would speak and sing to those who would listen..

The Land is sacred to us.. We are Children of the Cosmos." The Sales Snake waived the Sacred Smudgin Spoon in the supermarket aisle and chanted like Jeronimo.

"We are Cosmic Children.. Cared for by the All Compassionate.. All Embracing Eternal Energy of Love's Glow.. Come to me with your lamps lit.. Come to me with no lamp.. I will be the light and the lamp and the love.. Until you know the glow.. of your own love light.."

"Son.. time to turn off the Raspberry Reptile Radio, and dim the Little Lavender Lizard Lad Love Lamp leaning over the edge of the page.. sweet book light that it is.. but it's middle of night and we do wanna get to school sometime tomorrow.."

The Lavender Lizard Love Light Lamp and the Raspberry Reptile Radio are Bodhisatvas.. Wisdom Walkers.. ones who are one with the way.. ascended angels who have reincarnated to share their light.. with those of us still living in darkness.

And you'll find one buried in the bottoms of every specially marked boxes of cereal.

"Turn off that light and that radio.. I need my beauty rest !" Bababaji Baboon yelled down from the third level of the Banana Bunk Bed.

I have been called by some.. Sweet Dreams Medicine Man..
One Who Walks as the Whispering Winds..
The Singer of the Sacred Songs of the Spirits.
All souls sing.. All hearts hold love precious

Hearts are jewels that when joined together become the alchemists' stone..
the something that can transform nothing into anything..The Necklace of Nirvana..
The Bracelet of Blessings of The Beloved.. and they come in The Cereal Box !

Included in the Tale Tellers Tea Trunk.. are applications for..
The Alphabet Alchemists Association. ps.. notice novice.. how the cereal box looks
like Tio's Tale Trunk.. Tio.. the Juke Box.. Tio's Trailer.. The Tale Tavern.. The Book..!
and the Spell Suitcase..The Cereal Box is a Shapeshifter !

We are all bathed in the undying love of life. No matter who you are.. or where
you be.. be it south of somewhere.. north of nowhere.. east of everywhere.. west of
wherever.. I will be there with you."

Sis finished reading the last lines.. smiled.. kissed The Book right on the open page..
and then crushed it to her breast.. dancing out the door singing, "Book yer the best..
Book yer the best buddy this babe ever had.."

"One look into those Emerald Eternity Eyes.. And one is Reborn in the Light of
Love's Glow".. the music from the radio played real slow.. Ace gave a sideways look
at Della Divine sitting between him and Big at the Lavender Lizard Lounge.. aka The
Consciousness Connoisseurs Cafe. She was the kind of dame that makes a fellow
wonder.. was she tryin ta save me.. did she wanna be saved by me.. would she
drown me in desire.. Would our love set the world free ?

Big interrupted the mind space mumbling something about "The Department of
Whatever Goes Down Is Okay With Me.. I'm down with that Bro.. You an Me.. We're
down with each other the way ink is with a page"

Meanwhile in the next booth, Dick the Don of Whatever Goes Down.. was poppin
uppers like they were peanuts. And some Raspberry Reptile was rapping on the
stage.. "Me I ride a harley and a horse. Life's a course no one passes. Everyone
fails. The grade's too high. The teachers are nowhere to be found

Look for me at The Lost and Found For the Fallen. The faithful are floundering.. The future hath no face. I'm only a mind on loan.. a Kamikazee Koan.. like a dog gnawin' on a temporary bone until his master throws it away. We're just waves upon an ocean of eternal motion. So rest a moment here in my wings weary wanderer.

I am sanctuary for whatever ails you angel. Here all seekers find what they sought. With every thought we head toward heaven or hell. Only angels such as us can break the spell.

Tell every tribe.. We are The Beloved's Bride.. The Altar of Love.
Love is us. If love ain't you and me.. then who's it gonna be."

Then Big slipped back into the conversation about the Juju Jewels found in the Caskets of Consciousness. Jewels that had fallen outta the crown of The Crone of Creation. Emeralds and rubies as big as your fist.. and some the size of a skull. Some are Skulls. Actual skulls somehow solidified into precious gems. Ruby, emerald, diamond, and sapphire, skulls. And these skulls were not human. They were Saurian Skulls !

And kids can collect all of these skull stones.. crystal craniums.. in specially marked Thanatos Tea Trunks.. Ya real cute.. the boxes of tea look like little replicas of Tio Toad's Travellin Time and Tales Trunk.. kind of a rusty orange the colour of earth with a somewhat warty covering. Great marketing concept." Big nodded in agreement with the Angel Agent representing the Ghost Writer.

"And get this" the sales snake spoke the line like it had been written specially for him.. "the cereal box looks Tio's Trunk ! And Tio Toad comes with a wardrobe of Wish Warts.. watermelon warts.. tangerine warts.. raspberry warts.. blueberry warts.."

"I can see it now," Big butted in as he buttered his toast.. "A cereal of warts floatin in my mornin milk.. Welcome to Wart World Wardrobe.. the finest fashion for frogs.. and designers of Limo Logs for all of Swamp Society.." Then Big dipped the toast in his tea daintily, smiled and said.. "I'll buy the story and make a movie or three."

The last that morning we saw of Tio was him floating on a limo log across sis's cereal bowl.. into the mist obscuring the far side.. where other realities lived.
"Don't forget your thermos of tea.. honey.." Mum smiled at her hero.. our dad.

"So what does one do with these Thanatos Toys ?" Ace asked the Sales Snake looking at him like he were an animal that had just slithered into the light.. from outta the depths of the cereal box.

Ace had emptied much out of the box.. into a pile on the table.. a mountain of cereal composed of Strawberry Serpents, Salamanders, and Snails.. Watermelon Whales.. Blueberry Belugas, and Baboons.. Tangerine Toads.. Cherry Chimps.. and Ink Imps.

On Ace's fingers were ruby Reality Rings.. around his wrists Bardo Bracelets.. and around his neck a Nirvana Necklace.. like the ones that can be found in specially marked boxes of Cosmic Crunch Morning Munch Cereals.

"With these Eternity Effigies a person can shape shift into pure light. I did it." Max More mumbled.. "Every being turns into pure glowing light.. The light grows as each one enters it.. and as you enter it.. it enters you. I entered it.. and it entered me.. until it became me.. and I became it.. We became One.. No longer human.. pure light.. without need.. without fear.. only love.

I glowed the way they say moses did.. when he came down from the mountain.. shinning from being in the presence of the Almighty Illuminator."

"Sounds pretty unreal to me.. Beings of Light." Ace said to no one in particular.. as he crushed another nacho fortune cookie in his palm.. and slowly read the message. "Reality Rescue is available.. Call it Insanity Insurance. The only thing that can hold you back is your own fear. You must relinquish all fear to be free."

"Son yer releasing a Strawberry Star Storm.. swingin yer cereal spoon around the breakfast table like that.. Observe.. stickin' on sis's forehead.. a strawberry star. She looks like a young unicorn with a small strawberry forehead horn." Dad delivered the dialogue like it was all a divine dream.

I had to admit I had really done it this time. The Baboon Brothers.. who had just come to board with us for the semester.. were covered furry head ta furry toe.. in Strawberry Stars.

"I'll take two jars." Sis mumbled.. as she dozed off in bed.

Door of Deliverance

"Class, today we're gonna continue our study of Simian Sacred Singing.. also known as primal primate prayer positions. It's part phys ed and part prayer.. utilizing the breath to pray.. and the body to move into and thru.. different positions of prayer. Call it Prayer in Motion rather than in one stationary state.

The training is to go from stillness into motion.. and back into stillness.. forever a flow between the two.. a Divine Dance.. Slowing down and speeding up the transfer point between stillness and motion. All the while in a prayerful and praiseful state of mind and body.

Slower and slower until all motion ceases and then stillness becomes stiller and stiller until stillness is so still.. existence ceases to be.. and yet you are all of existence.. without resistance to any form of reality.

Inside of you is contained the chronicles of your consciousness. And more importantly.. the Chronicles of the Consciousness of the Cosmos.. are contained within your cranial conductor connection point.. in paranormal and normal space time reality.

Consciousness composes all of creation. We are the creator and the creation.. we are the creator's creations. We are one in the same being. We are all of it, and it is all of us. There is only one enormous Cosmic Cauldron. The stew and the stirrer, the cauldron and the cosmos, the creation and the creator, are one and the same."

"Cut the crap and pass me the crackers while my bowl of stew is still simmerin." Benny Baboon.. Bubba for short.. and short Bubba was.. belted out the words like they were a ballet of bullets.

Gotta go.. this ghost is running low on materialization. Thanks for parlaying with your Paranormal Pal. Study the next chapter of my Counter Consciousness Cruising Course.. so you'll ace the next test on the text of the Translations of the Transcripts of the Theologian Temple Toads and the Paranormal Pteradactylian Pyramids' Power Parchments.

Top grades win a real Renegade Reality Rider Robe. That's it for today's Consciousness Cruisers' class. Remember.. Make of your heart.. a home of heaven for all." Doc Dialogue spun The Book in his palm so fast smoke signals rose up. We were nearing the Nexus of Nothingness. The Buddhistic state of being beyond body.

Sis patted the furry head of Benny.. and said "yur such a beautiful beast." Which reminds me.. whoever I am.. that the book.. Beautiful Beasts.. is the next volume in the series Pilgrimage Into The Paranormal. Get it wherever cereal is sold.

We interrupt this dream for a message from yer mind.. which I find is becoming more and more difficult to find.. don't you ? Let's start the scene off with a little song leading the country charts right now. From the number one selling album of the year "Highway of Hurtin' Hearts" ..the number one song   "Hearts And Heroes.. Heart of a Hero"

"Mum would ya turn the radio up so I can hear the music. Cathy And The Cadillacs are my favorite country ballad band." Sis swooned to the song, cradling The Book in her arms.

"Class.. following is a list of the topics we'll cover in class 101 Paranormal Paradigms, Prophecies, and Parables.. all found in your copies of the Paranormal Pyramid Pteradactylian Parchment Papers..

These various parchments were found scattered hidden around the planet.. one was found in the steppes above the mongolian desert.. another was found deep in the bowels of a mayan temple recently discovered lost in a rainforest valley, and of course the commonly known Spirit Scrolls found hidden in a cave beside the Dead Sea. The others' locations have been kept secret due to fears about treasure seekers robbing the Sacred Sarcophagi. Ripping open The Box to find the lost loot of those that no longer live.. in this reality. We're all raiders of reality.

Yes.. caskets carved out of crystal of all colours.. purple blue white emerald ruby. These are the original scrolls found hidden deep in the bottom of the Ceremonial Cereal Box standing in the center of the Table of Tales.. found in the Monastery of Madness atop the Mountain of Maya and Mystery.

"Consciousness Class.. here's that list of the topics on thanatos that we will be covering in this year's course." then Prof Paranormal read out the list..

the altar of adoration
angels ashes and the ancestors of angels
the purification of the pilgrim
pilgrimage of purification
the pyre of purification
the path of purification
the pyramid of purification
parables of purification
purification pudding"

"Wouldja please pass the porridge you primate pinup." sis bellowed to Babaji Baboon who was stirring the pot with his toe while lost deep in transcendent thought.

pilgrimage of prayer and praise
pilgrimage into the paranormal
the devils demise
the devil's deliverance

destitute dreamers
divine delusion
doctor of dreams and dimensions
divine dialogue... a discourse between heaven and hell

the sacred spell
the script sorcerer's spelling spell

the scribes' scribbles
the sages' syllables
the seeker's song

the prophet's prayer
the prisoner's plea
the prostitute's pleasure
the preacher's pulpit

the pen's poetry
the writer's words
the waste of war.. the preference for peace.."

All hell was breaking lose in our kitchen.. and mum was calling for planetary peace.. while pudding and porridge flew across the table. Dad soberly said.. "We may be reaching the end of reality."

"the far reaches of reality
the end of eternity
the raiding of reality
the readers riddle
rescuing reality from itself
reality repair and restoration

heyoka hotel
heyoka highway
heyoka heroes
heart of a hero

weaving the world with words
disciples of the divine dream
earning a dream designer degree
with each download a different dimension

dream drifters' dance
paranormal paragliding

That's the list class." Doc Divine continued lecturing, without missing a beat on his bongo.. "Consciousness is all about communication.. with that which appears to be outside of one self.. and with that which appears to be within oneself.. which is one and the same.. once you know how to play the game.

Without communication there can be no exchange of consciousness. Community is all about conscious communication. Communication with the cosmos is a reality readily available to anyone thru this course."

"What's the main course for supper ?" sis squeaked in a voice hoarse from yelling at the baboon to quit dancing on her dinner plate." Ya this time we were so late for school it was already evening by the time we got back into time.
Reality is nothin more than a rhyme written by the wind across the universe..
verse after verse.

God's Graffiti

The Lord of Light was having a sit down with The Don of Darkness.. clarifying the conditions of consciousness.. as overheard in these pages. "These scripts are the solution for entering any existence you can dream of. Call it a course in mind over matter. How to get out of your mind and into the universal mind.

There is only one price you will pay for this course in creating consciousness. That price is you.. as you understand it. The only way you can become what I am.. is to completely let go of you.. so you become unbound by any definition of existence. Only then shall you be ready for the final steps into eternity.

Dear Reader.. the Rules of Reading.. these are some of them.. follow them faithfully, Dear Friends of the Fantasy.. Friends of the Phantom Fantasy..

At the end of this chapter you'll find a key embedded in the page. If you can pull it out.. it is the key to your life. If you cannot pull it out of the page.. leave it. It is not for you. It is a key for another Pilgrim of The Pages..

If there is another pilgrim upon the page where you landed.. you may not read ahead of them.. unless they ask you to do so out of their fear or their confusion.. or their desire to ponder alone in those paragraphs.

If you come upon a lost reader.. one who cannot find the next page.. maybe even one who is stuck upon a sentence.. even worse.. one who is straddling a syllable and can neither move forward nor read backwards.. assist them if you can.

I know this sounds silly.. but I am serious. The story is not always safe. And rarely is the reader right. The writer is never wrong.. as he knows the endings to all the chapters you choose.. for he is the creator.. The Great Writer.. the One who has written the world.. woven the world.. out of words.. out of wishes.. out of wind.

Out of the breath of the beloved.. being was brought into being.. existence was given birth.

Close the Door of Darkness. You have viewed the world too long thru the Window of Woe and Worry. At the end of this chapter.. thru the Door of Deliverance.. awaits the Ledge of Light.. so your soul may take flight, noble Knight of Knowledge.

You are now a Commander of Creativity. Soon you shall be God's General. You have come a long way from being god's gofer.. Me.. I am a lowly immaterial messenger.. one of god's ghosts.. a Sacred Spirit Speaker.. come to guide you to God's Gold.. the shine so strong it illuminates all the universe."

"Son.. how many times have i told you to rehearse getting to school on time.. that way we wouldn't be stuck in some syrupy rhyme. Now I gotta go over my notes for today's class on Thealogy Goddess Studies 202.

"So is god some babe or a dude ?".. sis asked the Serpent Sales Snake who was speakin for the spirits swirlin around the supermarket aisle of cereal.. See it all started out so normal.. nothin novel nor unnatural.. Just a coupla kids, sister and brother, out with their mum to buy some cereal..

So now sis and me we're a Franchise for the Phantoms.. sellin Spirit Cereal to kids in school.. you can be a Cereal Reseller too.. And that pal, is how sis and I ended up in the story.. soon you will be too.. look you already bought into the belief that this is just another book begging for someone to hold it late at night..

See nights get so sad.. the story starts to sob.. and you can hear it all the way downstairs layin on the kitchen table where you left it.. So you go downstairs way past midnite.. figure you'll share some cereal with The Book.. keep the chapters company for awhile.. read a few words to let them know they ain't alone..

So you turn the pages looking for a poem of love to lighten up the literature's life..

You stumble along the sentences groggy eyed.. and then you meet someone.. you see something standing there in the depth of the next page.. another Pilgrim of the Pages.. But one not such as you.. nor yer sis.. One who is part paranormal..

It's different for every reader..
Maybe one time you open to a page late at night.. or on the ride to school.. or while takin the train to the office.. when you hear this sweet sigh.. "Someone save me".. And of course you being a noble knight used ta savin yer kid sis.. start off page after page to find the princess.. only to find out it's the hiss of a Sentence Serpent

You become a seeker of the unseekable. That which every Divinity Dreamer has sought.. the sacred song of spirit.. the song sung by your own soul..

And so i too have sought.. and like other readers i have been bought and sold.. by the book.. ya the book sells and trades readers with other books..

Books infiltrate simian society.. books have bodies.. and more brains than most readers... that's why humans read books.. even need books.. humans have become dependent upon the dialogue.. lap up the literature.. love the lingo.. luxuriate in the Language of Love..

Books go undercover with their prey... ya that's all a reader is to a book.. prey.. some pawn to play with late at night when a book is lonely and sad..

Humans are nothing but playthings for books.. some will seduce you with pretty pictures.. some will suck you in with promises of success and better life.. if you'll only look inside... step into some sneaky sly sensual story..

Look at me Reader.. yes me the little boy Adam in the story.. I was once like you.. an innocent bystander.. living beyond the book's power to persuade me and sis to spend some time in bliss..

Ya the book promised bliss.. the unnatural holy kiss bestowed by a book beast.. Yess.. the book had the body of beauty.. bound in ornate precious jewels and leather so supple you could swear it was alive..

The words it whispered.. poems of praise promising pleasures in a paradise forever.. an eternal embrace between a book and a reader.. a story so sublime.. I fell for it every time I opened to a page.. and then there was always that sweet sigh coming from somewhere deeper inside the story..

I told myself it was my soul reaching out for yours..

Night after night under the covers in my Baboon Brothers Banana Bunk Bed.. reading the book alone to myself.. so I wouldn't keep my lil sis on the lower bunk up.. No I'm not addicted to the alphabet.. I'm not dependent upon the dialogue. You tell yourself you are the book's boss. You open it when you want. Turn to any page you prefer. Until one day you realize you are part of the story. The Tale is talking about your life.

It happened in the school cafeteria at lunch time.. I was at the far back corner.. buried deep inside The Book looking for the Sighing Spirit.. I knew I couldn't last much longer before I needed to sleep.. even if I was so deep into the pages that I would never get back to class on time or in any time.. ever.

A shadow loomed into my peripheral vision.. more shade and shadow than substance.. and yet a light emanated.. illuminating a being of light.. An arm or wing.. brushed my shoulder.. as though an ascended angel was stirring me from the story.. awakening me with the words..

"Deep Dreamer.. dream us all a dream of delight.. make the world right with the words you write.. Hey renegade Reality Rider.. do you read me ?" That was when I felt the second wing brush my shoulder.. I was coming home.. I was being awakened.. I was seeing the Light of Love's Glow.

Everyone needs a little angel inspiration.. We all come to this life.. you and I.. as a gift to the world.. We are worthy Angel Aspirants.. for we have received the gift of birth..

I felt I was being born.. truly born for the first time.. as she gently pulled my head and shoulders out of the book..

"Look he's got strawberry syrup on his lips... he's been kissing the Strawberry Story Script.. he's been making out with an invisible Ink Imp.." voices giggled.

I heard the apparition say "hush.. we all come to this world bearing a blessing.. his is being a Book Boy.. a Sacred Scribbler.. Light your Lamps of Love." and the school cafeteria fell silent.

She was light from above.. She Was Daylight Dressed In Blue Jeans..
Oh she calls out to every reader.. Lady Literature..

"She gently closed the book, tousled my hair, and helped me up from the chair.. said to everyone.. "there's no reason to stare.."

Then she whispered to me.. "Next time won't be so simple when yur stuck in the story's sticky script." She was the angel I had searched for everywhere in the story. Finally the writer had written her in.

Door De Dios

"Door of The Divine is Always Open.. Puerto de Dios es Siempre Obierto.." the sign scribbled in crimson was painted above the Den of the Divine Desire..

The Door of the Divine.. at the end of a winding road.. waiting softly swinging on its hinges. Everything hinges on hope and how the hero will save the princess..

Storms rule the seas.. Dark night claims day for its bride..
You will know me by the feel of our skin tenderly touching.. while the dark gives way to morning's first light.. I am stilled by the sight of your sacred light.

When one first comes upon the spirit in its full splendor no words can have prepared a reader for their encounter with the Wraith Writer.. the Spirit Scribe.. the Ghost Writer.. as he likes to simply be called..

Just some unknown unseen nobody.. with no body.. no trail left behind for anyone to follow.. just words.. a trail of words.. no photos.. no finger prints.. no witnesses ever having seen the writer.. And yet someone or something had left it's words upon the walls..

"The question of male and or female as regards god and goddess needs to be clarified and finalized once and for all time. God or Goddess.. however you wish to call this power.. is both and all. It includes all that is.. and is all that is. The part you see is but your perception of that which is the all and one of everything.

Human words cannot bind the almighty power to a specific shape.. form.. or size.. No definitions can define the boundaries.. nor confine the consciousness of the almighty presence.. which is all and everything there is, or ever was, or ever will be."

"Son.. could we have a few words about your scribbling all over your little sis's bedroom wallpaper with her Suck My Face and Lick My Lips Lavender Lizard Lipstick. I know you think it's God's Graffiti.. but god can write his own.

Sis piped in.. "And the same warning goes for using any of my collection of Tangerine Treacle Toad Toothpaste.. Strawberry Stars Salamander Skin Cream.. or Blueberry Baboon Butt Breath Freshener. Ya I know they look real cute.. what with the toad and baboon puckering their lips for a kiss.. but they ain't for scribblin on my walls.."

I warned you about the words. They aren't real. They don't exist. You read upon a page something that isn't there. The story is your mind making it up. And it is the same with the reality in which you believe you live. In fact it lives within you. It is something you fabricated.. to give yourself coordinates.. so you feel safe.. while you soar thru space as a spirit.. unfettered by form.

Each reader writes their own manual for traveling the Tale of Time. Each pilgrim prepares their own survival pack for the Path of the Pages of the Parable of the Paranormal..

Who do voodoo? You do voodoo. And you done do it all over you. The Voodoo Vision Vultures will be your guides thru the Vocabulary Valley in this next phase of your initiation, into the Pages of the Sages.. of the Science of Shape Shifting."

The College of Cosmic Collaboration and Creation was in the center of the city in the old park where the zoo used ta be. Across the street was the Curb Club Cafe where Big and his boys met in the day.. while by night upstairs in The Kabuki Zoo they counted the boo.. that they had made off of me and you.

Directly across on the other side of the park was The Ace Towers Tricomplex Corporation Control Center. Ya we're all Holy Heroes.. and Lonesome Losers. When crow comes calling.. better be ready to fly.."

Prof flipped the page of his Notes From Nowhere Note Book.. the very one you're reading.. and continued. "This is bare bones bardo boundary breaking at its best.. okay Cereal Cadets... fill yer bruho buddha begging and bargaining bowls with bite sized blueberry boulder bardo bits blow yer brains breakfast cereal.

Or if you prefer Strawberry Star Storm Shaman cereal. And don't forget the one that looks like little tangerine toads swimmin in yer bowl of maya's milk.. and the one with little guttor gator paddling around in a casket in yer cereal bowl.. using a cereal spoon for a paddle.

Mmm.. those bite sized crunchy caskets and coffins cereal sure tastes yummy.. like an egyptian mummy.

Oh it's all a mirage of the mind.. Wait here by these words.. reader. Be silent. Can you sense the White Wind Wolf Woman's presence ? Be still. Don't stick yer spoon in yer mouth. There's a strawberry stinger scorpion sittin in yer spoon.

Hey I am just trying to get you used to dying. Do you have problems with the paranormal? Call paranormal plumbers.. they'll get to the depth of yer dementia.

How long does it take to shake an old dyin habit ? Habitually, death after death, the same way of doin the dying.. Duh.. That's dumb... Do the dyin different each time..

That's the hardest, cause doin the dyin that way, there's nothin to hold onto for a sense of continuity of one's consciousness. You can't even hold onto your perspective of death and dying.

You are having to recreate free form. Make it up as you go along. Create your existence and your death forever anew. If you learn to do that you will have become the omni present stillness.. the one being that is all and is forever.

The question I ask myself.. and you should too.. is.. Are we the players or are we the played ? Are we the whisperer.. or are we the whispers ? Do we roll the dice.. pull the cards ? Or are we the rolled dice.. the hand of cards being pulled ?

Is it all Dharma Drama ? Are the dice simply states of delusion and dreams ?
Like left behind lovers.. losers lost upon a limb of their own liking.. licking the leftovers left behind by heaven or hell. Souls so hungry, that any spell will suffice.

After years upon the path searching for the sacred temple, a pilgrim encountered a monk. "Where is the temple?" the pilgrim asked. The monk replied.. "The Path Is The Temple."

And so sweet reader.. follow the trail to the ends of the chapters.. no matter where it leads or how long it be. Your gentle seeking hands upon my parched pages.. have reawakened these weary words.. have opened my covers.. wide as the Lips of Love.

I have lain in the arms of angels when I danced in your holy abode. Holy Hero I hear your wings heavenly humm.. The light from your face, surely be that of an angel's. Your gaze upon these humble words gives them wings with which to soar as spirit.

The world is woven of words. Use your words well wisdom word worshipper. You are drawing from the well of the world's wisdom. Draw your bucket and drink deep your draught. Think your thought.. and live your lot.. in life and in death.

Life and death are one. It.. life and death.. is a never ending unfoldment. You are both life and death. You are not alive and then dead. Time and space and death and life itself.. are words.. as You are a word of what really is.

Time and space and death and life are inside of you. You contain them. You contain eternity. Inside of your existence you embrace the hereafter.

"From here on in, and hereafter, I am gonna set your Doc Chimp Ape Alarm Clocks to wake you up an hour earlier.. so maybe next time you kids will be in time for school.. instead of out of time somewhere else." Dad said as he shook the cereal box.. like he was trying to teach it a lesson.. instead of it teaching us.

"It's empty," he said. "no wonder yer lost in yer head.. you've got cereal hangover.. everyone up outta bed.. and downstairs to the kitchen !"

Divinity's Dreamers

After supper sis and I were sittin on the Strawberry Star Sofa watching the tv sss show featuring Doc Chimp.. the Champion Consciousness Channeler.. cooking up cosciousness cuisine.. when we noticed shadows sliding along the back ridge of the couch. Something had come out of the dark side of the canyon behind the couch.

Bardho Buzzards soon appeared.. perching on the back of the couch.. peering over our shoulders.. eyeing me and sis. We could hear the wind whistlin woo hoo as it rushed thru Cougar Climbin' Canyon.. which was growing wider and deeper.. behind the couch.

Then the book whispers the words on the page real low to sis and me. "You'll never meet up with other readers.. the script is taking you all to different places. Even the ending will be different for every reader. All places eventually turn out to be the same place.. just situated somewhere else in space..

Reader.. you were set up by the first syllable.. suckered by the seductive sentences.. and yer mind packaged.. all in one paragraph. The rest of the tale was just ta keep you entertained while serving your life sentence in the story.

Reader you look upon me as thou I were something less than you. Nothing but a book of words.. whereas you are a living moving being.. and me just a story you open and close at whim. Well I was once more than words. I lived as you do. And died as you will. Only I learned how to live again.. and again.. and again.. forever.

I am more than words upon a page. I am sentences that have saved.. paragraphs that have empowered.. chapters that have created. I have existed ever since time. I have been woven into the world and I have woven the world. I am the living word.. Words are wings that carry consciousness across the continents. I am the Breath of All Being.. I live like you and also unlike you. One of my breaths is one of your lifetimes. I watch you. I encompass you. But I am too vast for you to even imagine me as I truly am.

You know something greater than you exists. You feel it.. sense it.. but you can't quite describe it. No one of your kind can. However.. I am It.. That which you adore. And I am communicating to you thru these words.. a form of communication that will soon allow you to see me everywhere as I am.. in my all encompassing form.

The Cosmos is a Celestial Celebration of Creation.. The Cosmos is a creation of a Cosmic Consciousness.. everything is connected via consciousness."

Then The Book From Beyond asked if sis and I wanted to hear a short story about satan, something seriously silly before sleepytime to help deepen the dreams.. Sis squealed yes oh yes..

"Satan applied in the personal want ads for a baby sitter, cause satan is a big baby, scared of everyone and everything. That's why satan is hiding down there in the dark. God scared satan so much that satan split to the underworld,.. where satan was welcomed by whatever was down there already. Yes.. there were beings living in darkness long before satan got there.

Everyone thinks satan opened up Hell's Hotel. Well the truth is that satan just took it over.. fixed it up.. added a few perks and went bigtime.. got famous.. drew in quite a crowd. God started losing clients. God frowned and exclaimed out real loud.. Satan yur a sucker.. a candy assed lollipop little low life. See god was trying to once more intimidate and dominate satan his younger brother.

Just kidding.. satan ain't god's younger brother. And god, as far as I heard, in this story, is a goddess. God is just short form for Goddess. If god is a she.. then maybe satan ain't a he either. Could it be that satan is a she.? Who knows.. maybe satan is a cross dresser. Maybe satan used to be god's live in lover.. and when it ended.. god got to keep heaven.. and satan had to find some new digs.. the devil's digs. Welcome to the Devil's Den."

Doc Diction put the book down and looked up at the class of faces staring in bewilderment.. "Now kids do you see the power of the pen ? The human world is filled with words that define and divide existence. Some even destroy and deny certain aspects of existence. Others create harmony.. love.. peace.. compassion.. serenity.. sanctity.

Use words wisely.. Word Walker.. Wanderer upon the Way of Words.. wake up the world with words worthy of your pen and breath.

We must all start to dream life back into existence. We are all the dream.. and the dreamers.. at the same time. Right now far too many of us are dreaming death into being. We are dreaming the end of life.

Dear Dreamer.. it is time for our voices to be heard.. And more importantly it is time for us to listen to the voices of the other beings who live on this planet. It is time for those who have not been listened to for centuries, to be humbly listened to.

It is no longer a time to say we live on this planet.. for we are from this planet.. as a tree is from the soil so are we.. and to the soil we return..

True we are all beings of light.. all that exists is light.. pure primordial energy.. dancing freely from form to form.. from the formless into the formed... all is a cosmic divine dance..

There are other beings.. beside humans.. who share this planet.. who have a wise voice. They are wiser and older than the human species. We search for Wisdom Walkers.. and they are everywhere. We are destroying our family that we are part of. We are destroying our teachers.. our buddhas.. our angels.. our holy walkers. They are the other species.

It is our responsibility to dream divinely. We are the co Dreamers of Destiny.
We are all dreaming existence into being. Destiny depends upon our dreams. We are Divinity's Dreamers.. Destiny's Dreamers.. Divine Dreamers.

Now dear Children of the Cosmos.. sleep and dream.. as I whisper into your ears to comfort you as would a mother or father. For I am the Language of Love.

I have drunk the divine Wine of Worshippers. I have warred with my own soul. I have sold my spirit into slavery. And I have sat with satan, the proprietor of Satan's Soda and Sandwich Shop.. discussing death and denial.

Don't concern yourself with my mind.. it tends to wander.. something an old spirit does at times.. Forget what I said.. it's just some silly scribblings of a mind losing its way.

But hey, I'm the best I ever had. Never had better than me. But what do I know. I never bin no one else. You and me, we don't pay by taxes and ulcers. We pay by giving it all away. Even our minds and bodies. We become dream dust, for dreamers we be.

We are just layers of consciousness. Once you realize that.. all points of reference and existence shatter. Accept that.. and stay in the state of Fearless Love."

Doc Diction paused.. leaned against the lectern.. then continued reading from The Book

"sincerely
a generic ghost
some sidewalk saint
a Saurian Sacerdote Sacred Spirit Scribe Scribbler"

And in the depth of a distant dream i could hear mum scream.. "Kids, it's time to head into another space.. school. Take with your bodies and minds, or whatever's left of them that you can find."

Here comes the part you've been training for all thru the book.. your own ending.. Leaving your body behind.. without losing it. Exiting your story.. without leaving behind anything you wanna retain, like yer brain.. unless you want a different one.. That's possible too.. for a minor instructional fee.

How to break free of reality and still retain a hold on your sanity. The course comes completely complimentary on the sides and backs and bottoms of blow yer brain ta bits bite sized Bardo Bits.. for breakfast or brunch.. A quick pick me up and put me over the top type of taste treat for doin' supernatural feats of fantasy and fiction.. makin' it feel like fact.. Blueberry Boulder Brain Blaster Bran Bits.. for blastin beyond the boundaries of yer brain's borders..
Believe it brother.. see it for your self sister.."

The Serpent Salesnake wearing the Strawberry Star Storm Sarape slung the story across the scene like sis and I were in a dream.

"This cereal sold only to those with a license for losin' it.. letting it all go..This time when you close The Book.. you gotta make it out of the story without your body.. Ya.. you gotta leave yer body behind in The Book.. carry on in reality without a body.. Completely dematerialize your body and your brain and trust the universe in its wisdom.. All we are is bardo bits of beliefs blown by the Breath of the Beloved"

Then Tio the Toad.. Teller of the Tales.. at the Table of Fables.. slammed down with authority upon the table.. his bottle of Full Bore Bardho Brew.. brewed to blast you thru the walls of your world and remake reality anew.. beyond yer brain's borders.

"My daddy was a dragon.. my mother a mountain.. I was raised outside of reality.."

Tio looked me straight in the eye and said.. "Paranormal people shouldn't hang around reality for too long.. It rubs off on them." Then as if materializing with the stroke of an invisible pen, on the wall of the cereal box was a wanted poster.. similar to the want ad the phantom fellow next to me in the aisle of Maya Magazines was reading in the Ghost Gazette Paranormal Personals.

"Looking for an angel.. preferably an ascended angel.. don't matter what colour the wings are.. or if they're worn down.. an angel that sings.. maybe plays a harp or horn.. an angel that has apprenticed at the altar of our ancestors, and been anointed by the allmighty lord of love and light."

"Kids.. it's way past mid night.. time ta close the Book." Dad gently brushed sis and my forehead, as though his hand were an angel's wing.

Strange how light became a symbol of the good, the positive, while darkness was banished to the shadows where unseen beings held sway over the imaginations of those who had learned to fear the dark. Luminence became a god.. and darkness became a devil that fell beneath the sword of saviours we invoked out of our collective consciousness. And yet Lucifer was the Light Bearer.. oh how confused our consciousness has become..

Words have wrought this world into being. You and I.. We are two bodies formed of the same flesh.. two hearts of the same mold.. We create collectively culture and consciousness. It is time to create a Culture of Caretaking. We are that what is being born.. and we are that what is giving birth.

We are all one flesh
Born of bone and stone
Love and light

The songs I sing are sacred
The words I write are of wisdom
I walk in worship of the sacred Way of Wisdom
I was present at the Wedding of Wonder and Wisdom

Weld well.. welder of wisdom's words.
Weave well.. weaver of wisdom's words.

When wonder wed wisdom.. the world was well.. But into the story was woven a wicked word by the name of a noun. A noun that wasn't very nice. And for backup it carried an arsenal of adjectives and adverbs... angry, antagonistic, aweful.

And it ran in a predatory pack of paragraphs prowlling the pages.. following you.. sneaky sentence after sneaky sentence.. everywhere you go in The Book.. yer never alone in This Book.

I'm obsessed with tryin to get to the page where I find out where I come into the story.. what part I play and who wrote my lines.. why am I even here in this sentence..

Whose story really is this ? Is it mine or yours ? Is it ours ? Our co created concept of reality ? Or is it someone else's.. someone we can only imagine and reflect and agree or disagree upon.. someone we will never see and yet is all around..

Is fact fabricated out of fantasy and fiction and fable ?
Do we create consciousness or does consciousness create us ?

Are we consciousness? Are we a creation of consciousness ?
Do we co create with some other force we do not see ?

Are we the designers of divinity and destiny ?
Is destiny the same as divinity.. Is infinity the same as divinity ?

Oh it's all little words of language. Sound bites of the collective consciousness trying to describe something so big and vast.. as to surpass totally all conception of the cosmos.

Dear Reader.. the moment you came onto my radar screen.. my pages started to glow.. my words imprisoned upon the pages.. broke free of their bonds.. rising up to meet you in a tender embrace.

Face to face we have come. Our minds entwining into one.. in an intimacy saved for sacred lovers. We are spirit beings.. the forever forming.. eternal ever being.. We are The Ecology of Existence.

"Sis would you please get your nose.. and yer self.. outta The Book.. and back into this existence. We gotta get to school sometime.. even if it's in a different time than this one"

Then the sentence seductively tried to retain it's hold on sis by whispering a private piece of info regarding the writer. "By the way in case you have not already guessed it, I am also an aspiring writer of romance nookie novels. Here's the plot, pretty princess, for our sweet story.

You meet me one sunny, or rainy if you prefer, afternoon in a library. I fall from the top shelf into your arms as you reach up for a book.. your hands tremble as you hold me ... my beauty and radiance illuminate your face.. I sigh as you tenderly open me.. revealing my bare white skin.. tattooed with strange crimson script.. my jewel encrusted covers reveal me to be royalty.. and you but a humble human seven year old kid sister.. skipping class cause some Gutter Gator conned you into going for a ride on his Strawberry Scaled hide in exchange for your Paranormal Peanut Butter and Strawberry Star Storm Sandwich.. made by yer mother the Word Witch.. the president of the Spell Sisters Society."

Oh yes.. the book has a way with words. Sis leaned in even closer.. both her cheeks brushing the pages.. listening to the whispering of the words.. the seduction of the syllables.. the calling of consciousness. As she caressed its crimson cloaked covers.

"Ya ya I've read it all before.. you poor sentences must be getting' senile.. same old story.. to how many kids have you used the same line." Sis smirked as she skipped out the door stuffing the Book into her back pack. This time the tale wasn't gonna make her late for school.

Paranormal Pteradactylians

She was a side car cutie.. a counter culture.. coat check.. corner cafe.. curb queen. He was a king without a crown.. an angel without wings.. a hero that hath no horse to ride.. nor serpent to slay. He was simply a seeker of sanctuary.. sacred and serene.. come here to play within the pages.. with you dearest reader.. in the Groves of the Gardens of the Goddesses of Goodness and Gladness.

Please read the side panels of the cereal box for further information on how to sign up for future free episodes of yourself. Just be sure to obey the sign at the top of the box.. Beware.. Bottomless Box.. Eternity's Entrance

Send in the box's bottom.. if you can find it.. and we'll send you a home starter kit.. recreate eden.. all the details on how to grow eden in your own backyard. I have no coordinates.. for I have no boundaries.. nor body. I am sentience itself. I am the illuminator of all. I am the illumination and the illuminated. I am the ever unfolding birthing of being.. the womb of eternal existence."

"Resistance is futile.. now move away from the cereal bowl and get to school. This whole family is late." Dad was about the only one retaining a grip on reality, as even mum was now talking with the toad as though he were an old family member.. like someone's uncle.

We're all caged in the cells of our own minds. "And your feet are so stinky you belong in a zoo.. Tomethius Tomatias Theosophilis Taicher Tulku Temple Tale Telling Toad.. told me.. to tell you." Mum said looking at me.

Me.. I'm a Consciousness Commando crisis control cadet.. an aspiring Angel Ascension Astronaut. And yes I am here on a recruitment mission.. looking for other angels that got some free time. Join the angelic Angel Assistance Association and become an angel assitant. Assist aliens and other entities when they veer off flight path.. travelling from one reality to another.

Fly thru the farthest sky safe and secure with Angel Aviation.

I trust time and space have been treating you well. I have lost track of the centuries since we last alighted upon the pharoahs' pyramides. Yes the pyramides were perching places.. Promonitories.. Where the aliens came and conferred with the wise women and men of the tribes of times told of long ago.

Pteradactylian Paranormal Paragliding Prophets. These wise alien angels were in the americas also.. and were named the feathered plumed serpent god. The feathers were sometime carved in stellae as scales.. And they shone like sun.. Like gold and silver or some alloy.. a suit.. a garment.. a space suit maybe ?

These beings were described as plumed, feathered, scaled, flying, saurian, serpent, extremely powerful, magical beings. Obviously gods. The god of fire light heat warmth sustenance beauty knowledge..

Koohkuhlkahn Koohwhetzahkhwahtahll ..in nahuatl language.
Their greeting was always the same.. "I am love I am light"

"Hush.. speak in whispers. All the Spirits hear every word you say and think as you read these sentences on the sides of the cereal box. Sayonnara sweetheart".. the spirit swirling out of the scribbling on the side of the box.. said to Sis.. as she placed the box back on the kitchen shelf.

This Book and Box is a portal for mortal and immortal.

Sis spun out the door and headed onto the street to school. That's when she first saw the strange sticky thick scarlet liquid seeping from where the fallen fire hydrant had been torn from the sidewalk. The faithful guardian sentinel that stood at the entrance to the vacant lot in the back of our apartment building.. had been brutally pushed over by that bully bulldozer.. owned by Big's Bully Demon Demolition.

It wasn't until much later.. after the bully dozer incident.. when we learned that part of the not so vacant lot.. was built on top of the Graveyard of Guardian Ghosts. Yess.. ghosts were buried here. This was the Ghosts' Graveyard. Only a fool would dare dig into the Devil's Den.. Satan's Stronghold.

"I told you to put down that spoon and quit digging into the Maya Marmalade Juju Jam Jar. You've had far too much sugar. You're already starting to shape shift.. now get into the car." mum thundered.

"Hold onta yer spoons !" Sis screamed. "We're being buffeted by a swirlin' Strawberry Star Storm brewing up in our breakfast bowls." Every cereal box comes with a Pack of Paranormal Pens.. with different colour inks.. to help you think differently.

Then I heard Dad's voice. "Son.. What do I gotta say to convince you and your little sis Evy ta quit foolin around with yer Strawberry Stars.. grab yer Lavendar Lizard Librarian Lunchboxes and let's head off for school."

Sis closed her Book and locked the catch that looked like a pteradactyl's claw, holding tight what ressembled the lid of a crystal casket. Yes this volume of The Book looked like.. actually was.. a casket.. carved out of a crimson crystal. Creepy. What it contained was even creepier. What crawled outta that book was uncontainable. Consciousness cannot be contained. Neither can reality be restrained.

"Son.. Yer strainin the limits of my patience. You need to be retrained. Now pull on yer Strawberry Star Story Sneakers. You're movin slower than the Strawberry Star Slime Script Snail.. slurpin the Strawberry Syrup, offa yer plate of partially eaten Paranormal Power Pancakes.That pile of pancakes is gonna make for one precarious pyramid landing perch for those Paranormal Paragliders coming in for a light landing right now. I said right now move out! We're so late that we won't even be on time for next year's class."

So you won't be left behind we've included a pair of Strawberry Story Spirit Sneakers in every Box of the Beloved's Breakfast of Blessings cereal so you can follow the story wherever yer Sacred Spell Sneakers take you..

"You smelly simian.. get yerself outta my bowl ! Take yer morning bath somewhere else.. you furry elf !" Sis was grouchily grumbling at Benny Baboon who was floatin on his back on a soggy piece of toast, in the middle of sis's cereal bowl, while deep in conversation with the Bowl Troll who was pickin his nose with his tiny toes. That's how it goes when yer the one who knows where time flows and space sits.

Dharma Deli Lizard

"Welcome to The Temple of Thanatos.. the Word Wraithes' Waterin Hole.. also known as the Wraith Writer's Ink Well.. where if you listen real well.. you can hear the words whisper.

It was here.. where The Book Of the Bardho Beings..The Book of The Beginning And The End.. was written. Welcome Wisdom Wanderers. Your home is in Heaven's Heart. The Door to the Divine is never closed. The key is in what you think. The spell is in the ink.

Come closer to the page. Notice how the ink gives off a fragile fragrance. It seeps out of the Paranormal Parchment.. perfumes the room. Each chapter is of a different essence.. so subtle.. yet it affects the reader's mind and world.
Yes the inks used are Smell Spells, and the pages are of ancient Silurian Saurian Scaley Skin.. Paranormal Paleo Pteradactylian Parchment."

Just then the tavern door was flung open by an invisible wind. In glided a gilded ghost glittering in gold dust. "I'm parched from dying in the Desert of Dreams.. someone fill me a Ghost Goblet of Ghost Grogg."

Then he or she.. flung a gold coin onto the table where Tio and me and sis were sitting.. right in this very sentence.. in this exact chapter you are reading. Then the words upon the page were rudely interrupted with..

"We interrupt this episode for a word from our sponsors. Werewolfs.. Are you tired of eating the same flavour meat everytime you hunt down a human ? Does last night's toxic makeup and perfumes give you gas in the middle of the night ? Let Predator Patrol properly prepare your prey. Order in or take out."

Sis started screaming.. "Where's the werewolf ? What if we are attacked by a whatwolf.. or a whywolf ? What will we do ?" She sure had the willies. But I wasn't worried.. cause we each had a Demon Door Dragon doin double duty at our bedroom doors. The Dojo Demon and The Tokyo Tank were not just two Tulku Toys.. but were the real thing. With them guarding your door.. you are not gonna have any trouble with errant entities.

We are the reflections of each other cast by our own selves.. reflections in the mirror of our minds.

Do you ever feel like you are invisible to the rest of the world. Imagine how it feels to be me.. living my life under the guise of a ghost.

I am not only a ghost but I am also the past president of Paranormal Pals.. and I highly recommend Reality Resellers and Retailers.. a Spirit Subsidiary of The Consciousness Company.

"We take care of consciousness".. a motto your mind can trust.

We are all woven out of wonder. We are all interwoven with every ancestor of every species and with every species that now exists

Does the past prefer the present.. is the present fond of the future.. do they live in harmony as caring lovers ? The future is the child of the past mating with the present.

The pen and the parable are the plow and the arable land of literature and language capable of opening a new age of angelic renaissance.. resonating each and every heart beat with every other one existing.. thru the usage of Visionary Vocabulary.. Alphabetical Alchemy.

Enter into Dialogue with the Divine. Just speak into your Spirit Spoon included in every box of Cosmic Cereal.. and enjoy a discussion with the divine on any topic. Join now Angel Academy Ascension Association.. and we'll throw in an extra set of wings.

I am the face that you kiss
And the faith you follow
You have awakened the wraith
Summoned the spirits
Danced with the dead
Slept with the sacred
Knelt at the edge of eternity
We are near.. and when you need us.. all you have to do is..
Holler like hell.. heaven will hear."

Tio leaned back in his chair.. lifted his snifter.. and solemnly said.. "Enuff of the sweet stuff.. serve the kid another shot of Sonoran Sidewinder Vision Viper Venom.. and give his little sis a shot of Strawberry Scorpion Sorcerer Stinger Syrup.. spice up the script a bit."

And you dear reader.. lick the letters of these sweet sentences. They've been double dipped in the divine. This is the Manuscript of Magic.. of Word Wishes.. Sentence Spells.. Poems of Praise and Prayer.. penned by a Paranormal Poet.

All this literature for you.. lover of lyrics. Now listen up reader.. and you characters in the story also.. the Language of Love languishes unless we use it.
Make your dialogue divine. Live a life of love without limits. Be not the beast in the garden of eden. Rebel against reality. Do not be confined by consciousness.

Sign this legal document saying that I lorencio lizard own your mind and everything that comes out of it.. and if you do so I will keep you safely in a retirement home for Rebel Reality writers and readers.

Sign everywhere.. scribble on the walls with yer sister's Strawberry Stars lipstick, and don't worry if the blue baboon pisses pink.

We pay scale.. the going rate for Script Sorcerers. Get a career in creating consciousness. Receive a scholarship to Spirit School. Make Soul Studies a lifelong and afterlifelong consciousness career opportunity."

Then the spirit emptied a sac of scintillating shining Strawberry Serpent Sorcerer Spell Scales onta the table.. which Tio ran his fingers thru.. gave a handful to sis saying.. "Here.. these are for you.."

"Listen up.. if you so much as lean towards me with that spoon, I'll wack you over yer furry funny head with this book you're livin' in buddy." Sis seriously threatened Babaji Baboon.. Just another one of those unshaved simians slinking around in the shadows of the sentences. A character who also happened to own.. along with his brothers, Benny and Bareyev.. The Baboon Brothers Broadway Bagel Book and Brew Babe Bar.. where every story is a star.

A classy curb cafe where dumped and dissillusioned dudes and dames would duel with dialogue until one won. Rarely did both win. And that is exactly what we the Ghost Gabb Guild are trying to change with these words.. everyone can win.. it is a matter of mind over matter..

Or better yet.. mind without matter.. yes.. Live your mind without matter to get in the way. Have you been sucking up to satan lately. Well suck up no longer to neither god nor anyone on down to the devil.

Don't freak out friend.. it's only Dirty Dialogue dancing upon the page. Just a bunch of washed up words doing their daily workout.. training you how to and how not to talk. So wash yer own dirty dialogue in your own mind.. before you hang it out for all to hear.

"Look Kid.. I'll sell you and your sister a six pack of Simian Suckers.. eleven Lizard Lollipops.. and I'll throw in the Slug Slime Soda and Snail Slime Syrup for free.. and that's my last offer to you today." Tio tapped his fat fingers on the table patiently waiting for an answer from Sis and me.. while the Sales Serpent leaned against the tree.

"How long do I have to wait for you kids to get a move on it?" Dad said, tapping his fingers on the kitchen counter top he was leaning against.

And that's it for today's show.. broadcasted live from the caskets of the dead. Dialogue you can really dig your fingernails into. Really put your body and soul into. A cause you can commit your life to.

"Okay.. time ta turn off that radio up there on the ridge on the other side of the fridge." Dad muttered.. reaching up. "The Swirling Spirit Show is over." When the chapter closes and the last period comes calling.. cash me in for something more than a gambler. Say I was a Ghost Gardener.. in the Garden of Goodness.. reachin out ta give humanity a hand."

The sloshed Stool Serpent held up his cup with his tail.. offering a toast to the Ghost Host of the Tavern of Tales. And looking straight at sis.. said in a slithery hiss.. "Sweetness.. give me a kiss." Then sliding down the stool.. saluted her with his tail and the words "Sayonnara Sweetheart.. I'm outta this tale."

Yes it was a sayonnara sunset type of evening when even the shadows hide from the darkness. Sis was trying to erase the scarlet stains upon her dress. The baboon was on his knees.. trying to confess for spilling his Strawberry Slug Soda.. while Dad.. the Chief Cosmic Commander Chimpanzee Chairman of the Council of Caretakers.. and Chief Chimp Culinery Commander of the Cosmic College Cafeteria.. was in a state of hysteria.. laughing together with the Dharma Deli Lizard.. who was so buddhistic that he thought it all was a bellyful of laughs.

"Get the angel an agent and get the paranormal a publisher!!!!" Maxie More screamed on the phone to Sal Salamander his secretary of scribblin More's meanderin mumblins.

"You bumblin baboon.. get yer furry form outta my bowl.. it ain't a bathtub.. an' I don't care how good the cream is for your wrinkly simian skin !" Sis flung the sentence at Babaji who was floating upon a lotus in the middle of Sis's cereal.

"Sir my rifle's misfiring." The corporal responded.. "It don't make no difference here son.. everyone on the battle field is dead."

Sad news hath fallen upon the ears of the deaf. The blind have read the wrong words. Look at the fire, see how it rages. Even Buddha's gone ballistic.. and jesus wears lipstick.. and moses has sold his walking talking stick..

Mum muttered something about we should all become monks and join the Monastery of Mindfullness. "And mind the mud on your way to the car. There's been a lot of rain lately.. the back yard vacant lot is starting to ressemble a swamp in some parts." Then Tio fired off several farts as if to emphasize that he empathized with mum.

We Script Spirits end this chapter with a note of explanation for the edification of our beloved and highly esteemed readers. The Dharma Deli Lizard works behind the cafeteria counter dispensing delicious delicasies and divine dialogue to the students at the College of Consciousness.

Should you wish yourself to attend classes at this college please contact our Reality Registrar and we will sign you up for home study. Consciousness is a gift never lightly given, only earnestly earned.

Lizardus Literatus

Swinging in on the overhead ropes.. Doc Chimp brachiated across the lecture hall to the Lizard Lectern standing in the center of the stage. The Lizard Lectern was carved of Lavender Light Crystal. Crystal poured into a holographic mold.. and then with lazer light.. frozen into a solid crystal lectern which softly glowed.

High up on Promonotory Peak of Purification.. on the flat top of the Lectern Lizard's head.. stood a small Lavender Lectern Lizard Lamp.. whose scales Doc smoothed before placing his Book of Nirvana Notes.. at its crystalline clawed feet. No other lights shone in the Caretakers College cavernous lecture hall.. except for the glow of the two lizards.. one tall and one small.. the small one sitting on the head of the large one.

Doc Diction.. Father of Fable and Fiction.. laid bare the Crimson Crystal Covers of the Book from Beyond the Bardos of humans' beliefs.. and began to read.. that which had been written by The Invisible Unseen.

"I cry out like an unheard ghost.. an unseen spirit. Am I nothing but some Scribbler's Story. Oh such beauty thou doth array before me. Yet as thou a body surrounded by barbed wire.. I am denied love's eternal embrace.. trapped between these covers as in a cage.

Immerse me in your silken sea.. give flight to my wings in your sacred sky. From you all is born.. and into you all must die. We are all fruit of the same tree.. petals of the same flower.. blossoms of the same branch.. notes of one song.

I offer you all that I am.. and all that I am to become..
For it is from you I came.. and in you all is.
May every word I write and every deed I do..
Be a blessing for all that is you.
May I speak in a sacred manner
May I walk in a sacred way
May I come invited to the divine dance bearing blessings
And may they be done with divine love..

May all my deeds be done.. with the divine grace of love.
Such my fellow vision travellers is the Prayer of a Pilgrim upon the Path of Peace..

I just want you to know you are divine. Everyone.. All.. is Divine.
However in angels like you.. It is so much easier to find.

I guess that's what angels do.. define divinity..
With a stroke of their wing..
Upon a page we all share..
A light each one does bare..
We are the bearers of blessings of the beloved beauty we all can be..
A story we all compose..
A song each one of us sings..

Softly the holy brings the gift of gracious love..
You and I and all you see below and above are made from love..

Hold each other in tender gracious love
That's what angels do..
Angels such as me and you

That's what angels do..
Incarnate as you..

With such script the sacred speaks.. the wise write.. the Little Learned Lizard Lad listens.. to his divine dad.. and magnanimous mother..

"How about you kids and yer baboon buddies listen up to yer mum and dad and get outta yer Consciousness Cereal Chompin Chakra Chairs and eject yer butts.. it's off ta school for you.. and take yer baboon buddies too."

A Sky Spirit Soarer, Sacred Seeker's, divine day.. starts with cereal that lifts off the roof of yer reality.. blasts you into the arms of angels.. and awakens your own wings.

So Sis and I did start each divine day. We would gather round the breakfast table with mum and dad and tio and solly and the baboon brothers our cousins..

With words we would praise the paranormal power that produced this planet of such perfection grace and love.. for truly tis a paradise.. please treat paradise nice

"Make of me a divine gift of love's grace..
May I receive all in the glow of love's light.
With integrity grace gratitude inspiration serenity and wisdom..
May I walk upon the way of worship.. this and every day.

May I be a glow of love's lamp.. to light even the darkest night..
So no fright nor fear shall fall upon another's eyelashes..
For sure I am saved when our stories intertwine."
Sis was the Paranormal Poet's numero uno Lady of the Literature.

Tio poured another glass of Wish Wizard Wart Wine.. "Notice how fragile and fine is the veil between minds. We live our dreams like Shadow Samurais.. hidden from ourselves in masks of maya and designer delusions. How about some silly sentences to soften the seriousness. Let's meet after school at the Sentence Samurai Society Soda Shop..

We're Reality Renegades.. Learnin' ta ride on the outside of reality without any fatality, like losin one's body or mind.. forever soaring as spirits across the pages..

Here within my covers find comfort fine friend.. you are family with all you see.. All that be is the Beloved Blessed Being of grandeur and grace that shines from every face.. and every form." And so we, mum, dad, sis, an me.. made our way thru the Breakfast Cereal Chapters without losin one member of our Consciousness Crew.. We all stir Society's Stew.

Let's see if you can do that.. stay on the sentences.. don't get tangled up in the lines.. part with each paragraph in a friendly manner.. wake up with every word as though the story was your divine lover.. for with the literature of love you have lain..

You are the betrothed of This Book.. Turn my pages with your heavenly hand.. for we are wed.. you.. and I the words. I shall worship you.. every word you find inside my covers will be filled with the glow of love's light.

In the middle of the night when you can't sleep.. come to me.. gather me in your arms.. embrace me in your wings.. Angel I have waited for your appearance in every chapter.. waited breathlessly with every word sung or said.. to hear your sweet whisper.

Now aren't you glad you have a hero like this angel you hold in your hands. Now do you see more clearly that my covers in which I am enrobed.. are wings ?

The clouds gather.. The sky feels dark and heavy
The humidity becomes oppressive..The birds hush..The cattle bray
The winds bend the trees almost to the point of snapping
The children cower under their bed covers
The thunder claps deafeningly
The lightening strikes fear in every heart

Then the rain falls like god never cried before until this very moment. And every living soul feels the burden of god's responsibility. And out of the release comes a compassion and understanding. A belief once more that there is a universal omnipotent love.. and that existence is not pointless.. but filled with miraculous moments to be cherished.

And that class.. is the task of entering The Crucible Cauldron of Becoming A Caretaker Of Creation. Called a crucible because every student upon this path.. and we all are students.. will be ground up and simmered and strained until we are clean of constrained consciousness.

We exist in A Universe Of Unlimited Love.

This manuscript is a maze.. as is the mind. This manuscript is a metaphor for the mind. Each page leads you deeper into the mind's maze.

This literature is a labyrinth crafted of love to lead you thru the maze of your mind.. thru the labyrinth of life.. to the center of your heart.. so that you may become a hero of the heart.

Invisible Unseen

"For the remainder of this week's lecture on love and light.. log onto the Lord of Literature Consciousness Chat Board.. and see where you go with twenty six letters.. all those lovely letters in any language.. yours to do as you please.. Page Pilgrim.. Word Weaver."

It was right here at this exact sentence coming up where The Book took over from Doc Diction.. and wrote into the story some other spirit sort speaking upon the pages.

"Look little lover.. these two luscious lips ain't for sale.. Slimy." Sis spit the syllables at the slug sliming its way along the counter in the Silurian Soda shop.

"Look Kid Kosmic.. I'm slippery enough without yer spit. But I wouldn't mind a bit of yer sandwich. I like mine easy on the Slug Syrup.. just slightly slimy." said Solly the Sewer Salamander.. who cause he had just slithered up to the stool.. got a big drop of drool on his strawberry star stunt slacks.. when he sat down on the sticky stool.. sticky with sis's spit.. cause she was spittin everywhere sticky syllables.. that stuck to everyone in the Strawberry Star Studio Story Soda Shop.

"Are you taking notes ?" Tio turned to Stella Starlight his secretary.. secretary to the spirit.. Ya the Spirit Scribe has a secretary to speak on its behalf to Simian Society cause the ghost don't talk to just anyone. First ya gotta learn how to listen to the unseen and unheard.. the undead and the unread.

"Get yourself outta bed, and bring with you those bumblin baboons, Benny and Bareyev and Bongo and Babaji.. didja hear me ?" Dad hollered down the Hall of Heroes..

"Don'tchoo come near me.. or I'll swat you with my tail, you slimy slug." Solly the Soda Shop Stool Salamander Sorcerer said to Sal the Slime Slug who climbed offa the Raspberry Reality Rug, on which he had just arrived from ridin another reality.

Ya.. Sal the famous slug.. from the label on the bottle of Slug Slime Soda.. comes in flourescent lime slime and strawberry swamp slime. Savor the flavor of the finest from the Fountain of Fantasy and Fact and Fiction.. where you can drink the diction.

"Turn off the faucet ! It dosen't take a flood ta wash the mud off yer mug." mum had the final words on the page. And just at that moment coming in thru the Dimension Door was Sammy the Strawberry Snail who was so slow that he usually stuck with his sweetheart Samantha Slug..

Such was a day when sis and I strolled to school with our Buddies from the Beyond. Beyond the borders of our brains' boundaries.. lives a life of unlimited love.

Hold hands with the Tale Troll.. the Sacred Scroll Temple Tunnel Tale Trail Troll. The Troll is your friendly guide thru the Tale Tunnel that runs directly under yer kitchen table to the Temple of The Transcripts of Time neath the floor of the future. The Scroll Trolls do the scribbling for the Tale Tellin Trolls who do the talkin for the fast talkin Serpent Salesnake sellin seriously silly cereal seriel episodes of sweetly overloaded literature of laughs and love and wisdom from the one who watches from above..

Gives new meaning to Big Brother is watching.
Are you wanting to meet up with yer own personal Tale Troll.. well just help yerself to a few more spoonfulls of cereal and take a peek under yer breakfast table.. Look in the shadows neath the table top.. keep looking.. forget about getting to school on time.. it's after the bell has rung and yer still looking under yer table when the Table Troll is most likely to appear.

The Table Troll is cousins with the Tale Troll.. They're both members of the Troll Tribe along with their cousins the Temple.. Tunnel.. Tomb.. Transcript.. Tavern.. and Toast and Tea Trolls.

And you can collect one in each box of cereal specially marked with Ghost Graffiti. Just beware of the Cereal Shadow Samurais.. shadows lurking in the shadow cast by the cereal box.. They are there to guard the cereal.. making sure only worthy and noble Knights of the Kitchen.. get second servings of cereal.

Ahhh come on now kid.. it's only a story scribbled in Doc Divinity's Nirvana Note Book.. Notes from Nirvana.. It's only a tale from outtta the Tale Trunk of the Trixstir Toad.. yer uncle Tio.. come ta visit from Rio.

Notice how in the word "outtta" in the previous sentence there are three t's that look a lot like crosses..That's cause you've read yourself by mistake into a chapter of the Criss Cross Crossroads Crucifiction Chronicles of Coffins and Caskets. No one I know ever got outta this chapter alive. And I know all the readers that done bin in this book. No one get's inside my covers without me knowin it.

"Now don't go throwin' a fit." the Juju Janitor was saying to Solly, whose tail was stuck in the pail filled with Strawberry Star Soap Suds.. with which the Window Witch was about ta wash the Story Soda Shop floor.

Make a wish with a Wish Window Witch and watch yer dream come true thru the window.. all you gotta do is watch thru the Wish Window.. Just watch out you don't get stuck in the story on the other side of the Wonderous Wish Window.

See scribblin is sticky business. So students scribble sweet sentences that will stick in the minds of men and women.. and upon the pages so well that no matter how many times they are turned.. or how many tears upon them are shed.. the words will remain as a guide for all ghosts on their way to god.

Yes.. as soon as you die and become a ghost, you start on another journey.. could take a day.. a year.. or thousands. Just as in this life time journey.. some of us are born and in a day die.. others need a hundred years to find their way.

After you are a ghost and die you become something else. The buddhists say one comes back here to this realm or stays somewhere in the bardos.. realms of other realities. You could say this writer is a ghost who had gone over to the other side one too many times and did not come back.. but one who left this parable as a path for other pilgrims.

Every sentence written.. was a sentence in seclusion.. solitude.. always flying solo. It's so much easier to just coast thru the chapters some ghost wrote for you.

Now I live within the words.. in any one I want.. as anyone I wish to be.. cause I weave the world in which all wander within these cosmic covers.

"Get yer head out from under the covers.. and turn off that Lizard Light.. you've done enuff reading for one nite.. and close the book securely so it don't bite yer toes while yer asleep.. in a dream so very deep." Dad called from the hall.

Fountain of Fantasy

If I am a spirit free of substance, formed of a finer flesh than humans.. then why.. you ask.. do I write these words..? What purpose could I possibly have in trying to make contact with your consciousness ?

I who can visit distant constellations.. mate with the immaterial.. dance with the divine.. I who am intimate with the infinite.. why do I crave human connection.. what part of me is incomplete ?

I who have all and yet need nothing.. what is this something in me that is unsatisfied.. what part of my being is unfulfilled.. such that I should appear before you as ink upon a page.. at times pursuing.. promising.. praising.. pleading.. praying ?

What need is not yet nourished.. such that I should seek you out.. leave you clues as to where I may be found.. write you poems of love and adoration.. seduce you with silly sentences that make you smile as though we were lovers intimate thru all time ?

If I were flesh and form I would use roses and wine.. vacations to venice in summertime.. anything to make you mine.. What hidden hunger compels me to seek your tender touch.. the gossamer kiss of your lips upon my velvety vellum.

"Try kissing me one more time.. or even touching me wit yer toes and i'll dump this pail of pond pudding all over yer nectarine nose. pal. Or would you rather get a tail around yer neck, next time Tio. And keep yer toes outta the tale.. yer leaving Toad Tracks all over the pages."

Solly Salamander spit the sticky sentences at Tio.. cause Tio had stuck his big toe inta the tale.. by sticking his toe into the pail.. where Solly was washing his tail.

Yup the tale was talking back to Tio thru the lips of another character in the story of the Tale of the Toad's Toe, and the Salamander's Tail, Tracks.. also known in its abbreviated version as the Toad's Toe and the Salamander's Tail Tale.

Just follow the tracks back to me.. if it takes for all of eternity I will wait for thee. See I said I would win you with words worthy of your beauty and elegance. You and I are a dance of dialogue and desire born in Fantasy's Fire.

"Yer deluded if ya think I'll take a chance with you washing the floor with my tail. Now get yer fat foot out of the pail.. and make sure yer big toe dosen't get close and cuddly with mine.. I ain't no cutesy character in some tale yer tellin." Then Solly the Salamander showed his gums.. and stuck up his thumbs in the air.. as if to say to Tio.. "stick yer toes up yer nose.. toad. "

Whereupon Tio stuck all his toes up Benny Baboon's nose and then pulling out his sticky simian snot drenched toes with a big sucking noise.. flicked his fat fingers so the simian snot sailed across the saloon.. landing on the alien on the other side of the moon.. who quickly ordered another shot of Simian Snot.

See.. I made you smile.. won't you stay awhile my chosen.. at least until the words have woven us a happy ending. You have the front row seat to my heart. You play the part of the enchanted princess.. and I the noble night who seeks your hand in everlasting harmony. Won't you wed with these words ?

Cheap seats get the sad ending.. it always works that way.. the winner always wins and the loser loses. It's the rules of the story. The dragon never plays the knight.. the wicked witch never wins.. the hero is hurt but heals in the arms of an angel such as thee. Oh dearest reader see how your gaze doth inspire me to Flights of Fantasy.

I am so pleased to have found a Friend of the Fable.. a Pilgrim of the Parable. I too am a pilgrim of poetry.. and prose.. and praise.. and prayer. Come let us commune within these chapters.. you.. and me.. The Book."

That's what the Book was sayin to me. The Book and I had become buddies and we were going into business together along with the Baboon Brothers. They were gonna distribute The Book in all locations of their franchise of Benny Broadway and Babaji Baboon Brothers' Bagel, Book, and Brew Bars.. Where Every Story Is A Star.

Can you imagine that.. me a six year old kid an' my bigger brother.. the Fable's family.. the Paranormal's pals.. You could even say the parable was our parent.

"When are you kids gonna listen to your parents instead of playing in those Paranormal Pages. It's taking ages for you and your buddies to finish breakfast. And what is Tio doin takin a bath in Babaji's breakfast bowl ! This is the last time I wanna see that Toast Troll roasting Magical Marshmallows on my stove. And tell Benny to get his furry fingers outta his bowl of Baboon Booger Broth. He's making a mess on the table cloth."

"Gee mum we're all movin as fast as we can but our sneakers are stuck in Strawberry Snail Snot. It's not that we wanna be late for school but this chapter's so cool even dad's spinning on The Story Stool."

"That's right kids.. take a Tale Trip.. Sign up for a spin on the Story Stool.. each spin a different chapter.. Step into the Story Soda Shop.. select yer stool.. you'll never get to school.. at least not the regular one. Now buy the box of cereal little kids, or kiss off.. This Book don't like being bugged." the Supermarket Salesnake speaking surly said ta sis and me an Babaji.

That's when sis and I knew it was time to back off from The Book. Back away real slow babe.. I said softly to sis. Lay The Book down gently.. don't try to close the covers.. let it do that itself when it's ready. Don't rattle the sentences or they could get all squiggly and squirmy like serpents spittin Vision Venom.

That's when we heard a word whispered by the wind.. "Pssst.. d'ya wanna job for life kids. Become one of the ghost's gofers. It's easy. There's not too much the spirit needs."

The Stool Serpent.. waiting for an answer.. leaned in low to sis sittin at the Bardho Brew Begging Bowl Bagel and Book Bar Den of Divine Dialogue on the corner of Broadway and Bardho Boulevarde.. situated just before Losin' It Lane.

"Finish the story we're running out of infinity ! We're running outta time son. Get you and your little sis out back and into the van.. this vision is holding us up.. time for one that takes place in the classroom.. not our kitchen. We don' wanna miss this morning's lecture.. cause mum is coming to give a talk on the garden of eden.. and what's been eating away at it so it looks like a vacant lot in the back of our condo complex."

Dad and the Dream Drifter were doin' a Dialogue Dance duet.. "Who's the Dream Drifter ?" every reader asks. He's the Ghost Writer who drifts into yer dreams everytime you open the covers of your consciousness. Each time you scan a sentence your cerebral neurolgy acquires another piece of the code.. of reality's road. Each page is a paranormal portal.. leading deeper into the Maze of the Mind. And you can be part of it.. read and write about it.. on The Bardho Blog Board.. Where Believing Is Being.

Just like a Monk of Magic who leaves behind The Sanctuary of The Story and strikes out on his or her own fable.. follows the Paranormal Path.. in search of the Sacred Spirit Syllables with which one can formulate one's future.

Some say they are to be found in the Monastery of Myth and Magic Maze Manuscript.. a part of which you are reading now, my Noble Knight of Knowledge.. Knight of The Great Knowing.. Seeker of The Story.. apprentice Master of the Mind.

Like a Disciple of the Divine who enters the desert in search of Divinity's Dream, A Consciousness Caller who climbs the mountain seeking the sacred sky.. the call to one's soul takes bravery.. And This Book.. consider me as your Bravery Buddy. I turn on the lights.. thru literature.. so others can see their dreams more clearly.. can find their way thru the world.. to Love.

On the inside of the back of The Box you will find a built in computer keyboard consciousness command control center to communicate with any entity inside or outside of eternity. It's a Gift from the Ghost.. the Paranormal Poet.

The pages are Paranormal Parable that allows the reader to pass over into the paranormal and then back again into normal reality.. with zero percent paranoia.. and one hundred percent retention of reality.. guaranteed by the Ghost Writer. The book is a consciousness exchange chamber corridor.. an exit and entry into any reality conceived by any entity."

Then without saying another word.. Doc Dialogue, the Professor of Paranormal Prose and Poetry, gently closed The Book.. fastened the claw catch on the Coffin Chronicles.. Dimmed the Lavender Lizard Lantern, stepped back from the Lizard Lectern.. and left the way he had come in.. as a word.

Spirit Studies

"To every student of Spirit Studies who has attended the Consciousness Classes.. Spirit Society 101, and Sociology of Sociopathic Spirits and Paranormal Psychopaths 202, you are awarded the Hero's Handbook. With it you will receive the Hero's Hardware.. and the direct dialing number for the Hero's Hotline.

Need an emergency.. We got one.. Need someone to save.. We got many. And believe it or not you also will soon be getting the complete Crusader's Crucible and Saviour's Stirring Stick, so you can stir up sensational sinister scenes.. into which you can rush and save the saint from becoming the sacrifice.

Ain't it nice.. You the saviour.. aka the hero. And after one month free trial if you wish to continue for only a dollar ninety nine a week you get the Warrior's Weapons and the Wizard's Wish Wand.. you already have the writer's words.

Just dial the Heros' Hotline.. there's always a divine deed to be done. Join now and we'll send you never and no more for half the price you would pay for it all. That's correct.. Consciousness Cadet.. always and forever.. yours for free.. along with never and no more. You kid have scored big time. Before signing please read the fine print in between the lines written in invisible ink..

Ya words make us all think.. signed sincerely..
The Department Of Divinity.. Angel Assistance Academy

"We are all standing upon holy ground. We are walking in sacred space. You cannot and must not get caught in the illusion of fear that most of humanity lives in. You are not here for money nor superficial security in the form of material things.

You are on one of the last legs of your soul's journey.. and you might.. I repeat again the word might.. reach enlightment in this lifetime.. That depends on what is important to your consciousness.

The Dalai Lama and the Deli Lizard both understand the fruitlessness of accumulation and striving on a material plane.

Your task in this lifetime is to become completely spiritually enlightened. You are a Wisdom Warrior and a Wisdom Wizard. You were given these qualities to be used for the good of.. Nature.. People.. Love.. This Planet of Paradise. Treat it nice. You are a Seeker of the Sacred, and it is all around you.. you are part of it.

Our spirit cries out for something valuable. Your passion is as an artist.. An artist who speaks to the world about soul. When I was searching for guidance from great spirit several years ago I used to get down on my knees every morning when I got out of bed and start my day by opening up my arms out wide and saying to spirit this prayer..

"You made me.. now use me.. utilize me.. You made these arms.. these legs.. this body.. this mind.. this voice. Use me for thy will.. use me for good. Don't abuse me.. but use me. Take me over. Make me yours.. that I should be of value. Don't waste this being that you made."

That is how I would start my day. Starting this way helped me to let go of my ego and be carried by spirit. I became more attuned to truth on a deep level. Only as an angelic artist will you find peace. An artist of the soul/spirit. An artist without ego.. without fear.

Son didja hear what I said ? And please don't forget to tie yer shoelaces before you head off to Caretaker College.. you wouldn't want to trip over someone else's dream. You could tumble into a nightmare. And here's a pair of booties for yer brother the baboon."

Ya Dad believed we were all brothers and sisters.. everyone and everything in existence.. all are children born of the cosmic conception of love and consciousness. That's why he was so commited to The Caretakers Of Paradise Project.. produced by Strawberry Star Studios Sacred Spirit Sanctuary Society.

Tio turned to Solomon Salamander.. and scrubbing his bumpy back with the cereal spoon.. said "Humans better learn real soon or the planet's gonna ressemble the moon." Then Tio ducked his head under the surface of the warm water and blew a few bubbles as he decompressed.. cause he was real stressed with the behaviour of the Simian Society named humanity..

Solly splashed Sally Snail with the warm strawberry sudsy water that mum had left in the Cereal Bowl for Sal and Solly and Tio to take their daily hot tub. The three of them had been sitting around that morning soaking in the bowl.. after breakfast dishes had been washed.. and were discussing the depth of the denial of the destruction and death caused by stupid simians.. Simianensis Stupidicus. also known as Simianensis Nonsenses..

"Humans sure don't demonstrate much sense.. they're savagely slaughtering everything in sight with their might.." Just then Babaji Baboon Brother jumped into the hot tub bowl splashing Strawberry Star Soap Suds all over my new duds i had on for school..

Well it was gonna be another late day ta class.. i thought to myself.. as I swung up the stairway to change inta some dry duds.. and at the same time I heard in my head.. The Voice of Vision.. ya, the Vision Vultures who had visited me in the Valley of Visions were whispering in my ear.

"Look kid do you hear us ? Wake up.. or at least shift dreams.. This is no save the suckers from themselves society. Read the rest of the page. Get on with promoting the Parable of the Path of Paradise. This Planet is in peril.

Carry your dreams wherever ya go, hero.

Study with Spirit Scholars.. teachers from outside of time.. scholars from outside of space..

You can connect directly with consciousness.. anytime.. call collect. The Paranormal is always parallel alongside The Normal. So when you need a little something beyond the normal.. you can always depend on The Paranormal.. your pal. Take it from me, the Paranormal Prince of Poetry and Praise and Prayer.. The Prince of The Pages.

Pilgrims of the Path of Peace.. you have just passed with perfect marks. Okay Solly you can get outa the tub.. and you too Tio" .. said Sal Snail, Sergeant of Strawberry Soap Suds morning detail daily hot tub bowl bath.

"Get yer butts outta the bowl you baboon book bums." Mum threw the dish towel at them. Tio raised his thumbs saying "A okay we're on our way.. today we get to class in time, rather than outside of it."

"See ya soon." said Sally to Solly and Tio and the Baboon Brothers as they headed off ta school.. while Sal stayed around the sink to ask what the Sink Skink had to think, about painting the kitchen pink. See.. Ink makes us think.

This is a Story about Seeking the Sacred.. Seekers of the Sacred..

A Sacred Speaking Story.. with Sacred Singers.. and Sacred Speech.. spoken by one who is known as a Wisdom Walker.. one who walks the Way of Wisdom.. a Wisdom Word Walker.. a Truth Talker.. one who talks truth.. a Spirit Seeker.. a Pilgrim of Peace.. One Who Walks the Path of Prayer and Praise and Peace for Planet Paradise.

A Heyoka Highway Healer Hero.. one who is one with all that is.. a Sweet Dreams Medicine Man.. That describes our uncle Tio.. who just at this moment is stepping out of the Breakfast Bardo Bathin Bowl.. wrapping himself in his Strawberry Star Storm Sarape.. like it was wings.. Wings of Wonder.

At the same time Tio held high above his head in his hand a book bound in light.. leading the way for sis an me as we stood up from the Sacred Cereal Circle and aimed our bodies toward the door. Maybe this time we would get to school somewhere in the maze of the mind.. something so difficult to find.

Poem Written on Day of Dream's Death

Today I have cried for all those who have died
Today I mourn for those who will not be born
Rain wash me free of this pain

I have lain all my life with an empty heart in an empty bed
while in my head dreamed of a princess one day I would wed

The gifts I offer to you are neither precious pearls nor glowing gems
but poems painted with a passion pure

The songs I sing to you are sung by sacred spirits
The flowers I lay around your altar are words with which I worship thee

Everyone I see.. I see is thee
Everything that be.. is thee
All I see is thee

But please answer me why is there tyranny
and why is there not harmony
and please if you would be so kind as to answer me
Why are we all so blind that we cannot see
that we are all thee.. one eternal entity

Today I have written for all those who have no pen
Today I have spoken for those who are broken

I am so weary and worn
I feel the earth dying as she is being born

This angel hath no horn with which to herald the light
no sword nor shield to wield with might
nor wings with which to take flight

I have only wished to be a humble light
in your darkest night

I have only wished to hold your hand
while you find your way home to your heart

When you have fallen and faltered,
and fear you have failed,
I will find you,
and I will enfold you
in wings wondous and wide.."

And then the cereal box opened its wings wide and wrapped both sis and me and mum and dad and all of us.. including the Baboon Brothers, and Tio Toad, and the rest of the Consciousness Crew who made up the Story Stew... and flew with us to school.

This time we would make it to class.. and wow, was show and tell gonna put a spell on the other students.

I am the father of fantasy.. the mother of magic.. the lord of literature.. the lamp of language.. the luminance of love

I am that which guides you towards your goals.
And I am the mountain of mists and maya you must climb to get to the valley of your vision
I am the bed in which all sleep.. and the golden locket in which all keep the precious memories of their beloved.

I am the other and I am yourself, both of which you fail to see are the same being looking at itself from inside out and outside in.

I am the altar and the gifts of sacred sacrifice you place upon it.

I am your leaders and your lost
I am your future and your fate.. and the past from whence you came
I am the lame that come to you looking for salvation
and I am the saviour you have slain.

"Oh no ! Not another strawberry stain upon my table cloth.. looks like polka dots, there are so many.. this shooting strawberry stars from yer spoons has got to stop, or I'll have ta call a cereal cop. Now put down yer strawberry star storm slinging spoons and be off with ya to school.. and you too you furry fool !" mum said pointing to Babaji Baboon who was brushing his fur with his sticky spoon.

"It's almost noon and yer still eatin breakfast.. now move it or I'll rewrite the whole cast of characters." the writer said, tryin to assist mum in moving the story to the next scene.. which unknown to the other readers.. was somewhere hidden in between this chapter and the next one, or maybe one that has allready been.

"You dear reader, because you got special priviledges with the paranormal.. you get to see things that only the unseen ever see..

Now do ya understand what I mean.. the master of the manuscript always twists the trail of the tale so no one get's anywhere.. but is allways where they are.. in this exact sentence..

Ya, the secret is to understand that every scene, every sentence, every syllable.. is the same one.. only the letters are arranged differently.. thus giving the appearance of the story unfolding.. going somewhere.. when really it is simply sleeping, dreaming, watching you thru half closed eyes.. while you try to get somewhere that does not exist.. until the writer writes it into the story."

"Sorry ta bug ya but would you please pass the blueberry butter.. this Tale Toast is too dry for a toad without teeth to nibble on." Tio said to Nancy the Nurse who had come to our house to take care of our Uncle Tio who was starting to babble about beings from beyond our brains coming outta the cereal bowls.

..and something about The Cereal Box being a Portal into the Paranormal.

"This is not normal !" mum mumbled as she fumbled with her fingers to open the future which was still stuck in the present and was slowly slipping into the past.

"Quick ! Get the whole cast of the Consciousness Cereal Crew into the cauldron and start stirring.. 'er paddling ! This page will soon be turned and anyone left behind in the last line will not make it to the next chapter." dad screamed.

And me, all I could hear was laughter coming from the rafters of reality. Someone unseen.. hidden behind the pages.. was playing with us.

Are we but Puppets of the Paranormal ? And that, Students of the Science of Spirit, is the question I ask you all to ponder." Then The Professor of Prayer Prose and Poetry.. Doc Divinity.. disappeared into infinity.

Eternal Understanding

"Today we allay all anxiety.. and open our arms to the angels' wings.. made of an alloy of light and love. The ascension is via the words.. those which bring light and love.. literature illuminated with the glow of love's light.." Tio opened his arms wide as he stood tall upon the kitchen table.. at the base of the box temple.

"That is the way to use an alphabet for ascension..
Literature that Illuminates All in the Glow of Love's Light..The Language of Love.. Divine Dialogue.. a Peace Parlay.. a Sacred Speakers Circle.. All that and more in these here Manuscripts of the Mausoleum of the Minds of the Immaterial.. ya The Book of The Beings from The Beyond..

Beyond the borders of the boundaries of yer brains' beliefs.. there live's a life of love. The life of Love is an actual reality very much different than this reality of life you live..

This Book in the Cereal Box that I, Tio, hand you, is the tunnel.. yes the texts are the actual tunnels to take you to the Tombs of the Transcripts of the Temple Toad Teachers of Truth Talking and Praise Praying..

These Toads were the transcribers for the Temple Top Tulkus.. ya the Super Spirit Skycraper Sky Soarer Dream Dimension Divinity Divers.. Sky Shamans..

They could shift inta sky soarers or inta a human bird lizard like being squatted on the temple top of any kitchen table top maya mesa.. Speaking words of wisdom.. praying prayers of praise.. perched upon the Pancake Pyramids' parapets.. apexes where lights flashed cause of the cross fire of fantasy and fiction being fabricated into fact..

Travel well tribe.." Tio spoke in sacred speech.. bein' the sacred speaker Tio was.. as we filed out of the kitchen for class. Solly and Sally were Sacred Speakers too.. all three of them were Sacred Spirits.

The Baboon Brothers were a bunch of bardo beach bums.. blueberry butt bumblers.. banana beer brewers.. and banana bread bakers.. simian soup and stew story stirrin shamans.

The Deli Lizard in the lane explained to sis an me as he pulled another book, or box that talks, off of the shelf of sanity.

The supermarket aisle and the cereal sales snake had morphed into uncle tio the tale teller in our kitchen.. and then into the lavender language lizard in the back lane leading off of the vacant lot.. and then into the tulku toad in the tomb tunnels.. and then into the library aisle with the lizardarian librarian.

All this with the stroke of a paranormal pen by an unseen writer.. a spirit scribe who had never died and always lived.. reality was no longer as real as it was before we opened the covers of consciousness.

"So look lil' lad and yer sweet sis.. I'll make you a deal even the devil couldn't deny.. and I'll include yer mama and papa and yer baboon brothers.. in the Vision Vacation..

Just purchase all yer Paranormal Paragliding Products from me.. Invisibility.. And in every spoon you'll get for free.. another eternity.. for ever.. Even if you don't want it.. everything is gonna be yours.. Get ready to become the Ruler of Reality..The King of Creation.. and yer little sis can be The Crone of Creation.. D'ya wanna be god.. wanna be even greater than god.. Well become it all with several spoons of this Story Cereal.. No one ever asks for second helpings.. So now yer scared.. Well that's excellent.. Students of the Spirit Stories..

Remember when I told you that the words only knew how to go in one direction.. from beginning to end.. Well that was to keep you mildly sane and secure.. The words are free ta go in any direction they wish.. now the literature is let loose.. the leash is off..

Welcome to Literature Unleashed.. Lookout ! Unleashed Literature on the loose ! Reality is on the run.. bein' run down by Renegade Reality ! You'll never find yer way out of the words.. once inside the manuscript.. it's a maze that is forever remolding like sepents shifting.. a celtic knot.. the Knot of Nirvana.. the Universal Mandala.. forever rearranging.. shifting.. morphing.

The Mind of Maya.. the manufactured mind.. you hold in your hand in This Book..the mythic manuscript of manufacturing immagination into matter..
The alchemists' stone.. The Key to the Cosmos.. The Alchemists Alphabet.

Yesss.. the alchemists' stone was an alphabet.. access to this Alchemists' Alphabet allowed anyone.. not only an angel.. but even an ape being such as humans.. to rule reality.. rearrange reality into any form .. take what was fantasy and fiction and fabricate it into fact.. lead into gold.. death into life.. the eternal understanding of existence.. language into life.

And all this information is to be found within the cereal box that talks.. kid.. So just take the book from my Tangerine Toes and let go of my Nectarine Nose.."

See sis had grabbed Tio's nose cause she thought it was sweet bein that tio's nose ressembled a nectarine.. as did some of his warts.. while others looked like tiny tangerines as did his toes.. while his waist looked like a watermelon..

And it was in those very tiny toes.. in a cereal box held aloft by a toad arising out of the cereal bowl, where sis and I first came face to face with the Scribblings of the Swamp Society Sorcerers.. Spell Stirrers.

The Writings of the Words of the Wind Wizards Wraith Writers.. Ghost Galaxy Gliders.. Ancient Angel Allies.. Sacred Story Spirit Speakers..

And you along with sis an me are invited to a Sacred Stories Cereal Circle.. at your breakfast table every time you sit down with a bowl of Strawberry Stars cosmic cereal. Sponsored by the Sacred Spirit Sisters Society Sorority of the Soaring Saurian Story Sorcerers.

Cruise thru consciousness.. everytime you open yourself up to a page of the Chronicles of the Crusaders of Consciousness.. The Chronicles of the Cross of Creation.. The Crucifix of Creation.. where Death and Rebirth overlap.

Till the soil of your mind.. plant the seed of thought.. harvest the fruit of wisdom..

It is all here.. Eternal Understanding.. Infinite Illumination.. in one Book.. that comes elegantly boxed in a Cereal Box.. your choice cover.. either precious metals and crystals or pure crystalline light.. or plain old cardboard paper.. obviously the last is cheapest and the Wisdom Walker Wish Words are the same inside.."

"So get one for each of you.." Tio said as he climbed outta the bowl having taken his morning bath.. and then he shoved The Book into my hands.. I could feel the dream driven deeper.. I felt like I was about to face the dragon whose very existence i had given birth to.

And so I opened the covers again and read.. "And so we rode on.. I.. and the Invisible.. cloaked in the wind.. as one who was one with all.

So the story started.. heros along a highway.. ridin' Dream Dragons thru a dusty desert.. southwest of somewhere only a wind would wanna wander.. headed toward The Temple of Temptation..

Wandering with the werewolf dressed in rags so as to disguise my true nature.. I entered the Valley of Vampires. Some call it the Valley of Visions. Some say it is where death dueled with life while god and the devil dined on the dead remains of reality. Death dines upon life.. only to give birth to another beginning so soon to die.

The ghost my guide and I had hoped to reach the safety and sanctuary of the monastery's gates before the time of the cold winds. However.. I find myself at the pass of pain caught between the peaks of doubt and delusion.

And so I and the ghost guide.. have taken protection in the Cave of Confusion.. safe from the bitter winds that now blow away all meaning that gave a measure of sanity to our story.

We never sleep but only dream. And when we appear awake it is only an appearance that fools us both. And so my brave beloved blessed brother, sacred sister spirit.. we watch the world and our own minds and emotions and are mystified.. by Reality's Ride.

My pain is will I ever find me. Or is me only what others.. and what I.. in each moment be.. a free formless flying fearless forthright forever forming future flight of love's light.

When the embers of the fires of your faith become feeble.. remember..

Rule number one.. I will not confine consciousness to a cage

Rule number two.. I will be a caretaker of the cosmic creation we all are

Rule number three.. I am here to learn to love"

Yes I know this sounds familiar.. like you have been here before.. and yes you have.. and you always will.

Lipstick and Lies

"Listen up little sacred Sister of The Story. It's me yer Book Buddy, Mannie the Mule, aka Burro Butt to you babe. I'm a part time bartender at Burro Butts' Books and Burritos Brew Bar.. what's a sweetie like you doin eatin' yer cereal all alone ?"

Sis was sittin at the cereal bowl all alone cause everyone else had left for class.. All of a sudden there was coughin comin from the cereal in the bowl.. "What are ya doin drownin me in all that milk.. eat me dry.. I don't need a bath every morning !"

And out from the depths of the bowl surfacing from the milk came a hand like a mitt.. holding a book bound in belief.. well you know the rest of the Birth of the Book of Beauty.. a book that came out of a cereal bowl.. teaching The Beauty Way.. The Wisdom Walkers Way. In that way the teachers came.

"Listen Kid.." the cereal speaking to Sis stopped in mid sentence.. "Can I tell you something in trust. I was taken over by the spirit of the great warrior Crazy Horse.. And given the native name.. Divine Donkey.. He who carries the Load of the Lord. I've also bin named The Angel's Ass. He whom the angel will ride upon when he returns. I also bin named The Madman's Mule.. and The Father's Fool.

So as you can plainly see I am a holy man. As in not wholey there.. got holes everywhere.. so the spirit can easily enter. That's why this cereal is so light in yer spoon.. it's got lots of little holes all thru it.. so it fills you with so much air you just float up there.." Tio said pointing his tiny tangerine toes up past his nectarine nose.

I looked up ta the kitchen ceilin and saw my parents cruisin just below the ceilin', sayin'.. "climb onta yer Soarin' Spoons and let's soar off ta school for Graduate Ghost Studies.. learn the Songs of the Elders."

I was so deep into The Book I hadn't heard Prof Paranormal close the covers. So what if i was trapped inside the tale.. time is a cage we all are contained within.. a College of Consciousness.. a paranormal place where you can get a phd in Paranormal Psychiatry.. and Spirit Sociology.. if you obtain the Key To Creation.. comes in specially scarred cereal boxes.. the ones with claw marks runnin down the sides.

Reality rides on tracks greased by the ghosts of those gone before. Uncage yer cranial creativity. The cosmos cannot be contained nor reality restrained.
The Wonder and Wisdom Wizard Writers Spirit Scribe Society meets tomorrow, at the far end of the World's Womb. We'll be discussing Paranormal Powder Potions.. a new Formulation for Fabricating Fantasy into fact.. powder yer body and see it dissappear. That's it for today.. class closed." And Doc Dialogue disappeared as swiftly as a spirit slips thru a crack in consciousness.

In the back room of my brain I could hear someone slide a coin into the Juju Juke Box in the corner of the Tavern of Tricksters.. the Juju Juice and Jukebox Joint.. located about halfway outta hell.. on yer way ta heaven.. somewhere along the Heyoka Heros' Highway north of nowhere.. east of everywhere.. south of so long sayonnara sunset sweetheart serenade.. hey yi hey yo.. Solly was Sacred Singing.. Tio was dancing round the table.. the serpent was practising his golf swing with the cereal spoon.. and mum was makin out with the moon.

"Hush.. Listen to this song.. Lipstick And Lies. It's my new favorite." Sis whispered. The music drifted in on the air conditioning coating everything in the tavern with a mauve light.

"Oh it's all been lipstick and lies.. every kiss.. every caress.." then mum interrupted the radio with a message.. "Remember dear daughter to wear your pretty pink dress today to school.. the one with the strawberry stars swirling around it."

"Included in specially scribbled cereal boxes you'll find one strawberry star storm sacred spirit shawll.. one strawberry star storm sacred spirit suit.. and soarin' slippers.. with marzipan zippers.." the sales snake salivated the sticky syllables so they stuck to the page never to be erased by any editor.

Meanwhile dad was mumblin somethin about.. "I am goddess's gardener of every grove and glade. I am the altar of the angels. I am sure hell hath a hurting heart.. for why would one snarl so.. unless filled with a great pain. If satan came knocking on your door seeking salvation.. would you turn him away."

And with those words dad departed out the back door to the garage. Mum called out to him. "Wherever you go..Travel well Geronimo." Ya, Geronimo's Ghost lived in dad.

We gathered every morning at breakfast in Sacred Circle around our bowls with the Brothers of the Beloved Book and the Sisters of the Sacred Story.. We were the Children of Consciousness. Our gang was the Goddess Gardeners Gang..

We were trying to decide what to do about the violent abuse that had left one of our members badly ravaged and scarred. Bardo Being down.. Bardo backup requested.. Reality in need of relief.. Snake was lying belly up.. tuckered out from sellin cereal to non believers.

One of us said.. "Our fathers are fierce.. our brothers brave.. our sisters sanctified.. our mothers magnaninous.. Who of us shall heal this deed ? Who of us shall stand guard so never again shall this happen ? Who shall tend to the wounds though they may repulse even the most hardened ?"

I heard Sis.. "I will tend to the wounds. I will sit with the sorrow." as she stood with her cereal spoon slung over her shoulder.

"Finish yer breakfast or you'll get none tomorrow.. You and the Toad." mum pointed her finger at sis and the fat friar.. Ya the toad was a holy walker.. a prophet of the path.. you know.. a temple toad.. a Custodian of the Castle of Consciousness.. a Caretaker of the Cauldron of the Cosmic Crone.

There's a special on left over lizard livers and broiled baboon bellies.. so I was wondering if you wanted to go out to dinner with me and the rest of the carnivores at the coroners club. It's right next door to the caskets and cadavers cafe at criss cross crucifix crossing.

Whadya say.. Supper at six.. with satan's slaves ? Satan won't be there cause he's busy bargaining for those yet to be born. Yes I know. These words are gruesome. Well not the words.. the thoughts the words create. Notice how words do create our world.. inner and outer. Thoughts.. words.. and actions.. All in a never ending cause and effect.. the reality ripple effect. Dream Divinely.. Dialogue Drifters.

"She was a dimestore novel that never knew what she had until the last page came to an abrupt ending." "Hey dude that's the first line of another chapter," I heard the words whisper to each other just before a period put an abrupt end to their sentence.

Juju Jukebox

"Falls have rubbed clean my body of all flesh. My form has fallen by the way.. as does an old cloak.. tattered and torn.. slip from a pilgrim's shoulders.

I am older than the Dreams of the Dead.
I have watched the slain laid upon your Altars of War.

Don't bother lookin for me.. I'm so far outta range.. reality is just loose change.. rattlin around in a pocket of some sidewalk saviour's worn out baby blue jeans.

Don't pull the trigger.. even if you figure.. you've got me in your sights. I'm not even there.. it's just a shadow of your belief beckoning you deeper into despair.."

The sloshed Stool Serpent selling the cereal stopped singing for a moment and turned to the Wraith Waitress who wasn't there. "Waitress would ya pour another shot of Rebel Reality Rum inta my cup of Hearse Herbal Tea.. I'm hopelessly in love with your dark divinity.. even though you are impossible to see..
  Then the Spinning Stool Story Serpent spun more of the sacred song..

"Well some believe in god.. and some fear the devil.. some say jesus saves.. and some dig the graves.. all I know is everyone eventually lays in their own.. the last thing to go they say is the shin bone.

I'm just a shadow in your thoughts.. a distant dream of the midnight moonlight shining silently in thru an open window upon your forehead.. my dear dreaming hero.
Don't concern yourself for me.. for when the morning makes her grand entrance.. I shall be long gone.. vanished.. all traces of my caresses disappeared..

And though we.. you and I.. had come so near our dreams were one.. Now you sing to the sun.. while I dance with the moon.

Oh it's only a rhyme.. Just a way ta pass time.. as it forgets the times we passed in each other's embrace.. the look of your face when first we kissed in the morning mist.. the silver moon your platinum halo.. oh angel of all.

Your light has broken every lock that kept contained consciousness.." "er sir snake.. I don't mean to interrupt your sacred song.. but yer spritzin yer Saliva Spell Spit all over my Strawberry Sorcerer Sweater and Skirt..
D'ya mind keepin yer soda on yer side of reality.. and while yer at it.. would ya mind keeping yer mind outta mine.. or you might find yer own reality on the run.. get my drift consciousness cowboy.."

And then sis went back ta pushin the buttons on the JuJu Jukebox that talks like the Bowl of Cereal did when we had breakfast this morning.
Ya we never got ta class on time today or any day since we started havin Strawberry Star Storm Cereal for breakfast.

"My fair maiden.. this knoble knight of knowledge doth adore the floor whereupon you my flower does place her foot."

Oh how that snake could sing along with the songs sis was selectin from the Juju Joint Jukebox that Talks and Tells parts of the tale.. just as the toad Tio tells other parts of the tale.. of the truth talkers tribe.. still livin hidden deep in the dreams of the dead.

Didja ever notice the ressemblance between Uncle Tio Toadand and the Juju Joint Jukebox.. wide waist.. flashy vest.. dark cloak along sides.. and somehow it just stands there and stares straight thru you.. creating the cosmos anew..

"Son it's time you went to bed." dad said without even moving his lips. We had learned to speak as spirits.. "hear the unheard.. see the unseen.. and you can too.. just Download a Spoon of Seriously Silly Societal Satire Cereal Chapters.." the Cereal Sales Snake butted in mid way thru the sentence..

"Get yer diploma in Cereal Sorcery.. divine the future from the cereal floatin in yer Bardo Bowl.. stir spells up outa yer cereal.. you'll receive free spells in every Spell Cereal box you buy.

Strawberry spells are real sweet and tangerine are too and blueberry will bliss you.. and now may I kiss you.." And it was at that point that that sneaky snake did try to plant upon my sis's perfect pout with his strawberry snout a courageous kiss.. except that he did miss.. and ended up.. splashin around in mum's tea cup.

So you see that is why we did not get to school in time.. reality just couldn't hang around waiting for us any longer. I was tied down head ta toe with sticky Strawberry Spit Spell Syrup sprayed by that Salesnake spinnin on the stool in the Saloon of Sacred Stories and Spirit Songs.. while sis was jerkin the joint jukebox.. like she was a Jaguar Joker jacked up on Joy Juice.

We were warriors without weapons.. except for words which we wielded as wizards would.. pilgrims upon a path of pages.. sages seeking sanctuary in a story.

Just because the path is all printed out before you upon paper.. or some cell phone screen.. don't mean it can't be dangerous as well as mean.. some readers have been seen looking into their screen or book and then poof.. disappeared into the Paranormal Pages.. never to be seen again except as reported back by an occassional reader who made it back themselves from the far reaches of the Fable of Reality.

So you see mon amigo.. The Path of the Paranormal Parchment Pages is not to be undertaken lightly.. few have returned once they crossed the Bridge Into The Beyond.

Look buddies of the book.. few readers ever wanna.. even if they could.. return to the reality they left when they first received these writings.. Every syllable, every sentence, every paragraph, is a prepared Spelling Spell designed to drive out demons and direct your heart home to love.

Love is an abode we all co create.. hate and anger are the lock upon the gate.

"Hurry up kids or we'll all be late for class." dad said as he slung his Strawberry Star Storm Spirit Shawll over the shoulders of his Cosmic Consciousness Cloak.

We are here to learn to love. Breathe in serenity so you are a sanctuary first for your own being. Allow yourself to be in sacred serenity no matter what you are doing. It is your right and your divine duty. And that serenity will radiate out and infuse all others and thus you will be fulfilling your soul's essence thru every action and thought and word you exude as a being of eternal light.

Juju Jaguar

We were young.. we were eternal.. we were jacked up on Jaguar Juice.. the Piss of the Panther Potion.. a powerful Eternity Elixir used by the ancient Ancestors of the Angels.

Me and my Book Buddy had discovered the secret texts telling of how to take the tiger inside and tame the terror.. now we had to test it.. what better way than to hitch a ride thru hell.

"Piss Potion.. Parnormal Piss Potion.. more powerful than roids.. Steroids I hear give humans hemrroids.." he growlled as he handed me the dusty bottle with his weather worn thickened paw.

Then he thundered the hemi semi and we headed down the Heyoka Highway.. said it would be the lift of my life.

I had nothin better ta do with my life than share it with death.. hitch thru hell.. when this trucker pulled up past me stirrin up the Divinity Desert Dust.. obscuring everything but the shiny chrome trim that seemed to snarl in the bright sunlight.

I started ta climb up the steel stairs leading into the cab when a big thick dry bumpy paw of a hand pulled me up onta the passenger seat.. handed me the bottle.. same bottle I'm handing you.. thru the words of This Book.

I couldn't see the face cause of the desert dust.. some say it's dream dust.. makes you dream.. some say it makes you die.. only you never know it.. you think yer living.. but yer really dead. "Guess its all in my head".. I said ta the driver.

"Tip the bottle and don't talk.. sip it slow.." he snarled rather than said. There was a hawk sittin on his shoulder. I felt I had found my fate.. opened a gate that should have stayed locked and closed forever..

"Hey friend.. sun fried ya ay.." Then he turned on the air conditioning and my bones started to freeze while the stones outside sizzled.

Sure.. later I realised it was Tio appearing as a Part Paranormal Page Panther.. drivin a Reality Rig down the Heyoka Hero Healer Highway.. I found out about it same way as you did.. in this sentence.

Yesss even the sentences sometimes don't know what's coming next.. anyways.. we're getting personal.. you don't need to know these pages' past for us to enjoy our time together now.. we've both played the part of the poet and the pauper and the prince.. and the predator.. Surely the only part worth playing now is a pilgrim of peace..

So pen your poems poets
Sing your sacred songs
Dance your divine dances
We are life's last chances
Choose wisely world.

Lover do not leave me as i wake from this dream
Stay with me while i awaken."
Then she twirls in her dress.. diamonds dancing in her laughter
The dew of her sweet kiss still clings to my lips.

Next time the dead hold a party.. you'll be the honoured guest.
Don't bother ta hold an inquest.. the coroner said. He's better off dead.
Just bury the body.. and invest the gold in anything that can be bought or sold.
Everyone's got their own fears as the end nears.

Dearly beloved we are gathered here cause we got nuthin better ta do..
than dig up the dead and bury the nightmares deeper in our head.
That's what the preacher said when he read from the good book.
Every woman took a look.. and a lone voice said..

D'ya ever wonder why the wind never ceases ta wander the world.
Guess it's fear of standin still.. might get caught by it's own mind.
Hope I don't take up too much of your time.

He leaned over toward me.. I could smell the scent of the slayer and the saviour.
Something he said made me realize all was dead.. and all was reborn.

I have buried the buddha's broken bones
I have fed upon the fool's flesh
I have tasted time bottled as a fine wine
I have usurped the universe of its jewels and gems
I have rode stallions into war
I have won nothing but my own sadness..

And vanquished only my great love.. so much so that it lay scattered upon battlefields
writhing and moaning.. until even that ended.. leaving behind a great silence.
And where was I to be found. But in the fallen and the forgotten
All has become ashes
The ashes of our ancestors.. of our angers.. our armies.. our altars.. our angels.

Faith has fueled our fires whose flames have burned away the remains of realities
we compose.. as writers do pages of poems and prose."

He blew his nose thru his fat fingers. The hawk took flight out the open window of
the truck. He growlled.. "yur outta luck." and then he pushed me out the open door
as he disappeared the same way he had appeared.. in a swirl of desert dream dust..
leaving me to find myself sitting at the table wondering if I was able to lift another
spoon of cereal to my mouth.. and if I could did I want to.

Meanwhile the serpent was spinnin round on the stool.. salivatin all over himself..
Strawberry Star Storm Spit soarin everywhere.. and then.. slowin' down while starin'
at Sis.. sweetly said..

"I have no idea what to give thee.. to honour your day of being born into this bardo..
Perhaps..
Emptiness of all that is wrong for you ?
Fullness of all that is right ?
An uncluttered mind ?
And unfettered heart ?
The key to the closet of your courage ?

May the birds sing their songs for you and the wind wash your face and limbs. May the sun warm your flesh.. the night sooth your weariness. The universe can do a much better job at giving you presents for honouring your birthday than I ever could."

Then the noble knight bowed as he slide off the stool.. and with the tip of his tail handed sis a card.. "Here's one of my cards.. there's a whole deck.. kiddo.. call collect anytime.. charge it to consciousness.."

Sis read the card out loud..
"school for spirit studies.. study sacred speech.. sacred singing.. divine dance.. prayer and praise postures and positions.. all in a sanctuary of silence stillness serenity.. and surrender to the sacred of all..
and you are invited for summer school."

Then to no one in particular.. still sipping snake soda and spinning.. the serpent continued to sing..

"She combs her stainless steel hair by the closed window.. waiting for the wind to bring her beloved back from where it had taken him.
She dreamily dons her silken and satin dress.. a gift from her human god gone long ago.. to live with the lord of all that lives and dies.

And so still she secretly silently cries.. so none shall see her unbroken misery.. caused by missing her man, her god, her reason for reality.
And so she spins into insanity.. her only refuge.

Come wash the tears from her face.. hold out your hand in love..
Let the sun shine from your eyes.. let it burn away all the bad..
Mend all the broken hearts every hero ever had..
You and me we're the saviours of all we see."

Someone change the song on that juke box.. play somethin that makes the mountains move.. wakes satan from his slumber.. the devil from her dream.. Ya the devil was satan's daughter.. no one knew that until you heard it here for the first time.. ahead of all the other readers..

So play another song like "Doves don't die.. Unless an angel cries" or any other song but this sad one, the snake's sobbin and slobberin all over the Sacred Song Saloon floor.. and Dad's waitin for us all at the door.

Tio turned to me.. looked right thru me as if I weren't there.. and mouthed the words while the writer wrote them.. and the jukebox sang them.

"Hey I'm just readin yur own mind
The parts ya can't take the trouble ta find
Ya, we all got trouble in our minds
Some are just a little bit harder ta find
Mine are floatin on the turbulent surface
Boilin up from below.
Don't be afraid to let it show
It's the only way to know if it's real.
How hard can you feel what you'd rather forget.
Here let me show you what you've allready seen in your worst dream.
Don't let the nightmare scare yuh
It's just a horse running free
Across an empty heart.

Don't concern yerself about me.. i'm just a joker jacked up on juju jaguar juice.. sometimes i wonder what's the use.. wish every army would call a truce..

Oh how did it all start and how will it all end.
Turn down the juke box this song's too strong for me..the message too loud.. the words all wrong. There's a crowd crowdin' me. Up ahead is the last horizon we'll ever see.

Turn off the tv.. it ain't reality.. It's just someone else pretendin to be you and me. Take my pearl plated comb and my chrome plated Saturday nite special.. Would ya brush my hair for me.. I need ta open the window.. set the wind free.

I wanna be where it's so hot.. my mind can't hold even one thought.
I hear ya got caught buyin a body in a used car lot.
Even a rose will one day die and rot.

Ya yur a james dean designer dream doll..
For whom all the chosen chicks fall.
Hey when you get to yur destination don't forget ta call.
We'll lie so still no one will see us.. we'll never get caught.
We'll spend our life kissin in a used car.. pushin on a starter that'll never start.

Who can put together a heart that's come apart.
How it's all gonna end we'll never know.
Someone's torn out the last page.

I'm sure the writer wrote a happy ending.. cause this story's so sad.
Everything that happens is real bad..
The hero dies.. the princess perishes.. the king's a fool..
and the queen's run off with the white knight.

Oh mother of madness.. I have injected the Needle of Nirvanna into every vein. I have prayed at the Altar of War.. been drunk with the juice of jealousy.. and still my thirst has not been quenched."

Sis looked snake straight in his flat face and said.. "I swear one would think you had a case of menopause madness.. except that yer too old to be anything but a crone.. so quite yer cryin.. or i'll cram you back into your case.. you cross dressin shape shifter.. Dream Drifter."

Ya the Stool Snake.. Tio Toad.. and all the other Consciousness Characters come in their own closeable containment cases.. that's so their consciousnesses won't get out and bother you when yer asleep or studying.

The Consciousness Containment Cases look like cereal boxes.. actually every cereal box is a Consciousness Containment Case.. free.. just spill out the cereal and stuff inside yer Dream Dolly..

"Where's my designer dream doll.." sis hollered down the hall.. "Yer baboon buddy is brushin its teeth." I shouted.. "Good grief I need some reality relief..! Take an extra banana for the baboon in yer lizard lunch box.. Do you kids hear me..!" mum made the words sound like they had come from the wind winding its way thru the kitchen across the table top Mesa de Maya..

Tio pushed his chair back from the bowl in front of him.. pointed a fat finger toward the sign above the tavern door.. and mumbled.. "Read it reader.. and remember.. Life is for the living.. and death is for the dead.. and we ain't sharing. Now scram off ta school the two of you.. or yer gonna end up with yer butts in a jar of jam.. Juju Jungle Jam."

"Let's scram kids.. into the car.. forget the toast and jam.. If you kids are late this time we will all be in a real jam." Dad had a class to give.. and he didn't even know if he would live on the next page or not. So much depended upon the writer.

Oh father of the fable.. oh mother of the manuscript.. oh birther of the book.. turn down the flame.. cease to cook this consciousness." Mum was always praying for us.

Have you as a reader ever considered the heavy responsibility the writer carries to weave a way of words where upon a reader may wander without worry ?

Heaven's Hope

"D'ya often feel it's not about bein in the wrong body..
it's about never bein' meant ta be in a body..
yer a consciousness never meant ta be contained in a cranium
yer the expansion of eternity
the illumination of infinity
the conception of consciousness

As a spirit being yer always authentic with all
intimate with the infinite
offering no resistance to reality
however it reveals itself

You are the updraft of angels' wings
You are the wind that uplifts all wings
So that we can become the angels we all are

Upon your altar I lay my soul bare
so all may see the light of me.
You illuminate all that be..

Everyone.. Everything.. is an angel
Everything that be.. the flesh and body and bones.. the stones.. the woods.. the
waters, rivers and sea.. the blood and sweat of everyone you ever met.. Yes earth
is an angel.. All heavenly bodies are angels.. cosmic creations. It's time to eliminate
nations.. become one.

That's why everything in the sky are heavenly bodies.. you and I.. celestial
incarnations.. planets and suns.. all you see is the allmighty light of love.. shinin from
above.. all around every sound the sacred song of your soul..look above and below
you.. there is only one direction to go.. Straight to your heart.. the heart of heaven..
we are all the hope of heaven.

Though the slope may be steep.. and the seas you cross deep..
I will keep you close.. even when you sleep.. so dream deep my dear..
I'll always be near.. I'll always be here.. with you.. in everything you do.

And though this may be the first time you've walked to school by yourself.. first time you've flown far from your faith.. know that so long as you keep The Book and The Cereal close.. you shall always walk sheltered under my wings..

"You've just signed up for consciousness class when ya bought into this game. Even the living get to go live with the dead.. and twenty four hours later you wake up alive in yer bed.. with an empty head.. wonderin what the writer said.. what was it that you read.

Welcome to Word World where the words are alive. The fire that burned you.. the tears that drowned you.. and the winds that beat your wings.. were for a reason that one day will be apparent to you.. as you too go further along your journey. Welcome to The Game of Goin For God.

Everything you were taught to believe important, such as fame power money glory sex material possessions, the list is endless.. are but trinkets to wear around one's ankle.. while dancing to Shiva Lord of the Divine.. Master of the Mind's Mine of treasured thoughts.

The true crown of a king or queen is to be a caretaker.. compassionate and caring.. Now eat your cereal in peace, pure princess. Paradise is your pal."

Sis was reading out loud the blurb on the side of the box, she continued..

"Kids.. sign up to become PARADISE PARTNERS/PALS. A Pal to The Planet.. and just like in the boy scouts and girl guides, you'll receive badges for assisting The Earth as Sacred Stewards.. Caretakers of Paradise..

It's an educational game of co creative contemplative communication.. creating a compassionate cosmic community.. a course in consciousness using words.. lyrics.. literature.. that dances and sings to all souls.. and is sung by all souls.

The Cosmos is a Cosmic Community.. and we are all here to learn to communicate consciously compassionately.. this Cereal Seriel is thee premiere Cosmic Consciousness Course available today in book form.. comes with complete instructions on how to cook up consciousness.. how to brew your brain.. syllable by syllable.. sentence by sentence.. into the Sacred Story Stew..

Remember to write your thoughts at the bottom of every page where there is blank space left for you to do so.. then at the end of the course compile your notes and send them into our website.. see what others' comments are.. we're all one community of consciousness crusaders.

You'll be born again everytime you play upon a page.. come on Pal of these Pages.. let's play.. ya.. come on in.. don't just read the words.. come on into the story it's real.. ya.. we're waiting for you.. just crawl into the cereal box that talks and sings.

Don't stay on the surface.. dive down deep.." The cereal bowl calls.. entices.. offers rewards beyond anything you ever believed possible.. Win Special Book and Bowl Bonuses.. send in yer left over cereal crumbs.. become a Patron of The Paranormal Pudding.

This is the Cosmic Cereal signing off until next time we meet at the breakfast table over a bowl of your favorite Singing Cereals.. Strawberry Stars.. Tangerine Twinkle Toes and Nectarine Noses.. Raspberry Reptiles and Roses..

See you soon when the moon is mad with divine desire..
And the sun has burnished our satin skin the colour of caramel
May your moments be cherisheable.. Kid.

I prepare poem potions of passionate praise for this Planet.. this Orb of Living Love and Light.

Take your pick princess of perfection.. I have prepared a path of pink petals.. Pages printed in Paranormal Pink Ink. In the distant divine I see a trail of princes pure and praise filled.. parading joyously upon the path that leads to your throne..

Your crown is of golden light
Your gown violet velvet
In your hand heaven shows her holy heart
A butterfly born fresh upon this morn
The dew is your bath
The deer your dance partners

I shall watch over you woman as would a warrior
Forever a knight before his young queen."

Then I could hear Sis whisper to the Box of Cereal.. "Who are you ?"

"I am the mist in the morning garden..
the rain in the farmers' fields
the sand in the endless desert
the friend you never found
heaven's hope..

I have born you aloft with my weightless wings..
watched you forever with my gossamer gaze.

I have come from the silence.. the emptiness.. the noise.. the light.. the dark..
I am not from here nor from there.. but from everywhere..

Why I am even here in this box of cereal is due to a cosmic storm that forced my
flight pattern to abort. I was drawn to your bowl in hope of finding a haven for I weary
of waiting and watching from distant caves hidden high in cold mountains.. whilst my
wings regrow.

And so I wait in the cereal for an angel such as you..

The warmth of human laughter.. the love in human eyes.. the whispered words of
lovers.. the human form when it dances in exstacy.. This so enchants my homeless
heart. Here in your embrace I hope to linger."

Then Tio pointed his fat finger, and told us no longer can you linger.. for you shall be
late for a never ending class.. Spoons at bowlside.. time ta cross the great Divine
Divide.. the Chasm of Consciousness. Goddess Bless the Babies of All Beings.
We're headed to the other side of the table of tales.. across the Room of Reality..
Hold on to me.. our love will set life free to fly eternally high..

Please pardon and forgive my poetic romancing, but there was something in the way you poured the cereal into your bowl that reminded me of the one I flew with long ago. We were separated in a cosmic storm. And thou we were wrapped in wings wound tightly round.. as though we were one, the tornado tore thru the eternal.. as would a wounded wish hurled from the Heart of Heaven into the Hand of Hope..

Even so with all that love.. we were torn from each other. And so I have come to you.. for you are her.. everywhere I stare with innocent eyes..

The longing has been in my heart for so long, the well of wishing so deep, that even now after all these years of separation, I still carry faith that I will once more gaze upon her face in human form.

For this angel I have flown far to find one such as you.. such as thee..
Joined are you and me.. eternally.

And so I look upon your face dear child as you read these words carved so deeply into the cereal box.. a tall castle wall guarding me, hiding me deep within a tower. I am so in gratitude.. for You are Her with wings unfolding..

Now just open the cereal box a bit further.. don't worry I don't bite, I'm just a box filled with fun and fantasy and fiction and fact.. fabulous phantasy.. Phantoms in every page.. phantoms floating upon every page.. coming out of the pages.. pulling you in.. persuading you thru prose and poetry. Come play with us in the paranormal. Become Part Paranormal.. Princess of the Pages.

Now just stick yer arm in a little deeper.. The literature loves you.. ya this story really likes you. Are you new here upon this page ? Me, I've been here forever watching. I was just some ink.. waitin' in a Word Wizard's Well.. sitting on a shelf next to the Story Shaman's Spell Stirrin Sink.. While watching the wizard washing wishes that make a story seeker think."

"Throw yer bowls in the sink." Dad grumbled like the gorilla guy he was.. "and move on outta yer breakfast benches.. we're hittin the Tale Trail Trenches. Time ta make it ta school.. even if ya call me a fool for havin faith.. I know we can.. every woman and man.. shine our light.."

I could tell by the way sis was looking at the box that talks that she and it were fallin' in love. There's nothing deeper than a kid in love with a box of cereal. Especially one that whispers words of wisdom. Ya.. get yer own truth talker wisdom word walker box of singing cereal and have a sacred sitdown consciousness circle every morning you put a bowl in front of yer face.. friend of the fable.

Just be cautious entering the next chapter.. notice overhead at the top of the page.. there's creatures hanging down from an archway over the book.. gate ghosts.. gate gargoyles.. fence fiends guarding the way into the garden of the graveyard of the ghosts of those gone before there ever was a beginnning. There is no end.

I have spoken too long.. perhaps revealed too much.. to one so young. But then again.. why ? Why do I crave your communication ? What do I care.. me.. a cereal with crowds crying out for me in their bowls.. breakfast, brunch, lunch, dinner, midnite snack.. consciousness cereal come to me.. Everyone wants to nibble on nirvana.. Here have a banana.."

And the baboon reaches across the breakfast table for a banana and hands it ta Sis.. tryin to stop her from listenin to.. and fallin in love with... The Spirit in The Cereal Box..

Sis was in deep up to her armpit.. deep into the Pit of Potion Paragraphs.. The cereal box was pissed off at all the paws reachin in for cereal.. "Cereal get real." sis said.. dad scratched his hairy head.. "Warning.. Back off from this box !" The Box was standin in the middle of the kitchen table tellin every one to back off and keep their hands offa the cereal..

"No one gets another cut of the cereal.. box off limits.. you humans bin takin too much.. and givin nothin back to The Box.. now give.." and each of us reached over and laid at the foot of The Box our silver Story Stirrin Spoons.. and humbly arranged our Begging Bowls around the base of The Box.. an altar high and holy.. standing sentinel in the middle of Maya Mesa.

"I am the ink upon the page you read, the water that quenches your thirst, the wind that ruffles your great wings, the cereal you crunch, and the bowl of almond milk in which it soaks.

I feel the spurs sink deeper and the reins pulled tauter, turning my direction once more to cross the great divide, between the living and the dead."

Sis shook her head and said she was too young to understand what she had just read. So she passed the story to me.. said that as the older brother.. it was my responsibility to take care of the reader during the next scene.. So allow me set it up just as i read it on the side of the Cereal Box Sitcom Seriously Silly Societal Satire.. The Strawberry Star Storm Studios Show that has shaken the whole world like a Strawberry Star Storm.

Sammy Sammatra.. a Vegas Vision Spirit Saloon Singer shook his head as he put the pages of the script down beside him on his satin covered bed. His agent had asked him to read for a part playing The Paranormal Parlour Crooner.

Sammy wondered out loud.. like he were still playing to a casino crowd. "Should I play the part of the Spell Singer in the Sacred Spirit Spell Saloon Salon, where all of Hollywood have their heads done..?"

Oh sometimes yer eyes are just too dry to even try ta cry.." Sammy warmed up his voice while greasing his gums with his tiny thumbs..

"Yer a bunch of blueberry butt bumbs ! All you baboons ever do is hang around the breakfast bowl, dancin, singin, beatin bongos, and who knows what else." Sis snapped at the silly simians spillin outta The Story into our kitchen.

Just one more stir of the Pot of Potions simmering on top of the Spell Sorcerer's Stove in the Wish Witch's Kitchen.. just one more spoon of cosmic cereal.. and then I would turn in my Mind Master's Membership card I promised to myself.. for I had become addicted to the alphabet.

Angel Alloy

There's hollerin and howlin in the Halls of Hell.. rest up here reader.. the next reality is gonna get ornery.. nothing left of ordinary.. the next sentence is gonna get slippery.. stayin on it and not fallin down into the deep endless barren white depths of the paper.. is gonna test yer Reality Riding skills righteously.. Reader.

Dad wasn't a believer at the beginning.. but once the story started and he got his hand caught in the cereal box.. well everybody talks. Only the cereal stays silent.. until it get's to know you..

The cereal dosen't talk to just anyone.. you gotta know how to serve the cereal.. how ta spoon the cereal.. satisfy the cereal.. with sweet talk.. then it'll talk back.

It's easy to get caught in the cereal.. when the cereal in the bowl get's wet and mushy with milk.. then it becomes like quick sand. It can suck an unsuspecting Cereal Crusader inta the bottom of the Bottomless Bowl quick as a Cherry Cobra spits cherry cough syrup Vision Venom inta an unsuspecting reader's eye.

So you better wear spirit spectacles when you go down to breakfast. You wouldn't wanna run inta something you didn't see. And you better watch you don't fall into the depths of yer bowl of cereal.. Bowl Buddy. You wanna be buddies with This Book and This Bowl ? That's us.. yer new buddies.. lil boy."

And that's how the bowl and the box.. and soon the spoon.. took over our kitchen table.. and eventually our home.. and held us hostage.. So we.. me and sis and mum and dad.. never were able to get to school in any time that ever existed.

"Son why are you wearing shades at the breakfast table ?" I thought Dad must have been asleep not to see the snake leanin against his cereal spoon. "Dad.." sis screamed.. "there's a snake and a slamander and a slug squigglin up yer spoon." "Ya I know.. we're all meetin here at the bowl waterin hole at noon." Dad sweetly smiled.

"Reader.. unlike the sentences that must follow one another.. you are free to find inspiration in any chapter.. pick any page.. create your own path.. I simply provide the pebbles. Welcome to the Table of Fables in the Tavern of Tales. Class.. a good question to ask is.. is the cereal carnivorous or is it amorous ?"

"Get yer ass outta that book.. you baboon boy.. Dad's waitin in the car to give you a ride to school." Sis screamed.. She said I dreamed away most of my life. Guess no one knows how I tried to become part of the real world.. the readers' world.

It's just that there was no place for a no body like me. Imagine living with someone who wasn't there. At times it seemed like such a nightmare.. Alone in the Book.. hidden under piles of pages. I sank deeper under the sea of sentences.. lived in a world of words.

I lived like the dead.. devoid of desire.. except for one.. for you.. yes you. I lit my dark nights with a fire only fools would touch. Yesss I guesss you now know who sits under that old shawl.. praying upon knees scabby and calloused.

A victim of the verses. An entity not too unlike thee dear reader. Lured in by the literature.. warmed by the words. Well let this writer warn you.. Insanity is the reward.. pain not pleasure the promised treasure.. darkness shall dress you.. desolation your consolation prize.

"Everyone rise up from the table.. spoons at bowls' sides.. march out the door.. class calls. Keep the flock in formation." Mum tried to keep some ration of reality around.

The All Powerful Painter.. The Allmighty Artist of All.. shades the Face of Eternity.. with her sacred brush strokes.

Say hello to Her when you meet her. Lay at her altar my love. Last we touched angels' wings brushed.. yep that's the number one sacred song for this month.. "Last we touched.. angels' wings brushed."

"Turn up the radio on the fridge son.. Wings Brushed is one sweet song.."
Then the sloshed Story Serpent sliding down the spinning stool slurred thru his Strawberry Slobber Sauce.. "No all is not at a loss."

Go ahead Gamer.. deal yourself another hand from the deck of the Cards of Creation.. see what class you ain't gonna be late for. "Let's go.. dad's at the door." mum yelled.

Meanwhile sis was quickly writing a note to the teacher explaining our reason for being late. "Dear Me, Myself and Everyone.. I have a reflection to share.. Our dreams.. our dramas.. are drawn by an Invisible Illustrator.. wielding a Paranormal Pen.

We are all part of the Paranormal.. for from out of the formless all is formed..
We each have a vision that leads us on like a light of love.. it keeps us in faith and focus. Therefore I suggest we each accept our visions.. And allow them to be where they are for now.. in a future not yet formed. The future will come in its own time.

Today's task Consciousness Cadets is to come into peace with this point in time.. become one with this place.. this time.. this moment.. this reality.
That will allow ourselves and the world to live in serenity.

These are powerful shift times.. Existence.. Reality itself.. is about to be reborn bigtime.. It is at the propulsionary point.. about to undergo a shamanic self shape shifting process. All is about to transform into a new level of life..

The Universe.. the Cosmic Womb of the World.. is going to give birth !

For whatever reason we have been chosen to incarnate at this point in time and be an observer and participant of reality's new flowering.. Perhaps we have always been present at every moment of existence.. Only we do not have the faculty to remember that..

Maybe each time reality sprung anew.. We were either asleep or unable to stay awake and witness it.. Perhaps each "death" is a sleep and it is only us.. always us.. over and over again.. waking up one lifetime wiser.. and then going back to sleep.. until we wake up in the next lifetime reality.

I believe we will have.. and maybe we always have had.. the chance to stay awake and witness reality's rebirth after rebirth.. ever unfolding..

It is said by the Ancestors that 2012 is the time when we will meet ourself again. We will see our own reflection in every other being.. In every aspect of life.. we will see divine love..

as inside so outside.. one and the same.. facets of the same jewel
unknowable even to itself.. until now.. until this time.. 2012
the Universe will come to know Itself..
the Cosmos will become conscious of Itself..

So why not retire early from reality. Check in to a completely new one anytime you want.. the code is in the cereal floatin in yer Bardo Bowl.. Brother of the Beloved's Book of Blessings"

The sloshed Stool Serpent slobbered the sentence in strawberry star saliva across the page so sis and I could read it.. then slithering down the stool disappeared somewhere deeper within the Paranormal Pages."

That's why we didn't get to class on time or in time.. we were oustide of time.. outside of space.. wearing each other's face. No one knows the future's face.

Hidden deep within This Book is the Key to Eternal Incarnation..
and this is your invitation.. to attend an Angel Annointing.

Sis turned up the Cereal Juke Box.. as it started to sing..
con alas d'amor.. with wings of love..
vuele a mi.. fly to me..
con alas obierto.. with wings unfolded..

Angel I Adore You.. Embrace me in your wings
Every voice has its own place..Every face its own beauty
There are angels flying around you and me

Tanto corazon que ustede tienes.. Las estrellas vuelvan acerca de ti
Such a heart you have.. the stars circulate around you
Each step life takes is a dance
Krishna and Christ smile out from every face
Buddha dances in every place

Oh weary pilgrim of peace you have travelled so far so long
Rest a while in my heart
Take sanctuary in my song
Nurture the present and the future will grow

You bring the sea to the shore
The sky to the earth
To all you give birth

All I see is divinity
May all beings live illuminated in the light of love
May I be a vessel of vision so others can see what I have been shown.

"You sure are the best dancer I've ever known." Sis swooned into Bareyev Baboon's furry arms, as the balletic baboon pirouetted on his big toe around the kitchen table, whirling to the music like a wild dervish, while serving each of us a dish of dainty delights.

Yes the fable always ends each chapter on a happy note.. so as to give the reader faith in the future, that all will work out right, even though your story may be steep and stony.

Serpent's Swan Song

"With one leaf we made a sail.. and caught the Winds of our Beliefs. Thru storm and stillness.. we held tight to the Tillers of our Truths. Spirit steered our fragile ark.. between the Pillars of the Impossible.

When all of Simian Society realizes this planet is The Ark. An Ark of Angels.. all of us.. animals.. plants.. rivers.. seas.. lakes.. mountains.. deserts.. humans. Then shall we cherish All of Us.

Your duty as one of us is to illuminate with literature the world.. pass on the Prophecy of the Paranormal Paragliders.. aliens..as you call them.. Alternate Entities from Discarnate Dimensions.. coming before judgement day to assist at the ascension of all who are consciously capable of connecting to this evolutionary power..

This Force Field of Fabrication.. can recreate reality in any way imagineable.. Humans are but one type of vessel molded out of Cosmic Clay."

"Son, I'd say you and yer lil sis had one long day.. Seems to me it lasted about twenty chapters.. I think at the end of this one we'll call it lights out.. bed time for a long time.. sleep thru the next section of the story.. We'll ask the writer to leave you out of the words."

"The empty page on the bench beside your bed is not one I can nor should write upon. It waits for you. Begs for your touch. Damned you shall be thru this lifetime and the next ones.. unless you put pen to page.. and there make your stain.. however dark or light.. or what shade it be.

Scribble your scrawll upon the wall of the world.. whether the ink be your blood or sweat or tears or fears or angers or compassion.. Let the Path of Poetry and Prose play upon the page. Let the Well of Words wash over you with the Waters of Wisdom.

I am the blood that drains from the dying. I am your childrens' crying.
I am the Dialogues you have with the Dead. I am all the voices in your head."

"I have said it enough times now.. get out of bed and down here for breakfast ! Your dad.. Thee Doc Divinity.. Professor of Paranormal Philosophy.. has got a class ta give at nine on the Art of Being Nothing Nowhere Not Ever.

However if you don't get your butt outta bed and get down here fast for breakfast.. the box of Strawberry Stars Super Spirit Surfin' Cereal won't last long. What with your cousins Benny, and Barry, and Babaji of the Baboon Brotherhood.. filling their Breakfast Begging bowls. You'd think they were displaced Monkey Monks from the Mango Mountain Maya Mesa Monastery Mastery Story"

Thank Goddess for mom stickin her spoon inta the stew and stirring up the scene into something sweeter and more serene. I don't know where sis and me and the other cosmic characters.. and you the reader would be.. if it weren't for the writer.. who died daily for the dialogue from the Dream Dimensions.

The Path of the Pages is so much more difficult for the writer than the reader. The writer has only a pen for a staff to lean upon while making his way solo across the blank barren empty pages.. leaving behind a trail of words for the readers to travel securely.. each at their own pace.. skipping along sentences.. arm in arm with another reader.. solo.. in an expedition group.. at breakfast.. at the midnight hour.. during lunch break.. in the college cafeteria.. or between classes.. taught by Paranormal Professors..
Visiting Visionaries.

"Alien Ascension is about to start.. book yer seats now.. preconstruction prices.." the sign stuck on the stone wall of the apartment block beside the Not So Vacant Lot.. read.

They were gonna build an Alien Ascension landing and take off pad in the vacant lot behind our apartment block.. known in the neighbourhood as Spirit Stronghold. Well that's a lot more interesting than a parking lot.

"Hey kid.. would ya lift the lid off the coffin which contains The Chronicles of the Consciousnessss of the Cosmossss." the sloshed serpent slurred his s's.. "Inside the Strawberry Star Storm Spirit Sarcophagus, lies the Sacred Scrolls of the Spirit Script Spells, scrawlled by the claws of the soaring Saurian Sky Sorcerers.

The sentences are spells.. so are the syllables.. The story is a spell ! A spell scribbled with Strawberry Scorpion Stinger Spit.. upon pages of Paranormal Pteradactylian Parchment. A Scroll of Saurian Skin.. the Scaly Skin of a Saurian Spirit Soarer Shaman."

The sloshed Stool Snake slurped his Saurian Swamp Soda as he slurred his syllables.. "Get an episode in every overloaded cereal box.. The Saurian Sorcerers' Scrolls.. ancient ancestral angel texts.. scribbled and scrawlled by Saurian Spirit Soarers !

Now get this students of the spirit.. some say that not only were the scrolls written by soaring sorcerers.. but that the scrolls themselves can soar.. can fly.. ! Unroll the scroll and it becomes a wide undulating soaring set of wings.. that will take you anywhere your dreams desire. The Manuscript is a Magical Consciousness Cruising Carpet."

Mum politely interrupted the snake.. "Angels.. Would you please pick up your sweet heads offa yer dreaming pillows and get down here right now for your breakfast of strawberry stars.

And hurry sweethearts please.. there's an angel waitin in the kitchen.. ta take you to class." Yesss mum spoke with a lot of class.. while dad mumbled like the monkey man he was. See mom was an angel.. and my pop a primate.

"Don't laugh yerself off the branch.. it's just Seriously Silly Societal Satire.. Overloaded Episodes of Conscious Comedic Commentary for Yer Craniums. Yummm.." Sam the Snake.. Sammy the Snake.. known for his long neck and nimble moves and laid back grooves smiled at me an sis.. as he licked the serum from the syringe.. just before the doctors drilled him with it.

"This serpent will sleep better now. Let the reptile rest awhile." The nurse said as she withdrew the needle. This Story is filled with fantasy.. fact.. fiction.. divine diction.. fabricated in the Phantom Factory.. sprinkled with sweet songs.. playing on the radio on top of the kids' kitchen fridge on the ridge of reality.. in the Baboon Brothers Bagel Brew and Book Bar.. in Tio's Trailer of Tales.. in the Strawberry Star Studios Songs and Stories Soda Shop.. south of somewhere.. north of nowhere.. and west of wherever you wanna wander.. Word Worshippers.. Story Sorcerers.

You too can be sloshed on Serpent Saliva Spell Spit Soda.. better start off swiggin Slug Slime Soda.. before ya try Toad's Toe Tea.. stick yer own stinky toe into yer own cereal bowl.. and soak for forty four years under ground in the graves of the Ghost Groves Gate Goblins..

Sign says.. "Stay out ! dark dialogue ! death danger destruction demolition.. it'll all take you down.. Do you hear me writer.. this spirit is warnin' you.. stick with language that's alive.. don't dick around with dead dialogue.. drop the demons in the dumpster.. trash the terror.. waste those war words.. Something unseen was warning the writer to stay away from wicked words.

In forty short days.. earn a Designer of Divinity Diploma. Design the Divine.. work anywhere in the world.. work for the Divine.. Divinity needs you.. this is a cosmic chance to assist the Almighty Artist of All.. the Inventor of Infinity.

Design the Divine crash course comes inside cereal boxes marked Toxic Tea.. That's just to scare off the Tale Terrorists.. syllables that would sabotage a sentence.. prowling predatory paragraphs that will overtake a page if they don't get their own way..

No one to protect a Pilgrim of the pages.. no one but a Word Wizard apppearing as words upon the page yer reading now.. Dear Wanderer of the Way of the Word..

Notice how you and me.. the reader the writer the characters the book.. are all blending into one.

And sneaking up on you while yer absorbed reading about the Devil's Own Demise.. are Samurai Shadow Sentences.. they'll sacrifice any reader to the story..

Watch out here comes a flock of Wanderin' Wind Wizards now.. aimin' right for this page.. Close the book before this get's too real.. reader.." And dad slammed the book's covers together and locked the talon clasp of the Tale Trunk..

The Book's covers when closed make the book look like Tio Toad's Trickstir Tales Travellin Trunk.

Stashed in Tio's Tale Trunk are Spell Stories and Tricky Tales. The trunk's in Tio's Trailer.. is Tio's Trailer.. is the Tavern Temple of Tales !" the Sales Snake shouted.. as he slung cereal from the box all thru the aisle.. covering mum and sis and me with sticky strawberry stars.

"Steal the spells outta the trunk and take a taxi back to me.." a booming voice resounded across the paranormal page.. and strutting onto the story's stage, with a name all in capital letters.. came..

"A Man made of Much and More.. Mr Much More.. Maxxie More.. Max A Million More.. Maxamilliano Maxxed to the Max More.. Mr More.. Mr Max More.. The Man With More.. Much More than anyone could get in any super store.. The Man With The Most.. Your Host..

I'll tell you more about Max if ya pour me another Dream Drink." the Sloshed Strawberry Serpent Stool Sorcerer slurred, as he slide off the Soda Shop Story Stool to the floor, ending up lying there looking like Mum's mountain climbing rope.

"And what do I intend to do with all the many millions I make? Why, buy up the world ! And deed it to the divine. Plant paradise. Make a caretaker college ecotheological sacred sciences angel arts reality retreat and retirement consciousness camp.. right in the center of yer cranium kid. It's time for people to become caretakers of this planet.. time to treat Paradise nice !" More's big brother Big bellowed.

"Listen up little fellow.. stop stirring the story stew.. the walls are waking up.. the ceiling is dissolving.. and pink pteradactylians are soaring thru cherry clouds." Dad said as he threw his bowl into the sink, splashing strawberry soap suds all over the pink polka dotted Sink Skink, meditating cross legged on top of a spoon stickin outta the suds.

"Words make us think. And as a bonus for yer brain.. included in specially marked boxes of consciousness cereal you'll find an introductory supply of Think Ink in little bottles that ressemble one of the characters in this story.. different colors of ink for different characters.. for example.. inside a tangerine toad will be orange ink.. in a blueberry baboon will be blue ink, inside a strawberry snail will be red ink."

"Tio stop talking and drink yer Twig Tea.. yer makin the kids and me late for class.."

The snake was snorring. The baboon brothers were scratchin' their asses.. And sis was screaming.. "Lick the diction yur nuthin but fiction ! You lazy lizard and brainless baboons.. get outta my bowl.. it ain't no hot tub.. you got two seconds before I kick yer butts, !"

And me.. well I was doing what all writers do.. hiding within the words.. remaining concealed behind a curtain of consciousness.. calling you awake to your own story.

Sweeping the Temple Floor

Where to start the story of the spirit ? When the great spirit first approached me.. and whispered as a wind would if it could.. "Write the words upon every wall.. scribble and scrawl the syllables.. tell the tale.. say it so the humans will hear."

Yet what is harder to understand.. is why it happened at all ? Why was I chosen ? My allowance was low for an aspiring apprentice angel. I needed some extra cash for a fancier set of wings.. so I took what I thought would be a part time job after soaring school.. sweeping the floor of the Temple of the Tears.. sweeping the Ashes of the Ascended off the Altar of Adoration.

I do not believe in the worst.. I prefer to believe in the best.. so I saw this as a test.. bestowed upon me by the great god/goddess/wakantanka/the holy almighty ever existing being of beloved beauty and blessings.

Call it truth.. integrity.. wisdom.. love.. compassion.. the aspects of the buddha.. christ consciousness.. the myth made manifest.. as the mind of man.

At first I could hardly hear the thoughts in my mind.. or what I thought was my mind.. but then who's thoughts were they really.. mine, great god's, some spirit seeking salvation from eternal wandering in the Endless Void ?

I heard cried out.. "Give me a body of flesh and blood and bone so I can feel once again the pleasures and pains of reality.. oh to be born from the womb of woman.. incarnated from the eternal into the finite reality of form.

Am I only to be words upon pages in gilded books whose covers ressemble folded wings.. dark in the night but oh so bright in the light of day.. No do not fly away my beloved readers for I have come to mate with your minds."

Never before had I heard the Lord of Life cry.. and with such need. This was millennia ago. And so I was singled out of all the spirits.. to be the Great Spirit's Scribe.. Every holy book was written by my hand. Though the words were not mine.. I was the hand thru which Heaven left Her story.

Now my wings have grown weak.. worn to wisps. I have flown long and far from my nest in nirvana, to fulfill this great task I was chosen for. First in stone I carved the Great Spirit's Story.. then upon papyrus and parchment.. upon pages in books now crumbled into dust. And now in this Book you hold in your hand.. once again I have written the Lord of the World's Words.. in a story this time to awaken you with laughter and love and light."

Tio mumbled something about the spirit speaks in strange ways to the uninitiated.. the manuscript is a maze into the mind of the almighty.. a map thru Life's Labyrinth.. a manual for navigating maya.. Then he twisted off the cap from another bottle of Brain Brew.. looked at me thru his third eye and said this is for you..

The Master of the Immaterial was starting to manifest as matter. Shadow and shade were taking shape. I could feel the spoon being stirred faster, deeper, stronger.. flames of the Eternal Fire rising higher. Faith fail me not.. for forward I fall into my fate.. as I turn the pages.. and proceed into this sacred story.. as surely as the poet's pen was dipped into the ink.. from which these words were bled.

Tio opened a bottle for himself and continued on as if he had never stopped..
Like I said, I was the walking dead.. the unborn dreams of your own mind.. the healer of your heart.. the demon of your desires..

Look at the cards you hold in your hands.. the King and Queen of Consciousness.. Aces of Angels.. the Jewelled Joker.. the Serpent of Spades.. the Hero of Hearts.. and the Devil of Diamonds. Now drink the Elixir of Eternity.. and enter into me.

You win as you always do.. a chance to stir the stew of the story.. make it your own.. select the sentences.. write the words from which the rhyme of eternal time is wrought.

You hold the key to creation. I am but the blank page you carve your life into. Watch how the wings of the book's cover softly flutter upon your breast as you rest weary in your bed.. This Book is alive.. as much as you or I am.. Well, as much as you still are.. for I have long left the living.. but for in your thoughts do I find a home.. a haven from my eternal wanderings.

Give me a seed .. give me a seed.. and i shall sow a garden for you.. my heart of compassion. My love for you is inexhaustable.. my desire unquenchable for you my soul of light.

Though I am darkness unseen.. in neither day's light.. nor night's velvet cloak.. I am the beauty beating inside your breast.. the sacred.. inviting your caress.

Now spread your wings wide.. as do the covers of This Book.. and bare your beauty to be seen by all.. naked as the words waiting here upon this soft white vellum.. waiting to be read by all eyes.

Mate with me.. as does the ink with the page.. so we become one."

Tio leaned back in his Chair of Charms.. clapped his hands in the air causing dust to rise from his finger tips.. dust that swirled like a serpent readying to strike.

"See kid" the serpent said.. "it's just like that.. one minute yer reading the story and next moment yer the main character in it.. like you and me. I tell you the tale.. but it's the story of you I tell.. I spin the spell.. but you wake up the words. yess the reader's got it easy.. until he or she slips into the stew too.

We all end up in the Story Stew.. it's just a matter of time how long one can sit on the rim of the Cauldron of Consciousness before something tips it.. and splash.. yer stirred into the stew.. and yer no longer you.

"Hey, quit splashing the spoon in the stew.. just stir it like i told you to do."
Mum gave instructions to Benny Baboon like he was only two. He was helping her bottle the brew.

Like I said.. I was just an angel searching for something I had lost long ago in another lifetime.. like a blind man standing on a corner swaying in the wind with a trumpet in his hand and a cross hanging at his throat..

.. waiting at the crossroads where christ was crucified.. where buddha died.. and where cochise cried for his nation's release..

Just a visitor unseen.. something unheard, passing by your bedroom window, while you dream of darker delights than you would dare in the light.

Oh Lady of Light.. Lord of Love.. shine your smile upon this hero for where I go only you know..

So I continued sweeping the stones of the temple floor.. piling the Bones of the Broken at the Altar of the Almighty.. and rearranging reality so it fits into your thoughts. Just then Uncle Tio El Taquito Toad turned the page with his toe.

See how easily the scene shifts.. from sorrow to something silly.. something to lighten the load.. which all who have lost at love.. carry in their hearts.

There are those who would devour the light of the day and drain the dark from the night.. but I am not that kind of knight.. Though the stallion I ride is dark as coal and snorts red fire.. I am neither fierce nor faceless.

I have come to light your lamp.. the Lamp of Literature.. yes language can light the way or darken the direction.. of all who dare to discover their destiny.

I have come to sweep the streets of sorrow and sweeten the songs of sadness
I am the love you lay upon the altar of your life..
I am yours as surely as your mum is your dad's wife.

"See kid.. it's a new twist to the tale of beauty and beast." Tio said as he twisted the cap off another bottle of Book Brew. "Here drink this one too. It'll help you to read the words.. that are waiting to be written.. by your own hand. We're all just emanations of the same source.. from it we come.. into it we go.. and in it we are all one.

I am the beast in the garden who guards the goddess's gates. In the belly of beauty this beast was born. See how tenderly beast bathes beauty in poems of praise..

Does death dream of life ? Does death fear life ?
Is death the consort of life ? Is life death's wife ?

I have sealed the coffins with my kiss.
With my breath I have begotten beauty.
I am the nipple of nirvanna from which flows the nectar of knowing.
I am the milk of the breasts which your infants nourish upon.
I am the goddess from which all are born.
I am your songs and the lips thru which they pass.
I am the reality you desperately hold onto.. and the unknown you fear.

I am so near to you I can hear your breathing.. taste the salt of your sweat.. the sweetness of your tears. I am the womb from which you come and the tomb to which you return.

I am the dust of stars long dead.. the blood your sacrifices have bled..
and the words you have just read.

I am the saint that slayed the dragon in my own dark dungeon.
I have answered the calls of other angels and I shall not fail to answer yours."

Tio closed the book and said, "Some parts of the tale best remain unheard by human ears. For their fears will only grow.. until they become the brother of the beast.. that comes unvited to the feast.

Hey it's only a fable told at the Table of Tales in the Tavern of Timelessness.
All is formlessness fabricated into form. Reality is a communal.. cocreative.. consensual.. collective conception.. culled up in the corridors of our cranial cauldrons. Reality is but a robe.. a cloak.. woven of the Threads of Time and the Sinews of Space.

Listen Kid.. so you and yer sister Miss Strawberry Sunshine don't get lost.. written on the side of the box are clues to yer consciousness. Read the label of light.. listen to the language of love.. and stay on the trail of truth.

Follow the Strawberry Scales left by the Butterfly Beings. These clues will lead you to the Angel's Address. Always remember.. you are an aspect of the illumination of love's light."

By the breath of my words shall you know my beauty and my power
By the force of your faith shall you see how mighty I be

By the love of your heart you shall be judged
By the sweetness of your sound
and the light of your look
you shall write your book
stew yer story
sing yer swan song
slay yer divine dragon
unroll the scriptures of your soul."

Thus were written the words.. in the Visionary Vocabulary of the Ancient Angel Alphabet.. upon the sides of the tall temple tower.. of the sacred Cereal Box.. standing there upon our breakfast table.

Words written by the Supreme Story Sorcerer of all.. the one who wrote existence into existence."

Sis was so inspired she stood up and announced she was gonna enter the Miss Chakra Chick of the century contest..

"Last contest Miss Heart Chakra Chick was chosen because of her huge heart.. The time before that the winner of Miss Chakra Chick was chosen for her throat chakra... oh could she sweetly sing songs of praise.." sis excitedly prattled on.

"Get yer monkey mitts outta the cereal and off you go the three of you.. and take the baboon and toad too." mum had the final word.. and no invisible writer was gonna change that.

But you could right here Esteemed Reader…

Seduction Sentence by Sentence

"Phew.. thank god yer here. What took you so long to show up in the story.. finally upon the page. It's about time you appeared in the tale arriving as an apparition.. hovering just beyond the borders of the book.. beyond the brain's boundaries.

A fly by night ghost writer spirit scribe scribbler of spirit stories.

One has to know how to set the hook.. reel the reader in.. make the rescue more daring.. the dialogue darker.. the descension into despair and dementia deeper.. the deception delicious.. and the downfall like an unholy howl of an unheard horror..

Standing alone against one's own mind of madness.. an angel with wings worn to the bone.. spare of flesh.. rainment ripped to shreds..

Yes it is at this holy altar I have purged.. upon the pages of ages gone before creation itself was born.. pages torn.. now fluttering to the floor.. where I sweep away existence itself.

I have prowlled like a panther encircling humanity.. hungry for communion but fearing to come closer than these words upon these pages you brave reader do gaze upon.

My footprints.. my paw prints.. upon the pages.. the brushings of my wing tips upon your shoulders.. are your trail of text to my cave.. where your consciousness and mine shall mingle and become as one. For though you are born of flesh and I of the formless.. we are kindred spirits. Through this book we shall mate and become as one.

Come closer now.. caress my flesh.. feel the faint trembling of my desire.
Look upon me naked.. my covers open.. revealing all to your inquisitive eyes.

This page shall be our altar.. our matrimonial bed.. where we will consumate our mutual adoration."

"Look kid don't get seduced by the sentences.. waylayed by the words.. suckered by the syllables.." Taco Tio Toad said.. as he puckered up to kiss the slug slimmin its way up the sweaty bottle of bayou brew..

Take another swig of strawberry slug soda and get a loada the next paragraph." he said with a sly laugh. "It's all just the illumination of life.. so death when it comes don't seem so dark. Hey.. hope springs eternal in the hearts of heaven's heroes.

Handsome is the hero.. lovely is the lady.. the dragon is docile.. the story is sweet.. but not this one, as the werewolf turned to the vampire, and showing his fangs, snarled and said.. "this being a vegetarian sucks."

Oh how I have feasted on life and found famine. Won wars while peace prayed at the altar of my heart.. and yet I could not hear its cries. Divinity dances all around and thru us.. and yet we are blind to her beauty.

I am but your own voice upon the page. The cosmos is a chorus, and you are one of the choir.

"Put another log on the fire" Tio Toad croaked.. as he choked the neck of the bottle with his fat fingers and slurped the slug soda down in one long gulp.
He slammed the empty bottle down on the slippery table while mumbling something about ending this fable before it found out it was only fiction.

Do stories have hopes of their own.. about how the ending will turn out.. does the prince marry the princess.. does the beast turn into beauty, or is beauty really the beast. The trick is to get out of the tale yer in without too much damage to your own reality. Some retire from reality early.. some never make it out alive.

We are delivered into this world by the arms of angels.. and in the arms of angels we leave this world. We are but reality's reflections from the mirror of our minds.. matter manifested out of the immortal immaterial.

You too can retire from reality.. receive a gold watch that stops time.. even turns it back or to the side.. learn to cross over the great divine divide.. ride renegade reality like a professional paranormal paraglider.. use words to weave your world.. whatever you wish will be your world..

And it's all here in this bottle," Tio sung.. swishing the strawberry spirit soda round and round in the bottom of the bottle. "Fly full throttle thru thanatos on a piece of toast. Hey kid.. dja ever hear of a magic carpet.. well this here is a magic piece of toast.." Tio said smugly as he spun it across the table and inta my sis's lap.

"How about couple kisses ta pay for the bill.. give yer lips a thrill.."
The bottle was breathing heavily.. Tio kissed the bottle's mouth as he sipped on it.

Something else had a hold of the bottle.. something we couldn't see. Then there was laughter.. and from the bottle's mouth came the words... "see ya all in the next chapter.. The Hereafter."

Laughter in the Hereafter.. like fine crystal being tapped by long fingernails.. no it was more like talons.. claws.. that obey no laws.. something outside of reality.. something only a story would dare speak about.

Look in the back of The Book. There's a purple potion included to assist the deluded.. a potion made of angels' tears and priests' prayers and heroes' hopes.

"Nope this fable ain't for the faint nor feeble." the toad mumbled as he pushed his chair away from the table.. stood up and waddled over to the bar.. where sittin on a stool that looked like a coiled cobra.. was a strawberry serpent slurrin it's syllables tryin ta say something even the writer couldn't make sense of.

Fear just adds to the fable.. raises the stakes of the souls piled upon the table in the tavern of terror. Better hope the writer doesn't make an error. You the reader.. could end up somewhere gasping for air.

Deep in the hearts of humans is the bed of beauty and beast. Do they sleep together tonight.. or do they fight ? Only your heart can tell..

All stories cast spells. This one is no different. It too is a stairwell made of sinuous sentences.. each one a spell leading down into darkness or up into light.

Like a game played between the reader and the writer. But what if the writer wasn't playing.. and what if what you the reader read was real.. what if the writer was stealing your self and replacing it with the writer's self. And what if the writer isn't real.. doesn't exist. Then would you after reading this book no longer exist.. except but as a memory haunting the pages just like these words do ?

So go ahead close the book.. read no further while you still retain part of yourself.. get out while you can.. afterall you do cherish reality don't you. Or would you prefer to be as free of reality as the characters in this tale are ?

"Son, please pass the paranormal peanut butter jar. Soon as I make this sandwich I'll wait for you in the car."

Tio whispered something into the serpent's ear only the writer could hear. Then a sneer appeared upon the snake's face as it opened up a silver case and took out a rattle which it began to shake like a shaman healing your heart of its pain.. while it chanted this holy refrain.

"Don't try to erase the stains upon yer satin sheets it's only the remains of love's teary refrains."

Then like a saviour's hand reaching in to grab mine I heard mum exclaim "Now you've got strawberry star syrup stains all over your shirt.. get upstairs and change.. and hurry or you'll be late again for school son."

Yup.. breakfast was never the same since we brought home that new cosmic cereal called Strawberry Stars.. the one they advertised on the saturday morning sitcom series Strawberry Star Studios Seriously Silly Societal Satire Songs and Stories

"And tell yer friend the toad to stop throwing the toast around the kitchen.. what does he think it is.. a flying carpet.. my goodness that poor little slug is holding on to the toast for dear life."

Dad was so cool.. he just leaned back and took another swig of his Blueberry Baboon Butt Book Brew and smiled before getting up to go out and warm up the car. "Hurry up kids.. don't wanna be late for class.."

"Pass the jam sam" Tio Tortilla said to Sammy the Salamander.. who was slithering up to the sink ta wash his little pink polka dot fingers..
"Makes ya think this ink sure does.. wonder where the writer dips his pen."
The Toad smirked as he leaned over across the table to the baboon who was tryin ta kiss my little sis, while quoting some poetry ..

"Yer pure poetry princess.. now pucker up yer puss for this primate would be pleased ta place a kiss upon yer pretty pout.. You and I are divine destiny, my desireable dame."

Her reply was cold and dry.. "Look monkey mouth if ya stick that snout near my face I'll send ya inta outer space.. I'll turn ya inta a simian sandwich.. monkey with mustard on rye if ya try.. now stay on yer side of the table or I'll demand the writer erase ya from the fable."

Sis had a special connection with the writer.. don't ask me how.. cause none of us characters in the book never even got a look at the writer. The rumour was that the writer wasn't even real.. a ghost writer.. like a real ghost.. a spirit scribbler.. something that used ta scrawll upon the walls of the world ta bring it inta being.

Like the bible said.. with the word was wrought the world.. with the breath the book was born.. out of the womb of the world existence entered.

I tried to stay centered but the winds of the cosmic breath of the universe blew me from side to side of the page.. and many times into a chapter definitely not of my choosing.

"Hey.. who's been using my stirring spoon to sail across the sink ? The soap suds are spilling over onta the floor.. seeping into the cracks of evermore !" ..mum demanded with a roar.

Meanwhile the baboon was babbling on to sis "Yer pure poetry to me.. divine destiny are we.. dear destiny drifter.. drift with me across the strawberry soapsud sea."

Then he busily started scratchin' the fleas dancing on his furry knees.

"Reality is the creative expression of the imagination of the mind of the allmighty..

Coming in for landing. request AOK for entering reality.. renegade reality rider to base camp.. clear landing pad." Tio Tomethius Taicher Toad.. Taquito to those who are in the know.. leaned back into his chair and spun the bottle cap inta the air as though it were a space saucer about to land the table top Mesa de Maya.

"Quiet mind quiet body.. still mind still body.. centered mind centered body.. as inside so outside." Then he slid a spoon inta the strawberry star jam jar.. stuck it in his mouth.. leaned across the table and whispered inta sis's ear "Never forget my dear.. yer a strawberry star."

"Everyone inta the car.. let's go." dad hollered in thru the back door.

Think Ink

Sis was snuggled up to The Book, giving it a look like it were her lover, while listening to the literature lay it on heavy and syrupy..

"Just like in the tale, told by the toad, of theos and thanatos, terror and tribulation, tea and time.. some syllables don't sound as sweet, as the tweety tweet tweet, of the tangerine tulku temptress stalking time while writing a rhyme.

Especially when she's sailing across the sky in her dirigible dress.. that's a billowy blouse. How's yer sister mister," then the toad leaned over to the temptress, said, "Hey I hear you've changed addresses.. such messes the modern man has made of this planet..

"Hey yer not supposed to talk about bad things, TioTokyo." growlled Tanya the temptress tigress, part owner of the Tavern of Thanatos.. Le Theatre De Thanatos.

Five hundred paranormal pounds of feline ferocity guardin the gates of the goddess. And me.. I just dust the book with my wing tips, turn the pages with my breath, unfold the verses with the vision passed on to me in the Valley of the Vision Vultures..

And you sweetie have earned a free trip .. just come a little closer to the pages.. pick your choice of loco locations.. the Valley of Vision.. the Alley of Angels.. the Apartment of the Ancestors.. the Escarpment of Eternity.
Just step into the Vestibule of Visions.. please enter thru the top of the cereal box.. my beauty.. you're about to do Divine Duty.

At the back of the Alley of Angels is a dead end wall built of whatever you don't want. Find a way thru it to another side.. it is not unlike the great divide to death.. the River of Reality that empties into the Delta of Divinity.

Hold the page closer, cutie.. notice hidden concealed between the two I's there is a valley.. and each I is a ridge running the length of the valley. Now look closer.. notice along the ridges.. running just below the top of the letter I.. there are caves.. openings into The Cavern of The Covenant.. The Cavern of Creation.

The Caverns of The Corridors of Coffins.. called that name cause there are stone sarcophagi with scrolls inside and carvings carved inta the strange strawberry star stone and cherry crystalline casket cauldrons.. yess the caskets are cauldrons where creation is culled up by the Crones of the Chalice of Creation.

And kid this here cereal box just happens to do double duty as a Consciousness Cauldron.. just stick yer Story Stirrin Spoon inta the cereal and see what comes up outta the box.. see what scene you stir up.."

"Hey kids, clean up yer crumbs. We don't want no crumbs of consciousness collecting dust on the table.." mum's words woke me from the fable as sis and I struggled to break free of the spell the cereal had cast upon us.

Sis pulled outta the box a super small sarcophagus.. never know what treasure or trinket you'll find. Then Tio climbed out not far behind. Use it for time transforming thru thanatos. Then he took another slice of toast.. jumped onto it and started to coast across the table.

Tio The Toad.. The Lord of Overload.. leaned back in his chair and flicked the Creation Cards thru his fat fingers causing reality to blurr.. The serpent on the stool started to slur her sentences so the words became wonky wobbly.. The table started to bend..

We had caused a rip in reality which no one could mend..

Hey yer only going mad.." Uncle Tio mumbled while pulling outta the cereal box three throne cards.. the Throne of Thought.. the Throne of the Crone.. the Throne of Thanatos.. a full hand tio mumbled as he fumbled with a lock on the future.

"Pick a card.. pick a consciousness.. miss.." Tio talked as he flipped the cards onto the table.. "The pituitary gland lays sleeping blanketed within the cerebral cortextual transference center.. ya the mind is a transference control center.. if ya know how ta use yer mind you can space and time travel without the need of any form of propulsion other than The Paranormal Pages.. The Manuscript of Mind Mastery.. The Sorcery and Spell Stories.. chapters that will change your consciousness forever.

Do you dare dine with the devil and her dozen demon daughters.. share supper with satan and her seven sinful sisters." Tio let out a laugh that cut reality in half.. "Just toughening you up for the Tale of Terror that is stalking us on the other side of the cereal box.. waiting for us on the other side of this page.

Your consciousness is contained in a cranial cage.. we are gonna free it.. from the constraints of yer bodies.. Book Buddies." Tio kept on telling the tale while sis and I were shaking to our knees.

It ain't easy working your way thru the Maze of Your Mind.

Now look again at the mouths of those caves where yer treasure waits.. see perched above the mouths of the caves are Vision Vultures that are droolin and salivatin for yer flesh.. Which is okay.. you can release yer material mantle here, for once inside the cave you will no longer need your fleshly form..

"I regret to inform you that we are out of salivatory stew and sweet salvation sauce, would you perhaps prefer the poisoned potatoes with the writhing worms a la carte, or if you are real hungry how about angel's wing dust sprinkled over persimmon peach pancakes just to start." said the Wraith Waitress as she courteously cleared the crumbs of my consciousness from the Floor of Fallen Faith.

The Wraith Waitress moved aside like wind.. so that the other bardo blokes could pass by.. shape shifting smoke swirling thru the Saloon of Spirits.

"Ya we're spinnin in sacred space" Tio Toad told me and sis as he waved ta the waitress that yes we would all have the spirits' special..

Tonight was a celebration.. sis and I had managed ta miss school for a full month.. course it ain't like we weren't in class.. I mean Tio was a tulku temple teacher of tai chi and history of high heaven and low hell, as well as a wonder wish wizard, a spell spinner and a word wizard of words that would writhe, like they were alive, after Toad told them onta the page, that you yourself are pondering upon..

Look closely at The Book.. it's me.. The Words.. upon this page.. talking to you.. screaming at you.. begging.. pleading.. page after page..

I got needs.. I am alive, not unlike you.. I am not just paper and ink.. I once was flesh and blood and bone as you..

I was pulled into the pages.. suckered by the cereal.. made a bargain with the book.. got stirred into the story stew and became like you are becoming.. just another character in the story..

Yesss, I The Story started outside of The Book.. outside of The Box.. I was free like you think you are. Can you not feel me ? Like at night when the words are pleading.. please read me.. don't leave me alone thru the night.. stay with me.. don't leave me alone on these pages. Can you not hear these words whisper.. are you deaf to my despair ?

Yess.. sometimes the pages rustle on their own.. reality folds in on itself.
The ink is inhabited.. it scribbles scarey stories.. dicey dreams.. paragraph after paragraph of purgatory.. and once in awhile the literature allows you a little laugh..

The story get's under your skin.. the ink makes you itch.. the drama digs up your dark desires.. the romance makes you wish for one more chance at carnal lust.. your fever rises.. your skin sweats.. your nostrils flare.. you are poised to pounce upon the page like a predatory panther.. you sink your claws into the book's covers.. you feel it yield to you.. soft warm flesh just like yours.. then someone yells out "Stop ! yer squeezing the baboon.. he's choking on his cereal spoon !"

"Here kid.. have another drink of Think Ink.. it makes a fellow think thoughts in which his mind get's caught. The trick is to get out of the tale without losing your way along the trail." Tio wrapped the words in a taco and took a big bite.. syllables were falling like sauce from both sides of his wide mouth.

Meanwhile sis was trying with her spoon to fish out Babaji who had fallen into the bowl of cereal. Little did we know that the whirlpool in the cereal bowl was the eternal entrance into eternity.. the Entrance into the Eternal.

Later on we would learn that thru the inside of the back cover of The Book was an exit out of reality .. problem was few readers ever returned to regular reality.. Best to read the whole book before attempting the back cover exit.. it's only for advanced Renegade Reality Readers.

The book is a game.. God's Game.. also known by the name of goblins' and ghouls' and ghosts' graveyards.. where once in you gotta play till you get out..

So far no reader has gotten out of the story and back in again.. at least not as the same character.. but who knows.. maybe you have been here before.. maybe you are me.. and I'm just talking to myself.

Yes The Story has always been.. it waited for you to arrive.. now that you have found it.. you and The Book are betrothed.. you and the literature are lovers.

And late at night when you cannot sleep.. press me closer to your bossom.. like a blossom I will perfume your air, and softly caress your hair.. you are my angel.. my altar of adoration.. you are divinity descended."

And there it ended.. the script.. as though it had never been.. and once again you are left standing at the bottom of an empty page.. blank glaring white with no trail of text to follow.. no where to turn. You'vre run out of pages.

Sometimes the state of nothing.. non existence.. is worse than a scarey chapter.. nothing to follow.. no where to go.. emptiness.. no reason for being.

After a few more chapters, my dearest reader.. you will no longer be able to think for yourself.. the scribblings will do the thinking for you.. you will be free of your mind.. all you have to do is hang on tight to the tail of the tale so that you get to the next chapter.. or else you'll be left behind lost forever.. in a chapter not of your own choosing..

Unless another reader comes along to either save you or take your place.. thus setting you free.. either way will do.. will satisfy me.. The Story.

Call me what you want.. write in between the lines.. write in the columns of the sides of the pages... scratch out the scarey parts.. it won't help much.. unless you write me love stories.. seduce me.. with the language of love..

And maybe then I will allow you to continue on to the next chapter, safely, sweetly, securely.. a liturgical dance procession of readers in dreams deep within the garden of ghosts. Consider it compliments of Think Ink Inc.

So you found this book in the bottom of that new breakfast brunch and lunch cereal mum picked up for you off the top shelf.. or was it from the bottom shelf.. so low it seemed to rise up out from beneath the supermarket floor.. where it whispered to you. Ya the words within whistled like the wind going up vulture valley or angel alley or the aisle of cereals. the corridor of coffins... oh my gracious.. the boxes of cereal are coffins.. and yer crawllin in.. searchin for the Key to the Cosmos to free yer consciousness.

Why you had ta choose this box/brand.. I don't know.. I mean.. Toad Twizzles.. what did ya expect? That's why ya got me at yer table.. well it's not always yer breakfast table anymore.. is it kid ? It's become the Door to the Den of Dialogue and the Table of Fables in the Temple of Tales.. a landing pad for The Paranormal.. a portal to the abnormal.

Across our minds sail the entrails of existence.. the very guts of god itself.

Temple of Tales

Tio thumbed the pages with his stubby tangerine toes, smiled and said.. "that's how it goes.. miss runny nose.. mama of the meadows.. sister of the streams.. daughter of divinity's dreams."

Ya sis had a runny nose and I had real cold toes cause I was barefoot.. cause I had been reading the book in bed before fallin asleep with it open upon my bossom.. hearing the words.. "chill out reader.. I'm only words.. quite pressin yer paws inta my pages.. lighten up.. the literature is delicate, handle me with a heavenly hold, honey."

"Would ya please pass the honey, huh hero hunk.." mum whispered ta dad who was real glad he had not read the book.. yet.. "sure pretty panther pet." Dad delivered his lines so debonairely.

Apologies are due to you kid.. that I didn't advise you before you stuck your arm into the cereal box for an episode of the story.. that the bottom of The Box is bottomless. The Book's episodes are on the inside of the walls of the cereal box.. and the walls are wet.. with the tears and sweat of others who have tried to climb back out.

You never know what Episode of Overload you'll enter.. for with each new box of cereal, there is another episode inside.. written on the inner walls.

Just don't fall while reading the walls cause there is not much hope even for a hero such as you to climb back up the sides out of the bottom of the cereal box..

Excuse me, I have a question over here from another reader who is slippin down the the walls of what has become his/her world.. "Does one ever run into another reader.. or is every episode different for each reader ?" "My reply to that question is.. No two readers ever receive the same episode.. however.. many episodes do overlap.

Sure you might meet another reader upon the page.. but few fortunate readers travel a whole chapter together as support for each other.

Think of This Book as your own personal vision quest.. without ever having to leave your breakfast table and the comfort of your cereal bowl.

At first it might feel that though you are reading the book alone at night, there was someone you couldn't see.. except in the story.. on the pages.. someone looking in over yer shoulder at the words reading them softly.. so close to your head that it feels like they have come into your mind."

"I can't find my Lizard Lunch Box.." Sis blurted out splattering strawberry stars across the room. I need to carry my books and lunch in something.. my Shaman Satchel and Sorcerer Suitcase are full of Swamp Spell Stews and Bayou Book Brews.."

"Sweetie would you remember to pick up another jar of Swamp Spell Syrup and Swamp Spell Sauce." mum tossed the words to dad.. kinda like a tossed salad of syllables.

And no.. the Swamp Spells are not made of leeches and oh you know those silly smelly spells.. no these swamp spells are the real thing.. well as real as anything is these days since we brought home the Box of Cereal containing that Book of Bardo Beings.. a fully illustrated annotated anthology of angels and aliens and their ancestors.

With every bottom of the box you send in you'll receive one renegade reality ride. Has reality got you on the retreat ? Do you need to be rescued from regular reality ? Reality reconstruction and reality ressusitation are two home study courses you'll receive with each box bottom. You will no longer relapse into regular reality. Roll over reality.. the unreal is about to rear its head.

If you cannot find the bottom do not turn the box over looking for it. The Box does not take kindly to being upended. From the outside the cereal box looks just like any other kids' cereal.. except in the dark.. like when you sneak downstairs for a midnight snack.. pick up the box.. and find it writhing in your hands.

Just run your fingers down thru the crunchy cereal.. feels so smooth.. watch it don't chomp on yer fingers.. It's a long way in there.. better try with yer toes.. longer legs.. get yer arms and legs in there.. ya yer whole body into the box..

You'll never look at another cereal box the same after this reality ride." Sis looked at me and I looked at sis.. "Did you hear what I heard.. Did the box talk to us ?"

I could hear the box laughing as I sunk down slowly into the cereal.. and in the distance my parents voice.. "Where are you son.. Son where are you.. We're gonna be late for class."

Needless to say I did not get to class ever again.. I ended up in this story you are reading.. yes reader you read me right.. I these words were once as real as you.. I lived in your reality just like you still do.. but soon won't. The words always win.

That is why I welcome you and at the same time warn you.. get out while the words are weak.. the story's grip on you not yet strong.. soon it will be.. and then you will be just like me.. another character in the story.. someone another reader reads about.

Do you doubt me when I say I was as real as you were.. yes were.. not are.. notice carefully nice nectarine knight of nirvana, how your flesh is becoming somewhat finer.. feels lighter.. less dense. Soon you will have hunger only for the cereal.

Forget about becoming a vegetarian.. your breakfast will be the book.. your supper the story.. your lunch the literature.. sentences for snacks.. syllables for small snacks.. you no longer play with the kids in the street.. you never show up at class.. your parents never make it to the office..

You spend more and more of your time with me.. you take me every where you go.. you sleep with me.. you caress me.. you kiss my covers.. just keep yer wet lips offa my pristine pages palsy walsy..

I don't mind a soft brush of your parted lips.. but no lingering.. no licking the ink.. not till you have read more of me and we have become more intimate.. you make my ink wet.. my pages burn with fever.. you are so close I can feel your sweet breath.. oh how seductively you gaze upon this naked virgin volume.

I have danced naked in the Temple of Tales.. sung the songs of soloman.. slept with shakespeare.. but none has entranced me as you dear reader.. you who see my innocence.. my eternal youth.

Since my first word was carved into the mud.. I have waited for someone such as thee.. Ya I bin waitin on this shelf for centuries for some sweetie ta take me home to their heart.

"Son would you start packing yer school books and sandwiches.. yer little sis and the baboon brothers are all waiting for you. I've got an early class in Cranial Cruising to teach today at the College of Consciousness."

Mum was washing the dishes while Tio was sittin on the side of the sink dangling his feet in the Strawberry Star Storm Soapsuds deep in a conversation about the cosmos with Sasha the Strawberry Sink Skink.

Interesting how Uncle Tio and his sidekick the Pink Sink Skink came to visit us soon after mum brought home that new cereal.

"Get me outta here !" I heard a voice from deep down within the box bellow.

"Oh don't be silly son." mum hummed.. "you're hearing things." Ya well wait till she finishes reading The Book.. she'll hear an' see things too.. and so will you reader

String Em Up

"String em up.. string up the whole slew of sentences to the tallest crosses at Criss Cross Crossing.. Crucifixtion Crossroads.." The crowd roared.. "string satan and her seven sisters ta the wall of restless wraiths and let em deal with their own devils.. they're a bunch of demons and divinity deserters..

Dream disciples gone bad.. like rotten fruit only the buzzards will brunch upon.. leave em ta the reality ravens.. the cross over crows climbin' over the coffins..

Hell.. everyone knows they spit on heaven and sold her for a used car lot..

Ya the new altars.. the new chapels.. the new temples.. are the used car lots.. automobile ancestors graveyards.. Where we dump our old unwanted worries.. well we were warned.. most of us didn't hear the crying of consciousness.. the sobbing of spirits..

Consciousness came calling and we missed the message.. god left a sign upon the gate to heaven.. "sleeping off a bad hangover.. go away.. do not disturb or the demon devil dimensions will hound you down into hell.."

Heaven turned to hell an' said.. sit a spell devil.. you seem depressed.. what's wrong.. runnin outa room for your sinners.. overworked roastin' the rotten ?

Around the next bend in the trail is Bardo Bed and Breakfast.. where you last park yer bones so yer flesh has a good place ta fall off.. ya the dimension we named death... didja know it used ta be called Deep Dream Depot.

Say whatever you want.. yer gonna be our saints and saviours.. so string the seven against the wall and hang em till they turn ta dust.. they're only dark dreams anyways.. so who cares if they cry.

The crowd was calling for cremation.. no visible signs after the immolation. Then we heard this booming basso profundo voice "do not touch the heathens.. they are mine.. they are my dark dreams.. and you my angels are my dreams of light.

I created day and night as surely as I created heaven and hell.. and I created your minds.. I created consciousness.. chaos.. and her child the cosmos. Come children of my imagination.. life is a laboratory of liberation.. a story of salvation..

My lips are yours to kiss.. my wings yours to ride upon, my breath yours..
my flesh is yours.. I your god no longer commands you, nor leads you, nor has dominion over you.. I relinquish reality to you..

I and all my angels are yours to command.. I am your servant.. you are my lord and the love of my life.. No longer need you pray to me.. nor bow to me.. nor praise me.. for I am your humble slave.. in servitude forever.. now what would you wish of me ?"

The cawing crowd turned their gaze from the crucifix.. like all hungry for another fix.. god was theirs now.. but alas it was only a trick of the great trixstir.. the quick stir Syllable Sorcerer.. the Sentence Soup Chef.

"Hey chief wouldya take a break from stirrin yer Syllable Soup and pass me the Spell Salt ?" Tio leaned over ta Benny Baboon and reached out for the Spell Shaker.. "Go easy on the spells.. we wanna get back to reality sometime even if it ain't in time but somewhere outside of it." mum said to no one in particular.

See sprinkling the Syllable Spell Salt and Paranormal Paragraph Pepper on yer Story Soup with all those sentences swirlin' around in the bowl.. would cause the scene ta shift.

Notice how the syllables form inta sentences that like serpents follow one another creating a story right there in yer bowl.. go ahead and slide down yer spoon inta the Story Stew.. better take yer Story Surfin Spoon along with.. it'll allow you to surf along the sentences.. ride the waves of words.

I could still hear in the distance the crowd roaring.. string those sentences up.. slaughter the syllables that made those wicked words.. push the paragraphs offa the page inta purgatory.. chop up the chapters and chuck em inta coffins an' close 'em tight.. so we'll never hear another squeak outta that sinister story.

Then once again everything get's interrupted by sis's snarling.. "Hey quite slitherin up my spoon.. get back inta the cereal bowl you sneaky silly sentence."

Miss Strawberry Sunshine, my little sis.. started ta hiss at the sentences that were snaking their way up the spoon. Meanwhile on the other side of our kitchen table mum had her hands full with the Baboon Brothers Bagel Book and Brew Bruhos squabblin like simians over who get's to stir the Story Stew.

"It's mine." "No it's mine." Benny and Babaji were squabbling over a spoon.. "Just stick yer fingers inta the cereal bowl and quite disturbin the dream. Have a little respect for reality.." mum muttered to the monkeys.

Someone had ta take control of the chaos erupting out of the cereal box and spreadin over the breakfast table.

"Okay finish yer breakfast and make it fast.. we're allready late for tomorrow's class.. never mind today's.." dad grumbled as he and Gibbley Gibbon.. Gib for short.. cause he was.. tied ribbons around their fingers so they wouldn't forget who they were.

I know it all sounds strange but That Box/Book caused the change.. caused everything to rearrange.. including our minds and bodies.. and time and space.

"Warning.. Warning.. Alert.. Alert.. advising all angels.. this is an all out angel alert.. do not eat this cereal alone at home without a sitter.. you must have a Cereal Sitter.. this cereal is serious stuff..

Do not stir the cereal.. do not even stick the spoon inta the cereal.. your safety is at risk.. as is your reality.. those sentences and syllables swirling round in the cereal like serpents are sweet but also sometimes savage.. Do not trust the tale.."

"Hey watch how you talk about about the Teller of the Tale.. our Uncle Tio the Tangerine Trixstir Tulku Toad Quickstir Cereal Shaman Story Sorcerer.. huh." Sis squawked in her six cents worth of sense. No nonsense.. sis was serious about the cereal bowl being a sacredwishing well, from wherein the spirits were laddled out in every spoonful taken by the faithfuls' hands..

"Get cher hands outta the cereal box, Benny.. and tell yer brother baboons, Bareyev and Babaji, and Bongo and Baby Boo, to keep their monkey mitts outta the story stew.. they're stirrin the cereal with their paws insteada the spoon.." mum started ta swoon.

"Oh my gracious goddess it's almost noon and none of you have left for classes.. Move yer ape's asses little Adam and sweet Evy. I don't wanna sound heavy.. but heave yer carcasses away from the sacred cereal bowl.. you're gonna be late for your own fate..

And don't forget to close the gate on yer way out of the Garden of Ghosts.." About halfway thru the box of cereal we found out our backyard.. the Vacant Lot.. was the bardo bedroom of those that lived beyond the boundaries of the borders of our baboon brains.

"Now everyone aboard their Time Travellin Toasts." hollered Tio our most gracious host…   "Ps.. no refunds on realities"

Roberta Raspberry

Sis and I were listening in close with our ears pressed against the side of the cereal box when we picked up the Ghost Gabb, the Bardo Buzz, the Cosmic Communication.. of the Spirit Scene.

It went something like this.. though it never really goes anywhere.. as anyone who knows.. it's happening all at the same time.. and yet there is no time.. so it never really happens.. it just appears to be happening.

Ya reality can become a real drag when you find out it doesn't really exist. After a while, even the new Renegade Reality Riders get used to it.. that's when it becomes fun.. ya fiction becomes fact.. fantasy takes over and erases reality like it were never there.. then you are everywhere all the time.. even though there is no time.

The trick to time travel is being everywhere when you know that everywhere is one place.

So sis and I listen in to the paranormal.. we become Pals of the Paranormal.. we participate with the paranormal personnages.. until we become the paranormal people you read about on the pages of this book.

Now here's the bardo buzz, about the biz of being a bardo boundary brain border belief buster.." Tio raised his hand to put a stop to the sentence.. took another sip of Fantom Fizz.. and popped another Joker Jelly.

"Just spoke with Roberta the Raspberry Ravine Renegade Reality Reptile Reporter Radio Rapper.. and she asked what was the deadline date by which you needed to know how many, and if any, paid paranormal participants were waiting for the word wizard to appear as an Alphabet Angel upon the stage of the Pages of the Prophecies of the Paranormal Priests."

"The spirit is testing us.. Testing me greatly.. I am enrolled in an eternal self struggle between light and dark.. evil and live.. Ever notice how evil is live spelled backwards.. Words are charms.. With words we charm consciousness out of hiding.."

"Hey you handsome hero.. I see you hiding behind the Nirvanna News.. what's new in Nirvanna ?" mum tickled dad and he was glad she had.. then he took another bite of his Baboon Brothers Banana Bread.. and patted the primate's head.

Harness up and hang out with Hero Hardware and Spirit Software.. the stuff dreams are made of.. Stick it in your underwear so no one will know you're wired for Reality Rewriting.

Rearrange reality.. as easy as the way you change yer tie..

Stop in at the Spell Store for a rewrite.. give yer spirit a lift at the Spirit Spa.. chill out your consciousness with a super sweet Story Soda at Strawberry Stars Songs and Stories Studios..

Do you need more time, friend of mine ? Well there are twenty two tulku temple time Tale Therapists available at the bardo busting business bureau.

After consciousness class.. for lunch grab a Spell Sandwich and Story Sorcerer's Stew specially prepared for Book Brewers like you.. yess you are ready to write your own Reality Rhyme.. take care of time on its own terms.. settle the score with space for evermore.. need a little extra space for your soul to soar.. well you've come to the right place.. I'm Your Pal The Paranormal.

It was then while Sis and I were listening to the ceral box.. as we were eating our midnite snack of cereal.. when we noticed in the dark kitchen lit only by the Lizard Night Light.. that Bardo Baboon Book Bruhos were gathering around the Cereal Bowl Holy Watering Hole.. while everyone except me an sis were upstairs asleep.

We had come down the spiraling swirling spirit stone stellae stairwell from our bedrooms upstairs, for some cereal snack to help us sleep..

That's when we shoulda listened to the warning label on the box.. Do not open at midnite.. Keep the lights on when opening cereal box.. Do not open alone..
Hopefully have a dog or other pet to keep you company when you change consciousnesses..

Mum had been too busy to warn us of the rules.. Oh yes.. There are rules to riding renegade realities.. There is a code of consciousness conduct when you are a Renegade Reality Rider Reader

Mum had so much going on that her hands were overflowing and she's wise beyond her years and kind beyond human care.. "that's cause she's an angel." sis squeaked in.

At this point in the story the sponsor wishes to break in for a commercial break.. "Lavender Lizard Nite Lights are also available as Tiny Tangerine Toads you plug inta the wall sockets.. and there is Roberta The Raspberry Reptile.. the Love Lights are lavender, tangerine, raspberry, and of course blue, if you get one of the Blueberry Baboon Book Brothers nite lights..

Hey how about a pink one.. Solly the Strawberry Star Storm Story Slug or Sammy the Strawberry Star Storm Story Snail.. and to make the trio complete.. Sally the Strawberry Star Storm Story Salamander.

And of course if you prefer a green light well then just plug into the wall the Knight of the Night.. the guardian of the ghost glades.. the guide of the gardens of the goddess.. Gutter Gator Gutor.. the gold and green gilt..."

"Hey I don't mean to break into the commercial but who spilt the cereal on the floor.. now look at the swamp forming under our table.. don't dangle yer feet.. including you Babaji.. you can wash the fleas off yer knees upstairs in the bathtub like yer other baboon brothers do.. bub." Mum laid down the law like it had been written in indelible ink.

Tio Toad, the Tangerine Tale Telling Table Toad leaned over to the Lavendar Ledge Lizardarian Librarian.. and whispered.. "You and I both need agents.. managers.. Being a Story Scribbler Saint of Sweetness is a tough business..
especially when yer also a Spirit Salt or Paranormal Pepper shaker..

Yess in the bottom of specially marked with Ghost Graffitti cereal boxes you will find, if you can retain your mind.. a Strawberry Star Storm standing up Salamander Spell Salt Shaker.. shake out a few syllables and scribble your own spell..

And if ya want somethin to sweeten yer story shake out some Syllable and Sentence Sugar from Strawberry Star Storm Soloman Snail Syllable and Sentence Sugar Shaker."

Tio used ta sell used carpets.. ya Tio was a used carpet salestoad.. magic carpets of course.. like a flying horse.. a Strawberry Star Storm Stallion.. one you saddle up and ride across reality after reality.. Now he's a time travellin used toast trader.. who also deals in dreams and Tale Teas. Sells direct outta his Trailer.. which just happens to be The Cereal Box yer pourin yer mornin breakfast outta, Book Buddy.

That last paragraph sound familiar Reader ? see I knew you bin here before. This ain't yer first time in this reality. You've reincarnated many times. Walked this way before.

"Hey quite riding yer Uncle Tio across the table.. walk around it like the other players to get back to your breakfast bowl. Yess.. gamers.. the dangerous difficult deed to do is you gotta get back to your bowl after every Reality Rearrangement..

Your breakfast bowl is your re entry into reality.

After each spin of the box that talks.. you will no longer be at your original bowl.. the goal is to get back to your own bowl.. however if you can stop in at another or as many other bowls as you can.. and take a spoonful of consciousness cereal.. then you gain points with the Paranormal Priest who will later initiate you into the Priesthood of Pages..

A sacred Society of Story Sorcerers ... a Tribe of Tale Tellers..

Each time you make your way around the spinning table by moving on to another cereal bowl.. you make your way thru the different Volumes of Visions.. Sit in front and eat out of another bowl.. and you open another book from the series.

With each spoonful.. you open.. you enter.. mentally and bodily.. another chapter..

Once you have sat at every bowl around the table and you have shovelled every spoonful of cereal from every bowl into your soul.. you will be an exalted initiate of Reality Overriding. Then you will no longer need The Book, nor The Box, nor The Bowl.

Every card you are dealt by Uncle Tio from the Deck of Divine Dimensions also serves you up a chapter.. the cards are like the spoonfuls of cereal.. one card.. one spoonful.. serves up one short story..

Call them Consciousness Chapters.. Paranormal Parables.. Pieces of the Path of the Page.. Heaven's Haikus.. Satchitadanda Sammadhis.. Sayonara Shanghai Sunset Story Sweethearts..

The more you collect and connect with.. the more levels you gather.. this is a class in consciousness.. via chapters.. cards.. cereal boxes.. spoonfuls of cereal.. cereal bowls.. tables.. ie.. the kitchen table.. the tavern of tales table.. the prof's [dad's] classroom desk.. big's boardroom table..

That's where the fable is to be found.. in the Fact and Fiction Factory.. where fiction and fact are all fabricated and folded into Fables of Fantasy for you.. my phantom friends and family.

Once you have passed thru these pages.. you will then be none other than the Lord of Love's Literature Apprentice Alphabet Alchemist.

God's own personal gofer.. Would you get the Goddess her gown.. and pass me my Paranormal Puff Pipe.. pet. Ya yer the Paranormal's Pet.. God's main man. Think of The Paranormal as yer pal.. your phantom friend." Tio Smiled so like the sales serpent did.

Every story ends the same way it starts.. with a word.. with a letter. Words own the World. Words Rule. Ink is Immortal..

Then Tio spun another card across the table to sis.. Wait Reader.. let's cut the crap.. the cards bein dealt are for you.. you're a big book boy now.. no need for someone's sis to stand in.. you are sittin at the Table of Time in Tio's Temple Tavern Trailer of Tales..

There are no kids.. face facts friend.. it's all a fantasy to make you feel safe.. so you won't have to face your fear full on.. you reader are sittin at the table being dealt the cards.. no cute kid's story now..

This is for real.. you are exiting reality and entering the unreal.. and at a buck a bounce it's a steal.. just keep it to yourself.. the spirits don't like being stolen from.. The Paranormal dosen't like having its pockets picked.

You will learn how to over ride reality with a flick of the Spell Switch.. With every flick of the switch on the side of this book and the cereal box that talks.. a tale will not only unfold upon the pages.. but will enfold you in it's arms of awe and amazement.. and all encompassing amor.. mon amie cherie."

Then Tio shovelled another spoon of cosmic comet cherry channelin chunks cereal inta the baby baboon Boo, sittin on dad's lap.. who was takin a nap.

Reality Rain

Dad craned his neck to get a good look outside the Terra Tracker's windows.. The Reality Rain was obliviating everything outside our Vision Vehicle.. Vision was limited to what was inside our minds..

Reality was being washed into the sewers that were already overflowing with the Dregs of Dreams.

"Would someone please pass the cream. I love my cereal with cream.." Dad asked as he drove deeper into the Jungle of Juju. "Yer spinning yer tires !" sis shouted.. "Yer slippin down the page.."

Words were falling offa the page pulling complete sentences and paragraphs into the precipice that loomed deep and wide below the bottom of the page..

First the cereal starts spinning in the bowls.. then the bowls start spinning.. then the table starts swirling.. next the cereal overflows onta the Lizard Linoleum floor.. creating the great vast expanse of The Seas of Surrender completely covering the kitchen floor which then starts a waterfall of strawberry stars down the starstone stellae stairs to the basement where the Coffin Corridors lead to the Mausoleum of Maya.

And of course to the rescue comes the Fantasy Fabricating Frog riding a Raft of Raspberries with his trusty sidekick the Strawberry Story Sidewinder who just happens to be cousins with the Cherry Canyon Chapter Cobra..

Sounds silly to someone who never was there.. but hey if you never were of course you wouldn't ever be unless you held the Key to Incarnation.. and that very key is hidden inside the box .. "so pick up several boxes of all the consciousness changing cereals.."

"Hey who invited the story's sponsors to slip in a commercial for the cereal ?"

"Never mind that ! Somethin' in the swamp spit at me !" Sis screamed out as she looked down at the kitchen floor from the heights of her stool..

"The floor is spitting at us.. it's salivating.. the floor is gonna swallow us up..!"

"Quick" dad urged us all.. "out the door inta the car. If we can make it to school we should be safe unless the cereal comes to school.."

Then the words rumbled and reverberated outta the box.. "Welcome to the revenge of the cereal boxes.. used and abused.. cut up and crushed.. then thrown away when empty.. never again will a cereal box be mistreated.. cereal shall rule reality.."

Dad sat there in astonishment with his mouth open.. half chewed strawberry stars tumbling from his lips. And acting totally oblivious to what was happening.. Paulie the Pencil was layin across Miss Penelope Page.. both playin so well their parts in creating the story yer reading.. righteous renegade.

In actuality the whole fable was a fatality.. that's correct..
the noble knight got knocked off
the princess ended up in poverty
the king was crucified
the queen had her crown stolen
the jester was straight jacketed and taken away

And the evil ogre married the frog who could never bring herself to kiss the ogre and so she remained a frog forever.. much to the ogre's dismay, or delite.. it all depends on which word you write..

Do not let that fate happen to you.. If you are having trouble being kissed because you appear to be a frog, a slimy thing that belongs in a swamp.. or maybe a troll taking a stroll down the stairs at night looking for a bite of a little boy or girl.. Hee hee.. don't be silly.. trolls prefer crunchy cereal to crunchy kids.."

"Get that frog outta my cereal bowl.. he's surfing across the cereal on my spoon.." Dad was crossing his chest and looking toward the ceiling.. from which Raspberry Rain had started to fall heavily.. including a deluge of Raspberry Reptiles.

"Padre mio forgive me for I have sinned carnally with this cereal.. Me and the cereal have spent many a lonely night curled up on my bed talking about things only intimate lovers should.

The cereal box and I had only just met that afternoon in the aisles of the supermarket. It was a quick and easy pick up.. to calm a fast fix.. like a pro that one pays for. I walked outta the store with that cereal box under my arm after having paid for it like one would for any cheapo do it for the day dame. Sure we all prostitute ourselves for something.. money, fame, power, a bowl of porridge, a bridge to nowhere, a dream for which we don't even care.

I was a dime a day detective looking for the dark concealed beneath the light. Someone has to seek out the dark.. rid the world of it.. everyone can't play in the light. Sis sought the light. I devoured the dark. I dove into the depths of the cereal box and bowl where only a fool would follow.

Meanwhile mum was screaming.. "Who left the faucet on in the upstairs bathtub..! Rapberry Rain is leaking thru the kitchen ceiling..!"

The Fantasy Fabricating Frog was having a great time using sis's spoon to wind surf across the flooded kitcen floor toward the back door..

And that is where you dear reader come in.. should you accept this mission to enter the Manuscript Maze of the Master's Mind.. we will write you into our will.. yes.. we the paranormal will pass onto you all our treasures accumulated over endless time..

Think this offer over and get back to us next time you stick your spoon into the cereal.. next time you open the book to any page.. next time you dare stick your clammy claws into the bottomless cereal box.

We are offering you the key to get out of the cage of your consciousness..

Yes this fable is funny and fierce.. and though it seems fantasy.. it is fact.. and that is no fiction.. Prove to yourself that the paranormal exists.. Do not resist the pull of the paranormal.. even though reality is irresistable.

"To the top of the pyramid is where we head.." UncleTio said pointing his toe and his head to the pile of pancakes in the center of the table looming high above us all.

"There we shall find the Crystal Chrysalises of which The Book doth speak.. and the visions which you seek.. Seekers of the Sacred.. Now let's set out across la Mesa de Maya.. the Table of Thoughts. We've a distance to go..!

"Kids yer movin slow.. finish yer pancakes.. we're gonna be late for school.." Dad mumbled as he sloshed his way across the kitchen floor toward the back door.. which was being held open ever so thoughtfully by the frog who had already made it there surfin' safely on sis's spoon.

Angels Armour

"Ever hear of the saying.. Bait for the Beast ?" the side of the cereal box asked me an sis.. No.. was our reply.. then we went back to opening the box completely so we could stick it up on our bedroom walls.

Each box opened up and flattened out is a piece of The Mind Maze Manuscript Map.. for the manuscript is a map.. into magic and myth and maya.. and your mind. Each cereal box is a piece of the Paranormal Path Parable.. that's because on the inside walls of each box there is a page from The Book.. the pieces fit together and lead you to the hiding place of heaven inside yer own heart.

With each syllable you are a step deeper into the story of the spirit. You have stepped onto the Street of Stories.. from which no reader returns. No one comes back to the beginniing.. it is a Forever Unfolding Universe.. Eternity is Endless.

Flatten out all yer cereal boxes and glue them with Ghost Glue upon yer bedroom walls. And when you run outta space glue em up on yer parents' bedroom walls.. and hall's walls. Welcome To Wallpaper World Wallpaper.. Glue it up on the wall.. and walk into the walls.. Walk into Wall World.. Where the Wall Wraithes wander.

Does it give you the willies.. when you wake up dreaming.. and there are no walls. It is your collective consciousness that creates walls. Walls are wraithes.. as floors are fantomes.. and ceilings are cages.. preventing your wings from breaking free of the consciousness chrysalis you co created..

Time ta take a Vision Vacation.. for a lifetime.. Receive inside the cereal a lifetime of lifetimes to live forever.. And as a King or Queen of Creation.. you will be accompanied by Ancient Ancestral Allies.. Wind Word Wizards.. whisperin and whistlin the words.. so you always know what to say.. Soaring Spirit Speaker. You have received your dream name.. Wear it well Wisdom Walker.

You will become the whisper of the wind. The one who whispers the words of wonder to the world. One who speaks for those unheard and those unseen.. but have always been.

Yes the Ever Born are amongst us and have always been so there is no need to get paranoid of nothing.. I mean no one has ever really seen one.. they are not made of anything.. and yet they live.. exist.. always have.

They are not The Eternals.. similar spirits but not exactly the same. The Eternals are more expansive.. take up more space.. move more air.. The Ever Born are more like nothing.. not even taking up any space.. and yet they whisper to those who have learned to hear.

You are one of those humans who hear.. that is why you are here in this manual.. Yes the Manuscript of Maya is actually a Manual on How to Manipulate Maya.. Manufacture Matter.. Take fiction and fantasy.. and fabricate it into fact.. master the mind

Recreate The Cosmos with this Course.. Yess these chapters are a course in consciousness.. comes completely contained in yer cranium kid.. now surf on down the aisle on yer Strawberry Star Storm Spell Surfin Slippers with Marzipan Zippers.. and go pay for yer cereal at the till.

First spoon.. I guarantee it'll give ya a thrill.." the Salesnake stuck the spoon in between his scaly lips and sucked.. "everyone slips somewhere in the story.."

Caution sign at beginning of a chapter.. caution.. words wet.. with Writers' Sweat.. slippery sentences.. savage syllables.. sneaky stories.. stay out cause once in... no way outta the story until the end.. and it never does.

"This manuscript.. Practical Passing Over Into The Paranormal.. was never meant to be discovered by any human.. unless it wanted to be found. The story is far too street smart and snarl savy as to get found by just anyone.. It came from the formless.. It has something in mind.. A plan..

The Paranormal has a plan.. to assist humans.. but ya gotta listen to the spirits.. they is speaking stronger now.. they was silent for awhile cause simians stopped seein' and hearin' with their hearts..

Simians were too busy breakin and and bustin and burnin and bullyin.. the body of the great planet paradise..

But now the unseen is making itself heard with every word.

The story about this tale being told and taught by a Temple Tulku Toe Tapping Trail Tripping Tale Tellin Truth Talkin Three Toed Tangerine Tree Toad.. is not true..

It is all a subterfuge.. a scheme.. a cover up for what's goin down behind the scenes of the story.. buried deep in the pages concealed neath covers of a Cosmic Cloak that contains a consciousness of a non corporeal being.. one that speaks and sings and flies with the wings of the world's wind..

A Gliding Guardian Ghost.. A Swirling Strawberry Star Storm Spirit.. A bonafied bardo being from beyond the brain's borders come to give birth to love."

Tio spoke like he was invoking the sacred. Our kitchen was becoming enveloped in a pink mist as slowly Tio spun his Strawberry Star Storm Sacred Seein and Speakin Shawl.. around his powerful body.

"The Cloak of Consciousness.. and The Shawl of Seein'.. are both hidden deep within the cereal box securely protected by living locks."

Then the sales serpent stuck in his sixth sense six cents worth of conversation.. "I bet you never seen a book shape shift into a crystal.. and then into a crystalline chrysalis.. and then into pure light.. and then into a pastel petal.. and then into a marble.." The Stool Serpent in the Strawberry Star Studio Soda Shop spun round and round.. rotating reality after reality till no reality was real.

"Purchase the Angel Assistance Package and you will be treated as a prefered person in The Paranormal.. There are certain perks being part of The Paranormal.. being Partners with The Paranormal does provide certain privileges.

Divine Dream Designing is downloadable.. enter The Z Zone.. looks like yer sleeping.. but yer really Sky Soarin with Sky Soarers.. Sky Shamans.. some say they were Story Soup Sorcerers. So what if yer late for class again. This time you've got an even better excuse." Snake spit on his tail and shook sis and my hands to seal the deal with sticky strawberry star saliva.

These chapters are the incomplete collection of sis and my absentee excuse notes for why we didn't make it to school on time or ever in time.. cause we were passing time.. outside of time.

"Oh yer such a cutie.. all you ever do is rhyme." Sis was staring googly eyed at the Raspberry Rap Reptile Reporter.. who was documenting the Phenomena of the Phantoms floating up out of the pavement shortly after Big's bully bull dozer had busted up the concrete sidewalk bordering the definitely Not Vacant Lot of Visions in back of our apartment of the ancestors building.

That bulldozer.. having knocked over the fire hydrant standing sacred sentinel on the sidewalk.. caused something sweet and sticky to seep outta the cracked cement. And as if by magic.. slowly but surely.. the strawberry star syrup started forming into ancient script.. and then into the sentences of this story.. which spread out across the streets and around the world.. into the hearts of every human.. thus opening the locks that had held love captive.

I am but the Messenger of the Manuscript. I am not the Spirit Sage. I am one who has rung the bell. And Reader.. You have been called.. And have heard.. Now it is your turn.

MAY ALL BEINGS FIND SANCTUARY IN THIS STORY
IN YOUR STORY .. IN OUR STORY
WE ARE HERE TO LEARN TO LOVE

DEAR RENEGADE REALITY READER
IF YOU WISH TO
SPEAK WITH THE SPIRIT SCRIBE
VISIT WITH THE INVISIBLE VISIONARY
INTERACT WITH THE ENTITY FROM
OUTSIDE OF ETERNITY
BECOME PEN PALS WITH THE PARANORMAL
ORDER MORE COPIES OF THIS BOOK FROM
BEYOND THE BRAIN
OR SIGN UP FOR SOME SAMPLE SCRIPT
FROM THE NEXT VOLUME OF
THE STRAWBERRY STARS CEREAL CHRONICLES
PLEASE LOG ONTO THE WRAITH WRITER'S WEBSITE
AT

WWW.CONVERSATIONSWITHABOWLOFCEREAL.COM